Also by David Michie

CONFLICT OF INTEREST

PURE
DECEPTION

DAVID MICHIE

TIME WARNER PAPERBACKS

A *Time Warner* Book

First published in Great Britain in 2000
by Little, Brown and Company

Published by Time Warner Paperbacks in 2001

A CIP catalogue record for this book
is available from the British Library.

ISBN 0 7515 3092 1

Typeset by Palimpsest Book Production, Polmont, Stirlingshire
Printed and bound in Great Britain by
Clays Ltd, St Ives plc

Time Warner Paperbacks
An imprint of
Time Warner Books UK
Brettenham House
Lancaster Place
London WC2E 7EN

www.TimeWarnerBooks.co.uk

To my dear friend, Kay Paddon, with love.

Power today has little to do with how much property a person owns or commands, it is instead determined by how many minutes of prime-time television or pages of news-media attention he can access or occupy.

Douglas Rushkoff, Media Virus

PROLOGUE

——

Alan Brent had never felt such terror in his life. Even half an hour later, hurrying through the night with shoulders hunched and collar raised, he had to fight to control the nausea, to keep down the acid rising from his stomach. *Clink, clink, clink*, came the sound from his trouser pocket. Steel on glass. He tried blocking it from his mind.

In ten years undercover he'd seen some sights – all manner of depravities and perversions and horrors. But none like tonight. Christ, no! Even though it hadn't been him trussed up on the floor, subjected to Larson's barbaric surgery, he'd scarcely been able to comprehend the sheer, stupefying viciousness of it. Behind their thick lenses, his eyes were still wide with shock. In his jacket pockets, he'd clenched his hands into tight fists to stop them shaking.

They were moving as fast as possible without drawing undue attention. One of the dark shadows was fifty yards ahead; the other man, fifty behind. This was Alan's first time out and they were taking no chances. They had been ruthlessly effective from the start, their actions planned meticulously to cover all scenarios, drilling each sequence in rehearsal, again and again. So when it had come to the actual operation, they were doing it for the hundredth time, and had carried it out with digital precision. Searing, heart-stopping torment had been inflicted with Teutonic efficiency. No wonder Larson thought he was untouchable.

As they rushed past shop windows lit up in the night, Alan told himself he should derive some satisfaction from the fact that he had at least been accepted. He'd broken into the inner circle. They'd never have let him anywhere near this if they'd had the slightest doubt. Going operational was a mark of trust, recognition – he needed that if he was going to penetrate the highest level of the organisation, though he hadn't counted on the cost. What had happened tonight outstripped his most lurid expectations – and there was nothing he could do about it now. He was way past the point of no return. Bile rose to his throat. It was all he could do not to retch.

They turned into his street. He paused, as he'd been instructed, while the front escort checked the way before signalling all clear. Alibis had been established and weren't to be wrecked by chance encounters – that was their reasoning and he played along with the game, knowing that, if it came to it, he could get one of the women from HQ to pretend to be his girlfriend.

The house was a typical Victorian terrace, indistinguishable from the other sixty in the street. He made his way quickly from pavement to front door, keys in his hand, and as soon as he was inside he shed his jacket, threw it over a coat-hook and headed immediately for the stairs. The sound from his trouser pocket as he ascended was a loathsome reminder. *Clink, clink, clink.*

Alan's kitchen was large and scattered with the detritus

of bachelorhood, cast in sepia by the grubby yellow glow from the streetlamp outside. Standing in the centre of it, spectacles glinting, he raised shaking fingers to push back the dark, wiry locks that fell dishevelled about his face. This was his first moment alone since the attack. It felt surreal to be back in the midst of familiar territory after what he'd just been through. As he stood there, heart pounding, and mouth vile, he still found it hard to believe. God Almighty, what had he let himself in for? In all the time he'd been working his way into the group, they'd never gone this far.

As he took a step forward, there came the sound from his pocket again – a single, unbidden *clink* – and with it, the unavoidable knowledge that the moment had come for him to deal with it. Trying to ignore it just wasn't an option any more. Wearily, he picked up a paper serviette from among the salt and pepper sachets and other remnants of number-less fast-food meals scattered across the kitchen bench. Unfolding the serviette over his right hand, he reached down into his pocket.

An hour before, the jar had been empty and clear; now its glass sides were sickeningly smeared. He set it down at the far corner of the bench without looking at it. *He'd been down on his knees when they'd made him pick them up. His skin-tight gloves were so fine, it had been like touching them with his bare hands. He hadn't felt nausea at the time – only shock. His fingers had shaken so violently he'd only just got them in the jar and was screwing the lid tight when he'd been ordered out.*

Turning, Alan made his way from the kitchen, trying to dismiss the jar from his mind. He wanted, more than anything, to leave it all behind. To forget about it completely. Climbing a final flight of stairs, he made his way into the long attic room he used as his combined office and bedroom; the place where he spent most of his days and all his nights.

As always, it was lit by the ghostly purple glow of his screen-saver, which was reflected in a series of Velux windows that ran along the ceiling.

He slumped on to the sofa and turned on the television with the remote control, at the same time picking up a half-empty can of Sprite from the floor and taking several, greedy swallows to flush the bitterness from his mouth and throat. He flicked through the television channels trying to find some absorbing distraction. But there was no distraction, he soon discovered, from his own raging turmoil. No matter what images appeared on television, he couldn't get what was in the jar out of his mind. Nor could he avoid the re-alisation, which came suddenly and nagged at him insist-ently, that he'd have to go back downstairs again. There was no way he could avoid it. He'd have to return to the kitchen, pick up the jar, and put it away in the fridge.

It was a warm night, after all. He couldn't risk the contents decomposing.

1

Right from the start, Mark Watson reckoned there had been a mistake. Making his way through the tinted glass doors leading off the pavement, he found himself in a vast, white atrium flooded with light from a domed glass ceiling six floors up. It was the kind of reception area that couldn't fail to impress, unexpected as it was completely incongruous. Most buildings in Soho were cramped and quirky – the offices of graphic designers and film producers and advertising agents to be found at the ends of dimly lit warrens and narrow staircases. GCM was utterly, improbably different. It was like stepping into an immense, bedazzling temple of glitz.

The reception desk, at the far end, was an endless curve of white, Egyptian marble, studded with clocks showing the time in every major entertainment market from Los Angeles to Tokyo. Behind it, four young women with supermodel good looks glowed, as though charged with post-gym endorphins. Above them, the GCM logo – a triumphal flourish in gold. Even before he'd got to the reception desk, Mark found himself thinking that someone, somewhere along the way had cocked it up. They'd got the wrong guy.

Promptly signed in, he was waved across to the seating area beside one of the chrome counters. Not that he was in any mood to sit. Instead, he walked around the walls, studying the float-framed photo-montages of famous actors and actresses holding aloft their glittering Oscars, superstar singers beaming with their Grammies, Broadway luminaries clutching luxuriant floral bouquets as they took their final bows. He picked up one of the glossy GCM brochures. Until that particular moment, he'd had no idea what GCM even stood for – but there it was, spelled out in embossed gilt lettering, Global Creative Management. And beneath the agency name, its client list.

As he scanned through it, he was increasingly impressed – and unfamiliarly self-conscious. Every single client listed was a major league player: pop stars whose records had gone platinum; household name actors. This was the 'A' league, no doubting it. There weren't any names here that were only vaguely familiar. No has-beens, wannabes or never-was-es. This was a list so star-studded, he could only be left wondering one thing: why the hell did they want to speak to *him*?

He'd received the phone call first thing this morning. Eight-thirty had found him behind his desk in the software support department of mobile phone company OmniCell, feeling less than bright-eyed and bushy-tailed; last night's *South Pacific* rehearsal in the Battersea Arts Centre had ended at half past ten, after which most of the cast had decamped to the nearby Slug and Lettuce for a swift one. But one had inevitably become two and even three in some cases – including his. He hadn't got to bed until the early hours.

So when the first call of the day had come through this morning, he hadn't bust a gut to get it. Instead, he'd let it ring awhile, hoping one of his colleagues would pick it up. Only when it became apparent they weren't going to, had he grabbed the receiver.

'Support,' he'd announced.

'Is Mark Watson available?' The voice at the other end was female, American and cool. Nothing like the usual Helpdesk callers, who phoned in various stages of desperation.

Mark sat up in his chair. 'That's me.'

Which was when Elizabeth Reynolds had said she was calling on behalf of Hilton Gallo from GCM. It was a blur after that, but the upshot was that he'd come to Hilton's attention and the GCM chief wanted to meet him. Would he be available later this morning?

Mark had felt sleepy numbness replaced instantly by sharp curiosity. He'd never heard of GCM – who were they, some record label? – and he assumed that Vinnie Dobson, his self-appointed manager, must have sent them a demo tape. But a high-powered meeting later this morning was the very last thing he felt up to.

'What about Wednesday?' he'd suggested.

The sleek voice on the phone swiftly cut that idea short: Mr Gallo was flying back to LA tomorrow morning. It was today, or nothing.

Mark had raised a hand to his brow, perplexed. He supposed he could wangle an early afternoon, but quite frankly, he didn't feel ready. He had no idea who this GCM crowd were, he was unprepared, and there was no way he was going to be briefed before he went in to see them – Vinnie was long weekending in France right now, stocking up on cheap booze. On the other hand, he guessed he owed it to Vinnie to go and see them – his manager had been sending out demo tapes for months. Eventually he told

Elizabeth, 'I might just manage four o'clock this afternoon.'

He didn't recognise the pause at the other end as arctic. Elizabeth Reynolds, every bit as smooth and svelte as she sounded, couldn't help pondering over the irony of it: Hilton Gallo represented more 'A-league' showbiz stars than any other agent in Los Angeles. He was a man with whom every studio head in Hollywood wanted to do lunch. Well-established celebrities of stage and screen would fly across America for the prospect of a mere twenty-minute slot in his notoriously crowded schedule. And here, she thought, was some complete zero, some London cybernerd, saying he *might just manage* four o'clock. She glanced down that afternoon's overloaded schedule. Hilton had made it very clear he wanted to see this guy. She couldn't afford to get heavy. Things would have to be shifted. After a while she said, 'Take down the address.'

Mark quickly unpeeled a yellow Post-It note and began writing.

For the rest of the morning, his mind very definitely wasn't on the job. He guessed he should be trying to dream up insightful analyses on the state of the music industry for when he went to GCM, or trenchant questions showing he kept up with the trade mags. Instead he kept wondering who this Hilton Gallo bloke was, and which demo tape he'd listened to. Mark had recorded a couple over the past year, about one of which he had decidedly mixed feelings.

He tried Vinnie a couple of times but, as he already knew, his mobile had poor reception in France. Mark understood that better than anyone – it was he who'd given Vinnie his mobile in the first place. OmniCell had been doing a discounted rate deal for staff and friends – and Vinnie had just had his mobile stolen. Mark also wondered what he was supposed to wear. Here he was, sitting in a Marks & Spencer suit and crumpled tie; he couldn't go to see some big shot from Los Angeles looking like a Helpdesk flunky.

It wasn't like Mark to get uptight. It was his easygoing self-assurance that drew people to him, a relaxed manner which came from not taking himself too seriously. Unexpected developments he took in his stride – with a job like his, he had to. But today's call from GCM was different; it was the first professional interest in his singing career he'd ever had.

At lunch-time he hurried back to his flat for a change of clothes so that when it was time to leave, he could head straight out to the Soho address he'd been given. In the end he decided to dress smart casual, and count on his broken-up face to see him through. While no one would have described Mark as handsome in the conventional sense, there was something about the way he looked which caught the attention – and held it. He was tall, rangy, with long, dark hair, but it was his face that was the reason for his popularity with women. Dominated by a long, prominent nose, jutting out at an angle as though once broken, Mark's craggy features gave him a battered, soulful look. Women responded to him as a man in need of loving. Macho, but at the same time vulnerable, he quite unconsciously provoked in them a surge of mixed feelings – intrigue, tenderness, lust. Men, taking in his height and rugged features, accorded him automatic respect.

Mark was aware of the impression he made on both sexes and hoped that today his natural bad looks would see him through. At least he could count on his hair, he thought as he left OmniCell shortly before three-thirty and headed to the nearby tube station. Thick, lustrous and down to his collar, his hair was his best asset – and women loved running their fingers through it. He'd opted for a dark linen jacket and black moleskin trousers, a deep-blue shirt and narrow tie, which he hoped did the business. As he descended the stairs to the Underground, he couldn't escape the irony. Here he was on his way to what could turn out to be the most important meeting of his performing career to date – the kind of meeting that would have got Vinnie all steamed up – and his 'manager' was nowhere in sight. After months of knocking on doors, sending out demos, trying to get in with the movers and shakers, now when someone was finally showing interest, Vinnie didn't even know it was happening.

It was Vinnie after all, who'd got him involved in the business. Mark had known Vinnie from way back, the two of them having grown up together on a council estate in Lewisham. After school they'd lost contact, Mark finding his way into computers through the guidance of his school's careers adviser, getting himself fixed up in a flat-share in Wimbledon and generally enjoying being a man about town. He'd always been close to his mum of course, and brother Lloyd, three years his junior. Growing up in a single-parent family, he'd felt a responsibility for them from an early age, and since he'd been earning, he'd enjoyed treating his mum to the kinds of things she'd never been able to afford when he and Lloyd were both kids, like dinners out, and weekend breaks, and indulgent gifts on her birthday.

And as the time approached for Lloyd to leave school, Mark had kept an eye out on the OmniCell internal appointments notice-board. When a trainee slot came up in new product development, Mark made sure that Lloyd's name was put on the interview list – and Lloyd had walked away with the job. That was three years ago, and since then Lloyd had advanced rapidly in the department, helped by his natural aptitude for computers combined with a creative mind.

Meanwhile, Mark's social life in Wimbledon had really taken off. A whole bunch of OmniCell's younger crowd lived in the area and used to get together at nights and over the weekends. There was a constant tide of people coming into town and going to parties and sleeping over. Discovering his own gregarious nature, not to mention his popularity with women, Mark had made the most of his independence – and it wasn't often that he woke up on a Sunday morning alone.

His singing career had started by accident just over a year ago. Mark had been out with a few friends at the Lamb in Balham where, by chance, Vinnie had organised a karaoke evening. Having been told in the past he had a good voice, and never lacking in confidence, it hadn't taken much egging on for Mark to be persuaded to take to the floor with Oasis's 'Wonderwall'. He'd been well received – extremely well received, Vinnie had thought, watching from the sidelines. It wasn't only the distinctive gravelly timbre he had to his voice, it was also his easy manner. He was clearly enjoying himself up there and good feeling was communicated effortlessly to the crowd. He had, Vinnie realised grimly, a lot more charisma than some of the 'professional' acts he managed.

Since leaving school, Vinnie had worked his way into the pub and club circuit as a music manager. Taking on guitarists and keyboard players who weren't too fussed about having to dodge the occasional beer can, he had a few acts on his books, ranging from acid-house artistes and late-night jazz crooners to mainstream rock groups who did covers of everyone else's music so that they could occasionally slip one of their own numbers into the mix. The hours were long, the pay was a joke and personal spats seemed endless. But Vinnie hadn't cared. He'd always believed in himself, and reading the music industry magazines – *Music Week* and *Billboard* – he would dream big dreams. It was only a matter of time until one of his groups came to the attention of music talent scouts. It was just a question of right place, right time, then he, Vinnie Dobson, would cash up big. He would come out from left of field and storm the industry. He knew he could do it – every week he read about guys heading in from nowhere to turn into major players. He'd get himself the Ferrari, the flash place in Hampstead. He'd be out at Stringfellows every night with a different woman on his arm. No doubt about it, Vinnie Dobson would be a name to be reckoned with.

Sure enough, his break had come when Swerve were signed up by Strobe Records, and 'She's My Lover' raced up the charts to number five. He'd created Swerve from the anaemic-looking, auburn-haired brothers, Oli and Steve Lamark, who hailed from a one-Porsche town in Lancashire. At a time when heroin chic was big on the catwalk, the Lamarks' look and their angst-rock sound had been perfectly in keeping with the times. It had been a first for all three of them and, when he looked back on it, there were things Vinnie would have done differently. But while it lasted, he'd been unstoppable. Okay, his commission hadn't stretched to the Ferrari, or the flash place in Hampstead – not yet. But he'd rented a flat in South Kensington and bought himself a second-hand Mercedes and all of that was a big step up. His confidence had been boosted as never before – people started calling his career 'meteoric'. Around that time he'd also signed up the Irish singer Siobhan O'Mara and Nigerian band Cha Punga, and music company executives started returning his calls. There was no doubting it, Vinnie Dobson was on his way to the top.

But when Swerve's follow-up number 'Wanting You' was

released, it barely made it into the top thirty, and after an initial burst of play-time, it was hardly heard of again. 'Too derivative' was the criticism that stuck – the Lamark brothers had imitated their own first hit too closely and that turned the punters off. Within days, Strobe Records were slow-pedalling the idea of an album – let's see how the next one flies, they said. And the initial buzz of excitement about Vinnie's other signings, Siobhan O'Mara and Cha Punga, died down into nothing.

Vinnie, who'd been spending money faster than it rolled in, quickly found himself staring down into the abyss. The Kensington flat had had to go, and he returned to his parents' place in Balham – 'while looking around for a place to buy' was how he played it. He'd fought to keep the car, as well as an aura of unassailable confidence – think big, talk big was how he operated. But, a year after Swerve's third single had flopped, and the two brothers had fallen out over some bimbo from Norwich, the big-time Vinnie front was getting harder and harder to keep up. Getting gigs in smoke-filled dens had never been a problem for him, but the real money was in record deals, and nobody on his books really stood out as a potential star. Nobody, that is, until he saw Mark Watson on stage.

Vinnie had bought Mark a beer after his karaoke performance and said he should think seriously about singing. Mark just laughed. That was the kind of stuff he'd dreamed about when he was fifteen. Standing in front of the bathroom mirror, hairbrush 'microphone' in hand, he'd had the same fantasy as every other teenage kid in the country. But that wasn't reality. Not the way he saw it.

Nonetheless a seed had been planted in his mind, and a couple of days later when Vinnie phoned to tell him a slot had become free next Saturday night in a club just round the corner from where he lived, and please wouldn't he consider it, Mark eventually said yes. It was only three songs with a back-up band. There'd be rehearsals on Saturday afternoon. Couldn't hurt.

That Saturday night Mark had enjoyed himself more than he'd ever imagined – and received a rapturous reception from the audience. He'd only ever thought of himself as just an ordinary bloke, but if he did have a musical talent, maybe he should develop it – he hadn't got such kicks from anything else before.

Which was why, over the next few months, he'd taken up proper singing lessons and started to perform. He found himself at folk evenings and in jazz back-ups and even in the bass of a baroque choir – his new singing teacher encouraged all his students to throw themselves into the widest range of musical experiences possible. In the meantime, at Vinnie's insistence, he let his former schoolmate book him in on a few gigs, and record a couple of numbers to send out on demo to various record companies. The idea of himself as a star in the making was a novelty to Mark, but Vinnie could be very persuasive, leaning against his sleek Mercedes puffing on a slim panatella. Vinnie who had got 'She's My Lover' to number five in the charts, and who always seemed to have a deal up his sleeve, Vinnie whose gregarious bonhomie was infectious – maybe he'd turn out to be right, thought Mark, glancing round the GCM atrium. Although he still couldn't avoid being sceptical about his present situation. Even if Vinnie *had* blustered him in to see Hilton Gallo, agent to the stars, Gallo would work out in an instant that Mark was nothing like all his other top-drawer clients.

'Mr Watson?' A voice sounded across GCM's magnificent reception area as he stood at a chromium counter, scrutinising the selection of crushed watermelon, mango and papaya. He turned to find an immaculately blonde woman in a black suit making her brisk way towards him.

'That's right.'

She delivered a crisp handshake before gesturing to a glass-walled lift at the side of the atrium. 'I'll take you up.'

The lift slid up the side of the atrium towards the glass ceiling, the reception desk rapidly dwindling in size below. Gliding all the way to the top, Mark realised that, despite his reservations about the meeting he was about to have, he was by now very curious indeed to meet this Hilton Gallo.

As the lift came to a halt, he was shown along the corridor of the penthouse floor, also brilliantly lit and expansive, its walls bedecked with autographed portraits of showbiz luminaries – actors, actresses, sitcom stars, directors and producers . . . who wasn't here? Then throwing open a door with a flourish, the black-suited woman gestured, saying, 'Do go in.'

The room was very long, and white, and all the way down its right side sliding doors opened out on to a garden glimpsed through muslin curtains, that were billowing like clouds in the late-afternoon sunshine. A polished, alabaster table gleamed down the length of the room, at its centre a vase containing the largest display of fresh-cut flowers Mark thought he'd ever seen. A hundred blossoms, exotic and multicoloured, splashed vividly against the pure whiteness of the room. At first, Mark thought he was alone. Then after a moment, two figures emerged towards him from the intense brightness at the far end. The first, a tall, lean, elegantly suited man, his dark hair cropped so short it was almost shaven, had a curiously monastic appearance. As he drew closer, Mark noted the narrow face, the acute eyes – he felt the man had summed him up even before he reached out with a strong handshake and said, 'Hilton Gallo. And this is my assistant, Elizabeth Reynolds. You spoke?'

'That's right.' Mark turned to shake her hand. Elizabeth was every bit as svelte as she'd sounded, with big, blonde hair and an azure dress, accentuating the unnerving dazzle of her blue eyes.

'Let's step outside,' suggested Hilton, 'nice day.' He brushed aside one of the curtains, to reveal the most extraordinary of gardens, green and lush, its central feature an Italianate fountain from which water cascaded into a round pond stocked with golden koi. At the far end, yellow honeysuckle foamed about a wooden pergola which overlooked the garden on one side, and Soho Square six floors below on the other. It was the most unlikely Arcadia in the centre of London.

'I heard your tape.' Hilton led him across to the pergola, in which a table and chairs had been set up, and a jug of iced orange crush with glasses. 'I was impressed. Very impressed.'

'Thank you.' Mark wondered which tape he was referring to – but decided to keep schtum about that for the moment.

'Drink?' Hilton was gesturing towards the jug.

'Thank you.'

As Elizabeth began pouring out drinks, Hilton looked over at him again, that same almost predatory observation, all-seeing, all-knowing. 'It would help if I told you something about us, yes?'

'It would.' Mark nodded.

'GCM is the most powerful talent agency in America, and therefore,' Gallo gave a small, dry smile, 'the world.' He handed Mark a glass of orange crush before picking up his own. Mark was about to take his first sip when Hilton asked him, unexpectedly, 'Any idea why that might be?'

Mark had half-expected to be grilled on the dynamics of agency power-plays and, quite frankly, didn't take kindly to it. But he'd go along with Gallo for the moment.

'I suppose all the stars you represent?'

'Exactly.' Hilton met his eyes with an expression of approval. 'And would you care to venture what it is that makes our clients so powerful?'

'Money?' He shrugged.

Hilton nodded once. 'I thought you might say that.' Taking Mark by the arm, he guided him on to paving stones which formed a border round the perimeter of the lawn. It looked as if they were going for an afternoon stroll.

'You know, Mark,' he began, his hand still resting on Mark's right arm, 'the world we live in, money isn't the issue any more.'

Oh, yeah? thought Mark, try telling his bank manager that. Or his mates. Or any of the people walking along the street outside. But of course the world Hilton Gallo was talking about was a completely different place. It was a world of Oscar-winning clients and transatlantic jet-setting, and assistants who looked as if they'd just stepped off the catwalk. And just for this incredible moment, he thought, it was his world too.

'There are those who have it,' Hilton was saying, 'and have it big. They sit managing their investment portfolios from their Holmby Hills mansions, or maybe out of town some place – the Aspen chalet, the château in France – and they're worth a hundred, maybe two hundred million. But,' he glanced over at Mark, his eyes lit with wry humour, 'so what?'

So what indeed, thought Mark.

'Did you know,' Hilton asked him, 'every year there are another ten thousand millionaires in the world?'

'I didn't.'

'Think of the effect. A million in the bank used to be the Holy Grail. Now being a millionaire is no big deal. It's the democratisation of wealth. No one cares what you say or do just because you have a few million.' Hilton halted and turned to him, fixing him with a look of searing conviction. 'Power isn't about money any more. It used to be, but no longer. Shall I tell you where the game's moved to now?' He took a step closer, as though about to disclose a thrilling secret known to only a select élite.

Engrossed, Mark nodded.

'Power,' Hilton's voice had lowered to one of compelling intimacy, 'is about how many minutes of prime-time television you command. It's about how many column inches of newspaper you can access. How much radio play-time you occupy. How many hits you get on your website. Media control is the new currency. Control the media, and you control the world.' He paused as though at the high altar of truth.

'You see, Mark, people out there,' he gestured to Soho Square and beyond, 'they have a voracious appetite for media. We're living through the biggest explosion of media channels in history. They just can't get enough of it. You know how powerful that makes our clients?'

Mark had never had things related to him this way before. But what Hilton was saying did make sense. It was so simple, so obvious – and the super-agent's zeal was self-evident.

'Because our clients are powerful,' he had started walking again, 'that gives us leverage. GCM has more muscle than any other agency to land the most lucrative endorsement deals, to hike up performance fees, to extract maximum value for intellectual property.' They were on the final length of their garden circuit, walking alongside the balcony railing which overlooked Soho Square. Then Hilton paused abruptly. 'Which brings me to you.'

Here we are, thought Mark, crunch time. The moment when he would be found out. Discovered as someone different from the person he was believed to be. But at least he'd got a walk round the penthouse garden with Hilton Gallo out of it, and a lecture on the true meaning of power.

'Like I say, we were very impressed with the tape.'

It couldn't have been that second tape Vinnie had persuaded him to do one Sunday afternoon when he had access to spare studio time. It must have been the first, thought Mark. But why had Gallo waited four months to respond to it?

'Few performances stand out like yours did.'

'Glad you liked it.'

'We more than just liked it. We found it very compelling.'

No need to over-egg the pudding, thought Mark wryly. But he supposed Hilton Gallo couldn't stop selling. That was what he did.

Hilton was studying him carefully, 'I sense a certain . . . reservation?'

He was tuned in all right, Mark had to admit, very observant.

'I s'pose I'm just surprised you think my demo tape—'

'It wasn't a demo tape,' Hilton cut in. 'GCM has a policy of returning all demos unplayed.'

Mark raised his eyebrows.

'We rely entirely on our own scouts. You were recorded at a charity concert a few weeks back.'

Well, this changed things! He knew the concert Hilton was referring to. An e-mail had gone round OmniCell asking for volunteer performers for a children's leukaemia charity supported by the staff association. Mark had put his name down for a singing slot, thinking it would be good practice. As it happened, the charity concert had provoked his one and only serious argument with Vinnie. Vinnie had been dead against it from the moment Mark told him about it and Mark hadn't been able to work out why. Until a few days later, when Vinnie had phoned to tell him he'd booked him a gig at The Three Troubadours in Notting Hill. Same day, same time as the charity do. Mark had told him, forget it, he was already taken. Raising his voice, Vinnie said he thought they'd agreed Mark would cancel the leukaemia thing. When Mark begged to differ, Vinnie threw a wobbly.

In the end, Mark had done the charity concert and Vinnie had growled at him for a week. But what else was Mark to do? He'd promised to do the concert, so he had to go through with it. What he hadn't realised until this moment was that there'd been talent scouts on the prowl.

'We prefer managing the search process ourselves,' Hilton was telling him now, 'avoids potential . . . complications.'

Mark guessed exactly what complications he was referring to.

'You had no contract regarding the concert?' Hilton confirmed now.

Mark shook his head.

'And you don't have any recording arrangement or agent at this time?'

'Not a recording deal. But a mate of mine has been setting up gigs and sending out demo tapes—'

'Does your management contract—' interjected Hilton.

'We don't have a management contract,' he returned, 'nothing official.'

There had never been any paperwork between Vinnie and him, and the fact was that Mark made a lot of his own arrangements which Vinnie disputed, like singing lessons ('Why bother? You can sing already'), *South Pacific* ('Different ball-game, mate') and charity concerts ('Total waste of time').

'Well, then,' Hilton raised his palms in front of him with a smile, 'we have nothing to worry about.'

You mean, *you* have nothing to worry about, thought Mark. He reckoned Vinnie would be none too pleased if GCM snapped him up for mega-stardom just like that.

'Anyway, it's not your representation we're here to discuss. It's you.'

Mark raised his eyebrows.

'Your voice. Your presence. The way you are. I think you could be exactly what we've been looking for.'

'What exactly *is* that?' Mark asked.

'Can't go into details right now,' Hilton was confidential, 'but let's just say that it's the kind of opportunity *any* male singer today would be very excited about.'

At that moment, Elizabeth's mobile phone sounded. She answered it before putting her hand over the mouthpiece. 'Julia,' she called over to them.

Hilton made a dismissive gesture. 'I'll call her back.' He frowned.

Hilton Gallo would rather speak to me than Julia Roberts? wondered Mark. Or was it some other Julia? Meeting Hilton's eyes now, he asked, 'I thought you only represented big-name celebrities?'

Hilton regarded him seriously. 'True. That's how we make them.'

Glancing away into the square below, he pointed to a large Peter Jones van crawling through the traffic.

'You see that truck down there,' he nodded towards it. 'Imagine a fleet of those pulling up outside our offices every night and loading up with celebrity. That's how it is. We *manufacture* the stuff. It's true you need to start off with the right material, but there's never been a shortage of that. Our expertise is in following the markets, predictive modelling, matching artistic resources to where the money's headed. We've been cross-referencing very intensively of late, and I think you could be the right guy,' he looked back at Mark, 'but I need to be certain. I'd like you to put down a couple of tracks for me in the studio.'

Mark had been following all this with mounting interest. For all his initial scepticism and his reservations about Hilton Gallo's super-cool style, there was no doubting what was going on: this man, on first-name terms with the world's biggest stars, was considering plucking him from obscurity. That was the deal.

'Now, if you're in agreement,' Hilton was leading him back to the pergola and putting down his empty glass, 'we've a studio round the corner on standby. Sound engineers, and keyboard back-up. What I'd like is for you to record a couple of songs, a ballad for sure, and maybe something fast. I'll take the tape back to LA with me tomorrow. I should have a response for you pretty soon.'

Less than ten minutes later, Mark was making his way back down the steps away from the white light of the GCM building. On his way to the biggest audition of his life, he felt his head spinning. Events of this afternoon had been like something out of a story-book, and as a council-house boy from Lewisham, Mark knew just how much story-books had to do with the real world. But for all his ingrained cynicism, his disbelief in sudden strokes of good fortune, that was exactly what was happening. So *this* was how it felt to be discovered? To find the world suddenly changed halfway through the afternoon? Of course, there were no guarantees. But what a ride he was having in the meantime!

The only dark shadow on the horizon was what to do

about Vinnie. If GCM signed him up, his self-appointed manager would be more than a little piqued. He'd be absolutely livid. Still, thought Mark, no use worrying about what might never happen.

2

'You've got your ballet shoes?' Isis brushed her daughter's hair into a pony-tail.

'Yes, Mommy,' replied Holly. Then, not wanting to be asked, 'And my tutu, and my leotard and stockings.'

'Good.' Isis snapped a bead band round her hair. 'And the stuff for Miss Adams's class?'

'That's changed to next week.'

'Okay.' She glanced at her watch.

'Are we going to be late?' Her five-year-old daughter was more conscientious about time-keeping than she was.

'Not if I have breakfast when I get back.' Isis flashed a guilty glance in the direction of the breakfast table with its wheatgrass juice, lactobacillus yoghurt and high-fibre muesli. Anything to delay that. 'Go brush your teeth. Quickly. I'll be downstairs.'

Making her way through the hallway of her Malibu home with its familiar, sweeping view of the Pacific Ocean rolling on to the private beach, Isis paused, giving herself the once-over in the mirror. The greatest sex icon in contemporary pop, according to this year's *Rolling Stone* magazine survey. Just as well they never saw her at seven-forty-five in the morning. Or any time, for that matter, in the past few weeks. Because although the blonde hair, the striking height, the leonine poise hadn't lost their impact, there was something else too – an uneasy apprehension which had come into her eyes of late and which she just didn't seem able to shift.

Isis had always operated on intuition. It was what had led her to her greatest successes. It was her guiding star. *Aphrodisia*, her massively successful album, had been a creation of her inspired sixth sense, the result of her understanding, at a premonitory level, what it was her audience most wanted to experience at that particular moment. Conversely, there had been times in the past when ignoring her inner voice had led to her undoing. When she'd pretended not to hear what wasn't convenient at the time – and had always lived to regret it.

In the past three weeks the sense that something was awry had returned with a disturbing intensity. What's more, she knew the cause of it; three weeks earlier, she had signed an endorsement with Berkeley Square, the global cosmetics manufacturer. The deal was to be made public when a male partner, promoting the men's products in the same range, had also been signed up. What Isis couldn't work out was, why the apprehension? The Berkeley Square deal had come up at exactly the time she'd needed it most. It had seemed like the answer to her every prayer. What could possibly be wrong with it? In particular, why the sense of terrible foreboding that seemed to threaten the most vulnerable part of her, something from her past she'd spent the last eighteen years of her life trying to put behind her?

Celebrity and secrets, she knew all too well, were a deadly cocktail. But despite a decade of intense media scrutiny, of journalists picking and prying into every corner of her existence, she had succeeded in keeping her most private secret to herself – and two trusted advisers. How could the Berkeley Square endorsement contract possibly lead her into danger?

Running a hand through her lustrous locks, she turned away from the hallway mirror. No point in dwelling on it now, she thought, pushing aside a tapestry wall-hanging and making her way through a concealed door, down a flight of stairs, past the bodyguard's living quarters.

'You ready to rock 'n' roll, Frank?' she called, as she walked past his door towards the semi-darkness of the garage.

'Coming right now, ma'am.'

Bodyguards were rostered for four weeks at a time – the security firm said that stopped them getting complacent. She could always tell what week they were in by how deferential they were. When they first arrived, they were always in total awe of her – the most famous female pop singer, who'd achieved icon status on account of her provocative sexuality. Whey-hey, she could almost see them thinking, this made a change for them from all those anonymous studio big-shots. Things changed pretty soon though. After a couple of weeks they had worked out she was just the same as anyone. Worse. She had a hellish temper.

Her current bodyguard, Frank Stenner, was still in his first week, so it didn't take him long to emerge from his quarters, resplendent in dark suit and tie, cellular phone and handgun tucked discreetly beneath his jacket. He hurried into the garage behind her.

'D'you want me to—'

'I'll drive. You sit in the back with Holly.'

'Yes, ma'am.'

Driving at least gave her something to do where she felt in control, she reflected, climbing her way up behind the wheel of the specially customised Range Rover. Its tinted glass windows were bullet-proofed. It was fully equipped with an automatic siren and tracking devices, and linked up to an instant alert centre which guaranteed helicopter gunship response anywhere in LA within twelve minutes. A microphone and loudspeaker had been built into the chassis behind the front wheel, through which to communicate without having to open any windows. It even had flame-throwers, operated by a red floor lever under each side, specially installed by a security expert from Johannesburg, car-jacking capital of the world. Having woken up one night to find a stalker in her bedroom, holding a gun to her head, she wasn't taking any chances.

She glanced in the rear-view mirror and saw Frank wearing sunglasses.

'Too bright for you in here, Frank?'

'Uh . . . no, ma'am.' It took him a moment to work it out, before he removed his shades and stuffed them in his pocket.

She didn't know why she got so tetchy with the staff. Even though her once-legendary retinue had been slimmed down to just a bodyguard and her housekeeper Juanita, she still felt awkward having them around. It went beyond the fact that she'd grown up poor. It was more that she worried if they hung around her long enough, maybe something in her long-distant past would communicate itself without her even being aware of it. Maybe they'd find her out.

In saner moments, she told herself she was being ridiculous. You couldn't tell about that kind of thing just by looking. Christ knew, she'd been ogled and leered at more than any woman in history apart from Princess Di. But there were only two people in LA who knew her secret, and she intended to keep it that way. Not even her former husband

and Hollywood heart-throb John Dettler knew. When she'd spoken to Hilton Gallo about it, Hilton had said best not to tell him. On a need-to-know basis, John hadn't needed to know.

Glancing at her watch again, she was about to hoot when Holly appeared, running down the steps into the garage, piling into the back of the car and slamming the door shut behind her. Noticing the smudge of toothpaste at the corner of her mouth, Isis tugged a handkerchief from her pocket and was dabbing it with saliva, but Holly, seeing the movement, had already licked the back of her hand and wiped her mouth. Then as Isis pressed the remote-control button to open the garage door, Holly looked up at Frank with a bright smile.

'Hi, Frank!'

'Hi, Holly! How're ya doing?'

'All right.'

She was tall for her five years and blonde, just like her mother. She had more manners than her mother had had at that age, and was a lot more mature. In fact, she was more grown up than most five-year-olds – she had to be, thought Isis, checking her daughter was belted in, before starting the engine and heading out into the driveway. Once outside, they went through the well-worn routine of waiting for the garage door to shut, before using another remote-control to open the two sets of eight-foot-high steel gates that led out to the street.

Isis was trying to give Holly as normal a childhood as possible, after all the interruptions. The dropping her off at school, the music classes twice a week, the friends who came round to play – in recent months they'd settled into a comfortable rhythm after the upsets of the past. During Holly's first three years, their family life had been one of relative normality, though John had frequently been away on location. But during the last two, Holly had been shuttled to and fro, not only because of the separation and divorce, but also because there'd been times Isis simply hadn't been capable of being a mother.

Glancing in the rear-view mirror, she noticed the child looking pensively out of the window. She was sure Holly sensed a lot more than she was capable of expressing, poor kid. It worried her when she went quiet. 'Doing anything special at school today, hon?' she asked to draw her out.

'Just the same.' Holly looked up at where Frank was scanning around them. 'I'm going to draw a picture of Frank.'

'That's cool.' Isis marvelled at how easily Holly adapted to their changing cast of guards, in contrast to her own uneasiness. Now Holly was looking at her in the rear-view mirror.

'Are you going out today?' She'd picked up on the make-up, thought Isis, and realised that leaving her home for a meeting was a big thing for her.

'Just to see Hilton about the new record.'

'Oh.' She was thoughtful again, before coming out with one of her disconcerting observations. 'Does Hilton think you're better?'

'Honey!' Isis glanced up in the mirror at Frank, resenting his presence even more. 'That's never been a problem.'

It was Hilton who'd found her that last time, bombed-out and comatose in her bedroom. She hadn't been responding to his calls and, by divine intervention, he had decided to take matters into his own hands, driving out to Malibu the morning after her accidental OD. Once he'd arrived, her bodyguard had confirmed she was in her bedroom. Receiving no reply to his persistent knocking, Hilton had ordered the guard to break down the door. And there she'd been, the drugged-out wreckage of the former Queen of Charts, minutes away from death.

That had been six months ago, though it felt like a life-time. And it was only when she'd hit rock bottom that the recovery process could begin. Only when she woke up in the Betty Ford Center, washed up, washed out, an intra-venous drip in her arm, that she realised she'd done exactly what she'd vowed she never would – she had turned into a cliché. Staring at the white walls of her private ward, the white furniture and white sheets, the white coats of the doctors and nurses, as she lay in her chemical strait-jacket, she was too numb to feel anything, much less shed a tear. All the same, she could hardly believe that she, of all people, had fallen victim to the entertainment industry's most con-tagious virus: fear of failure.

She hadn't exactly been a nobody before *Aphrodisia*. Her début album, simply called *Isis*, had sold a very respectable two million copies, its title track making it into the top ten of the singles charts. Her newly appointed personal manager, Alan Roberts, had generated hours of radio play-time and her ten-city tour through America, with the accompanying TV interviews, press hype and fan mobbings, had been not so much her first taste of celebrity as her first sit-down, seven-course, cordon bleu feast of fame. There'd been an effort-lessness about it all which she'd taken for granted. Surprised and delighted by her good fortune, when she'd scribbled a few tracks for a new album it had been almost incidental to her round of promotional concerts and interviews. Hilton had said he loved the new compositions – and for her second record had negotiated a major deal with Unum Music.

It hadn't been the only deal he'd swung. In those far-off, carefree days, he'd also introduced her to the up-and-coming Hollywood action adventure hero, John Dettler, and proposed marriage. It had seemed a wonderful idea at the time and their Waikiki beach wedding had been followed, a year later, by the birth of Holly, an event that gave rise to one of the most widely circulated anecdotes proving just how ditsy the Queen of Charts could be. No sooner was she admitted to the labour room than Isis had ordered a telephone and had a nurse dial up John, who was on location in Italy. For the next hour and a half her screams of pain had echoed to Tuscany via satellite link-up – she'd insisted he stay on the line throughout her entire labour, so he would never be in any doubt about the agony of childbirth.

Later that year her second record had been released. *Aphrodisia* was the album that made her – and at the same time, paradoxically, led to her undoing. For all Hilton's enthusiasm and the lucrative Unum contract, nothing had prepared any of them for what was to happen. There'd been a massive tug from the retail chains within a day of the title track release – 'Aphrodisia' the song rocketed straight to the number one slot of the charts that week. Featuring Isis groaning her way to orgasm, above a sensual mix of Caribbean rhythm, orchestral sophistication and crooning sax, 'Aphrodisia' was novel, provocative, and instantly controversial. And the video, in which glimpses of her nakedness appeared in an erotically charged montage of settings from tropical to Egyptian occult, only pushed the line even further. Her record was instantly condemned by the fundamentalist right, taken before the censorship board in Australia, and championed by every gay club from San Francisco to Sydney. Best of all, it had been hotly debated on *Oprah* – thereby ensuring it remained the most played record in America.

As sales figures poured in from every world market, Unum executives had been ecstatic. With the release of the album, and its instant trajectory to the top of the charts, there had been feverish rounds of meetings, before the decision was taken to strip out a second track for single release; 'All I Need' was soon soaring up the charts. Over the next three months it had been an orgy of celebration as successive hit singles prompted Unum to keep pulling off tracks for single release. This was another *Thriller*, they declared. The album had already broken all Unum sales records and was on course to take a tilt at Michael Jackson's. One week, four of the top ten singles in America were *Aphrodisia* tracks – that same week, Isis appeared on the front cover of *Time* magazine.

The media, of course, just hadn't been able to get enough of Isis, and at GCM five agents were installed under Hilton to work full time on the avalanche of interviews, endorsements, concerts, and franchise requests that flooded through their doors. Isis had found herself at the centre of a whirlwind of activity, operating at a level she'd never have entertained in her wildest dreams. As she sat in meetings at GCM to have the latest sales reports presented, looking round at the dozen or more high-powered suits – producers, agents, lawyers, accountants – she could scarcely believe that all of this revolved around her. She realised that she'd turned into a one-woman industry.

She'd also become fabulously rich. Just how rich, she'd lost track of after the first fifty million – every time she discussed things with GCM, the figures had moved up. But there was more than she could possibly spend. Which was when she'd bought the ranch in Santa Ynez and the beach-front house in Malibu – a home next to the ocean had always been her dream, and here she was, having just turned twenty-eight, living it. There were the smart cars, the furnishings, the designer clothes. The never-ending stream of investment decisions. Overnight she had acquired a travelling opera of investment advisers, personal trainers, off-shore lawyers, interior designers, wardrobe consultants, personal shoppers. And at the centre of them all, like a maestro in black tails, Alan Roberts, her personal manager, conducted the entire performance.

The Aphrodisia World Tour had been a whirlwind of mass adulation, with capacity crowds packing out the largest entertainment venues of America, Britain and the rest of Europe. By the time it came to a close, four months after it started, Isis had become the most controversial pop icon in the world.

But even on tour, the doubts had set in. It was as though everything around her, from the weekly sales schedules to the acres of magazine coverage, served as a reminder of *Aphrodisia*'s overwhelming success. Driving through crowd after crowd of adoring fans, instead of revelling in their admiration, she had one thought and one thought alone: how on earth was she ever going to top this? Having ascended the giddying slopes of success with such easy nonchalance, finding herself as though by chance at the very pinnacle of achievement, it began to dawn on her that there was only one way she could go from here.

At first she didn't admit to herself that she was losing her nerve. She tried not even to think about it. Though on her return from tour, when she started work on some new songs, comparing them to the *Aphrodisia* tracks proved irresistible. How did they match up, she agonised. How different should they be, or how similar? What if they bombed? What if all the adulation over *Aphrodisia* turned to derision when she released her next album? Would she turn out to be a one-album wonder?

Hilton had tried helping her through her deepest concerns. All his biggest clients, he reassured her, suffered the same fear – it was one of the hazards of success nobody

ever told you about. Apart from offering his own advice, and
urging her in the direction of Transcendental Meditation,
he'd given her the names of several therapists who'd helped
other clients wrestling with the same demons. But Isis was
determined not to become another self-obsessed, southern
Californian earth muffin, who couldn't open her mouth without spewing psycho-babble. And she couldn't see the point
of sitting about cross-legged on the floor, repeating the same
mumbo-jumbo over and over.

Her third album, *Eros*, had been far from a flop. The title
track ascended rapidly through the charts, and the disc went
platinum after just ten weeks. The album would have been
celebrated as a stunning success if it hadn't followed
Aphrodisia. The problem was that it had. And contrary to
Hilton's frequent appeals to her sense of perspective, there
was no escaping the anticlimax she felt every time she visited
GCM for the latest sales updates. In her own mind, if
nowhere else, she was on a downer.

In retrospect, the Broadway débâcle had merely delayed
the inevitable. Musical impresario Patrick Denholme had
approached her with an invitation to play the lead role in
his new production, *Seventh Heaven*. Hilton had been against
the idea from the start, but she'd lectured him that critical
acclaim was as important to her as the commercial rewards
of another album. In her heart of hearts however she knew
that the appeal of *Seventh Heaven* went much deeper. She'd
believed that her performance in New York would be something that couldn't be measured in terms of record sales. She
wouldn't be living from day to day according to the latest
retail figures. She was putting herself in a position where
nothing she did could be compared to what she'd ever done
before.

The naïveté of this assumption became all too apparent

the morning after opening night. Following an unprecedented blaze of media hype, she found herself subjected to the most vicious mauling of her life. Apart from the fact that she had no acting skills whatsoever, wrote the New York critics, the voice of *Seventh Heaven*'s leading lady lacked all substance and depth. Its flimsiness betraying a lack of formal training with every note, commentators were astounded she had been cast in such an exposed role. Stripped of sound engineering and special effects, they all concurred, Isis couldn't sing. Evidently the public agreed. After an initial six-week run, the show was boycotted by the New York public, and ticket touts found it impossible to persuade even Japanese tourists to see the show. Acrimonious publicity ensued, as cast members fingered her as the cause of all their troubles. The final indignity came when *Seventh Heaven* closed its doors after just eight weeks, having lost $5 million; it was Broadway's biggest flop in years.

She'd returned to LA, wearied and defeated, only to find herself on the brink of bankruptcy thanks to her long-time manager and confidant, Alan Roberts, who turned out to have been systematically defrauding her. She'd had to give up the ranch at Santa Ynez, the cars, the staff, all the trappings on which she'd so quickly come to depend. The threat of financial ruin had been accompanied by all the legal wrangles, and this collapse of her personal world had in turn destroyed the last vestige of her inner confidence. She had sought the fail-safe, white solace of Dr Coke, and for several months spiralled downwards in sharp descent, before the final drama of her rescue from death by Hilton Gallo.

The first time she and Hilton had met after her stay in the substance abuse clinic had been several weeks later in one of GCM's private dining rooms. He hadn't spared her feelings, subjecting her to an in-depth grilling on her coke habit, her rehab programme, her future intentions. She'd realised there was no place to hide, and had told him the whole, unedifying saga including a blow-by-blow account of the state of her finances. Getting back to work, she declared, wasn't just something she wanted to do – it was a necessity if she was to save her home.

Hilton had pretty much gathered most of this already, and in true Gallo style had already been active on her behalf. He'd begun though by lecturing her on a few home truths. Broadway had been a serious mistake. Quite apart from turning out to be the biggest PR disaster of her career, doing Broadway had also meant she'd been out of the music market for a while. And the markets had kept moving. The youth audience who'd made her so big with *Aphrodisia* was now three years older. She needed to be repackaged and relaunched if she was to appeal to former fans and the new record buyers who'd taken their place.

The solution he'd proposed, however, was audacious. A new Isis album was already in development which would carry entirely fresh material written specifically for her instead of by her. More than that, he was in negotiations with British beauty company Berkeley Square about a lucrative endorsement deal for a beauty product range which would have the same evocative name as her new album: Nile. As a brand, Nile was perfect. The name was inextricably linked with her own and it conveyed the same powerful images that had propelled *Aphrodisia* to such meteoric success. What's more, the commercial double-whammy he'd put together had never been attempted before. Nile products would appear on perfume counters amid a wave of endorsement advertising at the same time that *Nile*, the CD, went on sale in record stores worldwide. The endorsement deal alone would deliver enough up-front cash to ensure she could keep her Malibu home. What's more, Hilton had built in what she realised was an insurance policy; she'd be joined, both on the album and the endorsement deal, by an unknown male talent. While the beauty range was to include 'his' and 'hers' products, Hilton's intention was to broaden the market appeal of the new album. What he didn't say, but what she understood implicitly, was that if it all went terribly wrong, she wouldn't be left standing in the spotlight alone.

Not that she'd been wild about the idea of the 'unknown male talent'. Just how unknown was unknown? Hilton had argued that apart from following the well-established convention of a romantic duet, the singer would be British, giving the album extra sizzle in America and added impact in Britain. She wasn't to worry about being overshadowed, this guy would be a complete nobody. In fact, they didn't even know who he was yet, talent scouts were still scouring Britain trying to find someone suitable. In the meantime, he needed her help as he worked up to final contract stage on both the record and endorsement. She must stay clean, make a few carefully selected social appearances, and work to a carefully scripted story he'd devised for the media.

Which was why, in the past few months, she'd been going to parties like last night's *High Society* magazine bash, the kind of remorselessly pretentious ass-kissing *soirée* at which she wouldn't usually be seen dead. But there she'd been, bright-eyed and drug-free, circulating in a room of wall-to-wall celebrity, being seen by all the right people and, in particular, Ariel Alhadeff, CEO of Unum Music, with whom she'd had a brief but significant exchange, underlining her commercial credentials. Then there was the interview with the *Los Angeles Times*, her first in eighteen months, a back-from-the-brink, baring-of-the-soul portrait which had appeared last week and apparently sent out the right signals.

All this, the socialising, the media exposure, even the wheat-grass and lactobacillus yoghurt, she thought of as the Gallo Rehabilitation Programme. Much as it ran contrary to her nature to be little goody-two-shoes, she realised that right now she didn't have a choice.

'Mommy, when will Daddy be back in town?' Holly broke her from her thoughts as they approached school.

'Not till the weekend, honey,' she replied.

'Will he take me to Sea World?' The visit had been promised for several weeks.

'You'll have to ask him. He said he would.'

'I want to see the walrus put his flippers over his face.' She'd seen the ads on TV and was entranced. 'He's so cute!'

Isis smiled at her daughter in the rear-view mirror. Even in her darkest hours, she'd never forgotten how lucky she was to have Holly. There'd been times, to her shame, when she'd been overwhelmed by doubts and fears about her own career. But she'd never gone for long without remembering her daughter and the joy of being her Mom. All her adult life what she'd wanted most of all was someone to love and nurture, someone who'd respond to her with unconditional love. After getting to LA and embarking on her career, the prospect of that had seemed increasingly remote. In fact, she'd almost given up the idea as a hopeless dream. Then Hilton had introduced her to John, and when Holly had been born it had meant far more to her than any amount of public acclaim or adulation; it had been her deepest and most fervent wish come true.

Since regaining control of her life, she and Holly had grown closer. She was doing her best to give her daughter all the love and self-assurance she'd been denied in her own childhood. More than anything, all she wanted was for Holly to grow up as a well-balanced kid.

As they pulled up at the school gates, Isis turned to kiss Holly goodbye.

'Be good,' she told her, 'we'll see you at twelve-thirty.'

'Okay.'

Frank was already out of the car and going round to Holly's side, scanning the area as always before opening her door, and seeing her the few yards to the school gates. The Early Development Centre in Brentwood wasn't exactly the most convenient school to get to, but it did offer the best security. Behind all the lush foliage surrounding the buildings, eight-foot-high walls topped with an electronic security alert provided fortress-like protection for all the celebrity offspring attending the school.

Once Frank was back in the car, Isis did a U-turn before heading back towards Sunset, turning on the radio as she did. She paid barely any attention to a newsreader who was running through the usual litany of politics and crime. Then, out from nowhere, an item suddenly caught her attention. Something about an attack on the Chief Executive Officer of Berkeley Square cosmetics.

'. . . we cross now for a live up-date from London,' the anchorman was saying. Quickly reaching over, Isis hiked up the volume.

'Yes, John,' the voice boomed through the car, 'this is undoubtedly one of the most terrifying attacks carried out in London in recent times and people here are still getting to grips with what happened. It was carried out late last night at Jacques Lefevre's home in Belgravia, an exclusive residential area in central London, not far from Buckingham Palace. Police haven't released all the details yet, but we do know that a gang of five men broke into Mr Lefevre's home and assaulted him. Many people will know that Mr Lefevre's wife is the Gossamer Girl, Helena Defoe.'

Transfixed as she listened to the news item, Isis's eyes were filled with horror.

'What happened next has left the police here visibly stunned,' the reporter's voice faltered. 'They aren't giving out any details at present, but it seems the gang carried out some form of mutilation on Mr Lefevre.'

'Mutilation?' echoed the anchor.

'That's right. As I say, police aren't saying exactly what yet . . .'

'Jesus Christ!' Isis couldn't contain herself.

The Los Angeles anchor was asking about motive, and the London reporter replying, 'So far nobody has claimed responsibility, but police suspect an animal liberation group.' Before the item had even finished, Isis had pulled over to the side of the road.

'Frank! You drive.'

'Right, ma'am.' He climbed out of the back as she slid over into the passenger seat, wrestling her cellphone from her handbag, and dialling. Of all the beauty companies in the world, the crazy bastards had to pick Berkeley Square!

The phone at the other end rang only twice before Hilton Gallo answered.

'I've just heard about Lefevre.' Isis didn't conceal her alarm.

In the back of a GCM limo, on his way directly to the office from Los Angeles International Airport, where he'd just arrived from London, Hilton raised a hand to his face, pinching the bridge of his nose. If there's ever bad news to break, get it out yourself, was his dictum. But he didn't always get there first. He'd only heard the news himself less than ten minutes ago on the car radio, and was still waiting for someone from the office to phone back with the full story.

'It's only just happened, so nobody knows yet who did it—'

'Oh, great!'

'—or why.' He paused for a moment. 'It's important not to jump to conclusions.'

'What other conclusions are there except that there's a bunch of animal rights nutsos on the warpath of Berkeley Square?' Even as she said it, she felt a return of the anxiety that had been at the fringes of her consciousness these past few weeks. Only this time the sensation was closer. It had become an urgent, insistent gnawing in her stomach.

'Like I said, let's wait for more information,' Hilton continued, businesslike. 'In the meantime, I have some extremely *good* news from London. We've found you a partner.'

In the passenger seat, Isis was weary. She knew the distraction technique. She used it herself. She realised Hilton was trying to get her mind off animal terrorists. But she was too shaken to care about anything else.

'I'll have a video and some photos in the next few days,' Hilton told her. He didn't add that he was looking over some black-and-whites right now, and intended running them past a few colleagues the moment he got to the office. 'I don't think there'll be any problem pulling him over here at short notice.'

'Who is this guy?' She was still to be convinced this was good news at all.

'One of our scouts found him playing at a charity concert in London. Never recorded a thing. I doubt more than a couple dozen people have ever heard of him.' He picked his way carefully across her sensitivities. 'The Berkeley Square people watched him in the studio when he was recording. They reckon he fits the brief. The two of you will be sensational together.'

They ended the conversation with Hilton promising to

call her within the hour for a full update on Berkeley Square. Snapping his cellular phone shut, and slipping it into his jacket pocket, Hilton glanced at his watch. He hoped Elizabeth would get back to him quickly with some reassuring information on the Lefevre incident. The Nile deal was of great personal importance to him, and he didn't intend to let it slip out of his grasp. Not only would it deliver him a pleasingly astronomical personal commission, but much more importantly, with its audacious scope, it would secure his position as the most outstanding agent of his generation. A guru in the world of creative management. It was a ruthless profession, and Hilton had honed his skills to perfection over the years – this endorsement would be the pinnacle of his achievements so far.

He looked again over the photographs of Mark Watson spread out beside him on the back seat. He was perfect, thought Hilton, just perfect. His looks and his voice couldn't have fit the brief any better. On his last night in London, at his Green's hotel suite, the video had been delivered to him by courier, and immediately he'd slipped it in the recorder and watched. Mark had been nervous, of course. There were rough edges to be knocked off – the hair, for starters, would definitely have to go. But the overall package was exactly what they'd been looking for; the guy's dark ruggedness contrasting with Isis's fair hair and feline beauty, his husky bass timbre supporting her mellifluous alto.

He smiled, recalling his meeting with Mark. He'd been much taken by the young man's humility, his gratitude. He wondered how long it would take before he changed. Because once he signed the Berkeley Square contract, he would become suddenly wealthy, and Hilton had had plenty of opportunity to observe at close hand the effect that sudden wealth had on people. There'd be at least a million in it for

Mark from the endorsement, and another million plus coming in from the recording contract, a deal already well advanced. In a very short space of time – call it a month – Mark's life would be transformed. There'd be more money than he'd ever wished for. He'd be the talk of every gossip column and celebrity magazine in the world. He and Isis would soon be splashed on big-city billboards and advertisements in all the top glossies – Berkeley Square was funding a massive awareness campaign, which would culminate in the release of the *Nile* title ballad, destined to be a number one hit single.

Critics sometimes accused Hilton Gallo of playing God with people's lives, dabbling his fingers in the stuff of their souls. That wasn't the way he saw it. Instead, he regarded himself as the facilitator, the mover operating behind the scenes to bring plans to fruition, to make dreams come true. And one thing he knew for certain was that all Mark Watson's most lavish fantasies were about to be realised. In just a few weeks, he was going to be a star.

London
Tuesday, 31 August

'It probably won't come to anything.' Mark swilled the Carlsberg in his glass, across the table from Vinnie.

'What won't?' Vinnie was lighting up a slim panatella.

'What I'm just about to tell you.'

'Well, spit it out.' Vinnie's mouth curled into a broad grin as he exhaled a plume of blue-grey smoke. 'Talk about keeping a man in suspense!'

Swarthy, leather-jacketed, his dark hair brushed back carelessly from his face, Vinnie's man-of-the-world confidence took some getting used to. And his reaction to what had gone on yesterday afternoon was something Mark had considered with care. The truth was, Mark was still bemused by it all. Nothing so exciting had happened to him in, well, ever.

But even on his way home from the studio yesterday evening, returning to the familiar landscape after his recording session in Soho, as he looked out at the row upon row of grey, terraced houses curving into the distance, it was like coming out of a movie in which he'd played a walk-on part. It was then that the phrase had come to him, 'It probably won't come to anything.' Yeah, that was it. There was a certain gritty realism about it. He couldn't pretend that what had happened hadn't been wonderful while it lasted. It had been fantastic! But he supposed he shouldn't count on it coming to anything. After all, how many people did he know whose lives had been changed out of all recognition during the course of a single afternoon?

He'd got home to discover that Vinnie had responded to one of the messages he'd left on his mobile phone voicemail. Then later that night, during the briefest of conversations on a very crackly line, they'd agreed to meet at Vinnie's local haunt, the Lamb, the following evening.

And here they were. Vinnie had insisted on buying drinks and sitting down before Mark told him about the events of the day before.

'I called you in France yesterday,' Mark told him, 'because I got the weirdest call. A woman from GCM said a bloke called Hilton Gallo wanted to see me, pronto.' As he spoke, he scanned Vinnie's face for signs of recognition. The name Hilton Gallo didn't seem to register with him – but that of GCM obviously did. Before the look of irritation crossing Vinnie's face could develop into anything, Mark continued, 'I had no idea who GCM were. I thought they must be a record company and I reckoned you must have posted them one of the demos—'

'Got to be joking!' snorted Vinnie. 'Wouldn't send out stuff to the competition.'

Mark took a sip of his beer. For a moment he couldn't help contrasting the room in Vinnie's parents' semi-detached in Balham which currently served as his office, with the six floors of glittering opulence in which he'd found himself yesterday afternoon.

'Yeah, well—'

'Just tell them to sod off,' Vinnie interrupted. 'In fact, don't bother. I'll tell them to sod off.'

'It's too late for that.'

'How d'you mean?'

'Like I said, they wanted to see me pronto. Like yesterday afternoon.'

Vinnie was leaning back in his seat, a look of incredulity on his face.

'I don't believe it.' He was shaking his head. 'You didn't go, did you?'

''Course I did.' Mark looked him in the eye. 'I assumed you'd sent in a demo.'

All Vinnie's customary joviality had evaporated. Now he was shaking his head severely. 'You shouldn't have gone in without speaking to me first.'

'I did try.' Mark was caustic.

'Anyway,' Vinnie shrugged his shoulders, 'complete waste of time. Those guys are major league. Don't waste their time with small fry.'

'Well, thanks for the vote of confidence!'

Oblivious to his sarcasm, Vinnie blew cigar smoke thoughtfully into the distance, before taking another sip of beer. For just a moment, Mark wondered if he was going to drop the subject. As far as he was concerned, he'd said his piece, told Vinnie what he needed to. But Vinnie wasn't letting go.

'So what did they want you for exactly?' Meeting Mark's gaze, his expression was hawkish.

'They were pretty vague.' No need, thought Mark, to tell him Hilton's comment about how it was the kind of opportunity any male vocalist would be excited about.

Vinnie was scrutinising him closely. 'But they must have said *something*!'

'They did mention a kind of duet.'

'Oh, yeah. Who with?'

'Wouldn't say.'

'See?' Vinnie's lips turned in disdain. 'Like I said, total waste of time.'

'Yeah,' nodded Mark. As he'd expected, Vinnie's reaction hadn't been one of effusive congratulation. So he repeated the phrase, 'Probably won't come to anything.'

That, he trusted, closed the subject – at least for the moment. But Vinnie had fixed him with a long, brooding, dark-eyed intensity.

'And if it does,' he said after a long pause, 'they'll have to come through me.'

Mark took a swig of his beer. He had no intention of leading the conversation down *there*.

'So where did they get your demo?' persisted Vinnie. 'One of the record companies?'

Christ, thought Mark, here we go. He shook his head. 'Took it themselves.'

'At one of my gigs?' He flushed with indignation.

'No. At the gig I did for the leukaemia charity—'

Vinnie instantly realised the implications. 'So they're trying to poach you?' he exploded, voice raised and eyes blazing.

'I don't think—'

'What d'you mean, you don't think?'

'They didn't even talk about—'

'The bastards are trying to fucking poach you!' he yelled so loud that people at the other tables were looking round. Not that that bothered Vinnie. 'Well, I hope you told them you already have a fucking manager!' He jabbed Mark in the chest with his forefinger.

'I did mention it.' Mark remained cool.

'And what did they say about *that*?' he demanded.

Mark hadn't wanted this – any of it. He just didn't see the point of arguing about something that probably wouldn't ever happen. But if Vinnie was going to try pushing him around, he wasn't about to cave in.

'They wanted to know about you.'

'They did, did they? Like what exactly?'

'Like what kind of arrangement we have.'

'Arrangement?' Vinnie bellowed. 'How d'you mean, arrangement?'

Mark met his seething expression evenly before saying the word, 'Contract.'

The effect was like unleashing a jet of oil into a raging fire.

'I'll tell you what kind of fucking contract we have!' Vinnie yelled. 'I get you the gigs and you do the fucking singing.'

'It's not me that needs to be persuaded.'

'Of course it is!' he retorted. 'This is all about you.'

Mark shook his head. 'It's about GCM. They're the guys with all the aces.'

On the other side of the table, Vinnie couldn't help himself. Shoving his chair noisily back from the table, he rose to his feet. Seizing Mark by the shoulders, he began to shake him. 'So you're saying you're on their side?'

'It's not that.' Mark pushed back his own chair. 'I can't make GCM—'

'Yes, you can!' Vinnie jabbed a forefinger in his face.

'How?'

'Tell them to go fuck themselves!'

Mark was aware of some of the regulars, including his brother Lloyd, coming over to their table as he stood up. 'Are you seriously saying that if GCM offer me a recording contract, I should tell them—'

'If I don't get my cut, you haven't any choice! You're contractually obliged!'

'Oh, really?' Mark felt his own temper quickly rising. 'You want a cut of something you didn't have anything to do with? Something you tried your level best to talk me out of? Fantastic judgement you've got!'

'That's not the point!' Vinnie ranted. 'I'm your fucking manager!'

Mark delivered a cold, hard stare. 'Then where's the contract?'

Vinnie attempted a lunge at him but was held back by Cyril, the Lamb's manager, who'd seized him by the arm and was telling him to leave off. Lloyd and some of his mates were calling out, 'Give it a break, Vinnie!'

But Vinnie's face was darkening to a deep, dangerous crimson. Despite the efforts of all those trying to restrain him, he'd grabbed hold of Mark's lapels and was pressing his face into Mark's. 'Listen to me, you little shit.' He was shaking him. 'I made you what you are today. You're *my* property. Cut me out of this deal and I promise I'll fucking kill you!'

3

London
Tuesday, 31 August

He'd chosen an office block that had been deserted halfway
through construction, a vacant concrete and steel tower twenty
floors high that stood, a monolith of failure, among all the
glittering high-rise office and apartment blocks of London's
Docklands. Inside it was a wreckage of scaffolding and decayed
boardwalks. Up to the sixth floor internal dividing walls had
been constructed, forming a maze of concrete cubes and
passages leading nowhere. It was perfect. No security guards
on the building nor any closed-circuit television monitors in
the area. Visitors could come and go unnoticed. Four possible
exit routes from the building. And he'd familiarised himself
with its layout. He didn't expect any difficulties today, but he'd
planned for them anyway. He always did. Scrupulous preparation was one of the reasons Bengt Larson was wanted by police
forces in four different European countries – but had never
been caught. It was what would make One Commando the
most feared fighting machine in the history of the animal liberation movement. It was why last night's operation against
Jacques Lefevre had been such a spectacular success.

He glanced at the hands of his Breitling Aviator. A few minutes before eleven a.m. He was dressed in trademark black, which formed a sharp contrast to the short blond hair and pale blue eyes that belied his Swedish ancestry. Black jeans, black boots, black sunglasses and a black turtle-neck sweater followed the contours of his powerfully built shoulders and well-muscled chest. He spent an average of two hours a day in training to keep in peak physical condition. He always pushed himself to the limits of his endurance, knowing that one day that extra strength, that steel will, could make the difference between life and death.

Others in the movement had quickly recognised in Larson a level of commitment and discipline that was extraordinary. In organisations where fanatical ideologues held sway over constantly changing factions of supporters with big hearts but little stomach for real fighting, Larson had come sharply into focus as a man of action. Someone who could be counted on to make things happen.

Larson was as aware of his strengths as he was contemptuous of the inadequacies of others. His father – who had dreamed of a career in the military but had been rejected because of his asthma – had drilled into him as a child the importance of never showing any pain or fear. Tears were for silly little girls and punishable with a good hiding. It was important to be strong, logical and self-sufficient at all times, and to be better than everyone else at whatever task you were set. Larson had tried his best to live up to those high expectations. He despised all forms of weakness; it was the flabby complacency of his compatriots which had driven him, in his youth, out of Sweden and into the German army. Then when the end of the cold war deprived him of an enemy, he worked his way through various resistance organisations before determining that animal liberation was the last frontier. It was a cause where the battle lines were sharply drawn. A struggle equal to his leadership capabilities – a modern fight for a modern soldier. When he'd been approached by leaders of the Animal Freedom Lobby, a mainstream animal rights group, to set up a secret, paramilitary wing, Larson had agreed, on one condition; that he alone had total control over the organisation. The AFL had been in no position to argue.

He'd masterminded One Commando from the ground up, putting into practice all the lessons he'd learned during intelligence training with NATO forces. He'd begun with his own personal safety. Operating out of a network of safe houses across Europe, he seldom spent more than ten days in any one country, and was never in Britain for longer than three nights. All those he recruited to his élite corps were rigorously screened – he was well aware that the secret services, with too many agents on their hands, were now penetrating animal liberation cells. Which was why, even once they were recruited, he ensured that none of his commandos ever knew more than they absolutely had to. They didn't meet one another except in training for an operation. They didn't even know each other's names. At any one time Larson might be in touch with up to fifty contacts all over the world, none of whom knew the others, or how they fitted into his future plans. He was the master of compartmentalisation and took extreme care to ensure that nobody had any knowledge of the big picture – except for one. And that one was the only man in the movement Larson respected for being as smart as he was.

He'd seen the other man at meetings, not only of the Animal Freedom Lobby, but also of other animal rights and anti-vivisection groups. In the early days of One Commando, he'd gone incognito to the kinds of meetings where he was most likely to find recruits. Whether it was an anti-cruelty conference in Cologne, or a live-animal export protest in Dover, the other man always seemed to be there, his dark, elegant suits and clean-cut features setting him apart from most of the other animal rights sympathisers. Jasper Jones was what he called himself – an assumed name, Larson supposed – and through his contacts he discovered that Jones worked for some kind of advertising agency in London. And although he looked different from most of the AFL crowd, what wasn't in any doubt was Jones's standing among all the people who counted. He had no formal function in the main animal rights groups, but he was treated with evident respect.

Each man had noticed the other, but had deliberately held back until they'd both found themselves at the same meeting in Paris. Larson had taken the empty seat next to Jones's at the back of a crowded conference room, and struck up conversation. Things had progressed rapidly after that. Although both men were wary, Larson soon found that Jones was as driven by a strong desire to make his mark as he himself was. And while he, Larson, was the implementer, the doer, Jones seemed both willing and able to underwrite the cost of One Commando activities, as well as to suggest strategy. Each needing the other, they complemented one another perfectly.

The principled Jones had suggested they agree on certain rules from the beginning: they would only ever take action against a company when there was incontrovertible evidence that it was engaged in torturing or abusing animals. And they would only take action against those who were ultimately accountable for torture and abuse. Theirs would be an ethical campaign. A just campaign. The public might not always approve of their methods – but never would One Commando be open to accusations of falsifying evidence, or picking the wrong target.

Last night's operation, the Lefevre attack, had been their first joint effort – and the most daring operation in the animal liberation movement's history. Berkeley Square had become a One Commando 'project' after AFL activities failed; when anecdotal evidence had come to light, a few months earlier, of massive abuse of animals in a Berkeley Square laboratory in Spain, the AFL had written a letter of protest. Berkeley Square had responded with a swift and firm denial.

Realising that clear evidence was needed, it was Jones himself who had travelled to a laboratory outside Madrid and, posing as a delivery man, gained admittance for long enough to fire off some film. His photographs had shown the horribly mutilated and discarded bodies of two chimpanzees, and over a dozen rabbits on which the most barbaric vivisection had all too clearly been carried out. AFL activists had printed fliers with photographs, circulating them directly to the public outside Berkeley Square Head Office. Surely the company couldn't try to pretend now?

But the response from Berkeley Square had, once again, been instant rebuttal. Neither Berkeley Square nor any of its subsidiaries tested on animals, declared a statement issued by the company's media office. All such testing had been abandoned ten years before in accordance with the Code of Practice of the Ethical Pharmaceuticals Manufacturers' Association, to which Berkeley Square was a founding signatory. The mere repetition of such allegations was libellous, and Berkeley Square wouldn't hesitate to take action against irresponsible reporters.

To the AFL's consternation, the Berkeley Square statement had been enough to keep their evidence completely out of the media, with the exception of a few tabloid reports referring obliquely to 'allegations of animal testing'. How was it that photographic evidence could be so completely quashed? There it was in black and white – but no one would believe them! Frustrated at their lack of success, the AFL had asked One Commando to see what they could do.

Last night, One Commando had done just that. Never had such dramatic, direct action been taken. The response had been immediate and massive. The operation had dominated every evening news bulletin on radio and TV and had made the front-page headlines in every newspaper this morning. The work of a single night had created massive awareness – and it had been Jones's suggestion that had transformed what would have been an incident scarcely worth reporting into the most newsworthy event in the country. Jones, with his flair for the theatrical.

None of the group had known before the raid what had been planned. They hadn't needed to. And afterwards, they'd dispersed back to homes outside London and, in several cases, across the Channel. But there was one piece of unfinished business. A piece critical to the ultimate success of the operation, which was the reason he was here this morning.

At exactly eleven there was a noise from the main fire escape. From a secure vantage point he watched as Alan Brent climbed across a steel RSJ into the concrete tower. Slight of build, pale-faced and bespectacled, he seemed the most unlikely recruit to One Commando. But Larson hadn't brought him in for his physique – he'd hired him for his brains. Brent had a genius-level IQ rating and a photographic memory. But more important still was his special facility with information technology. Whether cracking advanced security codes or hacking into computer systems, Brent's abilities were unsurpassed – he was a cybernaut extraordinaire. Last night it had been Brent who'd disabled Lefevre's electronic alarm within thirty seconds, making the entire mission possible. And that hadn't been the only part he'd played. Because it had been his first operation, Larson had given him another assignment to test his mettle. A form of initiation. Brent had been shaken, that much had been plain to see – the shock had been visible in his trembling hands. But he'd gone through with it. He'd followed orders. And now, as instructed, he'd returned.

When Larson stepped out from behind a brick wall, Brent looked up with a start. Then in automatic response he pulled his shoulders straight and brushed a fallen lock of hair back from his face.

Larson nodded briskly, eyes concealed behind the black, reflective sunglasses.

'Good,' he murmured. Having learned to speak English from a series of American-trained teachers in Sweden his accent was a strange Scando-American. 'I have something for you.'

Behind his own thick lenses, Brent's face registered alarm as Larson reached into his bag. God Almighty, Brent wondered, had he walked straight into some trap? But as Larson extracted an envelope, he relaxed. It was of the brown, padded variety and an address had been printed on it. Accepting it, Brent stared at the address and the inscription beneath: 'From One Commando. Two eyes for many.' Realising what was to go inside, he asked, 'You want me to deliver this?' It was more an exclamation of astonishment than enquiry.

Larson acknowledged him with a brisk nod. 'The operation is all over the news. But not the reason. That needs to be changed.'

'But how will they know . . . ?'

This time, Larson extracted from his pocket a slim imitation-walnut case, wrapped in a veneer of protective cling-film. As Brent took it from him, he noticed the discreet gilt engraving, 'Jacques Lefevre', and remembered the case being extracted from Lefevre's jacket pocket the night before. Larson was also handing him a VHS tape labelled, 'Berkeley Square laboratories, Madrid'.

Staring down at the spectacles case and video, Brent swallowed. 'This ...' he was shaking his head, 'this is going to ...'

'Blow the place apart?' offered Larson, this time with a wry smile. 'My intention exactly.'

The afternoon editorial conference was already under way when the courier package arrived addressed to Patrick Harlow, Editor, *The Globe*. His secretary, Jenny, knew better than to let any such delivery sit on her desk for more than a minute while Patrick was in his office – conference or not. Tearing open the padded envelope, she found the spectacles case together with a videotape. The case was made of sleek imitation walnut, and she glanced at it briefly before standing to take both items in to Patrick. Glory, hallelujah! she thought. Patrick was always leaving his glasses in offices and sitting rooms – several times a week she'd have to get on the phone to track them down and have them biked back urgently. At last, it seemed, he'd responded to her frequent entreaties – not to mention those of his wife – and had bought a second pair.

She opened his office door without knocking. Around the large table extending from his desk, a spirited debate was going on about tomorrow's lead. Berkeley Square was the story of the week – the month! – and in the twenty-four hours since it had broken, *The Globe* and its tabloid competitors had been engaged in a frenetic scramble to track down family, friends, associates and acquaintances of the Lefevres, cheque-books at the ready, for any revelation – the more salacious the better – so long as it was exclusive. At this moment, *The Globe* had two options, both concerning Jacques Lefevre's wife, Gossamer Girl Helena Defoe, who'd been on a shoot in New York when her husband had been attacked. 'Helena: Supermodel. Mega-bitch' was based on the testimony of a model agency boss, and ex-boyfriend in Paris, who'd described her as a manipulative minx who'd set her sights on screwing her way to the top. 'The Heartbreak of Helena' was the alternative – a friend had described how desperately Helena had wanted Jacques' baby, but she'd had difficulties falling pregnant and was considering IVF treatment.

As Jenny slipped quietly into the room, Heather Samuels, News Editor, was arguing in favour of the IVF story.

'I agree it's a strong angle,' retorted Reg Frith, Deputy Editor, 'but that's not our market. Male readership, remember. They'll go for the "mega-bitch" story. We can run the IVF thing on page two.'

Jenny put the spectacles case and video down in front of Patrick.

'What's this?' Glancing away from Reg, he looked up with a querying expression.

'Just arrived for you. I assumed you'd ordered a new pair?'

Patrick shook his head, picking up the case, glancing at the polished veneer before catching sight of the fine calligraphic script. He opened the lid.

'What the—!' he exclaimed, recoiling from the contents in disgust as, beside him, Jenny's face turned into a portrait of revulsion.

Debate in the office ended abruptly as colleagues looked from Patrick to Jenny to the open spectacles cases. Then curiosity getting the better of them, they leaned or stood to get a glimpse of the cause of the consternation. Inside the spectacles case, gory with congealed blood, was, unmistak-ably, a pair of human eyeballs. Patrick regarded the horri-fied expressions of his colleagues for a moment before reaching for the tape. After a glance at its label, he leaned over to the TV in the corner of his office, slipped the tape into the video recorder and pressed 'Play'.

Bursting on to the screen shortly afterwards came images of whole batteries of cages containing rabbits in a laboratory-style warehouse. The date displayed in the corner of the screen was less than a month earlier. Close-up shots showed most of the rabbits had shaven fur and inflamed skin. The eyes of many were so damaged they were clotted with pus. Graphic, harrow-ing images, showing scenes of the most unspeakable suffering and pain, continued; an anti-vivisectionist's nightmare of stainless steel and surgical brutality. Shaking his head, Patrick fast-forwarded the video, his colleagues continuing to watch with him in stunned silence. The video continued its tour of the laboratory in relentless detail before freezing on a pile of dead rabbits which had been unceremoniously thrown into a plastic wheelie-bin.

Turning back to his colleagues, Patrick looked round at their shaken expressions.

'So much for Berkeley Square's denials.' His own expres-sion was disparaging. 'I think we have our lead. And we'd best call Scotland Yard.'

Los Angeles
Tuesday, 31 August

Hilton Gallo's morning regime was always the same when at home in Los Angeles. He'd rise at five-thirty and swim thirty lengths of the Olympic-length swimming pool he'd had specially constructed in the garden of his Pacific

Palisades home. Having performed his ablutions, he'd spend forty minutes in meditation, focusing on nothing but his TM mantra. By seven-fifteen he'd be prepared for the day ahead, exercised and energised, every sinew in a state of finely tuned readiness, reflexes acute and focus concentrated. Like a samurai warrior, peak performance was what he sought, and the stamina to engage in relentless, bruising battle. Because as head of GCM, every day was a constant struggle in a war without end. Competition had never been more fierce. In Los Angeles alone ICM, CAA and William Morris were all chasing the same deals as GCM. And right across the globe wherever GCM had offices – New York, Toronto, London, Paris, Rome, Madrid, Berlin, Beijing, Tokyo – were theatres of war for which he, as Commander in Chief, had ultimate responsibility.

Over a fruit platter breakfast, Hilton would go through the press. There were the two daily trades, *Variety* and *Hollywood Reporter*, as well as the *Wall Street Journal* and *New York Times* from the east, and the local *Los Angeles Times*. And of course, there were the faxes his secretary Melissa Schwartz sent through first thing when she arrived at the office at six.

By seven-forty-five he'd be on the phone in the back of his chauffeured car, catching the European offices mid-afternoon. As a man of educated tastes and a confirmed Anglophile, despite the milieu in which he operated, Hilton had always believed stretch limousines to be the very epitome of vulgarity. Even Rolls-Royces smacked, to him, of the nouveau riche and the crass. German and Italian marques he found respectively lacking in charm and impossibly flash. Which was why he set out to work in a Bristol, that exceptionally rare and luxurious hand-crafted motor-car that was the very model of subtlety. He'd had his Bristol customised for the work he did – a phone and television screen in the back seat enabling him to video-conference with colleagues around the world. What it lacked in panache, he used to think – and many found its appearance bland – it more than made up for in the originality of its design, and its constant ability to surprise. It was a car with which he felt in complete accord.

Some mornings he might go to the Peninsula for a breakfast meeting. For those deals too covert to discuss even at the office, he'd be driven to any one of half a dozen hotels in which a suite had been booked using an alias. But this particular morning, as he headed towards GCM headquarters, he received his first telephone call of the day from Elizabeth.

'I've just had an early-warning call from Stan Shepherd,' she told him. Stan worked as Media Relations Chief in their London office.

'Yes?'

'The story's about to break over there that "One Commando" have claimed responsibility for the Lefevre attack.'

'Along with a dozen others.'

'They sent Lefevre's eyes to the Editor of *The Globe* along with a videotape showing scenes of rabbits being used in lab tests, allegedly by Berkeley Square in Madrid.'

Hilton didn't miss a beat as he pulled a grimace. He hadn't known about the eyes. Nobody had. So that was what the British police had been keeping under wraps. He instantly thought what Isis's reaction would be when she got *this* news. She'd beaten him to the phone when the story first broke. He couldn't let that happen a second time. He had to preempt anything she might pick up from the media. He was determined that this endorsement would be the success he'd planned. His personal stake in it was too great to let some adverse news spoil it now. He glanced at his watch,

'I want you to bring my nine-thirty forward an hour.'

'Ross, Andy, Neil,' she confirmed the attendees, her own presence a given.

'Plus Leo,' he added their head of global media relations – he would definitely be needed after this latest news. 'And pull together a risk assessment on One Commando, won't you.'

'Do I speak to the Metropolitan Police in London?'

'They won't speak to us. Try Francis Hanniford at Berkeley Square. Human Resources Director. Lefevre has seconded him to liaise with Scotland Yard. He's also supposed to keep us in the loop.'

'Understood.'

'Monitor all news broadcasts till I get in. Let me know the moment the story breaks over here.'

The GCM building on Sunset Boulevard was a massive six floor block in white marble and dark, reflective glass, fronted by eight huge fountains with extravagant, five-metre-high plumes. Royal palms swayed and the flags of a dozen GCM territories fluttered outside. Constructed in the late eighties as a deliberate, glittering statement of corporate machismo, a more triumphal totem of GCM's success would have been impossible for architects to conceive. No matter how much it offended his own sensibilities, Hilton knew that he wasn't the audience being played to. As the Bristol pulled to a halt inside the Director's entrance, next to the executive suite elevator, he opened the back door and stepped out. Less than thirty seconds later, he emerged from the elevator on the top floor, turning left and heading towards his private meeting room. It was exactly eight-thirty as he opened the door.

The meeting was tight but high-powered. Ross McCormack was head of endorsements, and Andy Murdoch his counterpart for music. Neil Ferreira, one of Andy's top people, was working on the Isis deal and Leo Lebowitz controlled the media machine that lay at the heart of all GCM activities. All conversation stopped as soon as Hilton came into the room. He nodded once to them all, before sitting down at the head of the table. Elizabeth was already on his right-hand side, briefing pad open for notes.

'Two issues here,' he began in his quiet, precise tones. Holding up a finger he said, 'One: the commercial fallout from the Berkeley Square deal. And', raising a second finger, 'two: the security implications for Isis.'

Across the table, his eyes met Ross McCormack's. Ross looked every inch the advertising man he used to be. His crew-cut hair was very blond, and his thick-rimmed glasses very red, giving him the appearance of someone out of a Roy Lichtenstein cartoon. When he spoke, he was strong and persuasive.

'The starting point is that we were conscious of the animal testing issue before we even negotiated. The legal team in London checked out Berkeley and all its subsidiaries as part of our usual ethical vetting procedure. There is no question that any of them use animal testing – they haven't for more than a decade.'

'What about the video?' asked Hilton.

McCormack shrugged. 'Who knows where that came from. Wherever it is, it's not a Berkeley Square facility. I double-checked the due diligence report before this meeting – Spain was cleared. Anyway, yesterday Lord Bullerton, Berkeley Square Chairman, read out their denial in person, outside Berkeley House, accompanied, at Leo's suggestion,' he nodded to his colleague, 'by his wife. Lady Bullerton is on the Council of the RSPCA, a fact that wasn't missed by the media covering the event.'

'So the Madrid video's just some hoax?'

'An attempt at justification,' nodded McCormack. 'Berkeley's version of events has been accepted by most commentators, including animal rights groups. They've also received powerful support from the Ethical Pharmaceuticals Manufacturers' Association. But the best thing they've done to validate their statement is to issue an open invitation to the media to visit any Berkeley Square production site anywhere in the world. That kind of transparency,' he shook his head, 'it's impossible to beat.'

Hilton looked over at Leo Lebowitz. 'Hasn't been much commentary over here. It's been a British thing so far?'

Lebowitz was nodding.

'How has it been playing in the UK?'

Lebowitz, forty-something, and the only bearded man in the agency, had the smiling, enigmatic air of a religious mystic.

'Immediately after the attack,' he replied, 'questions *were* raised about Berkeley. It seemed inconceivable that the attack could have gone ahead without any justification whatsoever. But things changed pretty quickly. Bullerton's statement laid to rest all but the hard-liners. Of course, the video could change things—'

'Has *The Globe* released it yet?'

Lebowitz was shaking his head. 'The police have it now. They're not letting anyone near it – say it's too disturbing.'

'How is this going to affect the timing of Nile?' Hilton asked Ross McCormack.

'If there is a delay we're talking a week, ten days max. Berkeley just want to get this whole thing behind them.'

'Does that gives us leverage to up the stakes?'

McCormack shook his head. 'There's no more room. We got a great deal out of Berkeley Square already. But I do think we need to add an addendum on security.'

Hilton was nodding, before looking over at Elizabeth.

'Where are we on a risk assessment?'

'Scotland Yard have appointed a Detective Inspector Bennett to the investigation – supposed to come highly recommended. Specialises in underground eco-terrorism.'

Hilton's expression was grave.

'Francis Hanniford was very helpful.' She glanced at Hilton. 'Turns out he was at Eton with the British Home Secretary and has been given direct access to someone high up in Scotland Yard – I would think Bennett or one of his reports.'

Around the table the others regarded her with intense expressions.

'Hanniford's faxing over the intelligence he's received on One Commando. Apparently they're led by a renegade former NATO army officer called Bengt Larson.'

'Danish?' prompted Lebowitz.

'Swedish. Hanniford says that Scandinavians dominate militant eco-terrorist groups in Britain.' Elizabeth recalled his authoritative public school accent. 'Larson is wanted by Interpol on previous charges, so this isn't a one-off.'

Hilton had raised his hands to his temples.

'Hanniford said the Lefevre operation was carried out so effectively the group didn't leave a trace of themselves behind.'

'Was there *any* reassuring stuff to come out?' Lebowitz wanted to know, exasperated.

Elizabeth nodded. 'Hanniford did say there's no evidence that One Commando's activities extend outside the UK. And Larson isn't known to have been involved in activity anywhere outside Europe.'

'Still doesn't give us much to reassure her,' remarked Lebowitz.

'Quite,' Hilton agreed looking round at his colleagues. 'In a few minutes I'm going to have to break the latest news to her before she hears it somewhere else.' He met their expressions gravely. 'She's not going to let this go.'

McCormack's eyebrows twitched with alarm. 'You're not seriously contemplating withdrawal—'

'Difficult to make a judgement call with what we've got so far.' Hilton regarded him evenly. 'But Isis's safety has to be our top priority.'

The meeting ended a short while later on an inconclusive note. Everyone knew what had to be done. But there was no getting away from the latest disturbing turn of events. They would proceed with caution, they decided, while trying to find out more about One Commando. Hilton had the hardest task, preparing Isis for the sensational news about to scandalise the US media and trying to persuade her not to pull the plug on Berkeley Square. Ross McCormack was dispatched to see Blake Horowitz, the company lawyer, to review security clauses in Isis's agreement with Berkeley Square. And Elizabeth Reynolds had a phone call to place to Mark Watson; she was to arrange for him to come to Los Angeles without delay.

4

Isis sank back into the plush cream sofa. On the table in front of her, in an intricately patterned Royal Doulton cup, was a drink of camomile tea. As always when she visited Hilton, she couldn't help responding to the air of tranquillity that always prevailed in his office, in marked contrast to the ferocious activity throughout the rest of the GCM building. The uncluttered spaces, fresh-cut flowers and clear light were part of it, but the real source of the calm was Hilton himself, sitting opposite, cool and dark in charcoal Armani, his expression serene. Not for the first time in the years he'd represented her, she felt more as though she were on a visit to her psychiatrist rather than in a meeting with her agent.

'I haven't told you this before,' she met his gaze, 'but ever since we first talked about the endorsement I was . . . anxious about it.'

Hilton raised his eyebrows. 'Was there a specific—'

'No,' she shook her head, 'nothing like that. It was more a deep-down feeling.'

Hilton brought his hands together and raised them, prayer-like, to his lips.

'Then all this blows up,' she continued, 'and it just seems to prove everything I'd picked up from the start.'

'What are you saying?' He was solicitous. 'That it was a mistake to sign the Berkeley Square endorsement?'

'Yes.' She met his eyes briefly before looking into the distance. 'Well, maybe,' she shrugged. 'Maybe it was a mistake. Maybe I should pull out now before it gets any closer.'

'It's understandable you feel this way,' he responded.

'But?'

'And I've always respected your intuition. You know that.'

'But?' she persisted.

'Well,' he met her eyes with a smile, 'you had very good reasons for signing the endorsement. What I must ask you now is if any of those reasons have changed?'

Leaning back in the sofa, she closed her eyes. Hilton always went for the analytical approach, but analysis was something she'd been incapable of ever since hearing of the Lefevre attack on the car radio. The news item had come as a hateful confirmation of her own uneasy feelings. Worse. While her emotions, until then, had been unfounded and ill-defined, now they had a clear and terrible focus.

Within hours, every news broadcast had been full of the gruesome twist to the Lefevre attack – the delivery to *The Globe* newspaper of the spectacles case containing Jacques Lefevre's eyes. The media revelled in the ghoulish horror of it, photographs or video-footage of the now-famous spectacles case carried in all the headlines. The footage of One Commando's video had also been described – only to have its implicit accusations fiercely rebutted by Berkeley Square who had arranged immediate media tours of its facility in Spain. While journalists had failed to find anything like the horrors depicted on the One Commando video, had Berkeley Square really disclosed the whole truth?

Isis's fax spewed out pages from Berkeley Square – copies of media releases about the condition of Jacques Lefevre, as well as categorical denials about the use of animals in product testing. Alone in Malibu, Isis had been absorbing all this in a state of growing terror, when Hilton phoned to say they should meet.

Now, in the reassuring serenity of his office, as he worked through the reasons they'd agreed to the endorsement, everything felt so different. He talked about how Berkeley Square had delivered the money she'd needed to hold on to her home. How the deal would deliver a huge publicity advantage to the launch of her new album. Neither of those reasons had changed, she had to agree. He then went into why she shouldn't over-react to news of the Lefevre attack; did it make sense to call off one of the most important deals of her career over an isolated incident on the other side of the Atlantic? One Commando was a London-based group whose past activities had all been carried out in Britain – there was no reason to suspect they were about to launch attacks in America. What's more, Lefevre was the only person they'd ever assaulted.

Hilton was, as always, immensely persuasive. By the time he'd finished, Isis felt foolish for even contemplating backing out. For a while she sat, regarding him in silence, before she murmured, 'What you're saying . . . I wouldn't disagree with any of it. From a rational point of view, of course I should stay in the game. It's just that this isn't about reason or logic.'

He raised his eyebrows, queryingly.

'It's about instinct. My instinct.' She shook her head. 'And that hasn't changed.'

'You don't seriously believe Berkeley Square actually does test on animals, do you?' he wanted to know.

'Maybe they do,' shrugged Isis, 'but I doubt it.'

'Perhaps you have a sense that what happened to Lefevre could happen to you?'

'Perhaps,' she nodded, 'or maybe worse.'

Hilton leaned back slightly in his chair, exhaling slowly. He'd already guessed that Isis's response might be bound up in her ultimate fear of having her traumatic past revealed. Just as he knew that, if it were so, no matter how compelling his arguments, they would be of little use.

Meeting his eyes, Isis tried to smile through her grim self-consciousness. She had told Hilton everything when he'd first taken her on as a client. He had insisted he needed to know if he was to protect her effectively – and he'd never let her down yet. When she'd come to LA, she'd wanted to leave her past way behind her, yet because Hilton was the man he was, she'd found the experience of telling him her story powerfully cathartic. Having been brought up as a Catholic, Isis understood the power of confession. And when she'd confessed to Hilton it was as though the act had itself been a form of expiation, and after it she'd been free to live her new life. Yet images of the past still haunted her. No matter how much she sought to exorcise them, they would return, unbidden, at odd moments of the day and night when they were least expected. One particular scene would play and replay, reaching out across nearly two decades to fill her with apprehension whenever it returned.

It was a baking mid-summer Sunday, the blazing sunshine exposing that run-down suburb of Miami in all its rank ugliness; the rusted cars, the boarded-up windows, the over-grown gardens and fetid stench of dog excrement. This was where the Carbonis had ended up after emigrating to the land of the Almighty Dollar six years before, encouraged by earlier émigrés from Lucca, Italy. There was money to be made in America, they'd been told – easy money. To Isis's father, whose dreams extended well beyond the suffocating city walls of Lucca, the invitation had been irresistible. After a few months of reality, broken promises of employment, and a labourer's wages, he'd started to realise the move had been a mistake. But Giovanni Carboni was too proud, too stub-born to go back. Instead, he'd gone to work for Amtrack, and his wife Marina had taken in ironing, and they learned to survive in the new country by acting as though they'd never left the old one.

They began to observe customs to which they'd paid little regard until then – like Mass on a Sunday. Isis's mem-ories of those Sundays were of endless, incomprehensible incantations while she sat on an uncomfortable pew, in tight, scratchy clothing, the sharp tang of naphthalene exuding from her father's only suit. Although he invoked the names of both Father and Son with exasperating frequency, her father had no religious feeling, and it was all her mother could do to keep up the daily grind, with-out troubling herself about metaphysical questions. But going to Mass reassured them both of their roots, gave them a chance to spend time afterwards with others from Lucca and Florence and beyond. Traditions that had been of little significance back home took on a special meaning here. Having failed to make his dreams of untold wealth come true, her father had retreated into the strict orthodoxy of the old country, where a man's job was to earn a living by the sweat of his brow, and the woman's was to take care of the family, and acknowledge her husband as her lord and master.

Giovanni didn't believe in lavishing affection – that was for women. He regarded himself instead as the one who set the rules and saw that they went unbroken, imposing all the authority at home that he was unable to express at work. His temper worn by ceaseless toil, he was a man whose fury was easily provoked – and nothing inflamed him more than sexual deceit, a characteristic he regarded as uniquely female. After a few glasses of Chianti he would rail at the fickleness of women, hammering on the table about how it was their treachery that wrecked marriages and tore families apart. Two of his friends from back home had lost their darkly attractive wives to rich, blond Americans – the women were nothing better than whores, he'd declare, challenging his wife with a furious expression she knew better than to contradict. Isis was left in no doubt that as long as she lived under his roof, her own behaviour would be watched with all the patriarchal zeal of an obdurate archbishop, and the faintest stirrings of sexuality would be subjected to her father's wrathful scrutiny.

On this particular Sunday, the Carbonis had been invited to the Bazzanis after Mass. Most Sundays, several of the families would get together, the women arriving with polenta, salami, gnocchi and torte – always torte! – and the men bringing bottles of cheap beer and wine. The afternoons would be whiled away in an alcoholic daze amid the reassuring buzz of Italian. Isis had always found these sessions tedious and now, at twelve, having reached that awkward stage between childhood and maturity, had begun to resent the endless hours sitting in the corner, gangly and uncomfortable. So this Sunday, when she pleaded a headache, to her relief and excitement her parents said she could stay at home. Her mother gave her an aspirin and prepared her lunch. Her father sternly warned her not to leave the house. She stood, looking woebegone and in pain, until the moment they closed the front door behind them, at which point she pranced through the house on her tiptoes with glee. All she wanted was time alone. Time unfettered. In particular, time to try out something new.

Two afternoons before, when the gym class at school had finished, she'd been walking past Gabby Trinci's locker. Beautiful Gabby, with the deeply tanned skin and sloe eyes and budding figure. As she'd walked by, she'd noticed that Gabby had left her locker door open and there, sticking out of it, was the end of her brassière strap. Gabby wasn't the only girl in the class already wearing a bra, but her intricately patterned black lace underwear was the most beautiful. Of all the girls in the class, she was the one Isis envied most – there was something effortless about her burgeoning womanhood that was far removed from Isis's own confused feelings of anxiety and guilt. The glimpse of the bra strap conjured up something irresistibly sophisticated; the tantalising promise of what might be. And alone beside the lockers, Isis had found herself doing something she'd never done before. She'd hardly been able to help herself. Opening the locker door, she'd quickly snatched the garment and shoved it in her pocket before continuing on her way.

She meant to return it, of course. She hero-worshipped Gabby and wouldn't want to do anything to upset her. Early next week she'd leave it somewhere it would be found and returned to its rightful owner. Meantime, it was hers to savour.

In the Carboni household, there was no question of her being allowed to wear a brassière. She knew better than to even suggest such a thing. Despite her desperate yearnings and prayers for her body to blossom like Gabby Trinci's, it hadn't yet happened. And until it did, she would be denied her sexuality. Not so long before, her father had returned home to find her putting away her mother's lingerie after a trip to the launderette. Even though it was baggy and discoloured and nothing like Gabby Trinci's pretty black underwear, perhaps there had been a certain longing in her eyes because her father, responding to her expression, had stormed over to where she was kneeling, picked her up and wordlessly thrown her out of the bedroom. The only time she'd put on make-up, two years ago, he'd marched her to the kitchen sink and rubbed her face raw with a dishcloth.

But today she had Gabby's beautiful brassière and her parents had gone out for the afternoon! Quickly stripping off, she went to her wardrobe and extracted the stolen treasure from where she'd hidden it inside a jersey. She held it awhile, caressing it with her fingertips, closing her eyes as she felt the touch of it on her cheeks. Then, with some difficulty, she put it on, hooking it at the back and using tissues to fill it out. Her body lacked Gabby's firm pertness, but as she looked at herself in the mirror above her mother's makeshift dressing table, she could still admire the way the fabric enclosed her body, the patterns where the black lace pressed close to her skin.

She brushed her hair, all the while imagining she was Gabby, before reaching inside a drawer to find her mother's special lipstick – the deep red one she only wore to go to church or on special occasions. She held the gold tube like the illicit treasure it was, before twisting up the lipstick and running it lightly over her lips, careful to avoid any smudging. She didn't get it exactly right first time, and had to tidy it up, but she was pleased with the effect. The blonde hair and the deep, red lipstick; the blackness of the bra against her pale skin. She was so absorbed in her reflection that she didn't hear the front door opening, or the footfall on the carpet. So engrossed in this thrilling, grown-up image of herself that she was only aware of the door opening when it was too late. She turned round to find her father and Mr Bazzani standing, staring at her. She knew, in that instant, there would be hell to pay.

She'd been right. One way or another, it had been pay-back time ever since the horrific events following the opening of that door. But no one else knew it – no one, that is, except Hilton and Leo Lebowitz, who needed to know all of GCM's clients' darkest secrets. Back in Florida, her father and Mr Bazzani were now both dead, their ugly secret gone with them to the grave. Her mother was living in a retirement village, slowly forgetting herself, a victim of Alzheimer's. And here in Los Angeles her own version of an uneventful childhood in an anonymous suburb of Miami had long been accepted as the truth.

Regarding Isis carefully across his office now, Hilton wondered how best to salvage the Berkeley Square deal which he still believed was in her best interests, but which had gone so shaky. When he did eventually speak his tone was entreating. 'Can we agree, at least, not to commit ourselves to any immediate course of action on Berkeley Square?'

'You're stalling?' There was a note of cynicism in her voice.

'Only until we get more information.'

There was a long pause before Isis sighed. 'I'm just not happy about it.'

It was, they both understood, a reluctant agreement.

'I know you're not happy,' Hilton tried his best to reassure her, 'and believe me, I want to get this resolved one way or the other as soon as possible. All I'm asking is for a little time to consider our options.'

Our options, thought Isis sceptically. There were some things that just couldn't be put neatly into boxes to be wrapped up and stashed away. Some things that were just too dark, too all-consuming, that would resist all attempts at containment. And for the first time since beginning her new life in California, twelve years ago, she couldn't avoid the visceral sensation that she was about to be engulfed by the afflictions of her own, troubled past.

Los Angeles
Wednesday, 8 September

Mark pushed the airport trolley carrying his single suitcase through the green route at Los Angeles airport. He'd always thought that when people flew halfway round the world they were supposed to end up jet-lagged. But he didn't feel tired at all. Right now he was more excited than he had been for years. This was the first time he'd flown transatlantic, the first time he'd been up at the front of the plane; two firsts in twenty-four hours and he'd loved every minute of it: the luxurious seats, as much champagne as you could drink, being waited on hand and foot by drop-dead-gorgeous hostesses. Now as he made his way through the chaos of passengers and trolleys in the Arrivals hall he saw a line of greeters holding boards, one of which had his name on it.

'This way.' The Hispanic driver took charge of his trolley when he announced himself. 'Only the one luggage?' He was surprised.

'Didn't have much time to pack.'

'Plenty stores in Beverly Hills,' grinned the other.

Mark laughed. Ever since he'd checked-in at Heathrow he'd been made to feel important. Very important. And he felt more important still as the driver pushed his trolley in the direction of a stretch Cadillac and began unlocking the boot. Mark stared at the car in astonishment. You hardly ever spotted cars like that in London – you only ever saw them on TV at the Oscars or Golden Globe awards. Picking up his suitcase, he began carrying it over to the boot of the car – but the driver insisted he put it down, and let him do the rest.

'You picking up a group of us?' asked Mark, staring at the car as if it was too much to hope for.

The driver looked confused, glancing about them. 'You come single?'

Mark nodded.

'Then just you,' he confirmed, opening the door for Mark to climb inside.

It was dark and cavernous and the back seat was plush as a sofa. Mark glanced about, taking in the dark glass, the telephone, the TV – already switched on with a control set into the side panel.

'You want a drink?' The driver was behind the wheel. 'Bar is under the table.'

He glanced down at the door under the table to the left before opening it curiously. A half bottle of champagne and miniatures of every conceivable alcoholic drink were crammed inside, together with cans of mixers. At three in the afternoon he didn't suppose he should be drinking anything more dangerous than Coke. Then he thought, why the hell not? This might be the only time he got to ride in one of these things, so he might as well celebrate. Cracking open the bottle of champagne, he helped himself to a glass – real crystal, he noticed – before settling back into his seat.

As he raised the champagne flute to his lips, he looked out of the window at the passing city and offered a silent toast to Los Angeles.

The last week had been like one of those thrilling roller-coaster rides that just got better and better. For all his innate wariness about events that seemed too good to be true, there was no doubting that things were happening in his life. He remembered how he'd taken his Mum and Lloyd out to dinner on his last night in London. They'd gone to Le Palais in Covent Garden, a restaurant his mother had always liked the look of, but believed was far too expensive for the likes of them. 'Aren't you being a bit extravagant, dear?' she'd asked, when he'd announced where he was taking them. Mark had just laughed. GCM had paid him the equivalent of four months' salary from OmniCell. Four months was what he'd told Elizabeth it would take him to find a similar job when he came back. All his expenses in Los Angeles were to be paid for and if he signed various contracts that were 'in negotiation', he stood to make big money, Elizabeth had assured him.

How much was big money, he'd wondered? Since he'd got into this singing business he'd often thought about how much he'd get for a first album. Of course, he was an unknown and any label would be taking a risk. But he reckoned he'd definitely make ten grand and possibly up to twenty. Mark had never been one to count his chickens – he had no idea if he'd make any money at all in LA. What he knew for sure was that GCM had deposited nearly five grand in his bank account. He'd never had so much money to his name and he intended to enjoy it – he might not have this kind of cash again.

As he sat in the back of the Cadillac sipping champagne, he looked out of the window at the unfamiliar city, and realised he was in a different world now. On first impressions, Los Angeles wasn't anything special – just a vast, bewildering sprawl of freeways and warehouses, commercial estates and unfamiliar road signs. Though as they got off the freeway and drove up Santa Monica Boulevard in the direction of Beverly Hills, things began to change. Towering royal palms swayed in the afternoon breeze, glitzy office blocks in black glass and white concrete rose from lush, manicured lawns, gigantic movie billboards and signposts to Century City communicated the unmistakable combination of movies and money and corporate power.

Leaning forward, he asked the driver, 'Which hotel am I staying at?'

'Mammon,' came the reply.

Unusual, thought Mark, to name a hotel after the much-maligned god of money. But, hey, this was Los Angeles.

'Good place?'

The driver was shaking his head. 'Heeeey! Lots of big stars there!' He grinned in the rear-view mirror.

Mark smiled, taking another glug of champagne. Perhaps he'd get to meet some big celebrities, he thought with a thrill of anticipation. That would be something to write home about.

He could hardly believe his eyes when they pulled up at the hotel which turned out to be called Chateau Marmont. Was this really where he was to stay? It was like a private castle at the end of its steep driveway, with its gates and turrets and secluded courtyard gardens. Shown to the second floor, he found himself not in a room, but a suite, with a lounge, balcony and well-equipped kitchen – this must be costing GCM a packet.

On his coffee table, after his porter had gone, he found an envelope from GCM awaiting him. If he'd like to take an hour to relax, Elizabeth had written, a car would be coming to collect him at four for a meeting with Hilton. And, almost as a PS, here was his five hundred dollars cash per diem. Mark hadn't done Latin at school, but right at this moment he didn't much care, studying the wad of unfamiliar dollar bills before undoing the paper clip that held them together and throwing them into the air above his bed. The fizz might have gone to his head, but he was enjoying this, he reckoned – every bloody minute of it!

By four-thirty that afternoon, showered, shaven and still waiting for jet-lag to kick in, he was being whisked up in the GCM elevator to Hilton Gallo's office. This time he'd been prepared for an impressive display of GCM agency testosterone, but all the same he hadn't been able to help marvelling at the building, with its massive fountains and towering blocks of marble and reflective glass – it made GCM's Soho offices seem modest by comparison. Hilton Gallo was sitting alone at a meeting table in the middle of an office the size of a tennis court. When Mark came in, Gallo rose to his feet, stepped across to him and shook his hand with that strangely priest-like manner of his. Once again, as Mark met his eyes, he couldn't avoid a disconcerting sensation of the man's omniscience – as though he could see right through Mark into his very soul.

'Was your flight comfortable?' Hilton was solicitous as he gestured towards a chair opposite where he'd been sitting.

Mark enthused about the champagne and the air hostesses for a while, and then Hilton was asking him about the hotel. He hoped everything was to his liking? Were his rooms all right? Was there anything else he needed? Mark found it hard to believe that the boss of GCM, a man who obviously had wealth and power beyond his comprehension, was bothering to take such a close interest in his personal well-being. Once again, he felt a return of the uncertainty he'd experienced during their roof-top chat, the feeling that he didn't really know where he stood with this super-smooth operator.

'Tell me,' Hilton asked, having confirmed that every aspect of his accommodation at Chateau Marmont was to his satisfaction, 'what do you make of Isis?'

The question caught him slightly by surprise. 'Well, I'm a big fan,' he said, though that was a given. 'I bought *Aphrodisia* when it came out. I used to do covers of some of the tracks – always goes down well with the punters.' He shrugged, finding it hard to put into words what he thought of Isis. 'She's a legend. Amazing. I wanted to see her when she came to Wembley, but the tickets were a bit steep. Forty-eight quid each!'

Hilton nodded sympathetically.

Mark chose not to mention the poster of Isis he'd had taped to his bedroom wall when he was a teenager – no need to sound adolescent. Plus, he reckoned, he'd been no different from any other young bloods in fantasising about her. Sexual fantasy was, after all, what Isis was all about.

'There was the Broadway thing,' Hilton was saying now.

'Oh, yeah, read about it. But that was Patrick Denholme. His music's crap and everyone's sick of him.' The words tumbled out unchecked, before he suddenly remembered who he was talking to. Hilton was probably Denholme's agent.

'I mean,' he quickly corrected himself, 'it's not so much that it's crap—'

A rare look of amusement passed over Hilton's features. 'It's all right,' he held up his hand, 'I don't want you to censor what you say.' Their eyes met for a moment before Hilton continued, 'Of course, you know about the personal problems Isis had. She's through them now.'

Mark was shaking his head. Why was Hilton so keen to shoot the breeze about Isis? He thought he was here to discuss a recording contract.

'There were some financial difficulties. Substance abuse. Often goes with the territory.'

'I didn't know about them.'

'Her last album, *Eros*, did very well, but didn't reach the same heights as *Aphrodisia*.' Hilton was looking for a response.

Mark shrugged. 'How could it? No one's ever produced two albums in a row with half a dozen number ones each.'

Hilton leaned back in his chair and regarded Mark thoughtfully for a moment. 'It's good that you think like that.'

'Just common sense.'

'Maybe. But when you've achieved an extraordinary level of success, it's easy to lose sight of these things, to get the feeling you're losing your grip.'

There was a long pause before Hilton asked, finally, in an even voice, 'So I take it you'd have no problem recording an album with her?'

For a while, Mark was disoriented, experiencing the mental equivalent of being swept up in a crowd of Chelsea supporters and hurtled, out of control, towards the barriers. 'Me?' he managed after a while, 'I mean . . . Isis!'

'Let me be candid with you,' Hilton remained soft spoken, 'and everything said between us remains inside these four walls.' He rested his perfectly manicured hands on the table in front of him. 'Since *Eros*, Isis has had a difficult time of it in America. In Britain and Europe, as you have observed, her star is still very much in the north. You'll recall our conversation about celebrity being a product we manufacture? Isis's is a classic case in point. She's a brand that needs to be repackaged and relaunched in the local market, and refreshed elsewhere. Which is where you come in.'

Mark was still floundering as he tried getting his mind round this one, his expression a mixture of shock and elation. 'But my voice isn't anything like hers.'

'Which is exactly why we believe you'd make such a successful partnership.'

'What if Isis doesn't agree?'

'She's already heard the tracks you recorded in London. She liked them very much.' He paused deliberately, waiting for any further concerns, before saying, 'And there's another deal we need to discuss. You're familiar with Berkeley Square, yes?'

'The perfume people?' Mark met his watchful expression. 'My Mum wears Nightingale. Always has.'

'Core brand,' confirmed Hilton, 'what they built the beauty division on. They make a whole range of Nightingale products which are very popular with mature women. They're also a major pharmaceutical drugs manufacturer, though that isn't something we need to concern ourselves with. What Berkeley Square want to do now with their beauty range is reach a much younger audience, broaden their market base, which is why they're about to launch a radically different product line called Nile. There are still a few territories where the name hasn't been registered so it's not to be mentioned to anyone. We can't risk it leaking – the name is just perfect. Especially,' Hilton's eyes were gleaming now, 'because it will also be the name of your new album.'

Mark felt a rush of adrenaline.

'Nile is an aspirational brand,' continued Hilton, 'targeting eighteen-to-forty-year-old upwardly mobiles. And it's being manufactured in "his" and "hers" ranges. Berkeley Square have planned a major advertising initiative to support the launch, focusing on the endorsement by the hottest duo in the pop world,' he gestured towards Mark, 'Isis and you. We're talking three hundred prime site billboards across the UK and Europe, and a further five hundred in the States. Magazine ads running in fifty glossies from *Vogue* down, plus blanket TV and cinema support. The media spend behind Nile will be higher than for any beauty launch in history. They've really got to make this endorsement work for them.'

Already overwhelmed by the prospect of recording an album with Isis, these new revelations left Mark spinning.

'What would an endorsement of . . . Nile actually mean?'

Hilton nodded carefully. 'Strategically, it delivers an unprecedented opportunity to raise awareness of Isis and you at the launch of your album. We're talking here about the equivalent of a fifty-million-dollar advertising campaign.'

Mark shook his head, scarcely able to take it all in.

'Practically, it'll mean several photo sessions with Isis and you and a number of appearances – nothing onerous.' Leaning forward he murmured, 'Of course, and this is only if Isis and you decide to go ahead with it, it would also mean good money, Mark, very good money. Your own share would be something in the region of one point three, one point five million. That's US,' he added quickly.

The conversation had long since left the stratosphere of Mark's wildest fantasies. But this latest disclosure was just too much for him. 'One point three million dollars?' he almost stammered. 'I can't believe this!'

Hilton permitted himself a smile. 'I'll provide you with a full breakdown of royalty rates in our main territories. But by way of a ball-park figure you can expect at least another million from the album – that's being very conservative. If it goes off as we're planning, you'll be heading towards the double digits within a few weeks of launch.'

Mark took a deep breath. All of this was more than amazing! Hilton had him hooked all right – it seemed like his whole life was about to be transformed more than he'd believed possible. But even in the heat of the moment, his old instincts came kicking in: one day he's sitting behind his desk at OmniCell where he never expected to earn much more than two grand a month. Then a couple of weeks later here he is in Los Angeles talking about multi-million dollar contracts. It all just seemed too easy. There was no doubting, Hilton was getting him keyed up. But there was something he just had to ask, a burning question to which he'd kept returning ever since that first roof-top meeting: 'Why me?' he demanded.

Hilton raised his eyebrows marginally. 'You're right for Isis. Right for the part. As I said last time we met, we've been looking for someone to fit a very tight brief. I don't want you to be in any doubt,' he nodded once, seriously, 'that you do.'

Mark glanced down. It was true, Hilton had said it before, and he wanted to believe him. But he couldn't avoid his natural suspicions.

'This Nile endorsement deal. Is it definite yet?'

'As far as Berkeley Square and Isis are concerned it is. But the agreement still requires your signature. Before you sign, I suggest you have a read through these.' He touched a pile of documents in front of him. 'They outline in full all terms of the contract, and I'm also giving you a Security Briefing to take away.' Hilton had no intention of concealing the possible risk posed by One Commando, but nor did he have any wish to dwell on it.

'Of course, there are other things you need to consider about both the endorsement and the recording contract. You very rarely get pay-outs at the level I've just been talking about, without there being strings attached.'

Oh yeah, thought Mark. Here comes the downside.

'How do you feel, for example, about having a different performance name? Having your image managed by GCM? Having the media dredge up everything in your past?'

Mark shifted uncomfortably in his chair. How could he know how he'd feel about it? He'd never experienced anything like it.

'It's not something I've ever seriously thought about.'

Hilton paused a moment before meeting Mark's eyes. 'Then I suggest you do.' There was no escaping his seriousness. 'Your whole life will change. Overnight you'll become the target of intense media scrutiny. There'll be security considerations. And while I very much hope you become our client, there are limits to what GCM can do on your behalf. You'll need to appoint accountants; in time, lawyers. We can point you in the right direction, but these decisions ultimately rest with you.'

He spoke, thought Mark, as though initiating a novice into some arcane sect.

'Now, I know I've thrown a lot at you and you'll need time to digest it. What I'd like to do,' he pushed the pile of documents towards him, standing as he did, 'is give you copies of the recording contract, endorsement contract, the security briefing, more information about GCM, our standard client contract, a copy of the recording timetable, and the music and lyrics of the first six tracks of *Nile*.'

Mark got up from the table, collecting up the documents under his arm, and following Hilton to a side door which led through to another office in which Elizabeth Reynolds and Hilton's secretary, Melissa Schwartz, were working.

'If you decide you want to commit to these deals,' Hilton was saying, 'the next step will be for you and I to exchange signed contracts, followed immediately by a meeting with our media head, Leo Lebowitz. In the meantime, this is all completely confidential and not to be divulged to anyone. Even the most casual aside in this town is tomorrow's headline news.'

Mark glanced up at him with a flash of impatience. Hilton's manner made him feel as if he was already responsible for some major news leak. What did the bloke take him for, thinking he was going to rush out of here and get on the blower to the *News of the World*?

'When do you want an answer from me?' he asked.

'Twenty-four hours?' Hilton was showing him across to Elizabeth's desk, before retrieving a cassette tape from it. 'And you'll want to listen to this. Composer demo of the ballad we intend to be the number one hit single: the *Nile* title track by Isis and Jordan.' Then, responding to Mark's look of surprise, he smiled. 'That's you, of course.'

An hour later, in the sitting room of his hotel suite, Mark was still trying to work out what to make of it all. Still in a state of elation, disbelief, uncertainty. Isis and him – he could hardly conceive of it! Until today he wouldn't have had the audacity to so much as dream of the possibility. Signed up with pop's greatest sex symbol was just incredible – but there it all was in black and white.

The documents Hilton had given him lay open, scattered about him. He'd tried reading a few, but he'd only get through a couple of paragraphs then the words wouldn't register as he was too distracted to take anything in. He kept jumping up and helping himself to another drink from the fridge, and pacing the room feeling in turns triumphant, doubtful, hardly able to take it all in. As well as recalling all the good things Hilton had said at their meeting, he also remembered the warnings: how his life would change when he became suddenly famous. The media scrutiny. How GCM would want to manage his image.

He had spent some time reading the Security Briefing on the Nile endorsement, and remembered seeing something on the news back home about animal liberation terrorists attacking the Chief Executive of Berkeley Square. The briefing contained a few paragraphs on One Commando, who'd claimed responsibility for the attack. Sounded like a bunch of right nutsos, he reckoned, and though their fanaticism made them dangerous, and he understood the theoretical risk, the idea that they'd suddenly get all hot under the collar about him just didn't seem very real.

In fact, none of this right now was nearly as real to him as the alternative – going back to London and returning to the OmniCell Helpdesk. And no way on earth was he going to do that. He'd have to be crazy! It'd take a lot more than a vague security threat and over-zealous news hacks to put him off. In fact, the idea of being pursued by the paparazzi gave him a buzz. It had to be a whole lot better than being a complete nobody, even if his new name was 'Jordan Hampshire' as it confirmed in one of the documents he'd have to sign.

Two point five million, Hilton had said. Up towards double figures within weeks if all went well. What kind of choice was that to someone who barely cleared a grand a month? He already knew, straight away, what he was going to do with the money. He'd buy his Mum a flat in one of those mansion blocks she'd always liked the look of on Prince of Wales Drive, across from Battersea Park. He'd set her up so she wouldn't have to work another day of her life and take her on a shopping spree to buy some expensive new clothes. He'd do something for Lloyd too – probably sort out a flat for him, so he could spend his wages on himself instead of handing them over to a landlord. And of course there'd be his own new home. He'd always fancied a place overlooking the river – maybe in one of those fashionable apartment blocks in Chelsea Harbour, a top-of-the-range penthouse. Why not? He'd easily be able to afford it! Hey – even if he never worked again, after these deals he'd be set up for life!

Suddenly he felt like speaking to someone – but everyone he knew lived in London. Glancing at his watch he made a mental calculation, adding eight hours and working out that it was just after one in the morning; there was only one person he dared call at that time of the night.

Lloyd protested vigorously when he finally answered the phone. He'd had a late night, he told Mark, and hadn't been asleep for long before being woken by his call. Didn't Mark know what the time was?

Mark told him he knew exactly, but this was important. Then he told his brother about the GCM deal. Riding a wave of excitement, he could hardly contain himself. Lloyd soon forgot the time too and was gratifyingly excited for him, thought Mark – not to mention envious. The two of them had always had an easy, mutually mocking relationship – each making sure the other didn't get too impressed with himself. Mark got a load of it from Lloyd tonight, of course, but he expected it – somehow it made the whole thing seem more real.

Then he asked Lloyd what was going on in London. Which was when the conversation took a disconcerting turn; Lloyd told Mark about his discovery, made the night before, in a Covent Garden wine bar. He and a few mates from work had gone there for a drink, and who should he spot in the corner but Siobhan O'Mara.

'Seeing as Vinnie's been so quiet about her,' said Lloyd, 'I thought I'd ask what she's up to.'

'Too right!' agreed Mark. When he'd asked Vinnie, of late, about other clients like Siobhan, or that Nigerian group he was looking after, Vinnie had gone all mysterious, hinting at advanced negotiations and imminent signings, but never committing to anything definite.

'Turns out she fired Vinnie eight weeks ago.'

'What? Who's she gone to?'

'Nobody.'

'She fired Vinnie without having anyone else lined up?'

'Exactly what I said,' chimed Lloyd. 'She said she'd just had enough of him. He was getting out of control. She thinks he's losing it.'

'Not the only one. Did he want to kill her too?'

'Worse. Seems the dark side of our Vinnie isn't all talk. A mate of hers at Strobe Records told her Strobe are suing him. They've got him on video in their car park smashing up a producer's Ferrari. Keyed the paintwork, smashed in the lights and slashed the soft-top.'

Mark was speechless with shock.

'He'd been getting agitated about some Swerve master tape he claimed Strobe had lost,' Lloyd explained grimly. 'Last time he gets a contract out of them.'

Both brothers knew how utterly at odds this was with Vinnie's oft-repeated assurances that he and Strobe Records couldn't be closer.

'That's not the worst of it,' continued Lloyd. 'He also had a go at Pete Kelly.'

'Got to be joking!' The Soho club owner, an eccentric bohemian who frequented the streets in the company of his golden retriever, wasn't only the most affectionately regarded owner on the London club circuit, his club was an institution among music talent scouts.

'Kelly docked a fifteen per cent management charge

from some performance fee. Vinnie wasn't expecting it—'

'It wasn't Vinnie—' Mark was already dreading what he thought would follow.

'—who did the dog. Yeah. He told Siobhan that Kelly deserved it.'

Two months before, Kelly had emerged from his regular watering-hole to find his dog gone from the lamp-post to which he always leashed him. The frantic search that ensued had been to no avail. Returning home, Kelly had found his dog dangling from the front door – strangled by its own leash.

'Christ Almighty!' Mark was shaking his head.

Alarmed though he was, in a perverse way the revelation made sense of Vinnie's recent behaviour. It followed a pattern. Vinnie had believed he'd arrived when he'd had his first big success with Swerve. He'd been quite the big shot with his chart-topping clients and his Mercedes and his slim panatellas. But this act had become harder and harder to keep up since Swerve collapsed. Vinnie didn't have any signings to replace them. He was getting desperate. Hence the Ferrari attack. Pete Kelly's dog. The way he'd reacted down at the Lamb. If he kept this up, Mark thought now, he'd soon find every door in the music industry slammed in his face.

'How's he been with you?' Mark asked, getting concerned about his brother's safety.

'Only seen him once down the Lamb and he completely ignored me.'

'Just watch out for him.'

'Hey, I can look after myself. Anyway, it's you he's mad at.'

'I'm a bit far away for him to do much.'

Lloyd didn't reply immediately. They both realised that

Vinnie had revealed a dangerous and previously unsuspected tendency. Vengefulness fuelled by desperation.

'Maybe he'll cool down,' Lloyd said, finally.

'Yeah,' said Mark, staring unseeing out of his window at Chateau Marmont. 'I really hope so.'

5

_____

The e-mail Alan Brent received was short. Only one and a half lines to be exact. But the message it conveyed was cause for satisfaction. 'Congratulations' was the word Larson had used, referring to his special delivery to *The Globe* newspaper the week before. It was the first time Larson had sent him a personalised e-mail, instead of the terse, encrypted communiqués he usually issued to One Commando members. It was also the first time Larson had complimented him.

Every news bulletin on radio and TV last night and every national newspaper had reported his delivery of the eyes to *The Globe* newspaper the following day – an event that had given the Lefevre story a powerful impetus, providing, as it did, a shocking and savage revelatory twist. Until that moment the police had suppressed the details of exactly how Jacques Lefevre had been 'injured' – having first wanted to inform and advise Mrs Lefevre, who was flying in from New York.

But the genie had got out of the bottle now, and for over a week, One Commando had dominated the news media.

The contents of the video Brent had delivered had also been hotly debated – but despite the shocking scenes depicted, the media seemed strangely reluctant to accept that they had been shot in a Berkeley Square facility. Lord Bullerton's angry denials, together with threatened libel action, had had the usually accusatory tabloids siding with Berkeley Square. And when investigative teams from the broadsheet newspapers were unable to dig up anything to substantiate the One Commando video, it was assumed to be a hoax.

For all that, thought Alan, he was making progress. He'd almost got to the top. It had taken him six months, during which time he had closely scrutinised Larson's *modus operandi*, the clinical manner in which he kept every cell member separate and isolated. As military leader of One Commando, Bengt Larson was extremely significant, no doubting it. He was the most ruthless operator in the animal rights movement. But he wasn't the top man – of that Alan had been convinced from the start. There was someone above him who held sway.

For months, Alan's conviction about One Commando's unseen leader had been nothing more than a hunch. Then, last week, Larson had made a fleeting reference in a training session before the Lefevre operation. 'The powers that be,' he'd said, referring to the critical importance of the raid – confirming what Alan had suspected all along. And setting his ultimate objective. Alan didn't only need to win over Bengt Larson. He had to get right to the top of the organisation. If his mission was to be successful he needed to win the acceptance of 'the powers that be'.

Behind his computer, he glanced at his watch. Five to one. Just enough time to log on to the office intranet and file a report before his colleagues went off. They'd want to hear from him – and preferably without interrupting their lunch. Despite the nature of their work he'd long since discovered that most of the worker ants at HQ followed the same pedestrian regime of office workers the world over. In at nine, out at six. An hour off for lunch, at one. Endless meetings.

He never went into the office in person – under the terms of his contract he was specifically forbidden from going anywhere near the place. In fact, he'd only ever been allowed inside HQ once – ten years ago, when he'd been formally interviewed for the job.

They'd recruited him at the lowest point in his life. He'd just been fired from his first job, amid a welter of mutual recriminations, and he'd been feeling bitter, disillusioned, insecure. Having graduated from university cum laude five years before, he'd begun work full of big ideas and brave convictions. By the time he joined their operation, however, he'd been considerably more worldly wise.

His employers hadn't recruited him for his brains alone; apart from his near-genius-level intellectual prowess they also recognised in him a personality ideally suited to undercover work. Alan was a loner, always had been. He lived in his head, in the world of ideas, and working on his own suited him. It also kept things secure. Operating from home, he'd assembled, on his employers' budget, a collection of the most powerful computing and communications equipment available, all of which he'd installed in the large attic of his house which served both as office and bedroom. The vast majority of his assignments involved cyber-work, breaking through software encryption programs without being detected, as well as all the more routine stuff. Every day he'd spend hours at the keyboard, in an office lit by nothing but his customised purple screen-saver, and which was crammed with equipment, as well as empty Coke cans and polystyrene Kentucky Fried Chicken cartons going back more meals than he cared to remember. He only ever went out of the house for food or other essential errands. His life was as sealed off, anonymous and self-contained as it was possible to be in a major city. All of which contributed to his effectiveness as an undercover agent.

He was also scrupulous about safety. He changed his cyber-ID and e-mail address constantly so that even if someone did succeed in hooking on to him they would never be able to track his presence for any length of time. He had people from work come in every month routinely to sweep his house for bugs. They'd go through the entire place, from top to bottom, checking for any recording or transmission equipment. Sensitive material arriving in hard copy form – and substantial quantities of it would arrive by special delivery – he'd store electronically, before feeding the originals into the industrial shredder. Non-sensitive stuff he stored. And because he'd been doing this work for ten years, it meant his house had, little by little, turned into a vast storage repository.

His involvement in One Commando wasn't like anything he'd ever done before. But from the start he'd kept his usual careful records detailing every contact that was made by e-mail or phone, as well as the content of every conversation. Having penetrated the organisation, he intended finding out all he could about it – in particular, the power structure and who made the decisions. He'd also realised that analysis and intellectual insight on its own were not enough. If he was to achieve what he'd set out to do, he also had to be accepted – all the way to the top. Larson's e-mail was an important recognition and he would build on it. He'd use the credibility he'd earned to get more information. And he knew he was getting there. Very much closer, in particular, to answering the question that had increasingly become his preoccupation: who exactly was the puppetmaster pulling One Commando's strings?

London
Thursday, 9 September

Jasper Jones got up from behind his desk and stepped out of his office, instructing his secretary to hold all calls for the next ten minutes before returning inside, closing the door behind him. A senior executive at the Euston Road offices of Love Smith Ben David, his office was elegantly appointed and currently in near-total darkness, lit only by his desk light. Several television awards glinted in a corner cabinet, but he'd otherwise eschewed the breast-beating of his colleagues in the industry, who usually bedecked their walls with framed posters of their latest productions. Instead, his own office walls were hung with a few favourite prints – a couple of Kleins and a Magritte. There was a comfortable black leather sofa for visitors, a drinks cabinet containing a few bottles of spirits including his preferred tipple – Bombay Sapphire Gin. But there was nothing that so much as hinted at where his personal pursuits really lay.

His colleagues had no inkling about his involvement in the animal rights movement. If they'd found out he had any involvement in the Lefevre attack, they would have been apoplectic. Consequently, this past week he'd had to keep his private exhilaration under wraps. Never could he remember such intense media coverage of an animal rights operation. It was the eyes that had done it. If One Commando had knocked Lefevre unconscious, or sliced his face open, or even shot him dead, the story wouldn't have merited more than a few column inches in the national press, or a brief mention on the main evening news. But the gouging of Lefevre's eyes had struck a chord that resonated with a deep, collective fear. The notion that a grotesque mutilation could be conducted in the hallowed privacy of one of London's most genteel squares was a nightmare scenario that had seized the public subconscious, and raised the game to a completely different level.

Whether it was the simple horror invoked by the ubiquitous image of Lefevre's spectacles case, or whether the symbolism was understood – the destroyer of countless animals' sight is, himself, blinded – what had happened had spawned more news stories and features than Jones had ever counted on. In the last seven days, Jacques Lefevre's spectacles case had been so photographed, so written about, that it had already become an icon of the animal liberation struggle. In future weeks and months, its mere appearance would be all that was required to inspire a profound, public gasp of disquiet.

Not that Bengt Larson was satisfied. Jones had just received an e-mail from wherever Larson was currently residing in Europe; he was extremely upset by the turning tide of the media. Initial news, first of the Lefevre attack, and then *The Globe* delivery, had done little more than report events in scandalised tones. Since then the full weight of Britain's gigantic media machine had been brought to bear on what had happened – and the rapidly growing consensus of all the features, analysis and editorials was that One Commando was using a hoax video to justify its actions. Journalists had already been through Berkeley Square plants, not only in Spain but in every country where the company operated, and nothing had been found. Commercial rivals had done their utmost to verify One Commando's claims – but to no avail. So where had the footage come from? Flipping open his Psion Organiser and switching on its green backlight in the gloom of his office, Jones accessed a coded entry containing Larson's secret contact details. Finding his mobile telephone number, he picked up his telephone and began dialling.

Larson was vital to the cause – he had to be looked after. It had taken Jones months both to identify and win the confidence of the commando leader. He had spent a substantial part of his 'extra-curricular' hours in the last year getting to know all the main players in the animal liberation movement. He'd sat through countless night-time meetings and for more weekends than he cared to remember had travelled to conferences, rallies and protests all over Britain and on the Continent. Focusing on more established activist groups, all run by cabals of career protesters, once he'd proved his commitment with a few donations, doors had been opened and confidences begun to be imparted; he'd identified the Animal Freedom Lobby as the organisation where his own ideas would be best received. It was there he'd heard the whispers of a paramilitary organisation – the ultimate goal of his quest. Around the same time he'd been making enquiries about the tall, well-muscled Swede who'd attended several of the rallies he'd been at himself. It didn't really surprise him when he learned that Larson was the leader of the nascent One Commando – he'd looked and sounded the part.

At the other end, Larson's phone rang just twice before he answered it.

'I just got your e-mail,' explained Jones. 'You're worried.'

'Worried!' Larson barked at the other end. The word was wholly inadequate as a description of his state of mind. 'You've seen the newspapers, the TV! They're saying we're a gang of unprincipled terrorists! They're saying Berkeley Square are innocent. This is destroying us!'

Jones listened patiently as, at the other end, Larson vented his frustration. Extracting a pack of Gauloise Lights from his desk, he drew one out between his lips before flicking it to life with his gold Dunhill lighter and exhaling a stream of grey smoke into the semi-shadows. He didn't even try to interrupt. Instead he listened while Larson let off steam, making the occasional note on the briefing pad in front of him, and puffing on his cigarette. Then, after the tirade had abated, he waited a long while before saying, deliberately, 'That's certainly one side to it.'

There was a pause of disbelief from the other end before Larson finally managed, 'There's another side?'

'For the last week One Commando has achieved massive high profile coverage in all the major national news media.'

'For all the wrong reasons.'

'What else were they going to say?' asked Jones. 'You know what keeps every news organisation in this country going? Advertising revenue. How much revenue has the Animal Freedom Lobby poured into media coffers in the last year? Zilch. And how much money have members of the Ethical Pharmaceutical Manufacturers' Association spent in the same time?' He glanced at one of the revenue spreadsheets scattered on his desk. 'Six hundred and fifty-two million pounds. So whose side d'you think they're going to take?'

'It's as blatant as that?'

'You better believe it.' Jones spoke with cool conviction. 'You have some of the most powerful forces in business ranged against you. And you can be sure they're leaning heavily on the media to get their side out. Just because editors write things, it doesn't mean they're telling the truth. It doesn't mean Berkeley Square isn't testing on animals. It only means that, right now, they've got the media by the balls.'

'Bastards!' At the other end of the line, Larson's voice was choked with anger.

'You talk about credibility,' continued Jones, 'what about

the credibility of the people saying there *isn't* any testing? Bullerton, the Chairman of Berkeley Square? The Ethical Pharmaceutical Manufacturers' Association?'

'But what about this open invitation to visit any Berkeley Square plant?'

'They close down the site in Spain. So what? They just set up a lab under a different name and get the results fed through to them that way.'

At the other end, Larson fumed silently. He'd learned a lot from Jones about the plotting and scheming of big business. It was Jones, with his acute business brain, who'd explained to him how shareholdings worked and subsidiaries operated. Before that, he'd never realised how devious big companies could be or what a hold they had over the media. But he knew, better than anyone, where the video footage had come from; it was he who'd broken into Berkeley Square's Madrid laboratory just a few weeks earlier. Now, the realisation of how the media were being paid to peddle lies began to sink in. And his despair was turning to resentment. The tide of energy was welling back inside him.

'When you think of all we're up against,' Jones spoke with feeling, 'you realise just how much we achieved with the Lefevre raid. It put One Commando on the map. It got major national media coverage that even a month ago would have been inconceivable.' For a few moments he focused on the operation – the success of its planning, strategy and execution. How One Commando had successfully evaded police detection. How they had become, overnight, the biggest name in the animal liberation movement.

'You've got them on the run. They don't know where to start looking for you and they're terrified you're going to strike again. That's what all these headlines *really* mean.'

'I don't know,' Larson was less certain, 'it just seems that whatever we do, no one's going to believe us. But I was there! I filmed it myself. How can they all pretend it isn't happening?'

'Believe me, Bengt, I share your frustration,' Jones said grimly after a while. 'And it seems to me we're going to have to come up with something else, something different to make them pay attention.'

'You have an idea?'

Jones's expression was grave. 'Let's just say, I've been working on something.'

'Like . . . Lefevre?'

Jones exhaled another thin stream of blue-grey smoke into the darkness.

'Like it,' he confirmed, 'except much, much bigger.'

6

_____

Two days after arriving in LA, Mark was still buzzing. And still waiting for the jet-lag to set in. Yesterday afternoon, Elizabeth had phoned to ask if he'd had a chance to go through the contracts, and did he have any questions. Mark had said yes he had, and yes he did. But he would be signing. The truth was – not that he told Elizabeth – there'd never been any serious doubt in his mind. Once he'd convinced himself this whole story-book scenario was genuine, nothing else seemed to matter.

Elizabeth had sounded pleased with his reaction. He should sign the contracts, she told him, and bring them into GCM next day, where he'd meet Leo Lebowitz, head media honcho, so they could get the show on the road. Mark had put down the phone, amazed at the speed with which things were happening. Back in London, the major record labels took for ever to consider things. With GCM, the turnaround time on major deals seemed lightning quick.

Having waited in the GCM foyer for less than ten minutes, he saw Elizabeth step out of the lift wearing a white suit and looking very foxy. He found himself wondering about her, that way, but quickly checked himself. This was work, remember?

'Mark,' she reached out a welcoming hand. GCM people were always shaking hands, he'd noticed. He handed her over the envelope he'd had under his arm.

'They're signed?'

'Yeah,' he grinned.

'Good. I'll take them to Hilton and we'll get you counter-signed copies before you leave.'

He nodded, before asking the question that had been on his mind ever since Hilton had first told him about the record deal yesterday. 'When do I get to meet Isis?'

Elizabeth was hesitant. 'I'm not sure. We'll have to check your schedule.' Then, heading towards a door behind the reception desk, 'Seeing that you're now a client, would you like a quick agency tour?'

Mark nodded. 'I'd love that.'

She ushered him in, then through a steel security barrier, which slid open as she used a swipe card. Stepping forward, they came to a glass wall through which was visible a massive, open-plan office, with banks and banks of computer termi-nals stretching out into the distance. Smartly dressed exec-utive types were working at keyboards or speaking on phones in an industrious buzz of activity that reminded Mark of one of those exhibits you saw at the zoo, where you looked through a slab of glass into an insect hive.

'Accounts department,' she explained.

'Right.'

'We pride ourselves on having the quickest turnaround time in the industry. Four working days from cheques arriv-ing from the principals – that's the average turnaround time.'

He nodded. 'Reminds me of something,' he said, reaching into the breast pocket of his jacket and extracting an envelope addressed to himself. It had been sent by courier the day before and had contained nothing but a GCM compliments slip – and five hundred dollars in cash. 'There was a mistake.'

'Really?' A look of sudden concern crossed her face.

'You duplicated.' He was holding out the envelope. 'You already paid me.'

She looked puzzled, as she accepted the envelope. 'You mean?'

'When I got here. Then this came yesterday.'

Suddenly understanding, she smiled. 'That's right. No mistake. Five hundred is your per diem.' Then, responding to his confusion, 'Your daily allowance.'

'Five hundred dollars . . . *every* day?' He looked astonished for a moment. Then, 'That'll be for the hotel and everything.'

'GCM meets accommodation expenses.'

'So what am I supposed to spend five hundred dollars a day on?'

She couldn't help smiling. 'Oh, I'm sure if you practise, you'll get pretty good at it.' She stretched over, squeezing his arm. 'Most of our clients do.'

He was shaking his head ruefully as he accepted the envelope back. Then, glancing across to the other end of the Accounts department, he noticed for the first time that the entire far wall was the side of a vast aquarium containing golden koi – the same fish he'd seen in the fountain at the top of the GCM building in London.

'Biggest fish tank I've ever seen,' he remarked.

Elizabeth nodded, leading him back to the door. 'The building was designed by a feng shui expert. You know when you go to Chinese restaurants, they often have fish tanks near the cash register? The idea is to attract wealth.' She was leading him up a flight of stairs to the first floor.

'People here don't actually believe all that bollocks, do they?' he asked, astonished.

She raised a finger to her lips, and gave him a significant look. 'I wouldn't let Hilton hear you speak like that, if I were you.'

'You mean he really thinks—?'

'He believes in experimenting with anything that stacks the odds in our favour. You've got to admit, it's worked pretty well up to now.'

The stairs and lifts were at the centre of the rectangular GCM building. Arriving on the first floor, Elizabeth gestured towards the two wings to each side of them, clearly marked 'Film' and 'Television'. 'Like our main competitors,' she explained, 'GCM is divided into four main divisions – Film, TV, Music and Multimedia. Then we have services that run across all four divisions, like Media Relations and Endorsements.' She had led him into the Television offices, a maze of corridors with glass-walled offices behind which elegantly attired agents and their assistants were gesticulating on the phones, or talking in meetings with TVs playing. There was a palpable charge of energy about the place, thought Mark as he followed Elizabeth, a purposeful buzz of expectation.

'As of this week,' she was explaining, leading him on a brisk round-circuit, 'we have a hundred and eighty clients working on seventy different shows.'

'Actors, you mean?'

'Actors, producers, writers, directors. Sometimes the full package.'

Mark raised his eyebrows. 'How does that all work? How do you put things together?'

'Different in every case,' Elizabeth told him. 'Sometimes we'll pitch a sitcom concept to one of the networks, and they'll give us the go-ahead for development. Or they might have given creative approval to somebody else's idea, but come to us for casting. The start of it is always information.' They were heading out of Television now and into Film. 'You see this?' From one of the desks, as they passed by, she picked up a large, leather-bound file embossed with the GCM logo.

Mark nodded. He'd noticed a few files like it scattered about and had just assumed they were fancy telephone directories.

'This is the Film Bible. A database of every movie in English which is in development or production. Television, Music and Multimedia have their Bibles too.' She flipped open the cover to reveal a four-inch-thick wedge of computer printout carrying endless lists of names and titles and telephone numbers. 'Twice a week each division has full staff meetings, with video hook-ups to all our main offices around the globe. The meetings are part information exchanges, part brainstorms. We look at new books coming on the market available for adaptation, projects that studios are looking to develop, maybe a script which a producer client wants to get commissioned. Which directors want to work with which actors, or which actors have projects for which writers.' She tapped the file before replacing it on a desk. 'After meetings, all these files are updated, hard copy and intranet.' Then, leading him off round the Film offices which, to Mark, didn't look much different from Television, 'We guard our leads jealously – they're the lifeblood of the business.'

'Where do you get the information from?'

'Agents are out there all the time – breakfast, lunch and dinner meetings, industry bashes, private parties – and when they're not out circulating, they're on the phone.'

Glancing about at all the suited men and women, Mark noticed how many of them were wearing headsets with microphone transmitters as they strode about their offices.

'Two things done at once?' He pointed.

'Never enough hours in the day,' agreed Elizabeth, 'but we took medical advice after one of our top TV guys got a tumour in his ear.'

Mark looked at her in surprise.

'Agents make an average of a hundred and fifty calls a day. Sometimes we're on the phone for seven, eight hours.'

It was all a lot different from how Mark had pictured Hollywood agents. He'd always imagined their lives consisted of endless lunches with the rich and famous in chichi restaurants, after which they spent the day by the swimming pool in sunglasses and bathing trunks, sipping pina coladas with little umbrellas in them.

Looking around him he remarked, 'I always thought things in Los Angeles were more laid back.'

'In the bad old days. Now, most people in our industry work twelve- to sixteen-hour shifts.'

'How do you get to be an agent in the first place?'

'Interviews and psychometric tests like anyone else,' said Elizabeth. 'There are two hundred applicants for every one trainee job, and when you do get in, you literally start in the mail room.'

Walking through a maze of passages, Mark couldn't get over the scale of all this. Offices and meeting rooms and screening rooms seemed to go on for ever.

'After a while, once you get an idea how things work, with any luck you'll be taken on by one of the agents as an assistant. You shadow everything they do.'

'Like you and Hilton?' he risked.

'Exactly. But even when you get to be an agent, there's

no guarantee you'll stay. You have to bring in the deals – and this is the most fiercely competitive business in the world.'

'Sounds high pressure.'

'Which is why agencies attract a certain type of personality. It's not good enough just to be a super-salesman, you also have to have the right instinct.'

'Killer instinct?'

She turned, smiling wryly. 'You could say that.' Then as she led him back in the direction of the lifts, 'Some of our people eat a stem of garlic every day to maintain their aggression levels.'

'Bit off-putting for clients?' he guffawed.

'Not if you eat enough parsley.' Then sotto voce, as they waited for the lift, 'A few of my male colleagues say they practise semen-retention techniques to keep their edge.'

Mark had to laugh at the absurdity of all this. Testosterone-charged super-agents in their Armani suits and goldfish in the Accounts department – he'd heard it all now. Once they were in the lift, Elizabeth pressed the third-floor button.

'Music and Multimedia are on the second floor,' she told him as they ascended, 'same format you've just seen.'

'No chance of running into any celebrities then?' He'd been in Beverly Hills more than forty-eight hours and *still* hadn't seen anyone famous.

'Lord, no! It's the engine room down here – I just thought you'd like a peek. Regular client meetings are on the fifth floor.'

He nodded.

'We're going to level three, Media Relations.'

'All of it?' He was surprised. 'Must be a huge department.'

'Needs to be. It's the heart of our business.'

At that point the lift doors slid open on to a scene that was mesmerising for its sheer scale. A massive sprawl of open-plan desks ran the full length of the building, with glass-walled offices stretching down either side, like a vast airport terminal that had been converted into offices. Unlike the Accounts department, where executives busied themselves like worker ants, this place was a madhouse of yelled instructions and frantic arm gesturing, huddle-meetings around desks littered with media releases and, Mark noticed now, at least a dozen sound-proofed booths for live TV and radio interviews, all with their red 'Recording' lights on.

He was taking all this in with wide-eyed amazement when next to him Elizabeth said, 'About a third of all the world's biggest celebrity stories concern our clients.'

'I can believe it.'

'We have media contacts in every capital city on the planet and can get news out to them all within half an hour.'

'"Control the media and you control the world,"' mused Mark, recalling his first encounter with Hilton on GCM London's rooftop.

'One of Hilton's favourites,' she agreed.

'But how can GCM force journalists to say things?'

'We can't directly. It's a more subtle understanding than that. You see, when we contact journalists with news about our clients, or to arrange client interviews, we're always very clear about the information we're presenting and the spin we want on it. It's up to the journalist what happens next. If he turns in a hostile piece, we mark his card. Two strikes and he's out. He never gets another piece of news out of our offices again – not about any of our clients. Nor will he ever be allowed to interview them. When you look after as many clients as we do, a journalist is going to think very hard before slamming the door on GCM.'

Mark took all this in as Elizabeth led him through the flurry of the media relations offices towards the far corner.

'You said this department is at the heart of the business?'

She nodded. 'GCM trades on the reputation of its clients. Their appeal and ability to attract a large following. Those are all intangibles. They can be destroyed by the media virtually overnight. A well-managed image on the other hand . . .'

'What happens if you don't have an image?' he wondered, applying this information to himself.

She turned, smiling. 'Then you come here to get one.'

'You do?'

'That's exactly why Hilton wants you to spend time in Lebo-land. Leo Lebowitz is the best in the business.'

They had arrived at the doorway to a very large corner office, its high, white walls hung with sweeping and vivid abstract canvases, and from its window, a panoramic vista of Santa Monica Boulevard with its swaying royal palms. To Mark's surprise, there was no desk in the office. In fact, there was no furniture at all except a highly polished meeting table and, around it, a number of black leather chairs. On the far side of the office, headset strapped on, the bearded Lebowitz was on the phone – but gestured them inside.

'This is where I head back upstairs,' Elizabeth told Mark, 'but I'll see you before you leave.'

'Right,' he met her eyes and that impenetrable expression of professional cordiality, 'see you later.'

He stood at the door for a few moments while Lebowitz ended his conversation, removed the headset and turned to face him with a thoughtful smile.

'You must be Jordan Hampshire,' he offered his hand.

'Mark Watson is my real name,' he replied with a handshake.

'Reality's best left outside.' Lebowitz waved him towards the table, reaching behind him to close his office door. 'Let's stick to Jordan. Less confusing that way.'

Mark took a seat at the table opposite him and for a moment the two of them sized each other up. Lebowitz's intellectual authority, like Hilton's, was instantly self-evident, but unlike Hilton, whose manner lent him a certain detachment, Lebowitz was altogether more engaged.

'Hilton told you the purpose of this meeting?'

'Something about media management.'

'Whenever we take on a new client, we have a session like this to lay down the ground rules.' Lebowitz was stroking his beard reflectively. 'You see, we're all working as a team now, and it's important you know what your moves are, and what our moves are, when we engage the media.'

'Sounds military.'

'Has to be. When you're in the public eye, whether you like it or not, you have an image. Your only choice is whether to manage that image, or let the media manage it for you.'

Mark nodded. 'This image thing, why did you come up with the name Jordan Hampshire?' It was the first time he'd said the name out loud and as he said it, he didn't feel as if it had anything to do with him.

'My development team conducted extensive research using brand development instruments. An analysis of birth registers in ten major US cities shows that Jordan is the most popular name among eighteen-to-thirty-year-old A/B/C1 women. We also trialled twenty surnames, in focus groups, then using a quant. study, to find which was most closely identified with England. Hampshire topped it.'

Mark was astonished at how calculated it had been.

'We put the whole package into research, not just the name,' Lebowitz continued. 'Our psychographics came up with clear steers on image, wardrobe, hairstyle . . .'

Mark raised a hand to his hair automatically as Lebowitz opened up a flat box in front of him. This was something he hadn't thought about, he realised, feeling suddenly exposed. But of course, if these guys had come up with a name for him, they'd also have worked out an image, using all their fancy techniques.

Lebowitz was pulling out a selection of concept boards and sliding them across the table. To Mark's further concern, each board carried sketches of him – but not the way he looked right now, and definitely not the way he'd ever appeared on stage in London. The clothes Jordan Hampshire wore were altogether younger, a combination of retro flares and wide lapels with collarless shirts and crumpled linen jackets. The kinds of clothes only a real jerk would wear. And worst of all was the hairstyle. Gone was the lustrous mane of dark hair which he knew women went for, and instead was a short back and sides, so short he'd be almost bald, topped by a short, gelatined mass that looked like he'd just got out of bed. Walk into the pubs he used to frequent back home looking like that, he thought, and he'd find himself on the pavement in about ten seconds. Glancing up, he realised that Lebowitz had been watching his reaction closely.

'I'd feel a right dick looking like that.' He shook his head firmly.

Lebowitz seemed unperturbed. 'It usually takes time to adjust,' he said.

Something in his attitude nettled Mark. 'Maybe I don't want to adjust!'

'What, specifically, do you object to?'

'My hair, for starters. I've tried a lot of different styles. I know what women like and I know what suits me—'

'Suits *you*,' Lebowitz retorted. 'If it was thirtysomethings we were after, it'd be perfect. But that's not where the money is. The primary market is eighteen to thirty.'

'So you manipulate *all* your stars—'

'This isn't about manipulation,' Lebowitz was calm, his tone laced with a hint of humour, 'it's about accessibility. If you're not accessible to your market, you might as well pack up and go home.'

Mark wondered if Lebowitz's choice of expression had been deliberate, before deciding it was. Everything about this operation seemed calculated.

'So Isis's different looks . . . ?'

'Driven by the market. *Aphrodisia* was a flawless piece of packaging work. Exhaustive image engineering work. Pretesting. We're going to do the same for you.'

Mark was disconcerted by his penetrating gaze. 'Pretesting?'

'Before the CD and video release we run pilots. Get kids into observation rooms across the country and play them the stuff. If we've got the brief right in the first place there shouldn't be a need for fundamental changes. But there's usually some fine-tuning, maybe a revision of imagery or visual emphasis. Maybe some studio re-engineering. We need to be sure we've created a product with optimum impact.'

Mark was staring down at the concept boards in silence. None of this was anything like he'd imagined. After all the euphoria of the last few days, it was like flying into a wall at a hundred miles an hour. He thought GCM had signed him up because they believed he had something to offer. The way Lebowitz was explaining things now it seemed as if he was just to play a part, act a role that had nothing to do with him.

'This is all so . . . made up,' he was shaking his head, 'so artificial. Why can't someone just write bloody good music and be themselves?'

Lebowitz seemed amused by the proposition. 'They can,' his mouth formed a half smile, 'they usually do when they start out. But that's a pretty hit-and-miss way of continuing.'

'I s'pose you even use research to write the music?'

'We analyse what's worked well on the charts in the last six months and combine it with predictive modelling. On the back of that we briefed a couple of composers and they came up with several options which we played to our music panel – that's five hundred people nationwide. The *Nile* lead track is right on the button. Went down a treat.'

'What if Isis came up with a few songs of her own?'

'Oh, we'd test them. But we can't just let her do what she likes.'

'It worked for *Aphrodisia*.'

Lebowitz sighed. '*Aphrodisia* was three years ago. Isis was perfectly tuned in then. But the market's moved on and we can't risk her getting it wrong – there's too much at stake.' Then regarding his unconvinced expression, he looked serious. 'Unum Music is spending two million dollars on the video, eight hundred thousand dollars buying airtime and has an advertising budget of one point five million. *Nile* is going to be a number one hit. It can't be left to chance.'

So this was what Hilton had meant when he'd warned him about GCM having full artistic control. At the time it hadn't seemed a big deal, not when he was being paid over a million dollars for it. But now he realised just how much he'd be following orders. In reality, he was nothing more than a puppet on a string.

'The same goes for media relations,' Lebowitz was telling him. 'We have to avoid nasty surprises.' His expression was serious. 'The reason I kept this meeting private is so you'd feel free getting anything off your chest I need to know about.'

'What d'you mean?' Mark felt his heckles rise again.

'Anything that a tabloid newspaper or gossip columnist would consider interesting. I'm thinking along the lines of drugs, crime, sexual peccadilloes, domestic violence, unwanted children—'

Mark was once again infuriated by the way Lebowitz sat there, calmly reeling off a catalogue of intimate perversities. 'What if I've never done any of that stuff?' he protested, voice rising. 'What if I'm just a regular bloke—'

'Hey! Jordan!' Lebowitz leaned back in his chair and fixed him with a contemplative smile. 'I'm on your side, remember. If there are no skeletons in the cupboard, that makes my life a whole lot easier. But I have to say it would be a first. I've never signed up anyone who hasn't had some issue to manage.' Then as he met Mark's embarrassed expression his eyes turned earnest. 'One thing I don't want you to be in any doubt about is that in a few days' time your entire life will become public property. Journalists will be interviewing anyone who's ever known you – family, friends, enemies, ex-lovers, you name it. They'll be out after the dirt, waving their cheque-books, because that's what sells newspapers. If the first time I get to know that you were having an affair with your stepmother is when a journalist phones me for a quote, frankly, it's too damned late to save you. But if I know these things beforehand, I can put defences in place.'

The moment he'd started talking about friends and enemies and cheque-books, Mark instantly thought of Vinnie. If a journalist got on to him he didn't doubt that Vinnie would come out with the most twisted tale of duplicity and betrayal. You didn't have to imagine too hard to see the headlines.

'One thing I can guarantee,' Lebowitz continued, 'is that you'll be amazed what creeps out the woodwork. People you were at school with you don't even remember will come out saying you were best buddies. Girls you got in the sack will tell the most outrageous lies – even girls you didn't get in the sack—'

'There is someone you should know about.' Mark knew there was no point holding back.

Lebowitz gave him an enquiring look.

'Vinnie Dobson,' said Mark, 'used to act as my manager.'

Lebowitz unscrewed the top of his handsome Mont Blanc Meisterstück and held it poised on a briefing pad. Meeting Mark's eyes he said gravely, 'I need you to tell me everything.'

Mark finished fifteen minutes later, recounting his most recent conversation with Lloyd. Although there was no doubt in his mind that Lebowitz had to know, he didn't like having to do this. It made him feel like the school sneak who'd just been in the headmaster's office.

'Well, if that's the worst you've got,' Lebowitz looked up from his note-taking, 'we shouldn't have too many problems.' He scratched his beard thoughtfully. 'I'm sure we'll find a way to keep Mr Dobson out of mischief.' Then, looking up and meeting Mark in the eye, 'Are you sure there's nothing else we need to know about – embittered ex-girlfriends? Youthful indiscretions?'

Mark shook his head.

'On the subject of women – or indeed men,' Lebowitz leaned over, handing him a business card, 'here's the number to ring if you feel the need.'

Mark took one look at the shiny black card, with the

pink and gold lettering, before flashing back up at Lebowitz in annoyance, 'I'm not so desperate I've got to pay for it!' Was Lebowitz deliberately trying to piss him off, or was this just his style? He was about to flick the card back across the table when Lebowitz held up his hand.

'Keep it,' he ordered. 'Don't forget, everything is about to change for you. You're going to be a big star. You'll have to be wary of entrapment—'

'So for the rest of my life,' flashed Mark, 'whenever I feel like company I have to—'

'Georgia Klune is held in very high regard by this agency. She and those in her employ operate with the utmost discretion.'

'You mean, you refer all your clients to—'

'A lot of them.' He was nodding. Then, leaning back in his seat, he fixed Mark with that irksome, enigmatic half-smile. 'We all have our drives and our juices. Georgia provides what we think of as an insurance service. If any of our clients feel the need for relief, we prefer that they use Georgia's services, than be caught getting blow jobs from hookers on the Strip, or cottaging in the public lavatories. Whatever you're into, Georgia can provide it, and nobody will ever find out. That counts for a lot in my business.'

Mark regarded him, aggravated. This was all getting beyond weird.

'The deals will be announced in two days' time, and we're expecting serious media take-up. Before then, we've got a lot of work to get through. You'll also be needing a bodyguard.'

'Is that—?'

'Non-negotiable.' Lebowitz met his eyes. 'There's a lot of crazies out there who'd do anything to get on the news, including shoot someone famous.'

So this was what he'd signed himself into. A name and image that weren't his. Sex with women he'd never met. Security arrangements he didn't want. And none of it had anything to do with the main reason he was here – to record an album with Isis. So when Lebowitz said, 'Is there anything you'd like to ask?' he was quick to repeat the question he'd already asked Elizabeth,

'When do I get to meet Isis?'

'I've no idea,' the other was candid, 'is there any particular reason you need to?'

'Need to? If we're going to be working together, I'd like to get to know her.'

Lebowitz looked at him blankly.

'Or is that a quaint idea?'

The other shrugged – was that a trace of condescension? – before murmuring, 'It's a subjective thing.'

Mark shook his head, frustrated. 'Next you're going to tell me she's nothing like her image.'

Lebowitz grimaced. 'That's not a question I feel competent answering. Her image is all that concerns me.'

Then he was outlining everything that needed to be done in the following few days – clothes, hair, photo shoots for media pack development. An intensive schedule had been set up – there'd be no time now to enjoy the delights of Chateau Marmont.

Then, pausing, he regarded Mark carefully for a long while before saying, 'If I can offer you one piece of advice,' his tone signalled significance, 'you're going to see a lot of stuff about yourself in the media that I can tell you, right now, will be complete bullshit. Everything you say will be reported out of context, twisted and turned to support someone else's point of view. It'll help if you don't take it personally. Think of it as a game, a battle of wits.

When it gets really bad, and I can promise you it will, just try to remember it's not really you they're talking about. In fact, it's got nothing to do with you. It's a Jordan Hampshire thing.'

It was just after five that evening when Lebowitz was summoned by Hilton. Sitting on one of his large cream sofas, lighting subdued and the scene, out of the floor-to-ceiling window beside him, a panoramic night-time vista of Sunset Boulevard, Hilton looked like a man who'd just stepped out of his dressing room. As always, he had that air of calm order about him as though he'd recently emerged from an hour's meditation. Sitting, sipping his usual drink – hot water with a twist of lemon – he was the very picture of serenity.

'By close of play Monday,' he told Lebowitz once he was seated opposite, 'we'll be ready to go public. I'll have contracts signed by all parties to both deals. This afternoon Berkeley Square confirmed that Nile has been registered in every territory that matters.'

Lebowitz nodded.

'You've given some thought to how we're going to handle the announcement?' It wasn't so much a question, on Hilton's part, as an assumption.

'I believe a degree of unbundling is called for. I think we can take a couple of runs at this.'

'I thought you might.' A dry smile appeared on Hilton's face as he leaned back in his chair. Unbundling news into its component parts, to create several announcements instead of just one, was a strategy at which Lebowitz was Hollywood's master.

'First off is a major press conference. We go out with the record and endorsement deal fielding only the GCM media team.'

'No client appearances?' Hilton was surprised.

'Just photos in the media pack.'

Lebowitz's cavalier management of the media amused him.

'We want them to focus on the double-whammy. Same name record-signing and endorsement. Nile and Nile. Plus Isis and the new mystery man. There's plenty of news in there to keep them going a few days. Meantime every paparazzi in town will be hunting down Jordan—'

'We'll have to get him out of Chateau—'

'I've already put him in one of the guest houses. Nice and safe and also close to Unum.'

'Good.'

'When the time's right, we tip off the media for a joint Isis/Jordan photo-op. Script and package it for TV and tabloid front pages. By then there'll be a huge bounty riding on Jordan's head – every newspaper will be screaming for pictures. What we're looking at really is a global teaser campaign with a high-impact ending.'

Hilton regarded him with an appreciative expression. 'Excellent,' he said, 'the mileage we'll get out of this . . .'

'Biggest job we've ever done,' agreed Lebowitz.

Hilton paused for a moment. He always knew he could rely on Lebowitz to maintain tight control of the media. But there were other aspects of this operation where control would be more difficult. As he mused, his smile began to fade. 'What thoughts on Dobson?' he asked after a moment. The two of them had discussed the Dobson issue earlier on the phone, and come to a decision.

'Unum London will play ball.' Lebowitz nodded. 'Dobson will be getting an offer to sign a heavy-metal duo he represents on a session contract. Letter's going out in tonight's post.'

'Will remuneration be detailed?'

Lebowitz nodded. 'Forty grand sterling for a one-month contract.'

'Generous.'

'Unum are paying standard rate. We're topping it up fifty per cent. Small price to pay to neutralise—'

'Of course.'

'I'll have a follow-up call put in to him if we don't get a response on Monday. Unum have been co-operative.'

'I'll remember next time I speak to Ariel,' nodded Hilton, ever-conscious of the detail. The scheme to limit Vinnie Dobson's potential for damage had been straightforward; if he took the Unum money there was no way he could go whining to the media about being hard done by. If necessary, Lebowitz could make sure every news channel was aware that it was only Jordan's efforts that had secured his former musical partner a contract. Dobson would have painted himself out of the picture: end of story. The question was: would he take it?

'We'll have to see which way he's going to jump it before doing anything else.' Lebowitz reflected his own thoughts.

Hilton nodded, thinking this through for a while. Outside, the darkness was complete, bumper-to-bumper traffic down on Sunset forming an untidy line of moving red lights between floodlit office blocks and billboards. Then, turning to eyeball Lebowitz with a penetrating expression, 'Tell me, you haven't mentioned how your session with Watson went today?'

Lebowitz's eyes flicked over Hilton's shoulder and out of the window. 'Bumpy ride,' he murmured. Then, looking back to where Hilton continued to scrutinise him closely, 'If you want to know the truth, there's something about him I don't trust.'

Hilton absorbed this carefully. 'It's not just a matter of house-training?'

The other shook his head, adamant. 'No. It's more than that.' Meeting Hilton's gaze across the darkness of his office, for a long while he regarded him with a grave expression before saying finally, 'The problem is, the guy just asks too many questions.'

7

It was a quarter to eight in the evening when Jasper Jones slipped into his black Kenzo suit jacket, turned off the light in his office, and headed down the dimly lit corridor towards the lifts. Earlier that month, Love Smith Ben David had landed a new commission with fees worth in excess of two million pounds. Timing was tight, however, which meant all hands to the pumps. For ten out of the past fourteen days, he'd worked from eight in the morning straight through till midnight. Now as he headed out, even though he knew he'd done his fair share, he couldn't avoid a twinge of guilt knowing that most of his colleagues would still be here in another four hours. But it wasn't every day he had such a promising dinner party to attend. One of his fellow guests was to be Gail Sinclair, tall, blonde and beautiful. They'd first met at a Models Against Mink fashion show only a few weeks before. He'd instantly been attracted, and to his very great pleasure, the interest had been reciprocated. Which was why he'd prevailed on mutual friends to set up tonight's dinner.

Walking past the finance department, he called out

goodnight to Daniel Croom, who was always around long after everyone else had left. Receiving no reply, he slipped his head round the door. Daniel wasn't at his desk, though his light was still on, as was his computer, showing the Reuters screen-saver. It was more than Jones could resist; a news junkie through and through, he stepped across to scan the latest updates.

And then he saw it: just in from Los Angeles, the announcement from celebrity agency GCM that Isis and co-star Jordan Hampshire had signed an endorsement contract with British firm Berkeley Square cosmetics, to coincide with the launch of their new joint album, *Nile*. Jordan Hampshire, an unknown male vocalist, discovered by GCM, hailed from Wimbledon, south London. Jones had to reread the story three times to believe it. This was incredible, he thought, his mind spinning with the implications – the most astonishing turn of events. And One Commando could only benefit.

There was a sound behind him. Jones turned to find Croom at the door.

'Oh. Dan. Just popped in to say goodnight.'

The other stepped past him to his desk. 'Looking very pleased with yourself,' he observed Jones's smile.

'Oh,' Jones nodded towards the screen, 'just some interesting news.'

Making his way down to ground level in the lift a few moments later, he reflected that he'd planned to take a couple of bottles of chardonnay with him tonight. Scratch that idea, he decided. Make it two bottles of Dom Perignon.

But before he went anywhere, he'd be placing a call to Bengt Larson; this new, unknown star, Jordan Hampshire, had just stepped into One Commando's firing line. The sooner they knew a lot more about him, the better.

Mark stood in his bathrobe on the verandah of the Beverly Hills residence that was now his home, overlooking the lush green lawns, feather-leafed palms and glorious fuchsia baskets. 'Guest house' was the phrase Elizabeth had used. 'Mansion' would have been more appropriate. A double storey palazzo with four huge bedrooms, sumptuous entertaining areas, and a dazzlingly blue swimming pool, the place was equipped with every toy a man could wish for – spa, sauna, mini-golf course, billiard room, satellite TV, and a video library that occupied two entire walls of the viewing room. Situated high up in the hills, the GCM guest house had one of the most prestigious addresses in the suburb – and faced across the road to another home with a massive Italianate marble entry owned by a Hollywood studio.

At eight o'clock on a sun-drenched California morning, breakfast had just been served by his housekeeper. A dab hand in the kitchen, Mrs Martinez had prepared a trayload of fruit crushes and freshly baked croissants, accompanied by preserves and a percolator of full-roasted Columbia coffee. Not that he was in any mood to eat breakfast today. As he continued to pace about his multi-million dollar surroundings, Mark had never felt so angry in all his life. Exasperated was the way he was feeling. And, most of all, used.

The cause of his upset was sitting on the glass verandah table. It had arrived by courier at seven twenty-five this morning, a three-inch-thick pile of press cuttings, showing how the GCM announcement had been reported in that day's papers around the world. Most articles were dominated by photos of Isis and headlines about the double-whammy Nile endorsement and album release. All tied the news in with the One Commando attack on Lefevre: in signing up to Berkeley Square, were Isis and he putting their lives on the line, the tabloids sensationally demanded.

But it was all the stuff about Jordan Hampshire that was driving him crazy. Most of the papers had used those awful photos GCM had shot of him a few days ago, leaning against a Rolls-Royce, arm draped about the Spirit of Ecstasy and wearing a dreadful smirk and the even more dreadful hair-cut. As if the pictures weren't bad enough, the captions were worse. And all of them followed the same theme: 'Rags to Rollses,' trumpeted LA People; 'Lewisham to LA,' proclaimed the Mirror. According to the tabloids, he'd been down and out in London, living in an inner-city sink estate when he got his big break. He'd been abandoned by his father as a two-year-old, said most of the papers, while they all announced that his mother had brought up the family on the dole.

It was outrageous! You got the impression he'd been a no-hoper, a member of the economic underclass before Hilton Gallo had shown up on his white charger. And as for his mother – what an insult! What did they think she'd been doing for the last thirty years, working her fingers to the bone? He was especially disgusted to see the famous LA syndicated columnist Inky Mostyn repeating all that crap. Inky, whose column in a British tabloid he'd devoured every week, believing the dapper, bow-tied author to be the authentic voice of Hollywood. So much for authentic! He'd turned out to be just as much of a sleaze-bucket as the rest of them.

But that wasn't where the crap ended – not by a long shot. Continuing the rags-to-riches hysteria, some of the papers reported on his arrival in LA, how he was living a 'champagne lifestyle' at the Chateau Marmont where his suite was just down the corridor from Leonardo di Caprio's. Some determined hack from *The Globe* had interviewed Chateau Marmont staff who, the very model of discretion, had refused to divulge any information at all about him except that his favourite room service order had been smoked salmon bagels with cream cheese, and Cadbury's Fruit 'n' Nut chocolate. That was enough for *The Globe* to make out that the 'reclusive' Jordan Hampshire – where did they get that from? – led a solitary, Howard Hughes-like existence, alone in his luxury hotel suite, living off room service. They'd even commissioned a psychologist to analyse his eating habits. He was clearly insecure in his new environment, said the shrink, pointing out that bagels with cream cheese was classic 'comfort food'. He'd probably been suffering badly from jet-lag too – using the chocolate to pep up his energy levels.

If it hadn't been about him, he'd have laughed out loud at what a total aberration of reality it all was. He'd known before that you shouldn't believe everything you read in the papers, but he'd never had any idea it was this bad! And it was all very well for Lebowitz to tell him he shouldn't take it personally – but it wasn't Lebowitz they were writing about. Just laughing it off was a lot easier said than done. Anyway, there were other people involved. What about his mother? What about Lloyd?

Flicking through the press coverage – page after page of it – wondering what to do, Mark quickly became increasingly vexed. All of this made him feel as though he was nothing more than someone out of a second-rate soap opera, a character whose whole life could be fictionalised according to whatever story-line editors had decided on. They'd twisted so much about him already – and he hadn't even opened his mouth yet!

He was still wondering what to do when, behind him, there was a knocking on the glass verandah door. Mrs Martinez was pointing at her watch.

'Your driver is ready in ten minutes,' she reminded him.

He looked up at her, nodding blankly. He recalled the advice Lebowitz had given him: 'When it gets really bad, and I can promise you it will, just try to remember it's not really you they're talking about. In fact, it's got nothing to do with you. It's a Jordan Hampshire thing.' He couldn't say he hadn't been warned, he thought as he glanced over the verandah table one last time, before making his way inside and upstairs to his bedroom. He couldn't say he hadn't been briefed to expect it.

As he got dressed in Levis and a YSL shirt, all the unsavoury press details whirling through his mind, he was struck by a different thought; he could understand how the gutter press would sensationalise and exaggerate any story they were given. But there were some things they'd *all* got wrong. Like the thing about his Mum – that made him more furious than anything – saying the family had lived on the dole, when all the years they'd been growing up she used to come home grey with exhaustion from her long hours in the dry cleaner's. So why had all the papers run that crap? And where had they got the line about him living in some inner-city sink estate? Where had that come from? It was as though GCM had put out the angles and the press had all faithfully repeated the stories. But he'd given one of Lebowitz's sharp-suited henchmen, Philip Kaylis, his full life story during a briefing session, and anyway he'd seen the announcement media release when it went out, and it hadn't carried any lurid personal details.

Hurrying through to the bathroom, he brushed his teeth and tried not to look at his hair. Then returning downstairs and grabbing the lyrics and music for today's session he headed towards the garage, where Denzil, his large black bodyguard-cum-driver was waiting.

'We've got company today,' announced Denzil as he arrived, nodding in the direction of the gates.

'How d'you know?'

'Two of them have been up ladders already.'

After all the coverage he guessed it shouldn't be surprising paparazzi were covering all the options. One of the papers had said there was a bounty riding on his head – the media had been screaming out for a joint appearance by Isis and him at the press conference, but no such opportunity had been forthcoming.

'So what do we do?' he asked Denzil.

'Same as usual.' The bodyguard was opening the back door of the Lincoln limo. 'Maybe get under the blanket.' Then, seeing his expression, 'Just till we get out the gates.'

He felt more than stupid crouching behind Denzil's seat, shrouded in a black light-proof wrap. But he'd had his orders from Lebowitz: he was to stay strictly out of sight.

No sooner had the electric gates started sliding open than there was a flurry of activity. He could hear the clamour of shouted questions and clank of hastily moved aluminium ladders as the limo shot down the driveway, climaxing in a chorus of noise and flashing as they went through the gates, photographers holding flash cameras right up to the tinted glass and shooting off exposures. Denzil cursed under his breath as they accelerated down the street.

'What's going on?' Mark wanted to know.

'Bastards on scooters.'

'How far behind?'

'All around. 'Bout five of them.'

Mark was keen to shrug off the blanket. 'D'you reckon they'll—'

'Best you stay under there . . . sir.'

It was a less than comfortable journey into Unum that morning. Thirty-five minutes under a shroud while paparazzi weaved and curved alongside the limo. Then when they reached the studio, there was another media encampment to contend with. So this was how life was to be, thought Mark, until Lebowitz and the boys had decided the time was right: hiding behind security walls and under blankets in the back of cars while all the time those bastards printed whatever they liked about him.

When he finally got out at the other end he was disoriented and shaken. Denzil saw him into the studios, which were the usual hive of industry, with technicians, musicians, couriers and assorted suits moving about the corridors of the sprawling complex. In the last three days he'd learned to find his way through the labyrinthine maze to Studio 18, where 'the Isis album', as it was generally known, was being recorded. He was still adjusting to the light, after the pitch-blackness of the last half hour, as he made his way down a passage, when he noticed the group of people coming towards him from the opposite direction. Sound engineers and studio executives were jostling about someone at the centre of the group, every one of them with a line to pitch, or so it seemed. Until that moment, Mark's only thought had been getting to the studio – on his very first day, an Unum exec had been at pains to explain the punitive costs of every studio minute. But he couldn't help paying close attention as the group drew nearer, and he caught a first glimpse of the person who was attracting all the attention.

Amazingly, he didn't get it at first. Her very familiarity made her difficult to place. For a few instants he was trying to compute where he knew her from. Then just as they were about to pass, he realised! And halted. The next few moments happened in slow motion. He found himself saying her name out loud, half in surprise, half in greeting. Looking up from where she had been engaged in conversation, she turned to make eye contact. There was recognition – he could tell immediately. He was poised, focusing on her every action. It was the moment he'd imagined for so long, for years as nothing more than a daydream, but in the last few days as a far more tangible reality. He was stepping into the presence of his idol. The supernova with whom his name, as of yesterday evening, had become inextricably linked.

As they drew closer, he wondered what he should say – what she would say; this unexpected encounter had caught him unawares. But Isis was raising her right hand, her fingers straightening. He stood, as though mesmerised, taking in every frame of the action. Her hand drew closer to her face, her motion slowing as she came directly opposite him. Even so, it had happened before he'd fully realised it; she'd delivered him a salute. A salute! That casual gesture of acknowledgement you made to a neighbourhood acquaintance or while encountering someone vaguely known to you in the street. Before she'd even passed him, she was already glancing away.

He leaned against the wall, turning his head to follow the progress of the small group down the corridor. He could hardly believe it! She hadn't stopped! Hadn't even deigned to greet him by name. However insignificant he was compared to her, they were still partners in this album! But she'd treated him with the kind of flip casualness she might show towards a delivery man or the garbage collector. He watched the group as it reached the end of the passage and turned out of view. Not for the first time this morning he found himself wondering what in Christ's name he was doing in Los Angeles.

Moments later, he strode into the Studio 18 mixing room.

'Jordan!' Sam Bach greeted him, gesturing through to the studio. 'We're ready to start rolling.'

'I need to make a call first.'

Bach glanced pointedly at his watch. Mark pointedly ignored him. He'd just begun to realise what he hadn't fully realised before this morning – that despite the big deals and big money, he was just a commodity. A story for the papers. A voice to support Isis's. If he didn't stand up for himself, no one else was going to.

A short while later, he'd obtained from Unum switchboard the number of *LA News*, and was demanding to speak to Inky Mostyn. When Mostyn answered the phone, his voice was every bit as loftily acerbic as his writing suggested.

'This is Jordan Hampshire,' announced Mark, 'and I'm extremely pissed off about what you wrote today.'

Bach and several sound engineers had turned, and were looking at Mark in astonishment.

'You know, I actually used to be a fan of yours,' Mark continued, indifferent to their startled expressions. 'I used to read your column every week in London. I reckoned you had the inside track, you told things straight. Then this morning I open the paper and find you've written all this unadulterated crap—'

'Whatever do you mean?' prickled Inky.

'The stuff about my mother bringing us up on the dole. And me living in some "sink" estate.'

'To which details, precisely, do you object?' Inky seemed not to understand.

Mark shook his head. 'All of it! It's just not true!'

There was a pause at the other end, and the sounds of paper being shuffled, before Inky responded, 'If it's not true, then you shouldn't authorise your publicity agents to circulate it.'

'Publicity agents?' repeated Mark, taken aback.

'Global Creative Management,' Inky rumbled. 'It's all here, quite clearly—'

'But they showed me the media release.' His voice rose in indignation. 'It didn't say anything—'

'Wasn't in the release. It was in the Biographical Notes.' Then, responding to the silence at the other end, Inky sighed rather grandly. 'My dear boy, *this* kind of media release is merely the "hors d'oeuvres". It seems to me that GCM have passed you by on the entrée.'

Mark heard the click at the other end with a spasm of anger. Face darkening, he reached into his Levis, took out his wallet and extracted a card from it, before dialling the number printed there. Meeting Bach's gaze across the mixing room, his eyes challenged the man to raise objection to this second telephone call.

'Leo Lebowitz's office,' came the brisk voice at the other end.

'I need to speak to him right away.' Mark's voice was staccato with rage.

'He's in a meeting at this time—'

'Then get him out of the meeting.'

'He's not in the GCM building.'

'I want him to call me at Unum studios the moment he gets back—'

'Aren't you involved in recording? That's Jordan Hampshire, isn't it?'

'No. It's Mark Watson. And I don't care if we're in the middle of a track, I want to speak to him *immediately*!'

*   *   *

London
Thursday, 16 September

It had been a crazy twenty-four hours for Vinnie Dobson. The craziness had begun that morning with the letter from Unum Music. Completely out of the blue and signed by some guy he'd never even heard of, Unum were offering him a forty grand session deal for 'The Holy Black', a heavy-metal duo who played the South London pub and club circuit. The deal was worth eight grand to him in commission.

Usually any breakthrough like this would have him on his mobile within minutes, making sure all his industry contacts knew that Vinnie Dobson was moving and shaking, and still a force to be reckoned with. In other circumstances, he'd have been behind the wheel of his Merc heading directly round to see Rick and Headley, aka 'The Holy Black', a magnum of Dom Perignon at the ready.

But Vinnie smelled a rat. Unum was one of the world's largest music companies, and despite marketing through a dozen different labels, it was notoriously hard to penetrate, especially for new artists. He'd even read once that it was Unum's policy only to take on musicians who'd already made it with other labels – Unum had no interest in developing new talent. Which was why Unum was one of the few music companies Vinnie hadn't ever bothered to contact. So why this unsolicited offer? And why 'The Holy Black', who were virtually unknown outside their South London beat? Just exactly what was going on, and who was behind it?

He hadn't had long to wait. Within hours of getting the letter, mid-way through that afternoon, had come the phone call from the *Mirror*. It was the first Vinnie had heard about Mark Watson's record deal with Unum; the first he knew of his début with Isis. 'No comment' was all he'd managed, too shaken to say anything else. He hadn't known that GCM had even been in touch with Mark again – let alone that Mark had left London and was now in LA calling himself 'Jordan Hampshire' and signing up endorsement contracts!

No sooner had he hung up than the phone was ringing again – this time the *News of the World*. Repeating his 'no comment' line, this time with a flash of anger, he slammed the hall phone down, then reckoned he'd better go into his office and work out what to do next. But to get to the office he had to walk through the lounge, where his parents were watching TV.

'What's all this about?' his mother asked, regarding his furious expression as the phone began ringing yet again. It was exactly the wrong question at the wrong time. Because the full impact of what had just happened unleashed an anger Vinnie didn't even try to contain.

'That bastard Mark Watson! He's taken me to the fucking cleaners!'

'Language!' his father rebuked, as his mother got up to answer the phone.

But Vinnie was in no mood for parental edicts. Storming towards his office door, he raged about Mark's duplicity, going behind his back and cutting him out of deals, even though he owed his entire singing career to him.

When Vinnie's mother appeared at the door saying, 'It's the *Daily Telegraph*. They want to interview you', his father retorted sharply, 'He won't speak to them!'

Vinnie glared angrily at his father. 'Maybe I should!' he blazed, making his way back towards the hallway, 'Maybe I should tell them what a two-timing bastard—'

'You speak to any journalist,' his father roared across him, 'and you can pack your bags and get out right now. I won't have my family's name dragged through the press!'

The row that followed had been more acrimonious than any before. While Vinnie and his father raged, his mother had taken three calls from two more papers and a newswire before unplugging the phone in exasperation. Meantime, Vinnie's mobile was ringing insistently in his office. Such was his father's wrath that for a while it seemed as though the two of them might even come to blows – then it all got too much for Mrs Dobson who broke down. Leaving his father to comfort her, Vinnie strode back into the hall, seized his coat and left the house, slamming the door behind him.

That afternoon, Vinnie was sickened to find the *Evening Standard* full of the Isis and 'Jordan Hampshire' story. His mother tried plugging the phone back in the wall – but for only half an hour before pulling it out again. The media hadn't given up the chase. If anything, they seemed even more desperate to speak to Vinnie. Holed up in his office, sullen and resentful, he kept his mobile phone diverted to voicemail, receiving no fewer than twenty-eight messages from hacks wanting to speak to him. Much as he longed to vent his feelings, to tell the whole world the truth about the double-dealing shithead, he knew that he'd have to find a new place to shift out to first. The moment he did, he reckoned – like in a couple of hours' time – he'd get hold of that kiss-and-tell bloke to auction off his story to the highest bidder.

He still hadn't worked anything out when he went down to the Lamb that evening. To his surprise, the moment he walked in the door he was treated like a celebrity. The local hero. It caught him completely unawares; people just started standing up and clapping and calling out to him – even though they knew he'd had nothing to do with it, it was as though he'd pulled off the deal of the century. It was like he was a Mafia don strolling up to the bar as a wave of hand-clapping burst out around him and all the regulars surged forwards to greet him.

After all the hype in the *Standard*, Vinnie had relished the opportunity of telling things the way they *really* were. Mark Watson might have been one of the more popular performers at the Lamb, and his brother might be playing snooker less than ten yards away in the corner of the pub, but Vinnie had soon put everyone straight on just what a double-dealing bastard Watson had turned out to be. He reminded them how it was he who'd first recognised Mark's talents and given him his break in showbiz. It was he who'd given Mark a platform, and arranged the gigs and sent out countless demo tapes at huge expense. And how had he been rewarded? Mr High-and-Mighty only goes behind his back to GCM, doesn't he? He meets Hilton Gallo, cuts Vinnie out of the deal, and next thing they all know, he's jetting off to LA, leaving a trail of unfinished business and unpaid bills behind him.

Everyone remembered the row between Mark and Vinnie two weeks before. Once they'd heard Vinnie's side of the story, they were as pissed off as he was. Not that they needed any prompting. Torn out pages from the *Standard* had been circulating round the bar, showing photos of Mark in Los Angeles, standing next to a Rolls-Royce and sporting a new haircut. Everyone agreed he looked a right dickhead with his hair carved up that way, trying to be oh so cool and trendy. His clothes were even worse, producing hoots of derision – didn't he know what a complete ponce he was making of himself, dressed up like some yo-man pimp. As for the name, just who in Christ's name did he think he was? Regulars down at the Lamb didn't have any time for those who got ahead of themselves, and tall poppies were very definitely there to be cut down. Mark Watson might have acted like he was their mate once, but he'd obviously been taking them for a ride; he hadn't been the person they thought they'd known at all.

Downing a few pints before ordering a plate of curry, Vinnie revelled in being centre of attention and having everyone agree with him – made a pleasant change from all the crap he was getting at home. He didn't tell anyone about the Unum letter, currently safely folded in his leather jacket pocket. He still hadn't worked out how to play that one.

By nine o'clock, and a few more beers later, Vinnie was feeling better than he had so far that day. Watching some of his mates take over the snooker tables, he'd studiously ignored Lloyd Watson before managing a couple of sets himself. He was returning his snooker cue to its rack and was about to head back to the bar, when he was approached by a bloke from one of the other tables who asked him for a game.

'You're Vinnie Dobson, aren't you?'

Vinnie glanced up at the tall, solidly built foreigner with the red hair and beard and serious, slate-grey eyes. Although his accent sounded European, there was also a trace of an American twang. He extended his hand – Vinnie shook it briefly.

'It's a privilege to meet you,' the stranger said, with a respect in his voice that sounded as if he meant it. Vinnie just nodded. The bloke was a bit different, and while he felt flattered, he was also on guard.

'You a journalist?' he asked, suspiciously.

'Definitely not,' the other looked offended, 'what makes you think that?' He walked round the side of the table and slotted some coins into the ball release. The balls tumbled out in a noisy volley.

'Can't be too careful,' muttered Vinnie.

'Wise,' agreed the other, 'very wise.'

They began setting up the balls when the stranger continued, 'The real reason I came here tonight was to congratulate you on your judgement.'

Vinnie raised his eyebrows. He didn't know what the bloke was getting at, and he was still suspicious about who he was, but there was something intriguing about him, a powerful magnetism. The two of them began their game, Vinnie breaking, before pocketing a few balls with ease. Then, leaning over the table with his cue, the other said, 'You've a lot of supporters, you know.'

'Yeah,' Vinnie watched him pot a ball, 'the blokes have been great.'

'I don't just mean here. I mean all over the country.'

'Oh, sure, I've had hacks on the phone all the time.'

The other glanced up at him. 'I bet you have,' he said in that admiring tone.

'I've been keeping well schtum.' Vinnie was back on the table, clearing it with ease. 'You only need to open your mouth,' he said importantly, 'and these guys twist every word you say.'

The other nodded. 'That's what I mean about judgement,' he told him.

'Yeah?'

'A lot of other people would have been persuaded to sell their story to the *News of the World* or something.'

'Wankers!' declared Vinnie.

'Very few people understand you can be more effective keeping out of sight.'

Vinnie got the feeling this was more than just some casual chat. The other bloke seemed to be making a point, but he couldn't work out yet exactly what.

'When you say more effective?' he asked, rapping the table

with his cue to indicate which pocket he was potting into.

Moving closer, the other leaned across the table, voice lowered. 'You're not the only one disgusted by Watson. It would be understandable if you decided you wanted some . . . compensation.'

Vinnie looked up at him sharply. The possibility still lingered in his mind that this bloke might be a journalist trying to catch him off guard, or hoodwink him into saying something that would be turned against him. Although his manner was a lot different from any journalist Vinnie had encountered before. In a strange way, he came across like someone out of the army. After a pause, Vinnie replied, 'Do you have anything particular in mind?'

The other met his scrutiny as he murmured, 'Like I said before, you're very perceptive.' It was the stranger's turn again, but Vinnie, having almost cleared the table, had left him snookered. The black ball rolled across the table directly into the far pocket.

'What I want to know is, why are you worried about what Mark's done to me?' Vinnie removed the ball, and prepared to clear up.

'I'm not.' The other surprised him with his frankness. 'It's him signing up with Isis that I find . . . distasteful.' He watched Vinnie effortlessly pocket the two last balls, before saying, 'So you see, we find ourselves in the same corner.'

'We?' Vinnie turned to face him, curiosity now as strong as his suspicion. 'I don't even know who you are.'

Bengt Larson regarded him carefully. Vinnie Dobson had been a lot easier to isolate than he had expected. And although as prickly as he'd been warned, he'd also proven susceptible to flattery. What's more, while absorbed in his previous games of snooker, he'd left his leather jacket thrown over a bar stool. Conducting a routine search of its pockets,

Larson had discovered a letter he knew would make his job very much easier. He nodded in the direction of a quiet corner of the pub. 'Why don't we . . . ?' he suggested.

Vinnie followed, glass in hand, to a badly lit table at a bay window, concealed from the rest of the pub by a fruit machine. No one would see them talking. Standing in the semi-darkness, Larson continued in confidential tones. 'My name is Alex Heindl,' he said, 'but that's not important. What is important is the group of people I work with. And my backers. You'd be surprised how powerful they are.'

Vinnie regarded him carefully. 'What don't you like about Isis?'

Larson's eyes narrowed. 'She's just taken three million dollars off Berkeley Square to endorse their products. She should know better. So should your former client.'

Vinnie instantly recalled the attack on the Berkeley Square's boss just a few weeks ago – it had been mentioned again in this morning's papers. In particular, there were the descriptions of how the bloke had had his eyes gouged out. The attack had made a big impression on Vinnie. He vividly remembered the TV coverage. Now he met Larson's expression with a sudden, new respect.

'Are you the ones—'

'You're probably thinking along the right lines,' Larson interrupted him, 'but I can't tell you anything about who we are.' Then as Vinnie was about to protest he continued, 'Not here. Not now. Just like I wouldn't expect you to tell everything about yourself to a complete stranger. But we do have a common enemy.'

Vinnie was following him very carefully, remembering the way the police detective had described the activists on TV. They were extremely dangerous, was what he'd said, and highly likely to strike again. The idea of having a commando group take revenge on Big-Shot Watson was one that suddenly seized his imagination. His mind was a tumult of excitement as he stared at Larson with even greater compulsion.

'I'm sure you would like to see some harm come to him.' Larson spoke with assurance. 'What I need to know is – how badly?'

Vinnie took a swig from his beer glass. Nothing would give him greater pleasure than waking up to read that Mark Watson had returned to his luxury Hollywood bolt-hole one night to have his dick chopped off and shoved in his mouth – like in that movie he'd seen. There again, he didn't want to have anything to do with it if it meant putting himself at risk. 'Depends, doesn't it?' he said to Larson.

'Of course it does.' Larson held his stare. 'We wouldn't expect you to get your hands dirty.'

'No?'

'It would help us more if you pretended that all was forgiven.'

'You've got to be . . . !'

Larson stepped closer towards him. 'What we need, more than anything, is information. Intelligence. And you can get it for us. But no one must ever make the connection.'

Vinnie's thoughts were racing again, only this time not with images of vengeance – but cash in the bank. Eight grand. This could be the perfect arrangement! He'd sign the Unum deal and take the money. Make out that he'd put the past behind him. Meantime, Mark Watson wouldn't have any idea what was about to hit him.

'So what happens next?' he asked Larson, the breathlessness of his voice betraying his excitement.

'You and my group have to trust each other,' Larson's eyes darted about the pub, making sure they were still alone and unnoticed, 'and trust must be earned. First, we take one simple step. You obtain a piece of information for us. In return, I tell you our plans.'

Vinnie nodded. It seemed reasonable. Regarding the other's cool blue eyes with a sharp intensity he asked, 'What information would that be, then?'

8

It was Hilton Gallo himself who returned Mark's angry telephone call from Studio 18. Minutes after Mark had demanded Lebowitz call him, he was summoned from the studio, where he'd been running through initial sound level checks.

'I understand you were after Leo, urgently?' Hilton was cool as ever. Lebowitz's secretary, Mark realised, must have reacted to his tone and gone directly to the boss.

'Too right. I'm pissed off about all the crap in the media. I thought it was just the papers at first, but Inky Mostyn says you guys are putting it out.'

'Let me understand this correctly,' Hilton's voice notched up a tone, 'you're saying there are distortions in the material GCM released to the media?'

'I am.'

'I understood you had reviewed that material?'

'Only the media release. But all the personal stuff was in the Biographical Notes which I never saw. I phoned Inky Mostyn to complain about his column and he told me he was only repeating what GCM put out.'

'Well, in the first case, the Biographical Notes were prepared on the basis of your briefing of Philip Kaylis. Second, the notes would have been sent to you for approval if you'd requested them—'

'How could I request something I didn't know existed?'

'—and third, the terms of your contract specifically preclude you from talking to reporters without GCM's authorisation. Fortunately, we enjoy a very good relationship with Inky who I'm sure can be persuaded to ... overlook your conversation. If you'd spoken to the wrong journalist it could have been disastrous.' His tone was accusatory. 'Did you speak to anybody else?'

'No, I didn't, but—'

'Don't you see, in the wrong hands the media could present us as being at odds—'

'That's because we are!'

'Mark.' It was one of the rare occasions Hilton called him by name, and he used it now to convey a powerful combination of purported sympathy – and steely determination. 'It's possible that Philip misunderstood what you told him, or misstated some of the details, but we never intended knowingly to circulate false information about you – who would benefit from it?'

That wasn't something Mark was able to answer.

'You know, the worst of it is all the stuff they're publishing in Britain about my mother living off the dole.' There could be no doubting the strength of his feeling. 'I don't know anyone who works harder. I've never known her *not* to work. For three years when we were growing up she never took more than a four-day holiday. Couldn't afford to. How d'you reckon she's supposed to feel with everyone she knows reading about her being some welfare couch potato?'

There was a pause before Hilton responded, 'I understand

you're reacting from the noblest motives. And I want you to realise we are also concerned about your best interests and want to sort this out. That's why I'm calling you personally.'

'I just don't see where Kaylis got this stuff—'

'Nor do I. But you have my assurance that the moment I put the phone down, I will be asking questions.'

'Good, because my family will want answers. I haven't spoken to them yet and probably won't today because of the time difference. But it's not going to be easy—'

'Rest assured, I'll be back in touch before close of play.' Hilton paused before reverting to his usual businesslike tone. 'On the subject of media coverage, GCM is concerned by the strong reference to the One Commando issue. We were expecting some mention, of course, but the level isn't help-ful. Not to us, nor to Berkeley Square.'

With his own preoccupations, Mark hadn't paid too much attention to One Commando. But the animal rights group had been mentioned in most articles. He could see why the papers were doing it – it was a good chance for them to repeat the details of the Lefevre assault with lip-smacking relish.

'We need to shake them off the news agenda,' Hilton was saying.

'How can you stop journalists writing about them?'

'They've already milked the connection for as much as it's worth. They've said everything about One Commando there is to say.'

'So why are you worried about them?'

'Worry isn't the word I'd use,' Hilton corrected him. 'It's more *concern* that the market doesn't buy into all the tabloid hysteria. Our feeling is that if we put a different spin on the endorsement deal, the media will find it hard to keep on plugging away at One Commando.'

'That's something GCM will do, is it?'

'We'll provide the back-up, certainly,' Hilton told him, 'but you'll need to drive it.'

'How do you mean?' The warning bells were sounding. What did GCM want from him this time? Were they setting him up again for the media to make some ridiculous parody of his life? And was this why Hilton Gallo was calling him personally?

'I have no doubt,' Hilton's tone was significant as he looked over to where Lebowitz had been following the conversation from across his desk, 'you'll find the proposition, very, very interesting.'

London

Alan rushed up the staircase of his Clapham home, taking the stairs two at a time. Summoned unexpectedly by Larson just three hours before, his head was spinning from the events of the afternoon.

To begin with, when he'd arrived at the disused Kennington warehouse – donning a ski mask, as instructed, before entering – he'd found himself among a group of five masked commandos. He couldn't tell if any of the others had been involved in the Lefevre operation. In the fetid darkness of the vast corrugated aluminium shed, which was evidently used to store market stalls, they had assembled wordlessly before Larson who, powerful and dominating, explained One Commando's new purpose.

As he listened to the One Commando leader's extraordinarily audacious plans, he'd realised that Larson's ambition went way beyond another Lefevre-style operation. His new scheme would drive One Commando's objectives to a climactic conclusion. It would be the end-game, the final showdown; after the national furore following the Lefevre attack, he could scarcely conceive what fallout would follow Larson's latest plans.

As if all of that weren't enough, at the end of the briefing, Larson had pulled him aside from the others, leading him behind an ancient creaking market stall.

'I don't need to involve you directly in these operations,' he'd said. 'As a footsoldier your skills are surplus to requirements.' For one heart-stopping moment, Alan wondered if Larson doubted him. But surely he wouldn't have summoned him to the meeting if he didn't trust him? He stared up at where Larson's sunglasses glinted in a shard of light that fell from a hole in the roof, high above.

'What we need you for is intelligence.' He squeezed Alan's shoulder so hard it was all he could do not to grimace. 'We need all the information we can get – especially on our main targets. Do you understand?'

Alan nodded.

'Any contribution you make will be specially appreciated by the powers that be.'

There was that phrase again. And this time with a direct link to him.

'It is an opportunity for you to make your mark,' Larson told him, as though reflecting his thoughts. 'You'll be doing something for the movement which no one else can.'

All the way home, Alan had wondered how he'd play things. Larson was entrusting him with exactly what he sought – a project that would bring him to the attention of whoever really ran One Commando. The ideological force behind the group. The ultimate decision-maker. If he could deliver, Alan knew, he'd have set himself up as a key player. He'd be ideally placed to conclude his mission. But how could he give Larson what he wanted without opening up a whole new dimension of risk?

Reaching his attic workroom, he quickly logged on to his computer, opened up his e-mail package, and began to type.

Malibu, California

Isis was in her home studio when the phone call came through from Hilton. Standing, watching the sun slipping down behind the Pacific Ocean through the soundproofed glass, rehearsing her songs again and again, she'd been absorbed in her work when the phone introduced an unwelcome dose of reality. Something had come up, Hilton had told her quickly, and he needed to discuss it with her face to face. Might he visit her at home in, say, an hour? Isis had felt her chest tightening. She knew this must be serious. Hilton guarded his time jealously, and for him to come out to Malibu . . .

'Is it something to do with the Lefevre attack?' she'd wanted to know immediately.

'No. There haven't been any developments. This is more personal—'

'Christ!'

'Nothing you need worry about,' he reassured her hurriedly. 'It's actually very positive. But I think we should discuss it urgently.'

He'd arrived just over an hour later. Isis led him out to her balcony where they could sit in the shadows looking across to where the waves rolled in, washing the beach with silver.

'You got the press cuttings this morning, yes?' Hilton began, never one to waste time with small talk.

Isis nodded.

'Very strong coverage.'

'I know.' She didn't need Hilton to point out that the announcement had already generated at least three times the pre-publicity of her last album, *Eros*. Nor did she need to be told how all the hype was going to translate into sales. It was encouraging – extremely encouraging. Only, with the threat of One Commando given prominence in all the media, it was hard to feel upbeat.

'While all of that is very gratifying,' Hilton quickly read Isis's mood, 'Leo and I have also been giving a lot more thought to your concerns. In the last few days we've met several times for discussions. Leo's come up with a suggestion I think's well worth pursuing.'

In the shadows, Isis followed Hilton sceptically. Leo Lebowitz was indisputably the most ingenious PR spinner in LA, but she was highly doubtful he'd come up with any 'suggestion' that wasn't simply calculated to generate more air time and column inches.

'What we're looking at here is the issue of risk. You're worried about the risk of exposure.'

Isis didn't respond. She first wanted to see where this analysis was leading.

'As with any other risk,' Hilton continued, 'what Lebowitz is suggesting is that we do what we can to minimise the chances of your worst fears being realised.'

'This is starting to sound familiar,' her tone was cynical.

'Just hear me out,' he told her. 'If your name were to be romantically linked to someone, the result would be a highly effective diversion—'

'That would depend who that someone was.' There was a long pause before she demanded, 'Don't tell me you haven't got a name—'

'We do, of course.'

'Well?'

Hilton realised in her present frame of mind she was far from receptive. But there was no turning back now. Meeting her eyes in the darkness he murmured, 'Jordan Hampshire.' His expression was serious. 'Nothing long term.'

'Are you fucking crazy?' she exploded.

'We're talking six, eight weeks.'

'You're expecting me to let him stick his tongue down my throat—'

'It won't be necessary to go that far.'

But Isis wasn't listening to him. 'Make out with a goddam cellphone geek for a bit of publicity.'

'No,' Hilton countered, 'for the removal of risk.'

'You could at least have paired me off with someone a little more my type.'

'I know you don't like the idea of sharing the limelight—'

'It's not that.'

'I think it is. But you can't deny there's a certain logic to you and Jordan—'

'Oh, perfect logic if all you're looking for is constant media intrusion and harassment!' Her eyes blazed in the shadows. 'Why don't we just start a soap opera of my life and be done with it!'

Hilton waited a few moments before saying in measured tones, 'I've met Jordan several times and in my view he's a very personable young man. I would imagine he's been reticent in my company – no doubt in his own space he'd be a lively companion. If you were to meet him—'

'I already have.'

Hilton raised his eyebrows.

'I passed him at the studios this morning.' She remembered walking out from her early-morning session, in the midst of the usual retinue of sound engineers, Unum staff and security. The moment he'd appeared at the end of the corridor she'd recognised him. He was better in the flesh than the photographs she'd seen of him — bar the silly haircut. He'd looked spaced out, and as they'd got closer he'd slowed down with that jaw-on-the-ground groupie expression. Hilton was still scrutinising her carefully.

'Avoiding tough decisions has never been part of the deal,' he told her now.

'Hilton you're so persuasive.' She was facetious.

He shrugged. 'I'm just giving you an option. The rest is entirely up to you.'

She lowered her eyes, before glancing out to the surging breakers. Suddenly she felt like a wayward schoolgirl being carpeted by the headmaster. Hilton was the only one who ever made her feel this way. It was something in his detached style, she supposed, that made her face up to her own anger and suspicion. She supposed he *was* only trying to help.

'The point is,' he was saying, 'this is the risk we've had to live with ever since the beginning. There always has been the possibility that your secret—'

'I know! I know!' She was shaking her head. 'And most of the time I'm okay about it. But lately I've just felt threatened. The past few nights I've hardly been able to sleep.'

Hilton didn't respond, deciding instead to give Isis the opportunity to think over what he'd suggested. It was a long time before she spoke again, and when she did, her tone was fragile. 'What exactly would this . . . relationship entail?'

Bringing his hands together, he raised his fingers to his lips. 'A few dates. We'd want you to be seen out in each other's company at a couple of industry events.' Then, regarding her carefully, 'Timing is everything. The sooner the two of you are out somewhere together, the better.'

She absorbed this in silence for a long while before she asked, 'You think it'll be enough?'

He looked over at her imploring expression and wished he could give her the reassurance she sought. But there were no guarantees he could provide – she'd always known that. And it would have been wrong of him to pretend. So instead he answered, 'I think it's a good idea. And until we find out more about One Commando, it's the only real option we've got.'

London
Friday, 17 September

Lloyd Watson glanced at his watch in surprise when the doorbell rang. Just after ten in the evening. He wondered if his girlfriend Heidi had wangled an early shift at the hospital and come round to surprise him. Getting up from his chair, where he'd been sitting engrossed in *Inspector Morse*, he cast a critical eye across the sitting room: sleeping bags and crumpled pillows were strewn across the carpet from where two of his mates had been camping over. The remnants of his supper – a Domino's pizza box and several empty beer cans – littered the glass coffee table. Worst of all – Heidi's pet hate – all the ashtrays were still loaded from last night's post-pub party. He had to admit, it wasn't a pretty picture.

He walked through to the tiny hall, bracing himself for a tongue-lashing. The Banham front door had a security chain and fish-eye lens installed, although he never used them: why bother? But tonight, as he unlocked the catch, swung open the door, and caught sight of his visitor he felt a sudden tension in his throat. It wasn't Heidi on his doorstep. It was the very last person he'd expected to receive a visit from.

He instantly recalled his last conversation with Mark on the subject of Vinnie's vengeful streak. And his last encounter with Vinnie at the Lamb. He'd been among the group of regulars trying to calm him down – he hadn't doubted that Vinnie would have gone for Mark if it wasn't for all the blokes holding him back. Not that he'd have got very far; Mark could look after himself, Lloyd knew, just like he himself might have to right now.

But Vinnie was standing there with an embarrassed grimace on his face.

'Lloy-boy!' he greeted Lloyd with forced joviality, using the name he'd given him years before.

'Didn't think you'd want to come visiting?' Lloyd was direct. Looking him in the eye, he tried to figure out exactly what Vinnie was up to. He seemed calm enough though he'd probably had a few pints.

'Yeah, bit unexpected,' shrugged Vinnie. 'Can I come in?' He'd already stepped into the hall and was heading for the lounge, leaving Lloyd without much choice. Closing the front door, Lloyd followed him through.

'You know Mark's not here?' The thought occurred to him that perhaps Vinnie was after his older brother. 'He's—'

'In America. Yeah. I read the papers.' Vinnie sat back in the sofa, propping his feet up on the coffee table as he had dozens of times before.

Picking up the remote, Lloyd pressed the TV 'Mute' button, glancing at the screen as he did and wondering how long Vinnie planned hanging around. He decided not to offer him a beer. Lowering himself carefully into an ancient armchair, he looked over at Vinnie. 'You were pretty pissed off last time—'

'Oh. That!' Vinnie smirked. 'Yeah, well, that was then. This is now.'

It was a very different Vinnie from the one who'd been about to attack his brother. Very different too from the Vinnie that Siobhan O'Mara had told him about. Lloyd didn't try to hide his surprise.

'What's happened to change things?'

Vinnie shifted in the sofa before delivering one of his Big-Shot Music Producer looks. That had always irked Lloyd about Vinnie – he patronised him. Still treated him like Mark's kid brother, talking down to him and bragging about his exploits, expecting him to accept everything hook, line and sinker.

'This is to go no further than you and me.' Vinnie spoke conspiratorially, waving a finger between them.

Lloyd raised his eyebrows.

'I've just landed "The Holy Black" a forty grand recording contract.'

'That's amazing!' Lloyd exclaimed, thinking how pleased Rick and Headley would be. They'd been bashing away at the talent club circuit for years.

'So when's it coming out?'

Vinnie made a face. 'Session contract, not a record.'

'Who with?'

'That's the thing,' Vinnie eyeballed him, 'Unum Music.'

Then before Lloyd could react, 'I wasn't born yesterday. I know how things work. Let's face it, Mark probably put a word in for me.'

There was no 'probably' about it, so far as Lloyd could see. And Vinnie hadn't landed 'The Holy Black' a contract at all – Mark had got the Unum guys to throw it his way. Looking back at Vinnie, Lloyd said, 'Yeah. Mark's good that way.' He thought about his own job – he'd never have got his break into OmniCell if it hadn't been for Mark.

'So—' Vinnie was digging about in his pocket for a packet

of slim panatellas, before extracting one, removing the Cellophane wrapper, and lighting up, '—things have moved on a bit for me, you see.'

'I bet.' Lloyd eyed the panatella with distaste but decided not to be provocative by demanding Vinnie smoke it on the balcony.

'Foot in the door with Unum.' Vinnie was oblivious to Lloyd's expression. 'This is a first contract and I can build on it.'

'Sounds great.'

'Oh yes,' Vinnie couldn't resist it, 'just one of all kinds of new opportunities coming my way.'

'You mean, you've got other deals on the go?'

Vinnie gave him a secretive smile, thinking about his meeting with Larson. 'Like you wouldn't believe. New people, new deals – world's really opening up for me.'

Vinnie wouldn't divulge anything more and Lloyd wasn't going to give him the satisfaction of asking. Though he could hazard a guess about the 'new people' bit. Last time he'd seen him down the Lamb, Vinnie had been talking intently to a tall, bearded bloke with a strange accent. The pub got a lot of visitors, but the foreign man had sought Vinnie out. He'd played a few rounds of snooker with some of Lloyd's mates and, during the course of conversation, got to ask about Vinnie. Later, Lloyd had noticed the pair of them slipping out of the main section of the pub thick as thieves. Probably some hack wanting to buy Vinnie's story, thought Lloyd. Despite all Vinnie's bluster about not talking to reporters, it surprised Lloyd that he still hadn't cashed in on his former association with Mark. Even he had received calls from journalists promising large cheques in exchange for 'colour stories' about his brother. Had the foreign guy signed up Vinnie for some sort of exclusive?

'Way I see things,' Vinnie sucked on his panatella, 'I probably owe your brother an apology.'

He wasn't looking at Lloyd when he said it – which was just as well. This was so un-Vinnie that Lloyd couldn't conceal his scepticism.

'And thanks,' Vinnie continued, exhaling thoughtfully.

Well, those were two new words in his vocabulary, thought Lloyd. Next he was going to say he'd given his life to Jesus.

'Which is why I'm here.' He looked across at Lloyd's bemused expression. 'I tried to phone Mark, speak to him personally. Only problem is, when I called him at that hotel he was supposed to be staying in, they said he'd moved.'

'That's right. He's moved to a house somewhere.' Lloyd knew better than to say a mansion in Beverly Hills.

'You've got his number?'

Lloyd shook his head. 'Only spoken to him once since he moved and he called me. I reckon he can afford the long-distance rates.'

'Yeah.' Vinnie grinned, though his eyes weren't smiling. 'But, I mean, you could get his number for me?'

'Oh, sure,' Lloyd held his gaze. Of course he had Mark's number, but he had no intention of handing it over to Vinnie. Suspicions aroused, he didn't know what to make of Vinnie, except that he was up to something. Had his own agenda.

'He'll probably call me in the next week sometime. I'll ask him for it then.'

'Good.' Vinnie sat forward, tapping his ash into the opening of an empty beer can, before rising to his feet, mission accomplished.

'Coming down for a quick one?' he asked Lloyd, on the return to the front door, jerking his head in the general direction of the Lamb.

'It's all right, thanks. Need an early night.'

'Fair enough.'

Closing the door behind him, Lloyd returned to the lounge. He usually found Inspector Morse's investigations utterly engrossing, but tonight as he regarded the silent action, he had the unavoidable sensation that sinister events in real life had suddenly overtaken those on the screen.

9

—

Mark climbed into the back seat of the luxury Lincoln Town Car, pulled the dark blanket over his head, and braced himself for another round of flash cubes, car-thumping and yelled questions. He was less than ecstatic at being forced into discomfort once again by the very people at whose hands he and his family had received such a mauling. But it was for the last time. Hilton had promised him that.

'Less of them outside now,' Denzil tried keeping things upbeat as he closed the door behind him, 'the odds are stacked against them after dark.'

'Yeah.' Having laid his jacket out on the back seat, Mark was careful to avoid crushing his linen trousers. His clothes had been picked out for him by a wardrobe consultant sent over late that afternoon by GCM. And a stylist had spent twenty minutes fiddling with his hair, before applying various lotions and cosmetics to his face – none, he noted, manufactured by Berkeley Square – in preparation for what Hilton had described earlier in the day as the photo-opportunity of his life.

The GCM chief had phoned him, as agreed, after speaking to Kaylis about the Biographical Notes. It seemed there had been a genuine misunderstanding, he said. Mark had told Kaylis his mother lived in a council house. Not conversant with social services in Britain, Kaylis understood that to mean she was welfare dependent. As for the line about Mark living in an inner-city tenement, that's what Kaylis had taken him to mean by his use of the phrase 'housing estate'. Things had got lost in translation, concluded Hilton – and to prevent the possibility of such a thing ever happening again, he had instructed Lebowitz to ensure Mark received *all* media material in future, before distribution.

Mark hadn't said anything. Maybe it *had* just been a case of crossed wires. Then again, perhaps Lebowitz had deliberately sensationalised his past for the purpose of mass titillation. The fact was, he didn't think he could completely believe anything GCM came out with again. Meantime, Hilton's proposals to lose One Commando from the news agenda – and, at the same time, end his life in hiding – had taken him by surprise.

'We have in mind a photo-op,' he'd said.

'Hasn't that been on the cards?'

'Not the one we envisaged. We're planning to move things on a bit.'

'Yeah?'

'Leo and I have discussed this at length, and we believe it would be in your interests, as well as Isis's, for the two of you to be seen out together.'

'You mean,' Mark responded to his tone of voice, 'romantically?'

'Yes.'

Mark's astonishment was exceeded only by his certainty

about Isis's reaction to this. 'She'll never do it,' he told Hilton after a pause, 'she doesn't even like me.'

'What makes you say that?' Hilton moved automatically into damage-limitation mode.

'When I saw her at Unum she completely ignored me.'

'She's running to a tight schedule.'

'Not that tight!'

'I've already spoken to Isis and she's very willing.'

Quite the little cupid, Mark thought, but didn't say, still taken aback by the suggestion. After the current assault of half-truths and bare-faced lies, the prospect of another blaze of publicity in the near future didn't exactly thrill him. Especially seeing that it involved engineering his love life – or at least the appearance of it.

'Just think about it,' Hilton tried to enthuse him, 'intimate candle-lit dinners with the most famous pop chick in the world.'

Yeah, right, thought Mark. A few weeks ago he'd have been enthralled by the prospect. But now he knew nothing came without a pay-off.

'It's also a great way for you to make your first public appearance.' Hilton noted the silence. 'We'll put you into the right restaurant and by the time you come out every news organisation in the world will be waiting for you.'

For the first time in his life, Mark was beginning to realise why it was that famous people so often turned reclusive. After a lengthy pause he found himself asking, without really wanting to hear the answer, 'When did you want all this to happen?'

At the other end of the phone, Hilton was brisk. 'We've booked the two of you a table at Bianco Verdi tonight at eight.'

Now, as they drove out to Malibu, Denzil shaking off the

paparazzi, on the back seat Mark followed their progress on a Los Angeles street map. Looking at the map, it seemed hardly any distance at all from Beverly Hills to Malibu – but on the ground, the streets seemed to go on for ever, block after block of city that to an outsider's eyes formed an endless, anonymous sprawl. Once they'd got out to Malibu, however, it was something different, the affluence of the beachside community almost tangible. Denzil turned into a private driveway that led into what seemed like a fortress – he had to use his mobile phone to get the maid to open up the electronically controlled gates. Once inside, they found themselves sealed within a high-walled courtyard, requiring more security doors to be opened. While Denzil stayed outside with the car, Mark was shown inside to the lounge, where he was told to wait.

It was a strange sensation, finding himself in the home of the woman who'd been his idol, his fantasy. This view – a panoramic sweep over to where the silver breakers washed up on the beach – was the view that Isis looked out on during her private hours. These sumptuous damask chairs were the chairs she sat in. There was something voyeuristically thrilling but at the same time curiously matter-of-fact about being here. The room itself was long, cream carpeted and softly lit, opening out on to a balcony that overlooked the beach. Float-framed platinum discs bedecked its tangerine walls, and two Grammy awards stood on a corner shelf. On his way over here this evening, Mark had wondered if Isis would treat him any differently tonight than with the cool indifference of their studio encounter. But now as he stopped in front of each platinum disc, reading its inscription, he found himself wondering why he should have expected to be treated any differently. What was he to her, anyway?

When Isis did make her appearance, it was anything but grand. Rushing into the room, shoes in her hand, the first words she said to him were, 'Running late.' She was stylish in sculpted black, her blonde hair swept back, cleavage carefully revealed, and diamonds glinting at her ears and round her neck.

'We'll use the Mercedes.' She glanced over at him briefly, gesturing with the shoes that he should follow her. Obediently, he crossed the room, catching her scent as he did so – a warm, ambrosial fragrance that trailed after her in the hallway, through a door concealed by a large, tapestry wall-hanging and down some stairs towards the garage. By the time he'd stepped into the far side of the customised stretch Mercedes, Isis was already talking to someone on her mobile phone. Her driver, Frank, took them through security, first into the courtyard, then out through the gates. Mark sat silently as Isis ended one call before promptly beginning another, and the car glided back towards the city in the direction from which he'd so recently come. Any hopes he might have had of a tête-à-tête en route were soon ended. And while a powerful impulse made him want to just stare at Isis now that he was sitting so close to her, he didn't want to seem like a star-struck fan. So he just looked out of the front and side windows instead. Not for the first time since arriving in LA he felt that he was caught in some bizarre dream he had yet to categorise as fantasy or nightmare.

A short while before reaching the restaurant, Isis abruptly ended a call and turned to him.

'Now, how are we going to do the entrance?' she wanted to know.

It took him a moment to work out what she meant. Then he said, 'I thought the media will only get there later.'

'Bianco Verdi is one of the places you go to be seen,' she explained, making him feel awkwardly self-conscious. 'People there notice *everything*. They'll be interpreting every action.' As she met his eyes for the first time, her expression, thought Mark, was impenetrable.

'The restaurant's on my side of the street. When we pull up, the driver will open my door. You should get out your side, come round and give me a hand up – my left hand – then accompany me into the restaurant on my left side.'

He nodded.

'We'll hold hands, your right, my left,' she held hers out across the back seat and he reached out in response, 'fingers like this.' She demonstrated, before letting his hand drop. Mark had never choreographed his entrance into a restaurant before – he found the detail of it astonishing – though he was glad of the briefing when the time came. Bianco Verdi had a raised verandah overlooking the pavement, and behind the immaculately sculpted Luma shrubs interspersed in ceramic tubs along the railings, tables were packed out at this time of the night. He was aware of the theatre being created from the moment Isis emerged from the back seat of her car. He took her hand in his with an assumed ease of familiarity and, as they made their way towards the restaurant entrance, he noted the turning heads and interrupted conversations, the sudden movement of waiters towards a corner of the restaurant, quickly followed by the emergence of the impossibly named Romeo Casablanca, bouffant-haired, sports-jacketed and mincing over towards them with extravagant arm movements. 'Darling!' He approached Isis. 'So good to see you.'

Air kissing her on both sides, he stood back for a moment, still holding her arms, evidently enraptured by the spectacle of having her to dine in his restaurant. When he acknowledged Mark, it was almost as an afterthought, extending his hand while his gaze remained fixed all the time on Isis's face. Then he was hustling them to the most visible table in the restaurant, revelling in all the attention being generated. As they walked through the restaurant Mark couldn't fail to observe the unaffected gawping, as dozens of eyes focused intently on Isis, before taking him in too – he had never been the subject of such comprehensive eyeballing in his life before. And along with all the gawping, were smiles and waves from people Isis seemed to know, judging by the way she returned their greetings.

'You know a lot of people,' Mark murmured beside her.

'Mostly ass-creeps.' She turned to him, with a glued-on smile. 'Every time I come to a place like this I remember why I don't come more often.'

Then as they got to their table, 'Let's give them something to choke on their oysters about.' She tugged him towards her so he knew to lean over and kiss her. It was a brief kiss and felt perfectly natural, the kind of kiss any couple in love might exchange in a restaurant. They sat down at their table as waiters fussed with napkins and menus while the *maître d'* snapped his fingers for a complimentary bottle of Taittinger. When it had arrived, Isis made a fuss of inviting the manager to join them to toast Nile. After he'd finally left them on their own she told Mark, 'Ninety seconds and he'll have tipped off every major news channel in town.'

Mark's smile was wry. 'You're good at this.'

She shrugged. 'Practice.' Reaching out to where his hand was on the table, she slipped her fingers between his. 'Remember, it's all a performance now. Just keep it light. Plenty of bedroom eyes and stolen glances.'

'That doesn't need much acting.'

'Oh, very arch.' She laughed flirtatiously. 'Nothing saying you can't sometimes enjoy the performance.'

'Good,' said Mark, 'I plan to.'

Sitting opposite her for the first time, he was surprised how comfortable he felt in her company. After the way she'd ignored him at the studio, he'd come prepared for the worst kind of prima donna behaviour. But Isis was warm, engaged – even if it was all an act – and he found himself responding to her.

'How d'you feel the recording's going?' he asked.

'Mm,' she nodded. 'Pretty much on track. Recording's the easiest part.'

'Oh, yeah?'

'Media reaction – that's something else.'

Mark instantly reached up towards his hair.

'I had no idea what a circus I was getting myself into when I signed up.' He'd been wondering if he should get this off his chest, but it seemed all right now. Necessary, even. He didn't want Isis to get the wrong impression of him. 'It's been bad enough getting used to the silly clothes and even sillier haircut without having to read all the crap about my family and myself in the papers.'

She was following him intently.

'All that stuff about "Rags to Rollses,"' he was shaking his head, 'it's all such trash.' Pausing a moment, he leaned back in his seat. 'Sorry if I'm ranting. It's just so unexpected.'

'That's not ranting.' Her eyes glinted. 'Believe me, I *know* about ranting!'

'I s'pose you must be used to the media putting out rubbish about you?'

She shook her head. 'You never really get used to it.'

'So, what, I mean, d'you do?'

'You just keep going. You don't have any choice. Anonymity is no longer an option.'

She'd expressed something he wouldn't have been able to understand himself till a short while ago. In all the years he'd idolised the Queen of Charts, he'd never so much as guessed at the bizarre existence she had to lead, nor at how far removed from her public persona the real Isis might be. Small wonder she kept outsiders at bay. Remembering how she'd moved down the corridor at the studios, surrounded by the group of Unum executives, he realised now that the reason she'd ignored him had probably been nothing more than self-defence.

'It's inevitable you go a bit mad,' she said, sipping her champagne. 'I know there's plenty of people think I'm crazy with all my security gates and alarms. But you only need to wake up once with a blade to your throat, and you realise you just can't live normally. Too many nutsos out there.'

He thought of the Lefevre attack and his conversation with Hilton that morning. Not that One Commando was a subject he thought he should pursue.

Regarding him with an expression of enquiry, Isis asked now, 'I want to know what you were doing before.'

'Before Hilton?'

She nodded.

This was another thing he'd wondered how best to package. But he'd realised by now that she had a well-developed bullshit detector – there was no point pretending to be anything he wasn't.

'I was doing weekend gigs in clubs and pubs around South London. Like the papers say, no one had ever heard of me – that much is true. But it's not true that I was living in poverty on some council sink estate. And my mother wasn't living off social security. We've always been a hard-working family. We didn't have much,' he levelled with her, 'but at least I had my hair.'

He told her about how his father had left the family when Lloyd was only two years old, how his mother had worked in a dry cleaning shop and he'd had to take on responsibilities from an early age. It had been such an ordinary background he wouldn't have thought it would be of the slightest interest to Isis. But her questions revealed more than casual curiosity. She told him that she, too, came from a very ordinary family of Italian emigrants who'd settled in Miami. She hadn't always lived in a multi-million dollar home in Malibu. Mark felt a connection had been made between them – one he least expected. Recounting some family anecdotes from his childhood, and laughing with her, he forgot for a while that he was sitting opposite the world's sexiest pop chick.

Forty-five minutes later, Isis was in the powder room tidying up her make-up in preparation for the photo-frenzy that would accompany their departure from Bianco Verdi. The evening had gone better than she had expected, she found herself thinking through a blur of champagne. She'd been pleasantly surprised by Mark Watson's lack of pretension and his English humour. Unlike most pop star wannabes she'd met, he didn't come across as a self-absorbed boof-head. Instead, there was an all-round self-sufficiency about him that she thought was sweet. She supposed his looks helped; she was by no means oblivious to their powerful appeal. It might be easier to get through this make-believe romance than she had originally feared.

On her way back to the table, Romeo Casablanca hurried towards her, a-flutter with the news that a very large contingent of photographers were now encamped outside the restaurant. Was there anything he could do? He wrung his hands in dramatised anguish. Isis announced that she and Mr Hampshire would make their escape through the kitchen.

Back at the table, she explained the change of plan to Mark as he stood up and slipped into his jacket.

'But isn't the whole point of tonight—'

'They'll be waiting. Why d'you think I tipped off Casablanca? There'll be far more interest in the pictures if it's thought they're illicit instead of some PR job.'

Mark shook his head. He was still new to this.

'It'll also help if they have something to write about,' she said, pausing in the short passage that led through to the kitchen. Ahead of them, Romeo Casablanca was fussing and fretting, but now as she raised her face to Mark, he leaned down towards her, feeling her arms round his shoulders. This time as their lips met, to his surprise he felt her mouth parting. This wasn't something choreographed in advance and he didn't know if he should be taking liberties. But as she held him to her, he decided it should be treated like a moment of unrehearsed desire. Bodies pressed tightly together, his mouth searched hers. He was aware of several waitering staff passing by, but tried to ignore them, just like he was trying to ignore the fact that it was the world's greatest sex icon whose tongue was in his mouth. It felt good, no doubting it, the two of them melting together. But he'd hardly had any time to get used to it and she'd broken away from him and was stepping back. For a single instant their eyes met and he sensed a significance in her expression, though he couldn't place whether it was admonition or lust. Then she was directing him, ahead of her, into the kitchen, past a wide-eyed galley of chefs to the back exit.

Just as Isis had predicted, the moment they emerged their appearance was greeted with a flurry of flash cubes and excited calls from photographers. Doing their best to seem caught unawares, they hurried, hand-in-hand, to where the Mercedes was parked near by, engine already started for a quick escape. They pulled away with a squeal of wheels and several paparazzi photographers on scooters in hot pursuit. Mark glanced about at them.

'D'you think we'll lose them?'

'We don't want to. We came in this car for maximum exposure,' Isis replied, moving closer towards him on the back seat. Responding, he draped his arm around her shoulders amid another blaze of flash cubes. As the Mercedes purred out towards Malibu on that warm Los Angeles night with the Queen of Charts snuggled into his shoulder and the world's media in hot pursuit, Mark couldn't help but wonder at how quickly his life was changing.

Back in Isis's home, the garage door sliding shut behind them, Isis got out of the car and led the way back up the stairs and through the concealed entrance to the hallway.

'What happens next?' he asked her.

She turned. 'Hilton suggested you wait for an appropriate time before leaving,' she told him with a droll smile.

'Oh, yes?' he responded with a grin. 'And how long, I wonder, is appropriate?'

'Well, not five minutes.' She was leading him into her sitting room. 'So would you like a nightcap?'

'A Scotch would be nice, thanks.' He eyed her loaded drinks cabinet. Then as she poured them both drinks, 'I don't s'pose he gave you any other instructions, did he? Like, am I supposed to walk out of here with a big smile on my face?'

Turning, she met his eyes with an impish expression, handing him a tumbler. 'We could tousle your hair.'

'Ruffle up my clothes.'

'Lipstick and lovebites?' She snorted with amusement.

'I'll drink to that.'

They clinked their glasses and took first sips before meeting each other's eyes. Once again, he didn't know quite what to make of her. This evening may have been all role play, but he couldn't help sensing a tug of genuine attraction. Or was that simply wishful thinking? Here he was, late at night, with the world's most famous pop star looking into his eyes across the sofa of her soft-lit Malibu home. Of course he wanted to have those thoughts.

They continued their effortless conversation from the restaurant, Isis recalling the lighter side of her Broadway experiences, then after he'd finished his drink, Mark glanced at his watch.

'I've been here forty minutes. Do you think that's an "appropriate" time?'

'I guess.' Isis got up from where she was sitting. 'I'll leave you to head out the front door.'

Denzil was waiting with his car outside – and a bank of telephoto lenses, doubtless, already trained on the door.

'It's been a . . . great evening,' he approached her, 'thank you.'

Again, he sensed an energy between them, an intimacy that went beyond simple friendliness. He wondered if she'd show she sensed it too. Now was the time in the evening. This was the moment. He leaned to kiss her, preparing for embrace. But as he moved closer she turned, offering him her cheek. Then she was quickly breaking apart.

'I enjoyed the evening too.' She smiled enigmatically, squeezing his arm. Then stepping back, she gestured towards the hall. 'See you in the papers.'

Later that night, back at Beverly Hills, Mark noted from the array of clocks in the hallway that it was just after eight a.m. London time. He hadn't spoken to his family since the papers had come out. He reckoned he'd better make a couple of calls before turning in for bed.

He spoke to his mother first, concerned about how she'd been affected. She'd been at home the previous morning when the paper was delivered – the Watsons had always been a *Daily Mail* household. As it happened, the *Mail*'s article hadn't been too bad, but no sooner were they reading it than the telephone was ringing with reporters from other papers. Mrs Watson had been outraged by some of their questions – she'd let them have a piece of her mind, she told Mark. And when she arrived at work later, her colleagues were similarly indignant about what they'd read in the press. Any journalists calling the dry cleaner's were soon told where to go – none of the women there had any doubt that it was the papers who were twisting the truth, sensationalising what had happened 'just so they can sell a few more copies', as Mark's mother put it.

Mark hadn't been able to help smiling to himself when his Mum had said that – he should have known he could count on her sound common sense. No, she was very proud of him, his mother lectured him firmly, turning the tables on the conversation, and he wasn't to let the gutter press upset him.

Next he'd called Lloyd who, to his further relief, regarded the whole affair with droll amusement. The first he'd known about it was looking over fellow commuters' shoulders on the tube on his way to work the previous day. Arriving at the office, it was to find his e-mail 'In' tray swamped with notes from colleagues, with many ribbing references to one of the newspaper articles which referred to him as having been 'rescued from the dole queue by his generous big brother'. Later in the day, the publicity manager had put her head round the door and made a wisecrack about his older brother doing a celebrity endorsement for OmniCell.

Mark told Lloyd what he'd already warned his mother about – that a new wave of publicity was about to break, making Isis and him out to be an item. 'It's all just a scam,' he said, 'but for God's sake don't tell anyone that.'

'Just trying to stir up more publicity?' had been his mother's reaction earlier.

'Something like that.'

'Bummer having to get it on with Isis.' Lloyd had been facetious. 'Just how much selfless fucking is involved?'

'Keep your filthy little thoughts to yourself.'

They'd joshed about for a short while, then Lloyd had something to tell him. 'You'll never guess who came sniffing round after you last night.'

'Who was that, then?'

'Only your former "manager".'

'What?' exclaimed Mark. 'Round to your flat?'

'Yeah.'

'Did he give you a hard time?' Mark immediately thought back to their last conversation, and the revelations about Vinnie's increasingly violent tendencies.

'Nothing like that,' Lloyd replied. 'Came to tell me he'd just landed some deal with Unum.'

Mark was astonished. 'Would have thought that's the last thing he'd want you to know about. Anyway, I thought he wasn't speaking to you?'

'He wasn't. Not till his social call. Completely ignored me down the Lamb. Then he came round saying he wants to thank you and—'

'Thank me?' interjected Mark.

'—and apologise . . .'

Mark was beyond surprise. Unum deal or no Unum deal, Vinnie's nocturnal visit was way out of character.

'He wants something,' he told Lloyd after a moment's pause.

'Yeah. Your contact details.'

Mark absorbed this in silence.

'I didn't give them to him,' Lloyd added quickly.

'Why did he say he needed them?'

'Says he's planning to look you up. He's thinking of heading to LA.'

'Uh-huh?' That didn't ring true either. None of this did. Vinnie had always had a lot of front, but gushing thanks and gratitude had never been a part of it. And as for a visit to LA. It just didn't make sense, thought Mark – unless Vinnie was now working to a different agenda. In cahoots with someone else.

'Tell me,' he asked his brother, 'have you noticed anything else about Vinnie acting different?'

'Not really,' Lloyd shrugged at the other end, 'same old, same old.'

'He's not hanging out with a new crowd?'

Lloyd recalled Vinnie bragging about new people and doing new deals and remembered he'd seen him in the company of that foreign hack. He hadn't planned telling Mark about the journo – first of all he didn't know for sure that he *was* a journo, and second, even if he was, what could Mark do about it?

'There's been a few new people sniffing around for him,' was all he said now.

'What kind of people?' Mark sounded serious.

'Well . . . *a* person,' Lloyd corrected himself, 'and it might've been just nothing.'

At the other end, Mark wondered why Lloyd was being so evasive.

'Just tell me about the guy!'

'Well, I think he may have been a foreign reporter.'
Sensing Mark's determination, Lloyd decided to get the bad
news out of the way first. 'He and Vinnie were in a huddle
behind the fruit machines for about twenty minutes two
nights ago.' After a brief pause he added, 'I wasn't going to
mention it 'cause I don't know if the guy even is a journalist—'

'Hey, I'm way past worrying about what some foreign
language newspaper writes about me. The stuff in English is
bad enough.' Mark was pacing up and down.

'But if they paid Vinnie enough—'

'He'd say anything – I know,' agreed Mark. The Unum
deal had been planned as a damage-limitation exercise, not
that anyone was under the illusion it would stop Vinnie
taking a few snipes.

'What makes you think this guy was up to something with
Vinnie?' he persisted.

'He came looking for him. I was playing a few sets of
snooker with the boys when he sidles up and takes an interest, and before you know it he's asking questions about is
this Vinnie Dobson's local, and which one is he.'

'When you say foreign – was he a frog or something?'

'That's the thing, he had this weird accent, like half
American and half something else – German, or maybe
Scandinavian.'

Mark halted in his tracks. Euro-American accent. He
remembered reading the words, and though he couldn't place
where, he instantly sensed an uneasy recognition.

'Looked different, too. Really tall gym-boy – must pump
iron for hours a day – red hair and this goatee beard.'

As Lloyd continued, Mark's mind was whirring – until it
all suddenly slotted into place: the 'Security Briefing' on
Berkeley Square. The stuff Hilton Gallo had given him that

first day. The three-line profile of someone called Bengt Larson, he remembered, described him as being muscular in build, a master of disguise, and having a 'Euro-American accent.'

Aware of the pause at the other end, Mark's thoughts raced ahead. No need to tell Lloyd of his sudden suspicions, he reckoned, though an idea was starting to form. Breaking the silence he asked his brother, 'If you saw a photo of this bloke, d'you think you'd recognise him?'

'Oh, sure,' Lloyd was breezy. 'I spoke to him for a while and—'

'The thing is, he may have been in disguise.'

At the other end, Lloyd was surprised. He knew there was no end to what journalists would do for a celebrity scoop but he hadn't realised that dressing up incognito was one of them.

'You reckon you know who he is?' he asked now.

It was a while before Mark responded in a determined voice. 'No. But I mean to find out.'

Minutes later, Mark had walked through to the study, an expansive, book-lined affair, with shelves ranged from floor to ceiling down two whole walls, and the feel about it of a gentleman's club. In the lockable filing cabinet under the large, leather-topped desk, he kept all his most valuable documents – his contracts with GCM, Unum Music, Berkeley Square – together with anything else he considered important, including the Security Briefing. He'd soon found it, and was flicking through the pages to the paragraph about Larson. He remembered reading it that first day at Chateau Marmont, and how, at the time, Bengt Larson and One Commando had seemed an abstract concept, a theoretical threat if he signed the Berkeley Square endorsement. He hadn't had any idea that Larson might acquire a sudden significance in his own life. Could it be that within just ten days a violent terrorist, wanted by police forces of four European countries, was now trailing through his old London haunts?

This time as he focused on the paragraph about Larson he did so intently – there was nothing hypothetical about him now. It was only a short paragraph and didn't say much more than he remembered; as he read and reread it, he didn't know exactly what he was looking for, except for some clue, something that might signal where he could find out more about Larson, what he looked like – and what was being done to arrest him. The police of those four European countries must have photos of him, he thought. Identikit portraits at the very least.

He stared at the screen of his Compaq desktop, and a thought was suddenly triggered. The Compaq, complete with modem and dedicated phone line, had already been useful for exchanging e-mails with some of his mates back at OmniCell. Now he switched it on, impatiently waiting for it to boot up. Clicking on 'Internet' from a screen crowded with icons, as soon as he was connected he headed for the Alta Vista search engine, tapping a single word into the search field the moment it appeared.

On the support desk at OmniCell he'd had to be net-literate – most OmniCell product manufacturers kept detailed specifications on their websites, and responding to customer queries invariably required trawling through pages of electronic data. Mark had learned that the answers to most things could be found on the Net, if you had the patience to look, and now as a navy blue page with an impressive logo appeared, he wondered how far this would get him in his search for Bengt Larson.

The Interpol website, with its distinctive sword and scales logo surrounding the globe, had buttons ranged down both sides of the page. Glancing across them, Mark found one headed 'International Terrorism' which he opened up. It carried nothing more revealing than a few bland pages of definitions about differences between terrorism and crime – but at the bottom was a link to 'Current investigations'. This proved equally unexciting, providing nothing more than a round-up of major terrorist activities, all of which had already been well publicised. But once again there was an intriguing link – to 'Most Wanted International Terrorists'.

Hitting the button, Mark was soon looking at an A to Z of individuals, each accompanied by a photograph, as well as a summary list of the terrorism for which they were believed to be responsible. He scrolled rapidly down, hardly daring to hope for what he might find.

But there he was – Bengt Erik Larson, thirty-five, currently leader of One Commando animal terrorist group, but connected to a catalogue of previous terrorist activities which hadn't been so much as mentioned in GCM's Security Briefing. Prior to One Commando, Larson had been a member of a neo-Nazi anti-immigrants group in Munich responsible for a campaign of bombings, including the implosion of an entire four-floor apartment block, killing thirty-nine people, and the assassination of three Turkish community leaders. After apparently running to ground for eighteen months, his career in international terrorism had continued, bizarrely, with the Green Warriors, a militant eco-group. Mark vividly recalled the John F. Kennedy-style assassination of the high-profile Chief Executive Officer of one of the world's largest oil companies, gunned down in the back of his limousine while being driven through the streets of Amsterdam. That story had been all over the news media for weeks – though at the time there'd been no connection between Green Warriors, who'd claimed responsibility for the killing, and Bengt Larson, whom police had only subsequently identified as Green Warrior's mastermind.

The idea that Larson who, to date, had eluded the most strenuous efforts of Europe's police to catch him, might now have turned his attentions to him, just seemed too much to believe. And despite the Security Briefing, Mark had never imagined that signing a commercial endorsement deal could lead to such consequences. Now he looked at the photograph of Larson, taken nearly ten years before, when he was still an officer in the German army. He took in the direct blue gaze, the short-cropped fair hair, the straight, unsmiling mouth. He hoped to God he was jumping to conclusions, that Lloyd was right and the Lamb's foreign visitor had just been some Continental hack. But he couldn't afford to take any chances.

Within moments he'd sent an e-mail to Lloyd with Larson's photograph as an attachment. He asked Lloyd to get back to him a.s.a.p.

10

Isis's unexpected coolness towards Mark at the end of the evening had been far more apparent than real – a defence concealing her true feelings. In her private suite, she hurried through to check on Holly. Her daughter was sound asleep, lying in her customary foetal position, the sheet clutched to her chest and her long blonde tresses sweeping across the pillow beside her. Sitting on the edge of the bed, Isis reached out, stroking her daughter's hair back into place in an automatic gesture, before tracing down Holly's cheek with her fingertips. Looking down at the child's sleeping features, untroubled and at peace, seemed only to heighten her own feelings – a turmoil she had unwittingly provoked that evening. Because as much as she had enjoyed it at the time, her encounter with Mark, first in the restaurant and later at home, had snared her on a memory she wished to forget. A recollection that had carried her remorselessly back into the past.

*   *   *

That Sunday afternoon's humiliation, with her father and Mr
Bazzani, was the turning-point. Afterwards, nothing was ever
the same again. Her relationship with her father was irrevo-
cably damaged and she tried to make sure she was never again
left alone in the house with him. Even when her mother and
other people were about, she couldn't escape the expression
that sometimes came into his eyes when he looked at her.
So she retreated into silence and lived, more and more, in
the world of her own imagination, instead of the one she
shared with her family. It was a double life; no matter how
worried or at risk she felt, there was always another place she
could escape to, a place of safety where she could be who
she wanted to be, and no one could get at her.

She found a co-conspirator in her safe other world in
Gabby – the girl whose beautiful lingerie had led to her
undoing. Her father had, of course, destroyed the lace brassière. It had been his first act on catching sight of Isis as
she'd sat in front of the mirror – he'd torn the bra from
her body, ripping its delicate fabric. Isis had planned to
return it to Gabby the following Monday, but now that
wouldn't be possible, and there was no way she would have
been able to afford to buy a new one. So she decided to
take a chance and she confessed. Catching Gabby alone
in the locker room, she explained that her beautiful black
brassière had been a temptation Isis had been unable to
resist; that she'd only wanted to take it home before returning it. She didn't tell her everything about her father – not
then. All she said was that he'd found the bra in her school
case, assumed she'd stolen it, and destroyed it to teach her
a lesson.

Gabby had listened to all this without anger or recrimi-
nation. To Isis's tearful relief, she hadn't been at all upset
that Isis had 'borrowed' her bra without her knowledge, and

even less concerned about having it replaced – for a fifteen-year-old she had been wonderfully understanding. In fact Isis's confession had the effect of cementing their friendship. They hadn't been close friends in the past, yet they quickly became so. Inviting Isis home after school, Gabby had opened the door to the kind of family life she yearned for herself – a warm and generous home where childish pranks were regarded with indulgence, and exciting plans for weekends and holidays were constantly being hatched.

Isis's parents approved of the increasing lengths of time she spent with the Trinci family. Mr Trinci was a well-to-do businessman with two handsome sons as well as the pretty Gabriella – a love-match could prove very auspicious indeed. Meanwhile, Isis's adventures with Gabby were a lot different from the sedate, chaperoned outings she led her parents to imagine. Often, when Gabby's parents were away on one of their frequent nights out of town, she would invite Isis over after homework, and the two of them would pick out pert, sassy dresses from her extensive wardrobe, and spend ages applying make-up before blow-drying their hair. Then they'd go out to parties where they knew their presence would be kept secret, or to beachfront bars across town where they wouldn't be recognised. There were so many firsts for Isis from those clandestine excursions: her first drink – a frozen banana daiquiri; the first time she was chatted up by a man; her first kiss. She and Gabby would arrive back at the Trincis' house, high with teenage exuberance or crying with laughter as they recollected the excitement of the night's events. On rare occasions, Isis stayed over at the Trincis', and those nights she liked best, sleeping in the spare room beside Gabby's with the wonderful knowledge, as she closed her eyes, that she wouldn't be woken up by her father. But most times she found herself having to take off all her make-up, brush out her hair, and replace Gabby's pretty dresses with her own unflattering clothes before returning to the oppressive atmosphere of her own home. The Midnight Pumpkin, she used to call herself.

The most important 'first' from that period was one she didn't recognise at the time: even though she and Gabby used to set out in search of nothing more complicated than simply having fun, Isis felt, for the first time, an implicit acceptance of who she was. While her father continued to cast a dark shadow over her life at home, he was unable, she discovered, to extinguish her own sense of identity or to destroy her capacity to be happy.

Her friendship with Gabby meant more than simply the pursuit of high jinks. Gabby helped her in very practical ways too. Isis would never forget how it was Gabby who slipped a magazine into her desk, one morning at school, pointing out the title of a feature she ought to read. At lunch-time that day Isis sat in the playground, engrossed in the article which seemed to have been written especially with her in mind. It was all about girls who'd gone through exactly what she had, teenagers who were experiencing exactly the same trauma at home, and who faced the same feelings of isolation and despair. There were interviews with some of them and colour photographs. Psychologists and care workers gave their views – all of which Isis quickly devoured, before going back to the beginning of the article and reading it a second time. But best of all were the two lines at the end of the piece which gave the number of a telephone helpline which people like her could ring to get help.

She had, by then, opened up completely to Gabby, telling her all about her father, and her own emotions of unworthiness and self-blame. Knowing now that there was an authority, other than her father, to whom she could turn, and that she could take action to change things whether he liked it or not, held out the hope of an intoxicating freedom. But it was also terrifying. What if she picked up the telephone and called the helpline? What if she set in motion the things she now knew were possible? Nothing would ever be the same again. Even though she hated the way things were, changing her world completely would take special courage.

After school she discussed things with Gabby, and as usual her friend's confidence was persuasive. The way Gabby saw it, she simply had no choice but to act: she should call the helpline people as soon as she could. Whatever hardships might follow, they would be as nothing compared to the horrors she had already suffered. Besides, said Gabby, you'll always have me around to see you through.

If only that had been true. Later that same day when Gabby was walking home from school, a speeding driver had swerved to avoid a cyclist – and run directly into her. She'd been rushed away by ambulance, but her internal injuries were so severe that nothing could be done; Gabby had died within minutes of arrival at hospital.

A late night telephone call had broken the news to Isis, who had put down the receiver numb with shock. It just didn't seem possible – she'd been speaking to Gabby only hours before! That night, in defiance of her father, she locked her bedroom door. She knew she'd be unable to sleep, and as she sat, bereft, at the edge of her bed, face in her hands and tears sliding silently through her fingers, in her devastation she knew she couldn't carry on like this any longer. Gabby's final advice to her had been that she should make that telephone call. Tomorrow, she would do it, even though it meant ending her world.

*　　　*　　　*

Now as Isis looked down at Holly, she thought that she would probably never have made the call if she'd known the course of events that would follow. Ultimately, of course, it had been her salvation. She had learned to blossom as a woman and a singer, to fulfil a musical talent that had remained unexplored until her late teens. And of course the ultimate prize was Holly herself who was now the centre of her existence. But all this had only come at a price, and one she was still paying. Intimations of her past would catch up with her when she was least expecting them, bringing her face to face with the vulnerability she had never overcome. That kiss with Mark in the restaurant, and the moment of promised intimacy with him back at home were such reminders. Behind the worldly disregard that served as her persona, what she really felt was a silent, but insistent fear. Nothing terrified her more than the prospect of seeing exposed the pain that lay at the heart of her past.

London
Monday, 20 September

It was early afternoon when Jones's mobile telephone rang. Excusing himself from the informal meeting in his office, he answered it briskly.

'Checking in for the last time,' came Larson's distinctive voice.

'You're ready to go?'

'Ten-fifteen p.m.'

'Good.' In front of his colleagues, Jones dared not sound too enthused, even though Larson had, once again, demonstrated singular efficiency.

'This time tomorrow you will be watching it on the BBC and I shall be reading about it in *Le Soir*.'

'Excellent.'

Jones glanced over at where his colleagues were talking among themselves, coffee mugs in hand. It was at moments like these, amid day-to-day mundanity, that his involvement in One Commando gave him a particular charge of excitement, a thrill of clandestine pleasure.

'And if tonight's mission isn't ... persuasive enough,' continued Larson, 'I am planning the final onslaught.'

'You mean you've recruited that manager?'

'Dobson. He's playing ball.'

'I'd like to meet him.'

'I'm sure we can arrange it. I've also got Brent doing some research for us.'

'Oh.' Jones hesitated. 'I see.' He'd always been suspicious of Brent. It worried him that the intense young man might find out too much, get beyond himself. Mensa-intelligent Brent who could hack his way into any computer system in the world.

'You'll let me know when it's over?' he confirmed.

'I'll call from Eurostar tonight.'

Beverly Hills

Mark knew he was running late as he scrambled into his clothes. Seven-forty-five according to the bedside clock – he was due in at Unum by eight-thirty. The recording schedule was more intense than he'd ever imagined. He'd even had to put in a few studio sessions over the weekend – not to mention the informal rehearsals back home. Still – just as well, he reckoned. Recording *Nile* helped take his mind off everything else that was happening.

He hadn't heard back from Lloyd on the photo of Bengt Larson, though he needed to check this morning's e-mail.

As for Isis and their phoney romance, that had been all over the TV news over the weekend, and he reckoned there'd be another inch-thick delivery of press cuttings from Lebowitz waiting for him when he got downstairs. Not that the media coverage interested him nearly so much as what had actually gone on. He'd kept going back over everything that had happened between Isis and him, asking himself if it was possible any part of what they'd done for the cameras had been spontaneous, for real. There had been moments which had certainly felt like that to him. And what had happened later when he was leaving her home? Why the sudden withdrawal, the deliberate distancing?

He hurried downstairs to the kitchen. Mrs Martinez had prepared her usual fry-up, but there wasn't time for it. Grabbing a slice of toast and a mug of coffee, he headed in the direction of the study. Denzil was standing in the hallway, looking severe in dark sunglasses and gesticulating at his watch.

'Yeah, yeah,' Mark muttered through a mouthful of toast, 'give me five.'

He'd become far less enamoured and intimidated by The System than when he'd first arrived. Big names and big money had meant a lot to him then, but he'd realised, pretty soon, that if he didn't stand up for himself, he'd be treated like a doormat. Years on the OmniCell helpdesk had made him instinctively obliging – but now that he'd realised what he'd let himself in for, signing the Berkeley Square endorsement, it was no more Mr Nice Guy.

Behind the study desk he logged in quickly, opening up Eudora Light and entering his password. The eight-hour time lag between LA and London had some benefits, he supposed. If he sent an e-mail last thing at night, he could be pretty certain Lloyd would have replied by the time he got up next morning.

Up came the connector monitor, with five messages to download, followed in seconds by a bleep announcing that he had mail. Lloyd's was one of the e-mails and he opened it straight away.

'*The photo you sent me – that's the bloke from the Lamb!*' Lloyd had responded, unaware of the seriousness of his confirmation. '*He was older than in the picture and had red hair and a beard. Even if you hadn't warned me about the disguise, I reckon I'd have recognised those eyes anywhere! So who is this guy and what paper does he work for? And should I give Vinnie your contact details? I'll be seeing him in the next few days.*'

Shoving himself back from the desk, Mark felt giddy. Putting his head in his hands, he closed his eyes and took in a few deep breaths. Get a grip, he told himself. You have to think quickly!

He'd already decided that if this happened he must tell GCM; for all his suspicions about the agency's media agenda, surely he could trust Hilton when it came to security? Besides, this discovery wasn't only about him – it concerned Isis too. GCM would have to get on to the police – in Britain they'd put someone on Vinnie's tail.

Still feeling dazed, Mark sat up again in his chair and, leaning over, picked up the cordless telephone. He dialled GCM – the only number in America he knew by heart. When he asked for Hilton, he was put through to his secretary Melissa Schwartz who, recognising Mark's voice, told him that Hilton was currently in London.

'Shit!' he murmured under his breath. He hadn't considered that Hilton might be in London, but of course the GCM boss was frequently out of town.

'Is it something Elizabeth can help you with?' she suggested.

'No,' he was emphatic, 'it needs to be Hilton.'

There was a pause at the other end before Melissa told him, 'I'm looking at his diary now. He's in a client meeting for the next hour, then he's at a book launch in Piccadilly. If it's extremely urgent, we can interrupt the client meeting. Or we can get him to call you after the launch, which will be around eight o'clock – noon our time.'

'Only trouble is, I might still be over at Unum—'

'Studio eighteen,' Melissa confirmed briskly. 'I can get him to call you there directly?'

'Or I might have finished for the day.'

'What if I was to get him to call you later at your home. By then you'll definitely be wrapped up at Unum?'

Melissa was steering him away from interrupting the meeting, and maybe it would be better having Hilton's undivided attention. Alarmed though he was by his discovery, would it make any difference if Hilton only got the news about Larson later in the day?

'Okay,' he agreed with Melissa, 'get him to call me at home. But tell him it's serious.'

London

Hilton Gallo sat in his tastefully app⸏⸏⸏⸏⸏ at Green's, going through financials from GCM's European offices. He always stayed in the same fourth-floor suite, having found it, like the private hotel itself, through trial and error and, once found, returning to it every time he was in London, which was at least once a month. Simon Dubois, the Poirot-like character who presided over the hotel with his immaculate moustache, all-seeing eyes and Gallic charm, always made sure that every detail of Hilton's stay was to his client's satisfaction. Over many trips, Hilton's preferences had been noted and accommodated on each subsequent visit. Ahead of his arrival, direct telephone and fax lines were installed in the suite. The second bedroom was cleared of furniture, providing a quiet and spacious meditation retreat. And the sitting room walls were hung with the pride of Green's art collection, which included several Constables and a Stubbs. Whenever changes in furniture or décor were being considered, Simon Dubois always made a point of consulting Hilton, not only for the purposes of customer relations, but because, over the years, he'd come to respect the soft-spoken Californian's finely honed sensibilities and flawless taste.

This evening though, aesthetic matters were far from Hilton's mind. Rather, as he sat at the Boulle desk, shuffling through computer printouts from GCM's offices in Paris and Rome, he was unusually distracted by figures, wishing, for the umpteenth time that the French and Italian agencies would follow the rest of the network in adopting Excel software, instead of the chaotic accounting package he found so difficult to make sense of.

Glancing at his watch, he saw it was just after ten. Often, when he was in London, he'd enjoy an evening stroll before turning in. It was a private pleasure he'd discovered several years before – he'd take in the arboured squares and terraced houses of Chelsea, the cobbled mews streets and restaurants whose understated entrances belied their Michelin-star chefs. London, he often used to think, was far more his spiritual home than Los Angeles – it was so much more cultivated, restrained, civilised. If things had been different he would have moved here years ago. As it happened, his personal enjoyment of the city was restricted to those precious few hours when, business commitments discharged, he could afford the luxury of time to himself. His evening strolls fell into this category, but tonight, alas, there was no question of getting out for a walk. Thanks to One Commando he was considered high on the 'at risk' list, and his new security arrangements were particularly draconian when he visited London. They applied to every aspect of his activities, from his arrival at Heathrow, to the opening of his mail. Much against his own preferences, he was now accompanied round the clock by a security guard – currently watching *Wycliffe* in the hallway of his suite. So instead of a walk, Hilton went through to the bathroom, and splashed his face with cold water.

Just another half hour of maddening accounts, he promised himself, towelling his face dry and meeting his eyes in the mirror, then he'd call it a day. As always, when faced by a particularly irksome task, he tried to step back from the immediate difficulties and get a grip on the bigger picture. Whatever the frustrations of trying to understand French accounting, there was no question that, as an agency, GCM had got through the last week far better than he had feared.

Lebowitz's solution to One Commando's continuing media presence had been a great success. The joint appearance of Isis and Jordan at Bianco Verdi had pushed the terrorist group off the news pages. Media attention now switched to the burgeoning love affair between America's most famous sex icon and the tall, dark stranger from London. Video clips of the two of them had been flighted on all the celebrity news slots. Photographs of them sneaking out of the back entrance of the restaurant were plastered all over the press. There was much feverish speculation about the romance, with body language experts noting the powerful bond between the two of them, restaurant staff commenting that they'd hardly been able to keep their hands off each other, and astrologers divided on the issue of compatibility. Meticulously choreographed 'friends' of both parties were reported as saying how crazy they were for each other.

In the light of this latest victory, Hilton thought as he returned from the bathroom to his desk, his current difficulties with the European accounts were nothing if not trivial. Sitting down, he'd no sooner started work once again when he heard a knock at the suite door, followed by the sound of his bodyguard opening it.

'We have a delivery.'

Recognising Simon Dubois's distinctive French accent, Hilton got up from behind his desk and made his way through to the hallway. Simon stood, immaculately groomed as ever, accompanied by a young lad from room service carrying two hefty-looking documents. Hilton was surprised, but not greatly. He hadn't been expecting a delivery, but unsolicited scripts were a constant feature of his life.

'Good evening, sir,' Simon greeted him as he approached.

'Simon?' Hilton raised his eyebrows.

In all the years he'd been coming to Green's, he couldn't remember a single occasion when Simon hadn't greeted him by name. Now, as he met the hotel manager's eyes, he tried to place the expression. He seemed agitated, even angry. But why?

'You'd better bring them in,' Hilton nodded towards the documents.

Simon's assistant carried the parcels over towards the hallway table. Following him, Hilton reached into his trouser pocket, searching for some change, when he became aware of heavy footsteps down the corridor. Glancing over his shoulder he was aghast to see Simon shoved out of the way by a dark-clad, masked gunman. Four other figures, all brandishing pistols, followed immediately behind. Hilton's bodyguard barely had time to reach his own pistol before he was struck to the floor. He fell, heavy and unconscious, while two of the intruders made directly for Hilton.

'No noise, or you're dead,' one of them barked. They collected him up as though he were weightless and hustled him into the bedroom where they flung him on the bed, face first. Heart pounding, Hilton told himself to try not to panic. But he instantly guessed who his attackers were with a wave of sickening dread.

Time seemed to stretch out for an eternity as one of the men, standing over him, retrieved a roll of electric wire from his pocket while the other pinned him down to the bed, arms tugged behind him. They quickly rolled the tape round Hilton's wrists and ankles. Meanwhile, two of the other intruders were slipping round the side of the room, closing all the curtains. Behind him, Hilton could hear the man who was evidently the gang leader giving orders to Simon Dubois.

'Now, directly to the hotel entrance. Leave immediately, speaking to no one. Go to this address and wait. If there are no problems, we return your family.' Hilton recognised the accent from the Security Briefing – confirming his worst fears.

'When?' Dubois was asking.

'Go!' The suite door was locked behind Simon, then there were the hurried sounds of footsteps. Hilton, rolled over and jerked up by the shoulders, found himself staring up at a tall, well-built figure in a mask, wearing baggy, military-style trousers and a black jersey.

'So this is what a Hollywood super-agent looks like?' Larson loomed over him.

'Two hundred million dollars a year going through your hands, Mr Gallo. All that money must make you feel invincible. But look at you now.'

Hilton felt his heart pump so hard it threatened his whole system. *Stay calm*, he ordered himself. *Keep your head and work this out.* But cool composure became even more difficult as the man pulled out a hunting knife and, with the tip of the six-inch blade, traced a line around first his right eye, then his left, before flicking the skin next to his ear. A thin scratch line welled up, instant red.

'You're going to persuade your famous clients to cancel the Berkeley Square endorsement,' he said as a statement of fact. 'They will give up because of the violation of animal rights by Berkeley Square in Madrid.'

On the floor next door, Hilton's bodyguard had come round and was starting to groan. Ordering his men to secure him, the leader glanced back at Hilton.

'No amount of security and bodyguards can protect Isis and her lover from us.'

Hilton knew he had to keep this man talking. Create delay however he could and hope that someone, somewhere had worked out that things were amiss.

'If Berkeley Square really is torturing animals in Madrid, why can't anyone else find the facility?'

'Maybe they closed it down,' Larson retorted angrily. 'Maybe people aren't looking in the right place.'

'I think you underestimate their efforts,' Hilton risked further provocation. 'There are investigative journalists and cosmetics companies who'd love nothing better than to prove you're right.'

'I am right,' Larson's voice grew more heavily accented. 'I went there myself. I made the video!'

'Then help us find this place.'

Larson was shaking his head. 'You think I'm that stupid? You know exactly where it is! You're part of the cover-up.'

Hilton shifted his position on the bed. The electric wire was cutting into his wrists. Arms behind him, his back was arched with pain. He had to keep Larson talking.

'Isis and Jordan only signed the endorsement after due diligence. They'd drop the contract instantly if there was evidence—'

'You,' Larson was wagging the knife at him, shaking his head as he did, 'you already have evidence.'

'The whole world believes the video is a hoax.'

Larson's eyes flashed angrily behind the mask. 'Then I'll have to persuade you it's not!' His voice rose.

Seizing Hilton's face, he thrust him back against the bed, his grip like a vice about Hilton's forehead.

'This . . . persuasion,' Hilton choked, 'it could backfire. Isis and Jordan . . . may refuse.'

The other was leaning over him, the blade of his knife just inches away from his eyes. 'They won't refuse,' he snarled, 'not after they've seen you.'

11

'Trouble!' the radio on Larson's belt crackled to life.

Quickly standing, he seized it to his ear, pressing the red transmission button. 'What kind of trouble?'

'Company.'

All the commando members stared at Larson who stood, frozen for a moment, before rushing to the window, carefully lifting back the curtain, and staring outside. Everything appeared quiet. But through the stillness came the sounds of approaching police sirens. They weren't far off. Larson glanced quickly round, before ordering, 'Balcony exit!'

On the bed, Hilton wondered what they were going to do with him now. The now loudly advertised approach of the police could be a disaster! Every moment seemed to last an eternity as he struggled to watch what was happening. Would this precipitate a hasty end, he wondered? Would they shoot him dead?

Black-clad figures were running to where curtains concealed doors leading out to a narrow balcony at the side of the room away from the street. Pushing aside the curtains, they opened the doors. Now they were standing, in pairs, on the balcony, seizing the railings one floor above and hauling themselves up. Where was Larson, Hilton wondered? Moment by moment he waited, dry-mouthed, for a final act of retribution. Would it be some searing, unimaginable horror? Or simple, instant death?

The longer he waited, the more he felt he'd been completely forgotten. But after the tension, that seemed impossible! Weren't any of them left behind? After a few moments he raised his head to glance around him; had they all just gone?

Downstairs, the One Commando lookout monitoring police radio activity got out of his car, and walked directly, but not with undue haste, in the direction of where a back-up vehicle was parked one street away. It was a routine call that had alerted him. A police car had been sent out to investigate a barking dog disturbance in the same street as Green's. Moments later it had been instructed to disregard the previous order – PT 19 were on an operation in the area.

To his astonishment, Hilton found himself alone. He rolled over on his side, taking the pressure off his wrists. After all the adrenaline released into his system, the sudden calmness felt as surreal as the drama that had preceded it. Would they come back for him, he wondered quickly. How should he try to escape?

One floor above, Larson and his group were going through a well-rehearsed drill, collecting Green's letter-headed paper and envelopes from inside a drawer, and setting them alight before throwing them in a waste-paper bin and holding the burning papers up to a smoke detector. They triggered the fire alarm. As panic engulfed the hotel, they were quickly stripping off their black jerseys, masks and boots, rifling through wardrobes to find coats and bathrobes. Hotel staff could be heard running round each floor from room to room, hammering on doors and calling out for all guests to evacuate using the fire escape. The five terrorists were soon in the corridor, joining in the mêlée of guests, chambermaids, porters and kitchen staff making their way down the steel stairs behind the hotel.

The police arrived at the hotel in four rapid-response vehicles, two pulling up directly outside the front door and two squealing to a halt round the back. The tip-off had come less than five minutes earlier, and there'd been no doubting its seriousness. Firstly, the informant's credentials were impeccable – it was an inside job. Secondly, precise information had been provided on what action was being taken, where, when and by whom. Twelve police officers were soon scrambling from the cars and pounding through the usually hushed corridors, currently engulfed in chaos.

Two police officers had soon broken through the door to find Hilton sitting on his bed, working on the tape around his wrists, the left side of his face flecked with blood.

'Thank God!' he cried out with feeling as they rushed over to him.

'Are you all right?' The WPC was studying his face with concern.

Hilton was no longer even aware of the cut. 'They would have got my eyes,' he told them. Relief flooded through his body. He felt his jaw tremble from delayed shock.

The WPC was behind him, working quickly at the electric wire on his wrists, while the other policeman was at his ankles.

'How long were they in your room?' the WPC asked.

'Couple of minutes. I tried to keep Larson talking. If you'd been any later—'

'We were here within three minutes of the tip-off.'

'Tip-off?' His wrists freed, Hilton brought them round in front of him and was massaging them.

'That's right,' the PC confirmed.

'You mean?'

'Can't say more than that.'

Hilton raised his eyebrows. The policeman obviously knew more than he was letting on. Like why they had responded to the tip-off in the first place. He knew the police didn't react to every crank call that came in.

Ankles unfastened, he stretched his legs, before going over to the window where he stood for a moment, drawing back the curtain. Looking down at the gathering chaos of people – diners, residents, service staff, passers-by, a few policemen combing through them, in vain – he shook his head.

'They've got away.'

The PC joined him at the window, pulling a notepad from his pocket. 'It would help if we had some descriptions, sir.'

Hilton delivered a sideways glance. 'They're not going to march outside in military fatigues and ski masks.'

Then as the PC looked at him in surprise, he continued, 'They took control of the situation the moment they set off the fire alarm.'

'Perhaps you could tell us exactly what happened, right from the beginning.'

'Yeah.' Feeling his composure begin to return, Hilton's mind raced to assimilate all that had happened. Looking over at the policeman, he raised a hand to the muscle that twitched in his cheek. 'But I've got a couple of questions for you first. Like what in God's name are you going to tell the media?'

Los Angeles

'Elizabeth, it's me.' The voice at the other end of the phone was cool and crisp as ever. But Elizabeth Reynolds was startled.

'Hilton?' Both she and Leo Lebowitz, standing on the other side of the desk from her, looked up at the clock faces ranged across the office wall. London time was 1.30 a.m.

'Can't you sleep?' She was concerned. Hilton had caught the red-eye to London the night before and had, as usual, planned a full day's work at GCM offices in Soho. She would have thought he'd be exhausted by now.

'Haven't got to bed yet,' there was a droll note in his voice, 'we've had an . . . incident here. I need to speak to you and Leo. Conference call.'

'Leo's standing right opposite. I'll transfer to your office.'

Moments later they were sitting on either side of Hilton's meeting table, expressions aghast as Hilton smoothly recounted events of the evening, beginning with the ploy of the 'unsolicited manuscripts', the break-in by One Commando, and the eleventh-hour tip-off which had saved him. He told them about his midnight meeting with Detective Inspector Bennett of Scotland Yard, the investigating officer in charge, who had assured him that the police would respond to any media enquiries about events at Green's only with a standard form of words along the lines that an incident at the hotel had been investigated. After the meeting with the police, Hilton had returned to his fourth-floor suite at Green's, a replacement bodyguard in tow, where he planned to spend what remained of the night before catching the early-morning Eurostar to Paris.

Despite all the trauma, his equilibrium had evidently been quickly restored. Speaking with a calm detachment, it was as though he was describing a sequence from an action-thriller movie, rather than speaking as the victim of a terrifying attack. In fact, the only emotion he betrayed was one of concern about the outcome of the Berkeley Square endorsement.

'I've secured a news ban on what happened tonight,' he told Lebowitz and Elizabeth now, 'but One Commando is escalating this thing. They're after the endorsement contract, and Isis and Jordan are top of their list.' There was a lengthy pause before he answered the question that had begun to form in all their minds. 'The two of them will have to be told.'

Across the table from Elizabeth, Lebowitz put his face in his hands. 'She's gonna completely flip,' he groaned. 'It was bad enough with the Lefevre thing.'

'Do you see we have any option?' Hilton asked coolly.

Exhaling heavily, Lebowitz shook his head. 'No. We can't keep it from them. At least, not for long.'

'I think it would be best if I deal with the news myself, face to face, as soon as I get back,' said Hilton.

'Not a conversation I would relish,' responded Lebowitz. 'We're going to have to come up with something incredible to keep her in the deal.'

'Our only hope is a police breakthrough. But I couldn't get anything from the turkeys at Scotland Yard I spoke to tonight.'

It was rarely that Hilton signalled his disapproval so forcefully. Elizabeth and Lebowitz exchanged glances.

'Elizabeth, I need you to follow up tomorrow. I'm tied up in meetings all morning – I've told the police you'll be calling on my behalf.'

'Right.'

'We have to get a grip on what progress they're making with One Commando.'

'I'll speak to Hanniford again.'

'Find out what police briefings he's received.'

'Will do.'

'We need something tangible.'

There was silence for a moment before Lebowitz said, 'What if she wants to pull out?'

'You'd better discuss it with legal,' Hilton's voice was grim. 'Map out the options.'

All three of them were thinking about the Berkeley Square production cycle that was currently running at full throttle. Graphic design concepts had been signed off weeks before and with the photography now completed, the first colour proofs to be used in magazine advertisements, and on billboards, packaging and an array of promotional material were due any day. Intensive media schedules had been booked, and special guest appearances by Isis and Jordan already set up. For Isis and Jordan to pull the plug now would be a devastating blow, not only to Berkeley Square. GCM would suffer from massive and damaging fallout. Whatever the reasons given, Isis would be shunned by commercial sponsors for the rest of her days, and GCM would acquire an unenviable reputation as the agency that pulled out of the world's biggest endorsement deal at the eleventh hour. Plus, Berkeley Square would want to be handsomely compensated. It was the kind of scenario that was every agency executive's worst nightmare.

Signalling the end of the conversation, Hilton was about to hang up when Elizabeth told him, 'I've had a message from Melissa. Mark Watson wants you to call him at home.'

'Can't it wait till tomorrow?' After the events of the evening he was hardly in any mood for client calls.

'He said it was serious.'

*   *   *

Mark's recording session ended much later than scheduled, and it wasn't till mid-afternoon that he got back from Unum. Having been so completely absorbed in *Nile* had been good for him – he hadn't had a moment to dwell on that morning's e-mail from Lloyd. Though on his way home, he remembered his call to Melissa Schwartz and glanced at his watch; he wondered when he'd hear from Hilton.

As they reached the top of his street in Beverly Hills, he was astounded to see that the huge marble entry across the road from his house had been replaced by mediaeval-style gates. Gone were the white-plastered walls, replaced by towering ramparts.

'What's going on there?' he asked Denzil, staring across the road.

'New movie.' Denzil was blasé. 'Situational shots.'

'You mean,' he remembered the house was owned by a movie studio, 'none of that stuff over there is real?'

'Shit, no!' laughed Denzil.

'Had me fooled.'

'Would fool anyone who didn't know better.'

Back home, he took a swim before relaxing by the poolside with a bottle of Rolling Rock, and sheets of lyrics for the next day's recording. He had quickly learned the value of preparation and became so immersed in the music that the next time he glanced at his watch, it was after four-thirty. Which made it half-past midnight in London. Highly unlikely that Hilton was going to call him now, he thought, picking up his towel and making his way back indoors. For all Melissa Schwartz's promises, he thought bitterly, he obviously wasn't important enough to merit a transatlantic phone call from the venerable Hilton Gallo.

After another hour had ticked by, he became convinced this was the case. He was on the verge of phoning Melissa again to give her a piece of his mind when the telephone rang.

'I understand you need to speak to me?'

Mark looked at his watch. 'It's two o'clock over there!'

'Busy night,' Hilton was laconic. 'I would have called earlier but I've been unavoidably detained. Something . . . serious?'

'That's right,' nodded Mark. 'One Commando.'

There was a pause at the other end. 'What about them?'

'I don't know what's going on, but Larson has been in contact with Vinnie Dobson.'

'How, precisely?'

Mark told Hilton of his telephone conversation with Lloyd – of Vinnie's uncharacteristic visit to his brother's flat, and how the stranger Lloyd had seen in the local pub had triggered a memory from GCM's Security Briefing. He explained about the Interpol file and how Lloyd had identified Larson.

After listening intently, Hilton replied, 'Quite a piece of detective work.'

'If you pass the information on to Scotland Yard,' Mark continued, 'they'll put a tail on Dobson—'

'Of course,' agreed Hilton. 'In the meantime, if your brother sees Larson again—'

'Believe me, I've taken care of that. If Larson shows his face down the Lamb, the police will be down there before he's got his first pint.'

Hilton reflected on this soberly. 'You'll let me know—'

'Sure,' Mark was impatient. 'So what do *you* have on One Commando?' It was a while before Hilton replied, 'I was going to wait to tell you this, face to face, but there is something and it's not good, I'm afraid. Earlier this evening they attacked again—'

'Oh, my God! Who?'

'Me. In my hotel suite.'

'I don't believe—!' Mark was incredulous. 'You mean . . .
Are you all right?'

'Just. The police arrived minutes after One Commando.
Apparently they'd had a tip off.'

'I don't . . . !' Mark struggled to take it in.

'Still getting over it myself.'

Even in his state of shock, Mark registered the connection between Jacques Lefevre and Hilton Gallo – and in
that instant realised that all the sensational tabloid predic-
tions had proved to be right. One Commando *were* after
the endorsement deal. And if they'd already tried getting
to Hilton Gallo, their ultimate targets had to be Isis and
him. No wonder Bengt Larson had been on his tracks in
London.

'Did they say anything about the endorsement?' he asked
Hilton.

'They want you to drop it.'

'Christ! Does Isis—?'

'Not yet.'

Mark hesitated for a moment. Isis had made no secret of
her security fears. When she heard about this she'd go off
the deep end.

'So, what happens next?' he asked.

'I don't want to rush a decision. The police here are taking
this very seriously – they're under huge pressure to act. Your
information could also be a breakthrough.'

'You said something about a tip-off?'

'That's right.'

'Well, I mean, do they know who it was? Or why?'

Hilton drew breath before saying, 'I intend to have more
on that by the time we speak again.'

'When will that be?'
'I get back to LA in two days' time.'

London

The emergency exit had been a textbook operation. As it should have been, thought Larson. He'd drilled the team through it, just like he'd drilled them through every step of the operation, planning for every contingency then rehearsing, rehearsing, rehearsing till they responded like clockwork.

They'd encountered no difficulties escaping down the fire escape of the hotel and down into the street below. There, bewildered hotel staff, most of whom had never been through a fire drill, were doing their best to appear in control as they rounded up equally bewildered residents and diners. When the police cars, blue lights flashing, screeched to a halt outside the hotel, most of the uniformed officers had hurried indoors though several of them had begun combing through the gathering crowd of hotel guests, employees and curious onlookers. But Larson and his team had no difficulty slipping round a corner into the quiet mews street where the fallback getaway vehicle was waiting, engine already started.

It was a Federal Express van stolen from a depot late that afternoon, and its absence wouldn't be noticed till the following day. In the meantime, its passage through town aroused no suspicions as it duly made its way up Old Brompton Road, past where Harrods was lit up like a birthday cake, and towards Piccadilly. Not long afterwards, it pulled into a cul-de-sac just a few hundred yards from Leicester Square, where there were no closed-circuit television cameras to record the occupants emerging, now dressed in anonymous jeans and sweaters. They'd kept their surgical gloves on, of course, until the very end. The police didn't have prints of any of them – and they didn't want to start a collection. Within twenty seconds they'd dispersed in half a dozen different directions, mingling with the late-night West End crowds of teenagers and tourists.

Larson himself made directly for a public telephone where he soon set up the present meeting. As he walked along the Islington terrace now, the door to one of the blocks of flats opened and a figure emerged, crossing the street.

'What went wrong?' asked Jones a few moments later, pulling out his Gauloise Lights and offering him one.

Larson waved the pack away. 'We'd just got into Gallo's room,' he said, 'then we had to abort. Long stop warned us the police had been scrambled.'

The two men were walking along the street.

'Tip-off,' said the other, exhaling a stream of smoke. It was more a statement of fact than a question.

'Had to be. But who? Couldn't have been anyone at the hotel. We got right in there without being seen.'

'Are you sure about CCTVs?'

'First thing I checked out on our recce. The place was clean.'

'Which leaves only one possibility.'

Larson glanced over at him. 'That's what worries me. But I checked them all out.'

'How many people knew about tonight?'

'Six. The four I took with me, and the two who took care of Dubois. Brent also sat in on the first briefing, but I stood him down. I need him to take care of the research.'

Jones looked at him challengingly.

'I'm cultivating him. The guy's a genius when it comes to electronic security systems.' He felt the need to justify his decision. 'He can hack into anything on the internet – he can even break into Scotland Yard files and access police records. He's useful.'

Then, irritated that Jones wasn't agreeing, 'Look,' he wore a determined expression, 'I know Brent. He's rock solid.'

'I don't like it,' Jones was shaking his head.

'You think I do?'

'Got to be Brent. Where else could the tip-off come from?'

It was the question that worried Larson most. The one to which he had no answer.

'What d'you want me to do,' he retorted angrily, 'blow him away when we don't know for sure—'

'I'm not saying that,' Jones sucked on his Gauloise, 'I'm not saying you should blow him away.'

They walked on in silence for quite a while, Jones finishing his cigarette and flicking the butt into a drain in the roadside before he turned back to Larson again. 'All I'm thinking is that you should double-check. You want to believe Brent. I want to believe Brent. Let's double-check.'

'How?'

'Have him in for an interview. A formal interview.' Jones nodded meaningfully. 'See what comes up.'

'Yes?' Larson met his eye.

'Sure. We hope he's clean, but if he's not . . .' It didn't need spelling out.

As they walked on, Larson realised he didn't have any choice. Tonight's operation had gone belly up because of a security leak. It was up to him to fix it. He couldn't afford to lose Jones's support. And what Jones suggested wasn't unreasonable. He nodded once. 'I'll talk to Brent.'

'Good man.' Jones was brisk.

'Do you want to . . . assist in the interview? Second opinion?'

Jones considered this for a moment. 'I would, of course.

But best we keep things as we agreed, with me behind the scenes.'

They turned down a road to the left, and shortly afterwards, left again, making their way back in the direction of Jones's flat.

'I tell you what I *would* like,' he nodded to Larson. 'I'd like to see a recording of the interview. See for myself.'

'Of course,' Larson shrugged, 'I can arrange it.'

Los Angeles
Tuesday, 21 September

At three a.m. the morning after Hilton was attacked, Elizabeth Reynolds was woken by her alarm clock. Getting out of bed, she made her way through to the kitchen and poured herself a glass of milk before dialling the number she'd brought home from the office. In London, DI Bennett sounded unsurprised to be hearing from her – time difference or not. No, he didn't have any fresh information for Mr Gallo. But he would keep her posted, he assured her.

Later that morning at the office, when she still hadn't heard back from him by ten a.m. – six in the evening, London time, she called him again. He gave her the same message again – this time delivered in brusque tones. So she phoned Francis Hanniford.

Put through by his secretary, she heard the Berkeley Square director get up to close the door of his office before returning to the phone. Greetings exchanged, she began to explain what had happened to Hilton, before Hanniford cut her off in mid-sentence.

'So I've heard.' Hanniford's cut-glass accent conveyed a natural authority.

'DI Bennett?' She was surprised.

'Good heavens, no. Hilton spoke directly to Jacques earlier today.'

Elizabeth shook her head. 'Hilton's asked me to follow up on his behalf. But Bennett,' she was frustrated, 'he just won't tell me anything!'

'He wouldn't,' Hanniford was direct. 'With all due respect, my dear, he isn't going to reveal himself to a publicity assistant in Los Angeles. But that doesn't mean investigations aren't well under way.'

'Well, what *is* happening?' Elizabeth's voice rose in exasperation.

'I'm not as close to this one as I am to the Lefevre follow-up,' confided Hanniford. 'But, fortunately for both of us, there's a common element emerging.'

At the other end of the line, Elizabeth was listening intently.

'Confidentially, what we are seeing here bears all the hallmarks of a classic MI5 operation.'

'You mean there's someone—'

'Inside the group.'

'The source of the tip-off?'

'Exactly.'

'Scotland Yard have confirmed this?'

'Absolutely not. And they never would – directly. It's more insinuated than that. One has to understand the signals. My Yard connection went to considerable lengths lecturing me on how, after the cold war, the secret services were redeployed, and that included tracking more extreme animal rights organisations. He also said the services would be highly responsive to incidents like the attack on our CEO.'

'But if this is true,' asked Elizabeth, 'and there's an MI5 agent in One Commando, why weren't the police waiting for them at Green's?'

'This is where it gets interesting. It is probable that the police, our DI Bennett included, have no authority to close them down. Not their operation. It may well be that MI5's man on the inside has only recently been accepted by One Commando and has been charged with the task of finding out something specifically—'

'And until he does, One Commando can do what the hell they like!'

'Oh, it's not quite as bad as all that,' Hanniford replied with wry amusement. 'There may be a few close shaves, but they can't risk another Lefevre-style attack going ahead. Nor another Green's. Not again.'

Los Angeles
Thursday, 23 September

Mark and Isis strode down the corridor at Unum Music. The moment they had been summoned from the studio, Mark saw apprehension cloud Isis's face. During the past two days behind the microphones, they had deliberately banished all conversation about One Commando and had focused instead on their work; what was going on in London couldn't be allowed to interfere with the recording of *Nile*.

Studio 18 had become like an oasis amid all the anxieties following Hilton's attack. Having recorded most of the album separately, there were several tracks Isis and Mark needed to sing together – including the duet ballad designed to become the hit single 'Nile'. They'd done most of this work in the last few days. For Mark, it had been the most intense experience of his singing career. Even as he and Isis performed, he'd catch himself out wondering how it was that he had come to be in a Los Angeles studio, singing with his pop-star idol. More than that, how was it that as they rehearsed and performed 'Nile', he felt a return of that same connection he'd experienced the first time they'd met – except this time, even more powerful. They gazed intently at each other, voices rising and falling with the ebb and swell of the melody, and it felt, to Mark, as though there was an intuitive force at work. Surely Isis must be feeling it too? During the breaks in their recording sessions they had relaxed together in the lounge area, and Mark had realised that all the hype surrounding Isis and her career had fooled him into believing that she was some kind of superwoman. But over the past forty-eight hours his wariness and shyness in her presence had evaporated, and a tentative trust had been established. They had chatted and laughed over silly articles in the glossy magazines laid out for them on the table along with the mineral water, and Mark had discovered that Isis was just a human being like him, with her own everyday concerns. He was intrigued by the way she didn't really talk about her past, as he did, and he respected how she was trying to bring up her daughter with as much normality as was possible under the glare of the media spotlight. And he had to admit, the more he saw of her, the more beautiful she seemed. Her blonde hair and feline blue eyes were in complete contrast to his own dark looks. He was captivated by the difference.

Mark wondered if the growing closeness between them was all the more powerful *because* of the danger that threatened them both. No longer simply partners in an album, they were now also the joint targets of One Commando. Carried by the lyrics of the song, powerful and poignant, and the melody that brought their voices together and lifted them apart with an intensity that grew and grew, each inspired the other as they reached towards the final, thrilling climax. There was a charge going on in the studio, a sensuality that was potent, undeniable – Mark knew he wasn't the only one aware of it. He'd seen it in the way Isis held his eyes as they performed together – and avoided them afterwards, as though self-conscious about what she'd revealed of herself. He could see it on the faces of the sound engineers when they went into the mixing room to hear their takes. It was as though they'd been caught, like embarrassed voyeurs, witnessing a private intimacy; it took them all a few moments of chair shuffling and averted glances to get back to usual.

It was during their final playback session of the day that Hilton arrived – and the mood suddenly changed. As they walked through to the meeting rooms, it seemed to Mark that with every step they took, the sense of apprehension was heightened. Hilton had come to Unum directly from LAX, and was waiting for them in his dark Hugo Boss suit, crisp, white shirt and Hermès tie. Looking up at him as they shook hands, they could hardly avoid the narrow red scar to the side of his left eye.

'I know you wanted to pull the endorsement last time spoke,' he got down to business right away, looking Isis the eye, before glancing over at Mark, 'and that remain your prerogative. However, I thought I should let you know that we have some new information.'

'Arrests?' asked Mark.

'Not as yet.' Then, reacting to Isis's dismissive shrug, 'What we have found is that the British secret service, MI5, seem to have an agent in the group. That explains the police tip-off when I was attacked. It should also give us all a measure of reassurance that even if an attack was being planned against both of you, it would never be allowed to go ahead.'

'You mean, like the attack on you wasn't allowed to go ahead?' Isis was sardonic.

'It didn't get very far.'

'Well, pardon me if I'm not crazy about having armed terrorists rampaging through the house while I wait for the police to arrive—'

'I'm not saying we're in the clear—'

'What about Vinnie?' asked Mark. 'Are they following that up?'

'I gave the lead to Bennett—'

'This is hopeless!' Isis interjected, shaking her head firmly. 'Berkeley Square isn't worth it. Nothing's worth it!'

'We need to consider—'

'I'm sick of considering!' she snapped. 'I'm sick of weighing up the options. Putting my life on hold. This endorsement has been a nightmare right from the start, and I want out.'

'Isis, you know that's not true,' Hilton's tone was even. 'You shouldn't forget the benefits that came with the signing.'

'What are you saying,' demanded Isis, 'that I should ask Berkeley Square to sign up for another ten years?'

Hilton gave her time to cool off before saying in a low voice, 'I know you're not going to like my advice. But I don't think you should pull out because of what happened to me.'

'How many more attacks do you want me to wait for?'

'Don't forget there's an MI5 agent in this group.'

'Very reassuring!'

'It should be. And there's no suggestion One Commando even operate outside of London, let alone in Los Angeles. You need to be aware of all the implications – both of you,' he added, fixing Mark with a severe expression. 'The production process for the endorsement advertisements is way down the line. If you decide to withdraw now, Berkeley Square won't just be looking to you to return the money.

They'll be suing for production costs and commercial damages.'

'Just wonderful!' exclaimed Isis.

'Obviously, we'd have a very strong case with direct terrorist intimidation, but it would all go legal.'

She collapsed back in her chair, hands pressed to her eyes.

'What you're saying,' Mark resented Hilton's tone, 'is that we can sit and wait to be attacked by terrorists, or get taken to the cleaners by Berkeley Square?'

'What I'm saying,' Hilton replied sharply, 'is that while there's a lesson to be learned from my own ... disturbing encounter, it's to keep a grip.'

Isis was shaking her head slowly. 'That's what you said last time,' her voice was choked, 'when Lefevre was attacked. But things haven't gotten better. They just keep getting worse. And what if they start delving into my background?' she blurted. 'They could destroy me without coming anywhere near Los Angeles!'

'What background?' Mark demanded. 'How could they destroy—'

'That's got nothing to do with One Commando.' An uncharacteristic heat came into Hilton's voice as he flashed an angry glance first at Isis, then Mark. 'It's not at all relevant.'

'If it's relevant to the endorsement,' Mark wasn't going to be bamboozled, 'it's relevant to me. What's this "background"?'

Isis was staring down at the floor, unusually self-conscious.

Hilton exhaled slowly before regaining his usual expression of calm detachment. 'Isis gets confused about something that happened a long time ago, which doesn't mean anything to anyone any more. What she seems to forget' – although he addressed Mark, he continued gazing at Isis, unwaveringly

– 'is that she's been the biggest name in pop for years. People have been trying to dish the dirt on her from the minute she got to be famous. Why should anyone start looking there now?'

12

Alan Brent worked on the research assignment the way he always worked on any project that compelled him – the only way he knew *how* to work at things: obsessively. *The powers that be*, the phrase had kept on running through his mind like a mantra since his last meeting with Larson. This was the break he'd been waiting for, his chance to find out who really ran One Commando. To make himself useful, gain acceptance, accomplish his mission.

He had no idea where his investigations on their behalf would lead him. But his brief was simple: to dig up anything and everything that might help One Commando in their mission against Isis. And he had the most powerful information technology equipment with which to do it. As a student, working with an ageing IBM in the university library, he'd managed to break through meticulously constructed fire-walls into the most advanced security systems in the world to penetrate classified files at Los Alamos National Laboratory in America, the Bank of England – he'd even hacked into Paramount Studios to play around with scripts for episodes of his favourite sitcom *Cheers*.

The Isis project was far from straightforward. For starters he didn't even have Isis's real name to go on. Not that he was daunted. The only thing that really bothered him was what he'd do with any information he did retrieve. He supposed that if he dug up anything really interesting, his first duty would be to notify his boss before he contacted Larson. It would be up to him to decide how to play it.

He'd started by trawling the archives of US counterculture music e-zines. He knew none of the mainstream music titles ever mentioned the name she'd been born with – her publicists had succeeded in keeping that out of common currency. But he'd come across a few self-styled 'cult' e-zines in the past; sporadic and usually short-lived publications run out of bedrooms and public housing basements by disaffected twentysomethings who'd failed to make it into the mainstream music industry, and who'd turned their critical abilities instead into undermining it. His search through back issues confirmed that the 'crass commercialism' of Isis's music was a core target. In themselves the vitriolic critiques were of no interest to him; what he sought, quite simply, was a name.

It had taken him several hours to get it. Eventually he found it in a 1993 issue of the *Beat Meat* edited by one A. Henkshaw of Baton Rouge, who related a conspiracy theory to conceal Isis's past and even her real name. Henkshaw claimed to have evidence that her family name was Carboni and she'd been brought up in a middle-class Italian household, in Miami, Florida.

Alan quickly established that *Beat Meat* had been through a number of ownership changes since 1993, and that A. Henkshaw had long-since ceased to have anything to do with the title. He doubted that speaking to him about an article researched so long ago would be of the slightest use But he needed corroboration. Using a search combining bot 'Isis' and 'Carboni' he found confirmation sooner than he expected, and from the unlikeliest of sources; a piece contemporary culture and 'Who influences the influence had appeared in the *Wall Street Journal* two years ag. It carried a pen-sketch of Isis including the information that her real surname was Carboni and that she hailed from 'down-scale suburb of Miami'. The revelation that she had been born into an unexceptional Italian émigré family carried with it the full weight of the *WSJ*'s authority.

Alan left that lead, he could come back to it later, and looked up the on-line telephone directory for Miami. It included over two hundred Carbonis. Trying to find a link in that lot was virtually impossible. Even if she had a family out there, they were probably ex-directory and almost certainly wouldn't speak to him. So he printed off the list before turning his attention to locating the Registry of Births for Miami Dade County. That was plain sailing; the county had its own website, and he clicked his way directly into public records – only to find that they went back no further than 1990.

Births, births, births, he thought, where else would they be recorded? Swiftly accessing a media-list directory from a press-cutting bureau in New York, he surveyed a complete list of publications for the state of Florida, from the *Miami Herald* to the most obscure trade and hobby journals. But as he looked through the list he was already discounting it – if her family really had come from a slum, they were hardly going to announce the birth of their child in the *Miami Herald*.

Baptisms. If they were Catholic Italians they would have

had her baptised – there had probably been at least one exclusively Italian Roman Catholic church in Miami in the late sixties to early seventies. He was already searching for names of Christian churches in Miami. It was a long shot, he realised – most of them probably weren't mentioned on the internet. But his search revealed one overtly Italian Catholic church site, St Columbus, presided over by Father Marvin Robieri. The Catholic priest was evidently a big fan of the net – links to St Columbus, the Italian Family Church, appeared over a dozen times in search results under different references. And his church's own website bore an impressive logo, as well as a full-colour photograph of a beaming Marvin in all his ecclesiastical glory, with a gold crucifix, white doves and blue-clad Mary Mother of God, all in lurid hues. There were links on the site to a whole range of activities – church events, fellowship groups, fund-raising activities, mission work and a host of others, signposted in either English or Italian.

Alan glanced over them all, more amused than anything. On the surface, Father Marvin's Italian Family Church was exactly what he was looking for. But there was nothing that suggested baptismal records could be accessed – though they might be, he supposed, if he phoned. He was scanning down the links when the word 'Bollettino' caught his eye – probably worth a click, he supposed.

'Bollettino' was an electronic e-zine, no less. It was in Italian and appeared to serve as a kind of notice-board of events in the parish community of St Columbus. He couldn't understand very much, but scrolling down several pages, his eye was caught by subtitles 'Battesimi', 'Matrimoni', 'Funerali', with names and dates recorded beneath. Raising his eyebrows, he glanced along the list of links at the bottom of the page. Were any of these archives, he wondered, clicking one after the other. Did 'Bollettino' go back any further than Father Marvin's all-singing, all-dancing website?

Moving his cursor on to 'Archivi', he clicked into what was clearly an archive retrieval mechanism, and keyed in a date at random – February 1969 – before entering 'Search' and holding his breath. The down-load indicator of his computer was flashing, and Alan shifted his chair closer to the screen. It was such a long shot he didn't dare hope for anything. But to his astonishment up came 'Bollettino' for that month. A poorly reproduced and dog-eared image of a typewritten newsletter. But it was legible – and Alan was astonished that it was available at all. Father Marvin had evidently spent days, if not weeks, painstakingly scanning in all the past editions for posterity.

For the next few hours, Alan went through every one of the newsletters from 1968 to 1974 – no one knew Isis's age for certain – writing down the names of every Carboni ever baptised at St Columbus's. There had been eight in all, five boys and three girls, and Alan immediately set about trying to find the girls, beginning with his favourite tracing technique – the tax return records of the Internal Revenue Service. It was a method with which he was thoroughly familiar, and he had soon hacked effortlessly through the encryption devices designed specifically to keep out un-authorised visitors. Because of the strong possibility that the women he sought would have married, Alan searched through tax records from the period of their early twenties, before following through. And it wasn't long before he'd tracked down two of them, one a teacher in Delaware, the other a police officer in Florida. There was no trace of the third, Maria Chiara Carboni. Could she be Isis? Knowing the inadequacies of the Internal Revenue Service systems, Alan decided to look elsewhere, hacking into the files of educational institutions and police departments to track down Maria Chiara.

Later, Alan thought how ironic it was that when he'd made his discovery about Isis, the really big discovery, he hadn't even recognised it. The full significance of what he'd hit upon continued to elude him. Turning to medical institutions, in and around Miami, he hacked his way, with only a minimum of trouble, into the computer records of the Salmacis Hospital – one of those he'd found listed on an on-line directory. He had no idea if Salmacis was a private or public institution, and the records, such as they were, revealed little. But he did find, in 1984, several entries for patient M.C. Carboni, treated by Dr Robert Weiner. Alan printed off the page. Right then he didn't attribute any special significance to it – there was no telling if this was Maria, or Mirella, or for that matter Marco, and even if it was a Maria, was it *his* Maria or not?

It was only after a number of his more sophisticated tracking techniques hit dead ends, that Alan realised he'd failed to try the most basic. Going to the Yahoo homepage of an internet search engine, he keyed in the name Maria Carboni. There were dozens of matches, but within minutes he'd found one Maria Carboni in Miami and with her own website, advertising 'Paws on Miami Beach – offering both pooches and pussies the Purrrfect Pampering'. There was a photograph of a beaming Maria, holding a closely cropped, pink-rinsed poodle to her cheek and surrounded by red heart cat cushions and designer leashes. It was a gaudy, tacky image, but he had no doubt that this was the Maria he'd been searching for. Flopping back in his chair, he let out a low sigh. So this was the upshot of over ten hours on the net – a poodle parlour in Miami Beach!

As he sat, slumped in his chair, staring at this Maria, he

wondered though if there was not something about her face that was reminiscent of Isis. Was it an Italian gene-pool thing, he asked himself, or was it that after too many hours in front of the screen his eyes were just playing tricks with him? Leaning forward, he concentrated harder. The more he stared, the closer he could see a resemblance. Were they sisters, he wondered – but if so, what had happened to the record of Isis's baptism? And what exactly was it about Maria Carboni's face that held the key?

Lloyd spotted Vinnie the moment he stepped into the Lamb. A creature of habit, Vinnie was propping up the bar in his usual corner, talking to the manager and a few of his usual associates. As he busied himself ordering a round of drinks and taking them back to his table, Lloyd didn't pay him any special attention, though their eyes met across the pub and Vinnie delivered a nod. Lloyd still found it hard to believe: Vinnie Dobson in cahoots with one of Interpol's Most Wanted Terrorists. When Mark had given him the news, he had dismissed it at first as impossible. But he'd checked out the Interpol website for himself, and there it all was – including a photograph of Larson minus the red beard. Mark had asked him to try getting information out of Vinnie on the sly. Play it low key, he'd insisted. Give him my mobile number and tell him I'd like to hear from him. Find out *anything* you can about his new 'business contact', but whatever you do, don't let him think we're on to him. It's got to be casual.

Lloyd reckoned Vinnie would come over to him during the course of the evening. They hadn't seen each other since the surprise visit to his flat last Friday; he reckoned Mark's 'grateful' former manager wouldn't be able to resist approaching him. And sure enough, about half an hour later, he felt a tap on his shoulder.

'Thought you'd been avoiding me.' Vinnie cocked his head.

'Nothing like that.' Lloyd noted the surprised expressions round the table. Last time he and Vinnie had had anything to do with each other, the latter had been threatening his brother's life. Now he was motioning that Lloyd should get up and speak to him alone. He was doing his Swerve-manager, wheeler-dealer act which Lloyd usually resented, but which tonight he reckoned could be useful.

'Speak to him?' Vinnie wanted to know.

'Couple of days ago. Told him about your visit.' Lloyd was aware of Vinnie's impatient expression, and thought he'd play along with him for a while. 'He knew about your Unum deal—'

Vinnie raised a confidential finger to his lips.

'Oh, sorry. Yeah, he's pleased things are going so well for you. He asked how you were doing. I told him you were pretty flat out at the moment. That's right, isn't it?'

'Sure, sure.' Vinnie glowered before prompting, 'What about the phone number?'

Lloyd nodded innocently. 'Oh, I got that.' He touched his breast pocket. 'Right here, in fact.'

Vinnie visibly relaxed. 'Did he say anything else?'

'Just that he'd like to hear from you.'

'I'll be calling him all right,' the other said and took a swig of his bitter.

'You must be doing really well, heading out to LA?'

Vinnie nodded. 'Part of the jet-set now,' he said, only half in jest.

Lloyd looked suitably deferential. 'That's with the new business contact you mentioned?'

Vinnie shot him a sidelong glance. 'Pretty much.' Then,

unable to contain himself, 'You're talking big league. Seriously big league.'

'What – big league in London?'

'Christ, no. All over the place. He flies in. Does the business. Flies out again. Never in the same place more than a couple of days at a time.'

'Bit difficult to do business with if he's always on a plane?' he prompted.

'Oh, he stays in touch.' Vinnie patted the jacket pocket in which he kept his mobile.

'Sounds intriguing? What line is he in?' No harm in asking, thought Lloyd.

'Now that, Lloy-boy,' Vinnie touched his nose conspiratorially, 'is what you'd call classified information. And you know me. I like to keep things under wraps.'

Los Angeles
Friday, 24 September

Twenty-four hours after getting back to Los Angeles, Hilton Gallo was showing uncharacteristic signs of frustration: there'd been no further news from Scotland Yard on One Commando. DI Bennett was maintaining his wall of silence, despite the eleventh hour tip-off which had put the police hot on the heels of the group; despite the presence of an MI5 agent within it; despite the Vinnie Dobson lead. There was not so much as an inkling that arrests were imminent or that the group was about to be closed down.

And that meant he was going into this afternoon's meeting with far less certainty than he would have preferred. Ranged about him in the GCM Boardroom were the endorsements head Ross McCormack, and his counterpart in music

Andy Murdoch, plus GCM's in-house lawyer, Blake Horowitz, and Leo Lebowitz. Across the table from him Elizabeth was ready to take notes.

'The endorsement,' began Hilton, eyeballing Ross McCormack, 'where are we on the critical path?'

McCormack fiddled with the bright red frames of his spectacles. The prospect of Isis and Jordan Hampshire pulling out of the biggest deal he'd negotiated in his life was more than alarming. It had been giving him sleepless nights. If this deal went pear-shaped, no matter what the reason, he might as well kiss goodbye to his job and his career.

'Production's finished and artwork has been sent by Berkeley Square's agency to fifteen of the thirty magazines on the media schedule.' He tried hard to project his usual, brisk efficiency. 'The forty-eight-sheet posters have been sent to media agents in each of the twelve participating countries for installation. We're all on schedule for the campaign to break in a fortnight's time.'

Hilton nodded. Usually he would have been reassured that McCormack and his team was so well on top of production, but on this occasion the prospect that the endorsement was now slipping beyond control was less reassuring.

'And what about the matter we discussed last night?' He turned to Blake Horowitz.

Blake hadn't got to bed last night till three, after a marathon session at the offices of GCM's attorneys Mitchell & Curtin. Now he massaged his tired eyelids.

'There are three main points to this,' he began in measured tones. 'The first is the very practical one that at some point this campaign reaches the point of no return.'

All eyes turned to McCormack.

'As I said, the artwork's already gone.' He raised his shoulders.

'Artwork can be recalled.' Hilton looked over at him, steel-eyed.

McCormack's eyebrows twitched nervously. 'The posters, sure, we can pull those out even a few days before. But the magazines will be going to print any day now.'

'I want you to find out which day, specifically.'

'For all thirty of them?' McCormack's pale cheeks were rapidly colouring to the shade of his spectacle-frames.

'Yes,' retorted Hilton, glancing back to Horowitz. 'Carry on, Blake.'

'The second point is the basis on which our clients would revoke their endorsement contract. Having carefully checked the articles of the Berkeley Square contract,' he fingered a thick document in front of him, 'I find there is no specific clause that explicitly or implicitly allows for withdrawal on the basis of intimidation. I've discussed matters with Mitchell & Curtin and we believe there is precedent for such a withdrawal. However,' he looked up significantly, 'we would need to establish a threat. Evidence of terrorist intimidation would have to be provided to substantiate our clients' actions. And as far as I'm aware, we have no evidence as yet beyond your own experience,' he nodded at Hilton, 'which would be regarded by the courts as hearsay.'

Hilton looked down at the table, tight-lipped.

'The only other way out,' Horowitz continued, 'is to establish that Berkeley Square has, in fact, been testing on animals, and that our clients' reputations would be damaged by association ...' That was a line he didn't need to continue. 'The third issue to raise is that of commercial damages. Berkeley Square would seek the three point five million they've paid our clients. Production costs we estimate at half a million, and media costs at nearly eight million.' He glanced over at where Ross McCormack was nodding in agreement. 'Damages would be significant, especially having already announced the clients' endorsement. Depending on jurisdiction, and looking at the scale of awards paid out in past endorsement disputes, we're looking at damages equiv-alent to the endorsement cost, at the very least. Then there's the potential legal costs of the other side should we not succeed. In round terms we could be looking at twenty million plus.'

Hilton looked up to find all eyes on him.

Ross McCormack was shaking his head. 'That's some hit.'

'It's a monstrous penalty to pay,' retorted Hilton, '*if* there's no danger posed to our clients. But if it's the only way we can guarantee their survival . . .' He glanced round the table seriously. 'What we need right now is more information.'

Heads were nodding, though not McCormack's; the man wore a dyspeptic expression.

'Elizabeth, can you get Bennett on a conference call. You'll have to get him at home.'

A short while later, Elizabeth had brought a telephone over to the table, having dialled the policeman.

'Detective Inspector Bennett. Hilton Gallo. I'm with several colleagues wanting to know where you are with One Commando?'

Bennett sounded surprised. 'As I told your assistant yester-day, we're using every means at our disposal to bring this to a swift conclusion.'

'Just how swift? I got the impression, after my attack, we were talking hours?'

'It could be hours,' the voice at the other end was even, 'but it could be weeks.'

'Weeks?' Hilton's voice was choked. 'How could it be weeks? You know who these people are!'

'There are extenuating circumstances.'

'What extenuating circumstances?'

'I'm not in a position to divulge that information.'

There was a lengthy pause before, at the end of the table, Hilton drew himself up to his full height, clasped his hands in front of him, elbows on the table.

'Inspector Bennett,' his voice was sharp with authority, 'allow me to outline our position. Our two clients top the target list of a violent terrorist organisation. The terrorists are threatening them unless they cancel their endorsement contracts. It seems to me there are only two solutions. One is to apprehend the terrorists. The other is to cancel the endorsement contracts. I'd like to share with you, confidentially, the figure just passed on by a colleague, who tells me that any such cancellation will cost my clients twenty million dollars. Now perhaps you understand why I'm so eager for any information which will help resolve this problem?'

'Indeed,' came an unimpressed-sounding Bennett from the other end after a pause, 'and you must understand I am equally committed to protecting the means by which I have come to acquire certain information—'

'You're talking about the MI5 agent?'

'I'm unable to confirm or deny—'

'Let's cut the crap, Bennett.' His colleagues had never witnessed Hilton in such wrath. 'We know about the agent, no thanks to you. So, what are these "extenuating circumstances" that prevent you from arresting the group?'

'That's not something I'm allowed to divulge.'

'And what about Dobson? Has he led you anywhere?'

'The Metropolitan Police run a very tight ship. We have few enough staff to conduct surveillance of known criminals without committing our resources to following individuals in London pubs who have *allegedly* been seen in the company of Interpol suspects—'

'You mean, you're doing nothing about it?'

'I mean, we're pursuing the most fruitful lines of enquiry.'

'But you're not prepared to tell us what those lines are?'

'Mr Gallo, we're in the business of saving people's lives, not saving Hollywood money.'

Hilton jabbed the speaker phone off, furious. It was rare, in his negotiations with others, that he wasn't able to advance the interests of GCM and its clients – or at least leave the door open to the possibility of future advancement. But Bennett was in a separate category from those with whom he generally did business. GCM's dominance in the entertainment industry meant nothing to the policeman. Exasperated, Hilton was wondering where to take things next when Melissa Schwartz came through with a note: Mark Watson wanted to speak to him urgently.

'Put him through,' Hilton was curt.

Lloyd had phoned Mark to report on his conversation with Vinnie as soon as he got home from the pub. Mark had insisted that he relate to him every detail. The revelation that Larson was so highly mobile was extremely disturbing, and even though Lloyd and he didn't discuss it, they both realised the implications: Bengt Larson could be in America, even as they spoke. Right now he might be holed up somewhere in Los Angeles, planning the next attack. Despite what Hilton had said to Isis and him the day before, One Commando wasn't just a UK-only group. They were international.

For the first time since arriving in Los Angeles, Mark had felt at risk. Looking out of the windows of his Beverly Hills home, across the lush lawns to the flower beds lining the perimeter walls, he found himself wondering just how secure his home really was.

Now he reported back to Hilton on Lloyd's conversation with Vinnie. Hilton, who had him on speakerphone, sounded tense from the start of the conversation, and was even more uptight by the end of it. He *had* to realise, thought Mark, that this latest revelation meant the end of the endorsement. Last time they'd spoken to Isis, it had taken all Hilton's powers of persuasion to keep her in the deal – and even then she'd been far from happy. If she'd known that Larson's activities were global, she would have *insisted* on bailing out; Mark had no doubt that the end of this whole débâcle was only one phone call away for Hilton. As soon as he got on the line to Malibu, that would be it.

But there didn't seem any foregone conclusion as far as Hilton was concerned. Far from acknowledging that the time had come to draw a line under the whole Berkeley Square fiasco, he was moving the conversation smoothly on to security arrangements. He would instruct security specialists employed by GCM to conduct an immediate assessment of Mark's protection, he told him. They would be ordered to upgrade all necessary measures. No expense would be spared to ensure his safety. It was all very well, thought Mark, but why bother if they were going to call off the endorsement?

His suspicions growing, he waited until Hilton had ended before asking expectantly, 'And what news on Vinnie Dobson? Has he led them anywhere useful yet?'

There was a snort of impatience from the other end before Hilton admitted, 'I've just been on the phone to Bennett at Scotland Yard. They're not keeping Dobson under surveillance.'

'You've got to be—!'

'Bennett claims they don't have the resources. I think there's a very different reason.'

'But he's a direct lead to Larson!'

'So is their inside man. That's what they're not saying. It's my belief,' Hilton tried to convey more certainty than hope, 'they've got an operation under way they don't want to compromise—'

'I'd say it's more a case of the Plods not knowing their arses from their elbows,' retorted Mark. It wasn't a sentiment he'd expressed yesterday in front of Isis, but the fact was he'd lost all confidence in the Met when he was twelve; there'd been a break-in at home in Lewisham, and even though the police knew the suspects, and confirmed their fingerprints, they said they didn't have enough to go on to secure a conviction. He'd realised then, you couldn't count on the Met.

'This really is the end of it,' he was exasperated.

There was only silence from Hilton.

'Let's face it, when Isis hears that Larson's mobile she'll pull the plug.'

'That's by no means a certainty,' Hilton's tone was clipped.

'Come on, Hilton, I was there. I saw her face. She wants out.'

'There are good reasons for her to stay in.'

'Oh, sure. But as soon as I tell her about Larson—'

'As you'll have gathered by now,' Hilton swiftly interjected, 'she's a very . . . complex lady. This needs to be treated with sensitivity.'

'Meaning you don't want me to tell her?' He was sardonic.

'It's difficult news.' Hilton's response was frosty. 'It's best if I break it to her.'

'So in the land of the brave and the free, you can't talk to people about direct threats to their lives?' Mark's cynicism about Hilton's information control was now complete.

'That's not what I said.'

'Sounded like it to me.'

'All I said was—'

'That I shouldn't mention it,' his voice rose, 'so you can cover the whole thing up!'

'Let me spell this out,' Hilton's voice had sunk to sub-zero, 'I've known Isis since she arrived in Los Angeles fourteen years ago. You've known her a few weeks. I've worked closely with her. I understand her. I know her strengths – and her blind spots. When it comes to breaking difficult news so as not to cause undue distress, I'm better placed than you to do it.'

'So long as you *do* "break the difficult news,"' retorted Mark.

'I've already said that I will.'

'Oh, yeah,' Mark sounded disbelieving.

'You have my word,' Hilton intoned deliberately, 'and if I can give you some advice, I suggest you be a little less hasty in the judgements you form about people.'

13

For Alan Brent, the timing couldn't have been worse. Shortly after six in the morning he got the phone call from Larson; the One Commando boss wanted to see him. A taxi would be coming to collect him from his flat in ten minutes.

It was typical Larson – urgent and unpredictable. For security reasons Alan supposed it had to be that way. But following the revelations of just a few hours ago, he wasn't sure what to do; how much of his discovery should he reveal?

He hadn't been able to let go of the Isis riddle. It had got under his skin. The mystery of her identity – who she was and where she came from – had had him intrigued, infuriated, utterly absorbed. It was an intellectual puzzle he was determined to solve. The fact that he'd been commissioned to dig up this stuff by Bengt Larson, that he planned to use it to come to the attention of *the powers that be* became almost secondary to his main purpose; he *had* to discover the enigma of her past.

As it happened, the key that unlocked the door had come to him when he'd stopped looking. At the end of a long session of fruitless hacking that had gone on until one this morning, he'd shoved himself back from the computer desk, walked across the attic room, stripped down to his underpants and collapsed into bed. He had lain there, physically tired, but mentally perplexed, his mind performing high-wire gymnastics with the unrelated bits of data he'd assembled so far, but getting nowhere; 'Paws of Miami Beach'. Maria Carboni. Salmacis Hospital.

It had been as he was falling asleep, when his subconscious took over the problem that his conscious mind had failed to solve, that the realisation had come about. It was only once he'd stopped trying too hard, as he drifted between consciousness and sleep, that it came without any effort at all, jolting him awake.

Suddenly, he was too excited to sleep. In the dark, he glanced at the hands of his watch – a quarter to two in London made it a quarter to nine in Miami. He was soon up at his desk, getting phone numbers from international directory enquiries, and placing calls. He didn't get far by phoning Salmacis Hospital direct – Dr Weiner was no longer full time at the hospital, he was told, having set up his own practice elsewhere. No, they didn't have the number for that practice right now, but if he'd like to call back during normal working hours . . .

Back at his computer, Alan chased down several more dead alleys before finally getting his breakthrough shortly after three in the morning. He'd succeeded in tracking down Robert Weiner through the American Medical Association website. Now fifty-four, Weiner was still practising in Miami, operating a practice with two other specialists in downtown Miami. Short résumés of all three doctors were provided. Hardly daring to breathe, Alan scanned down their details. All worked in complementary disciplines. Any one of them may, or may not, be required to attend to a particular case. But each of them was a specialist in the same field of counselling, and treated patients emerging from the same tunnel of horrors. Alan found it hard to believe. But there it was, right in front of him, staring him in the face.

Surely Isis hadn't been through that?

'I want you to tell me about the Gallo operation,' demanded Larson, tugging him through the door almost as soon as he'd knocked. The flat was on the first floor of a derelict council block in Kensington Olympia. Stark, graffiti-sprayed walls were lit from a single naked bulb dangling from the ceiling. Even paler and more dishevelled than usual after a sleepless night, Alan blinked in bewilderment behind his thick lenses.

'But I – I wasn't even involved. Why me?'

On the way over, he'd wondered what was going on, tried to work out the significance of Larson's latest, and typically unanticipated, demand.

'You tell me.' Larson was accusatory. Dangerous.

'I'm n-not sure what you mean. I don't know anything about it.' He felt his mouth go suddenly dry. He should have seen this coming. Having got this far into the organisation, he should have prepared for confrontation. But he hadn't. He'd been so absorbed in the Isis assignment he'd forgotten about most other things. Now he felt alarmingly deficient.

'That is strange,' Larson began to circle him slowly, all the while staring intently at him. 'Your mates seemed to know all about it.'

'What mates?'

'Don't fuck with me, Brent,' Larson growled in his ear, 'you know who I'm talking about.'

'I don't.'

'All this while you've been tagging along with us, making

yourself useful, you must have thought you were being very clever,' Larson had returned to face him, and was eyeballing him from six inches away. 'Meantime, it turns out you're nothing but a spy. A snoop.'

It was then that Alan became aware of the red light of the camera. Installed in one corner of the room, it dangled from a hook that had been screwed into the ceiling. What was going on? Was this a set-up? He tried remembering what he'd learned about conflict resolution. He took a deep breath.

'There's obviously been a mistake,' he began. Appeal to reason, he recalled. Always appeal to reason in the first instance – and introduce an element of surprise. Yeah, well, he could do that all right.

'The Gallo operation – I don't know what you're talking about. And I'm not a spy. How could I be? Why would I spend hours getting incredible stuff on Isis if I was a spy?'

'What "incredible stuff"?'

'The research I've been doing.' He wished he could come across more confident. More controlled. But a nervous tic had developed under his eye. He felt his whole cheek twitching.

Larson met his eyes with a long, cold stare.

'I th-thought that was why you wanted to see me.'

Larson was leaning back with his arms crossed. 'Oh, yes?' His tone was disdainful. 'Exactly the kind of answer I'd expect from an undercover agent. There's only one problem with what you say. This information you talk about – I never got it.'

'That's because I only had the breakthrough last night.'

'How *very* convenient for you,' snorted Larson.

'But if you let me tell you now you'll see there's no way—'

'I think you'd better.'

Alan swallowed hard. He was radically revising his plans

by the second. The proper procedure would have been for him to relay his findings to HQ for their considerations before even hinting at their existence to anyone else. And in this instance he was in no doubt that his discoveries would have astounded all the head honchos there. But there was no way he could follow standard procedures right now. He didn't doubt for a second that Larson meant business.

So he told Larson everything. From the tracing of Maria Carboni right through the detection process to his final, astounding discovery. It was the first time he'd put his findings into words and said them out loud, and as he spoke he was aware how bizarre they must seem.

Larson stood listening to him, expressionless. When he was done, he glanced up at the ceiling for a few moments before saying, 'Well, either that is the most incredible thing I've ever heard, or it's the desperate tale of a worm wriggling on its hook.'

Alan felt beads of perspiration starting to slide down his forehead. 'I d-don't know where you get the idea of a . . . spy from.'

'The police were tipped off.' Larson's voice was steely. 'I didn't tip them off. It wasn't anyone in the group. Only one other person knew—'

'But you're missing a motive!' protested Alan.

'There'd be a motive if you were a spy.'

'But I'm not. You vetted my b-background. You know how committed I am to the cause—'

'Do I?' Larson was disbelieving.

'Well, you know how much I hate Berkeley Square.'

'Oh, yes. You joined them as a graduate,' his tone was mockingly schmaltzy, 'and they stole your big idea. They made you change departments. Such a sad story.'

'It's true! You know it!'

'It seemed to be true. Just like your discovery about Isis seems to be an amazing piece of detective work.'

'Go ahead. Ch-check it out!'

Larson leaned over him. 'I will,' he said, staring into Alan's eyes from just a few inches away, 'because you know what I'm going to do if it's not true, don't you?' He was nodding slowly. 'That's right Alan. I'm going to kill you.'

Jasper Jones sat on the kilim-patterned sofa of his well-upholstered sitting room, poring over the Sunday papers, while breakfast news pumped out of the TV. He seldom bought only one newspaper at the weekends. And this morning he'd bought the lot. Slipping out of bed carefully so as not to disturb Gail, who'd stayed over with him last night for only the second time, he'd gone down to his local newsagent just after eight o'clock. There he'd bought the *Sunday Times*, *Sunday Telegraph*, *Sunday Herald*, *Independent on Sunday*, *Observer*, *Mail on Sunday*, *Sunday Express*, *Sunday Mirror* and *News of the World*. With all their supplements and colour magazines, they stood over eight inches high on his coffee table. But Jones was not interested in anything but the news coverage – and particularly that on the front page.

He'd first become aware of it last night as he and Gail had returned from a party at the home of PR agency boss Mark Maritz in Hampstead. The radio of his Saab convertible was tuned in as usual to Capital Radio. During an advertisement break had come the unexpected announcement that tomorrow's *Sunday Herald* would carry an exclusive account of a second attack in central London by animal terrorist group One Commando. Included was an interview with Simon Dubois, a hotel manager whose family had been held hostage in the attack. Read out in breathless tones and making much of the police news blackout that had prevented reporting of the incident before now, the *Sunday Herald* puff-piece was tailor-made for sensation.

Jones had had a hard time keeping his feelings concealed from Gail. Having closely monitored the media immediately after the failed attack, he'd quickly realised the police had blanketed the whole thing. Monday night's disruption at Green's had evidently been explained to all those involved as a false fire alert. And that had suited him fine; he hardly wanted to see One Commando's failure trumpeted in the press.

As the week wore on and there was still no word of the attack, he'd begun to think the story might never surface. But thinking hard as he'd sped through the mild Saturday night, he had realised that this could only be wishful thinking. All it took was a casual exchange in the supermarket, a playground conversation, and the media, with eyes and ears everywhere and cheque-books at the ready, would pounce. Word had evidently got out from the Dubois family: had it been a calculated cash-in by Simon Dubois, or something more accidental? How much would be revealed? And now the cat was out of the bag, how many other Sunday papers would be hurriedly remaking their front pages?

He wanted, urgently, to get on the phone and find out just how this story was breaking. That was, of course, out of the question with Gail sitting right beside him. Slim, blonde, beautiful Gail with whom a new and very gratifying relationship had begun after the dinner party they'd both attended ten days earlier. But even as he drove her back to Islington, the inviting prospect of a night of passion ahead, he thought that, if the truth be told, he'd rather be heading for Wapping to pick up an early edition of the *Sunday Herald*, or spending the next few hours monitoring the twenty-four-hour news channels he received by satellite TV. He'd rather be getting a grip on what was going on; the One

Commando project meant a lot to him. He'd invested too much time, money and energy in it to see it all go belly up.

This morning as he'd flicked through the papers on his way home from the newsagent, he'd soon confirmed that all the late editions carried news of the Dubois interview, with the *Sunday Herald* adding to their front-page headline splash with a double-page spread on pages two and three. Back in his flat, he'd closed the sitting room door and turned the television on, volume low, as he continued to scan through each of the newspapers, tearing out any articles referring to the attack. He didn't have long to wait until an ITN news round-up repeated news of the attack, together with a clip of Dubois climbing into his car the night before, remarking that he had nothing more to say.

Recording all this on video, Jones took in every word in a state of total absorption. Then came his detailed reading of the *Sunday Herald*. They'd covered it as a human drama piece, with much made of the 'terrifying ordeal' suffered by Dubois's wife and two children, photographed looking traumatised on one page, with Simon Dubois appearing every bit as gaunt on the other. The family had been at home on an ordinary school-day afternoon when masked gunmen had burst through both the front and back doors simultaneously and ordered them, face down, on to the carpet. Shock had initially prevented them from doing anything but obey orders. But as soon as she'd recovered the power of speech, Mrs Dubois reported that she'd told the intruders they must have the wrong house: what interest could they, an ordinary middle-class family, be to a group of evidently organised militia?

But the gunmen hadn't been inclined to make conversation. They had apparently been highly disciplined and kept communication to a minimum. Mrs Dubois and her two children had been ordered to collect warm clothes and coats, before being handcuffed and bundled into a panel van which arrived down a laneway at the back of their house. In the darkness of the van, being driven through South London, Mrs Dubois had remembered the One Commando attack on Jacques Lefevre – or so she claimed. Clutching her children to her it was all she could do, she'd told reporters, to keep herself from breaking down, to stay brave for her kids' sake.

Scanning the rest of the piece, Jones turned to the interview with Dubois himself. There was nothing in here that hinted of One Commando's real target. The *Sunday Herald* – presumably at Dubois's request – hadn't even mentioned Green's by name, although none of the other papers had felt any such compunction. All that was reported of the main event was how Dubois, held to ransom over his family, had provided access to the hotel in an attack that had been foiled by the early intervention of the police. No mention was made of One Commando's intended target, though it was stated that Hollywood celebrities frequently stayed at the hotel.

Jones quickly recognised the *Sunday Herald*'s ploy: sensational though it was, what they'd launched here was a teaser. They'd deliberately kept back enough revelations to feed to readers, piecemeal. Rather than use up all their ammunition in one hit, they'd started a *Herald*-exclusive soap documentary which they'd use to beat down their opponents over the next week in the unending circulation wars. This was a story set to run and run. Jones was livid.

It was only moments after this recognition that the sitting room door opened and in came Gail wearing his bathrobe. Clear-eyed, hair brushed and even, if he wasn't mistaken, wearing a touch of make-up, she came over behind where he was sitting and put her arms around his chest. 'You work too hard,' she whispered, kissing his cheek.

'Not usually.'

Her hands roamed down his chest. 'Only since you met me then, eh?' she smiled.

He put his hands over her arms, as though to massage them but in reality to prevent them descending any further.

'I expect you've worked up quite an appetite?' she asked knowingly. 'I thought I might cook some breakfast. That is, if there's anything in your kitchen to cook?'

'Very nice,' replied Jones, relieved to be free of any further encumbrances. 'There should be some eggs and bacon and . . . things.' Then, glancing over the papers strewn all over the floor, 'I've got an important phone call to make.'

Bengt Larson was surprised when Jasper Jones's number showed up on the display of his cellular telephone. It was rare for Jones to initiate contact between the two of them, and unprecedented for him to call early on a Sunday. Stepping out of the derelict West London flat, he flipped open the phone.

'So, what do you make of the papers?' Jones exploded at the other end.

Larson had never heard him so angry. 'What d'you mean?'

'The *Sunday Herald*!'

'What are you talking about?'

'Christ Almighty! It's even worse than I thought. You haven't seen it?'

'No.'

Jones let out a long, steady stream of smoke from his Gaulois before telling Larson what had happened.

Larson paced up and down the corridor of the derelict council block.

'This is terrible!' he kept repeating, as Jones explained how the story was being played out in the media.

'You'd better believe it!' There was no mistaking Jones's accusatory tone. 'It goes completely against our strategy! We agreed, right at the beginning, we'd only act against direct targets. Now the whole world knows that civilians have been hurt – it plays into enemy hands.'

'But you agreed to the Dubois operation!' protested the other.

'I considered it acceptable collateral in securing Gallo.'

'But we never got that far—'

'And why not, Bengt – that's the point I'm making. Because of Alan Brent, that's why. Because he's a spy. He tipped off the police. And what have you done about him?'

'As a matter of interest,' Larson's usually impeccable English was cracking under pressure, 'I'm interviewing him right now.'

'What d'you mean?' Jones was caught unawares.

'Only that he's sitting, strapped into a chair, and I'm asking him . . . difficult questions. I've had him here for the last three hours.'

'You're filming it?' confirmed the other.

'Yes.'

'And?'

Larson paused a moment before exhaling heavily. 'You were right. He's guilty.' It took a lot for him to admit, but he couldn't ignore the evidence. Brent had looked like he was going to piss himself from the moment he'd arrived. 'He's the spy. The mole. I'm sure of it.' He paused before going on. He hadn't planned getting on to the next bit until he'd had time to follow up Brent's claims. Investigate first, he'd thought, before telling Jones. But with Jones about to spontaneously combust at the other end of the phone, he decided he'd better tell him right away. 'But there's something else,' he murmured. 'It may be misleading – I still need to check out the story.'

He told Jones about how he'd commissioned Brent to investigate Isis's background, and what Brent had found out about Maria Carboni, Salmacis Hospital, Dr Robert Weiner. As he spoke he detected a change in attitude at the other end of the line.

'This . . . information,' when Jones finally responded his voice was low, 'if there's any truth to it at all—'

'Of course,' Larson didn't need to be told, 'very useful.'

Useful? Jones's mind was going into overdrive.

'He told you this morning?'

'Correct.'

'Who else has he told?'

'No one.'

'You're sure?'

'He only found out himself a few hours ago.'

'Hmm,' mused Jones.

'There are only three of us who know about it. Brent. Me. And now you.'

There was a long pause before Jones finally retorted, 'Strikes me that's one person too many.'

Looking back to the door of the flat in which Brent sat cowering on a chair, Larson agreed with Jones's implied edict in just four words. 'Yeah,' he grunted eventually, 'he's gotta go.'

Minutes later, Jones emerged from his study to where Gail was standing in the kitchen frying up a mixture of onions and tomatoes.

'Smells delicious,' he observed, coming up behind her and slipping his hands into the bathrobe. 'Looks delicious too. After breakfast I'm going to have to reward you. One good turn . . .'

She turned with a grin. 'I'm pleased you're not working

all day. All work and no play makes Jack a dull boy.'

'True. But there are some things in life,' running his finger-tips up her taut silky thighs, 'you just can't ignore.'

Across town Bengt Larson slipped the mobile phone into his pocket and extracted a pair of black leather gloves which he tugged over his hands before opening the door.

Alan Brent squinted myopically at him in the semi-dark. Earlier, Larson had dashed his spectacles to the ground and stamped on them in a fit of rage.

'What's happening?' he wanted to know.

Larson stepped over to him and was lifting him to his feet.

'Interview terminated,' he told Alan.

'What does that mean?' The voice was so thin it sounded about to break.

Summoning his assistant with a jerk of the head, Larson dragged Alan off his chair by the scruff of his neck, and thrust his back against the wall.

'Guilty as charged.'

14

Flight BA2
Monday, 27 September

Mark sat near the back of First Class, sipping orange juice and flicking distractedly through the latest issue of *Men's Health* magazine. In the past, before Los Angeles, he'd always thought that flying up front must be one of the most glamorous experiences in the world. Now as he sat among a passenger roster of anonymous businessmen and the odd semi-celebrity, he reflected wryly on how times changed.

He'd travelled to New York earlier in the day, and this flight would get him to London just before five in the afternoon, local time. Lloyd would be out at Heathrow to collect him, then they would make their way down the M4 and through rush-hour traffic towards South London. With any luck, they'd be ordering their first pint down at the Lamb before eight. It was a high-risk visit; if things didn't go well for them tonight, they wouldn't have a second bite of the apple. He had to return to LA to continue his recording schedule on Wednesday; as he'd soon discovered, session work was a twenty-four-hours-a-day, seven-day-a-week business in

tinseltown. He'd had to get permission to leave from GCM
– it was like being back at school.

It was a radical idea, he supposed, but drastic times called
for drastic measures; this seemed his best and maybe only
option. After his terse exchange with Hilton Gallo it had
become all too apparent to him that no one had any grip
at all on One Commando. The MI5 insider had come up
with sweet FA. The Met weren't even following up the lead
he and Lloyd had given them. It was disarray all round.
Meantime, Isis was hiding out back in Malibu while Hilton
was up to his usual control freakery, trying to avoid telling
anyone what the hell was going on.

There was nothing for it, he'd decided, but to take matters
further into his own hands. So that was why he was heading back to London, with a very specific aim in mind. The
idea had been triggered when Lloyd was telling him about
his encounter with Vinnie down in the pub – Vinnie had
remarked on how Larson stayed in touch with him by phone,
and gestured towards his mobile. The OmniCell mobile.

From his days on OmniCell Customer Support line, Mark
was intimately acquainted with every aspect of mobile phone
operations – he'd had to be. Thinking about how they might
be able to track down Larson's whereabouts using Vinnie's
mobile, he soon realised how difficult that would be. Even if
Vinnie *did* have a contact number for Larson – and that was
unlikely – and even if Lloyd could get hold of his call log,
trying to identify one number among the dozens of other mobile
numbers would be like looking for a needle in a haystack;
Vinnie was what OmniCell termed a 'high-traffic user'.

It was only later, when the thought of the mobile returned,
niggling at his mind, that he recalled Lloyd telling him, not
so long ago, about something the software boys had developed, which enabled up to three hours of conversation to

be recorded and downloaded on to a computer file. From there it could be played back, as if through a tape recorder, or alternatively a voice recognition programme could be used to generate a written transcript. The idea was being developed for the business market, but Mark began to wonder about an altogether different application.

Late on Friday night, Mark had phoned Lloyd to ask him more about the device. Bleary-eyed and heavy-headed on a Saturday morning, Lloyd had been surprised by Mark's interest in software development stuff – but the reason had soon become apparent. And when Lloyd confirmed that Vinnie was still in London, there seemed to be no option.

It was just after seven-forty-five when the two brothers stepped into the Lamb. Within moments the place was bedlam. Lloyd hadn't told anyone about Mark's visit – it had only been confirmed the day before – so his appearance was a bolt from the blue. Just the way they'd planned it.

Everyone in the pub was suddenly crowding around Mark; friends, drinking mates, Lamb regulars, all wanting to shake him by the hand, slap him on the back, buy him a drink. Those who had been most outspoken against him when stirred up by Vinnie were, Lloyd noticed, among the first to lead the rush to welcome their showbiz celebrity back to Balham. There was no mention of 'moronic' hairstyles or 'oikish' clothing now. Instead, it was all Mark this, and Mark that, and won't you sign my sweatshirt, Jordan Hampshire, ha, ha?

Lloyd had picked him up from the airport, on schedule, and they'd made good progress on the roads. They'd have been much quicker by Underground, but Mark hadn't wanted to get caught up with people. Besides, they needed to discuss plans for the evening in private. They'd already worked out the overall strategy on the phone, but as they drove into town, turning south down Earl's Court Road, they talked through the detail. What they were attempting was highly illegal and used leading-edge kit but, Lloyd assured Mark, wasn't technically difficult. Using a welter of jargon which Mark used to spend his working hours translating for the benefit of the public, Lloyd evidently regarded this evening's operation as presenting only a minor challenge to his capabilities. What's more, he'd left work that evening fully prepared for all eventualities, as was evident from the bulge in his coat pocket.

The technical side was, however, only one aspect of the overall plan, and the most straightforward. The practicalities were different, and would require opportunism, meticulous timing and a great deal of care if the whole operation – the only reason for Mark's trip back to London – wasn't to be blown. Vinnie couldn't be allowed to suspect, for so much as a minute, that they knew he was involved with One Commando, much less that they were about to turn him into an unwitting double agent. And the only card they had to play was the element of surprise.

In the Lamb, Mark looked round the sea of eager faces. In other circumstances he guessed he would have found the adoration and inevitable wisecracks a real ego buzz. He would have pushed the boat out, enjoyed a few drinks and just let go. But tonight's visit to the Lamb wasn't social. Scanning through the group that had formed around him, it took him a while before he caught sight of Vinnie who was perched at his usual place, pretending not to notice his arrival.

'Vinnie!' He headed in his direction, taking the still-forming entourage with him. Some of the regulars, remembering the last furious encounter between Mark and his 'manager', followed proceedings bright-eyed with expectation.

Vinnie turned to meet him, a droll smile appearing on his face. 'Mr Hampshire!' He shook Mark's outstretched hand and thumped him on the shoulder, 'The hero returns!'

'Yeah, well, don't feel much of a hero with this haircut.' Mark raised a hand to his head.

'Oi! Vin, aren't you going to punch his lights out?' demanded one of the Lamb's stalwarts provocatively.

Vinnie just laughed. 'Hey, I'm proud of this man.' He thumped Mark on the shoulder again before turning to the manager. 'Line up a pint for him, will you, Cyril.'

A group had formed around them, just like they'd figured. Lloyd had moved into position on Vinnie's immediate right, although Vinnie had not acknowledged him – there was too much else going on.

I only need twelve clear minutes, Lloyd had said. *Fifteen at the outside*.

Mark reckoned it wouldn't be too difficult to keep Vinnie occupied that long. After his visit to Lloyd's flat, and the whole story about how grateful he was to Mark over the Unum deal, Vinnie was hardly going to change his line. He needed to keep in with the Watson brothers to be any use to One Commando. No matter how much he hated it, he'd have to keep up the act.

Vinnie was a creature of habit, so they'd counted on him behaving true to form tonight, and he hadn't let them down. Monday nights had always been quiet for him. 'The show-biz man's Sunday,' he used to quip, and he customarily spent it down the pub. What's more he was wearing his trademark leather jacket – a designer garment bought from a leather shop on King's Road, with pockets which, though deep, were easily accessible from where it hung loose at his sides.

In the first few moments after Mark had approached Vinnie, while his attention was firmly elsewhere, Lloyd took advantage of the jostling crowd and hearty handshakes, to slip his hand into Vinnie's pocket, find and extract his mobile.

The movement escaped the attention of nearly everyone else – most of them were too focused on what was going on between Vinnie and his former protégé. But Mark noticed his brother stepping back from where he'd been pressed beside Vinnie and retreat behind the crowd. So far, so good, he thought.

In the Gents', Lloyd quickly shut himself inside a cubicle, kneeled on the floor and, closing the toilet lid, used it as a surface to work on Vinnie's phone. Opening up mobile phones was all in a day's work and he knew precisely what needed doing. Whip off the housing, install the chip. A couple of minutes reprogramming then on goes the housing again and it's back to the pub. The chip he'd brought with him was in a small, sealed plastic pouch and when the time came he inserted it using the pair of tungsten-tipped tweezers he'd brought specially for the purpose. The chip had been customised to store both incoming and outgoing conversations, and the reprogramming that followed ensured that every time the 'End' button was pressed, the file containing the most recent call would be automatically transmitted back to a computer at OmniCell. This would mean an enforced three-second delay between calls. But nothing on the display would register that anything unusual was happening. And meanwhile, back at OmniCell, Lloyd had already ensured that every incoming file from the phone would be securely stored on computer and instantly accessible by Mark, wherever in the world he happened to be, via the Net.

Back in the pub, Vinnie handed Mark the drink he'd just bought him, before raising his own glass and clinking 'Cheers'.

'What about your drink?' Mark asked, as Vinnie swilled down what remained in his glass.

Vinnie pointed at his watch. 'Got to go, mate,' he explained. 'Session in Soho with a talent scout. Eight-thirty. Could be worth a lot of money.'

Oh, Christ, thought Mark. *This is all we need!*

'Lloyd tells me things are looking up?' He had to keep him talking.

'Too right!' Vinnie thrust his glass down on the counter.

'I'd like to hear about it.'

'Yeah, sure. When are you leaving town?' Vinnie's eyes were bearing into his.

Mark shrugged. 'Can't say. All depends when they want me back.'

'You're staying with Lloyd?'

'That's right,' he lied. He had no intention of issuing One Commando a gilt-edged invitation.

'Tell you what,' Vinnie turned away from the bar, 'I'll buzz you tomorrow. We'll set something up.' Thrusting his hands in his pockets, Vinnie searched for his keys. Mark watched, trying not to appear transfixed, as he fished about for them. They were a large bunch attached by a sturdy chain to a silver Mercedes logo, and having taken them out of his pocket Vinnie threw them up in the air before catching them again – one of his little habits. Glancing back at Mark, he was about to head out when a look of sudden alarm crossed his face. Dumping his keys on the bar top, he dived into both pockets again before confirming his suspicions.

'My mobile!' he exclaimed.

Now he was checking his breast pockets, and trousers. 'I always keep it . . .'

Across the bar Cyril asked, 'Maybe you left it at home?'

'No,' Vinnie was shaking his head vigorously, 'called someone on the way here.'

As he quickly became desperate, Mark was working out the best way to keep him from going.

'Why don't you phone your mobile number?' someone was suggesting. 'You'll soon find where—'

'Some bastard's probably nicked it!' Vinnie was resentful. 'Wouldn't be the first time either. Last time this happened it cost me big-time. *All* my contacts call me—'

'Try phoning it,' the suggestion was repeated.

'Yeah! Not a bad idea. Cyril!' Vinnie was turning.

Mark knew he had to interrupt. This couldn't be allowed to go on. Lloyd hadn't been long gone – if he was at the reprogramming stage and the mobile rang, that would completely screw things up!

He grabbed Vinnie's arm. 'Your car. What about checking there first? Probably find it just slipped out of your pocket, you know how things do . . .'

Vinnie looked over, with a doubtful expression.

'Where are you parked?' persisted Mark.

'Just outside,' he gestured.

'If you're going anyway—'

'I might have to cancel the fucking thing. Last time some bastard rang up a hundred quid of calls!'

'No need to panic,' Mark tried humouring him, 'it's probably sitting on the floor of your car.'

Some of the others were agreeing with their newly returned celebrity.

Looking round at their expressions, Vinnie shrugged. 'I guess it's worth . . .' he started in the direction of the pub door.

A few of them, led by Mark, followed him. Glancing at his watch, Mark wondered how long Lloyd had had. It didn't feel like any time at all. *He had to keep Vinnie occupied for another ten minutes.*

The Mercedes was parked almost directly outside, and Vinnie had soon pressed the automatic unlock switch. As he opened the driver's door and was leaning inside, some of the others looked beside the passenger seat.

'Nothing here,' Vinnie was tight-lipped. Having checked the floor and side, he now had his hand under the driver's seat. 'Not a fucking thing!'

Elsewhere around the car, the others were saying the same thing. They rummaged about, increasingly hopeless, until Vinnie ordered them out.

'Forget it!' He slammed his front door shut. 'This is a fucking waste of time.'

'When did you last use it?' someone was asking.

'I told you!' he barked, 'I called someone on the way here. I parked the car and we talked for a while. Then I finished and came inside. It's been nicked!' he looked directly at Mark.

'Sure looks that way,' Mark agreed.

'Best phone yourself up,' someone was repeating.

'What's the point? It's been nicked!'

'Yeah,' agreed Mark, 'they're not going to answer it, are they? And even if they do, what's he going to say?'

'But it might be lying about somewhere?'

'Can't do no harm, can it?'

'Just give it a go!'

The group was moving back inside, Vinnie with a face like thunder. Trying his mobile number was the best thing he could do and Mark realised he couldn't keep up the argument against it – not without seeming daft. Back at the bar, Vinnie was asking Cyril for the payphone he kept behind the bar and rifling through his pockets again – this time for change. Before he'd found any, however, one of the regulars was offering him his own mobile to use.

Distancing himself from the group, Mark made his way across to the Gents'. Inside, the place was empty – except for the one cubicle.

'Are you finished in there?' he asked in an urgent whisper.

'Just about.'

'He knows it's missing! He's trying to ring the bloody thing!'

'No worries—'

Mark heard a jangle of instruments as Lloyd got up from where he'd been kneeling.

'—volume's right down, mate.'

Less than two minutes later Vinnie was, once again, leaving the pub in high dudgeon. This time, Mark and Lloyd were the only ones following him.

'I'm going to be late!' he fumed, thrusting the pub door open with far more force than was needed. 'Late for my appointment and no mobile. What a fucking joke!'

'Yeah, well . . .' Mark watched him climb in the car and shove his key in the ignition.

The car had roared to life when, beside the driver's window, Lloyd called out, 'Hey! What's that?' and was gesturing under the car.

Moments later, Vinnie took back possession of his mobile. Still angry and upset, he managed only muttered thanks.

'Don't know how that happened!' he grunted, glancing at Lloyd only briefly.

'Or how we missed it before.' Mark adopted a bewildered expression.

'Yeah. Speak soon.' Vinnie jerked his head, before pulling away into the night traffic.

The two brothers watched him head down the road, and turn left at the first set of traffic lights.

'Sorted?' Mark turned to Lloyd.

'Oh, yes. Mr Dobson is now upgraded with the very latest cellular technology.'

'Good man.' Mark put an arm round his shoulders and gave him a squeeze. They were turning back towards the pub when he continued warily, 'I wonder if he's calling them right now?'

'We'll know about it, soon enough.'

Pausing before opening the pub door Mark continued, 'And what's with the eight-thirty appointment on a Monday night?'

'Yeah.' Lloyd shared his questioning expression. 'Don't reckon we should stick around here too long.'

15

It was social services who alerted the police to the problem on the derelict Olympia housing block. Drugs and gangs had destroyed much of the surrounding estate. Most flats had been trashed and were boarded up. There were, however, a few residents who hadn't been able to leave, who had no other place to go and the council hadn't been able to relocate them. Old Mrs Mills was one. She lived with half a dozen padlocks on the front door and only ventured out of her home twice a week when her son came to visit. But meals on wheels called by, regular as clockwork, and it was one of their ladies she first mentioned it to.

'There's something funny going on upstairs,' she'd told the volunteer.

'Yes, yes, dear.' The meals-on-wheels lady didn't pay too much attention to Mrs Mills's ramblings. She was losing her mind, poor thing, and after five years living behind bars was given to paranoia.

But when the social worker came round to check on her that same afternoon, he paid closer attention to Mrs Mills's complaint, and noticed something the meals-on-wheels lady hadn't. It was an odour, as faint as it was unmistakable to someone who'd smelled it before.

'That funny smell is probably from where someone has illegally dumped rubbish round the side of the block,' he told Mrs Mills, not wanting to alarm her. 'As for the noises you heard upstairs at the weekend, well, people are using these places for squats all the time.' It was, they both agreed, a disgrace she still had to live there.

As soon as he was back at the office, the social worker called the police, who dispatched two young PCs in a car to investigate. The social worker didn't give precise directions to the flat above Mrs Mills's, but none was needed – the PCs' sense of smell was all that was required. Nor did they need any equipment to break into the flat. Making their way along an exposed outside passage, they found the door unlocked and ajar. After stepping through a small hallway, they entered what had once been the main living room. There they halted in their tracks. They'd come here expecting a corpse – a corpse in a slum block. But what they were looking at was very much more complicated. The man's body dangled from a noose, head slumped forward and face hidden behind a mass of dark, unruly hair. Around his neck, the crude, cardboard placard attached to a piece of electric cable bore the single word 'SPY'.

One of the PCs turned to speak into the radio strapped to his shoulder.

'We're at the flat. Bit pongy,' he told the control room, viewing with distaste the excrement spattered on the floor beneath the dangling body. 'Our chum here's been dangling from a rope for two, three days?' he glanced at the other PC who nodded back, expressionless. 'Best send over a SOCO.'

Alerted to a suspicious death, within minutes a scenes-of-crime officer was dispatched to the flat, which was quickly taped off. Donning white overalls, he was soon photographing the body, before cutting it down, then going carefully through every room in the derelict flat. A police surgeon arrived, and shortly afterwards, a team from Forensic with a zip-up body bag.

Detective Sergeant Morris, large, hardboiled, and short-tempered, was put in charge of the case; several hours later he was reading through the pathologist's report for the benefit of his two subordinates in his office back at the station. The report wasn't long. The victim had died of a broken neck, consistent with the circumstances in which he'd been found. The victim's clothes were now sealed in plastic bags on the DS's desk, along with the placard which had been found around his neck.

'Spy,' mused the DS after finishing the pathology report. 'But for whom?'

'Drugs operation?' ventured White, the older of the two DC's.

'Forensics checked all the clothing and scene of the crime. No evidence of drugs contact. And the MO ... too ritualistic for a drugs killing.' The DS leaned back in his seat. 'Looks to me like a gangland killing. But something's not quite right.'

'ID?' queried Detective Constable Brewer, new to Morris's team.

'D'you think I'd be sitting here now if we'd found a passport in his back pocket?' glowered the DS, jerking his head at the plastic bags. 'This is all we've got to go on.'

DC Brewer sifted through the bags, before picking up one that contained a pair of spectacles, one lens of which had been smashed, and the other badly cracked.

'Thick lenses,' he remarked.

The DS leaned forward in his chair with a grunt. As he

turned over the bag in his hands, he noticed the manufacturer's name down the side of the glasses, but nothing to
distinguish the spectacles from a million others – except for
the thickness of the lenses. In the meantime, Brewer was
glancing at all the other bags on the DS's desk, before he
noticed one containing a spectacles wallet. It was a cheap,
black plastic sleeve without any markings on the outside,
the kind that was handed out by high street opticians
throughout Britain to purchasers of glasses of all kinds.

'Can I open . . . ?'

The DS nodded.

It was unlikely, but worth a look. Unsealing the clear
plastic bag and extracting the spectacles wallet, he opened
it up and glanced inside. There *was* a white lint cloth at
the bottom, the kind used for polishing lenses. He tugged it
out between his fingers and when he unfurled it he found,
printed in faded green ink, the name of a well-known retail
chain – Super-Specs – together with the address and phone
number of the Clapham branch. Meeting the DS's eyes,
Brewer said, 'They couldn't prescribe too many glasses with
lenses this thick.'

'Well done,' the DS's face was dour. 'Now check it out.'

The manager of Clapham Super-Specs was overworked,
harassed and had no easy answers. Customer computer
records were ordered by name, not prescription, he
explained. And while the lenses were more powerful than
most, they were by no means unique; he'd have to go through
all 3,500 customer records to pull out the two dozen or so
which closely matched the prescription. Plus, of course, it
was quite possible that the customer had acquired the case
and polishing cloth when buying a pair of sunglasses.

That night the Super-Specs manager worked into the
early hours, clicking through every computerised index card

in his customer records. It was a chore he could do without, he'd told the police. The hours were bad enough just trying to run this place without having extra stuff dumped on him. But they'd told him they were investigating a murder. He and he alone had the means by which to make a critical identification. He was legally obliged to assist.

When his list of twenty-eight names came through the next morning, the two DCs immediately began checking them off one by one. It was the least rewarding and most tedious line of enquiry. But they had no choice; the spectacles were their only lead.

Just before knocking off time, DS Morris summoned them for a status meeting. The list of names to be eliminated was down to five, the two DC's reported. They'd printed them out in alphabetical order.

'Before beating down any doors,' Brewer regarded Morris's testy features, 'we ran their names through the computer.'

Morris raised an eyebrow, questioningly.

'Nothing on four of them. But we picked up something on the first one. He had a restraint order slapped on him a few years ago. It might be nothing; we're still waiting for the full report.'

As Brewer continued, Morris glanced back at the list of names, focusing on the one at the top: Alan George Brent. Should it mean anything to him, he wondered?

Los Angeles
Wednesday, 29 September

Isis hadn't moved from the security of her home since Hilton's visit to Unum music studios over a week earlier. She'd needed no further warning to take extreme care, both of Holly's security as well as her own. Confining herself to her home studio, she focused on her music, rehearsing the few tracks she still had to record and spending a lot of time on the phone to her producer Sam Bach. Holly took the stay-at-home routine in her stride, Isis explaining that the unscheduled break from school would only be for a few days; her daughter soon had Juanita and Frank running round in circles at her bidding.

Despite the feeling of normality in the house, however, Isis's thoughts were haunted by One Commando. It was the first thing that entered her consciousness when she woke in the mornings – and the same thing that made it so hard getting to sleep at nights. Apart from the hours she spent with Holly, or rehearsing her music, or in some other convenient distraction, she couldn't drive the fear from her mind. They were after her – there could be no doubt of that now. The Berkeley Square endorsement had put her top of One Commando's list.

What Hilton had told her about the undercover agent *did* make a difference. It was her one consolation, her one hope that something could still be salvaged from this ordeal. Now it seemed that One Commando were no longer only the pursuers – they were also the pursued. How long would it be before they were closed down? She put calls into GCM every few hours, where Hilton and Elizabeth were in constant touch with the UK. It's only a matter of time, Hilton kept repeating the same phrase. Don't make any precipitous decision. There's a massive police operation in play.

In the meantime, life in the outside world went on and she knew she couldn't stay in limbo-land very long. Sam Bach had rescheduled an already intensive recording timetable to accommodate her and couldn't hold out much longer – she'd have to go into Unum early next week, to complete all the stuff Mark was doing. Ross McCormack and Andy Murdoch had been on the phone to discuss meetings and travel arrangements leading up to the launch of *Nile* in just a few weeks' time.

Most of all, Leo Lebowitz was becoming increasingly anxious about all the pre-launch publicity she would lose if she remained reclusive. She'd already passed up on a high-profile modelling agency launch the night before, which Lebowitz had wanted her and Mark to attend. She could just imagine the GCM boys hammering their calculators as they worked out the future sales she was losing through reduced visibility. She and Lebowitz had had a long conversation when he'd tried to persuade her to go to the function; yes, she knew One Commando were hardly likely to attack her in a room that was awash with celebrities. And she had no doubt that the vehicle escort GCM could provide would ensure her safety. It was, more than anything else, that she didn't feel up to circulating with the shiny set when she was just so worried, so hollow. Anxiety, she told Lebowitz, was an emotion very difficult to conceal.

That was when he'd suggested Panama Jacks instead. A casual family diner in Malibu, it was a short drive from her home. He'd have it vetted thoroughly by security immediately before the visit. She could be there and back within an hour and she wouldn't have to see anyone – it would just be Mark and Holly and her, dropping by for a weekend brunch – though he'd make sure a few photographers had been alerted in advance. The proposition was hard to turn down, especially as Panama Jacks was Holly's favourite, and Isis knew she couldn't keep her daughter cooped up at home much longer without respite.

Mark would play ball, Lebowitz assured her. He'd been on the phone to her singing partner who had just returned from an unscheduled supersonic trip to London. Back in town to continue his recording schedule, Mark was worried about her, said Lebowitz. Isis remembered how Mark had reacted last time they'd been together. She'd let slip about her 'background' and he'd instantly wanted to know all about it. It had been a foolish mistake, but in the heat of the moment, with Hilton pressuring her into staying in the endorsement contract, the words had come tumbling out before she could stop herself.

And that, she supposed, was exactly why she needed to keep Mark at arm's length. She had done her best to suppress the mutual attraction she'd sensed since their very first 'date' at Bianco Verdi. There had been times, especially in the last week as they worked in the studio together, when she had felt they were sharing an intimacy almost as great as love-making. But letting anything develop with Mark would be dangerous. Life could not be allowed to imitate art. If it did, and in a moment of tenderness she allowed all the barriers to come down, she knew she risked revealing the terrors of her past. And once she did that, once she'd confided her secret, she'd no longer be able to control it.

It was the same burden of emotion she'd had to carry ever since arriving in California. While in certain relationships she'd succeeded in enjoying sexual intimacy without having to give of her innermost thoughts and feelings, there were some men, she knew, with whom that couldn't happen. Mark was one of those men. His most attractive quality, his sensitivity, was also the greatest threat to her composure. If she gave herself to him, she knew she'd end up giving away much more than she should. For that reason she had no intention of getting romantically involved with him; it wasn't even a possibility.

*   *   *

Panama Jacks was a casual family diner on the opposite side of the road from Malibu beach, on the ground floor of a small ribbon of shops. Decorated in maritime theme, its walls were washed sea-green, and suspended from the ceiling was a low canopy of fishermen's nets, gathered up about brass lamps. Artifacts from shipwrecks had been placed about a room which buzzed with families, mostly local, but a few tourists as well.

Mark, whose body was still on transatlantic time, had reluctantly agreed to come when summoned by Lebowitz. Eager though he was to spend time with Isis, he was feeling fatigued – and knew he had to conserve his energies for a demanding studio session later in the day. What's more, lunch out with Isis accompanied by her daughter and both their bodyguards wasn't exactly the kind of encounter he had in mind. But Lebowitz had been insistent. It was critical to the publicity effort, he'd said. And what was forty-five minutes in the rest of his life?

Arriving at Panama Jacks with Isis, Mark couldn't help comparing their arrival here with the entrance Isis and he had made at the irredeemably self-infatuated Bianco Verdi. There there was no mistaking the whispered excitement and turning heads when they were ushered in by their body-guards – who had spent ten minutes reconnoitring the place beforehand in the company of other security experts – but after they were shown to a back table by a bug-eyed teenage waiter, the place soon calmed down. Apart from the occasional sidelong glance, and a couple of photographers' flashes – business done – people seemed happy just to leave them to their meal undisturbed. This was Malibu, thought Mark, where seeing stars in your local restaurant wasn't a big deal. He only wished they didn't have to sit down accompanied by two bodyguards in black suits with conspicuous bulges at their hips – but it was a whole lot better than not going out at all. Holly certainly thought so, excitedly demanding that the children's menu be read out to her twice before demanding her favourite potato wedges with garlic and chives.

A couple of times he met Isis's eyes across the table and tried to work out the expression in them – friendly, but distant. 'A complex lady,' Hilton had said about her the day before – that was no exaggeration. In fact, he was half-surprised she was still in the Berkeley Square deal at all after the discovery of the day before. Hilton's well-honed powers of persuasion had obviously kept her in play, though for how much longer he wouldn't care to speculate. Despite her efforts to appear at ease, he could detect she was anxious and on edge, and he didn't think he was just projecting his own feelings. The fact was, they were both caught up in a waiting game – waiting for the British police, or for MI5 to announce a breakthrough. But as every hour passed, and still nothing happened, how much longer were they expected to wait?

They were taking first sips of their drinks when their waiter returned to them, kneeling at their table, his striped pinafore clustered with buttons.

'Sorry to disturb you, Isis, ma'am,' he began, 'but you have a phone call.' He pointed towards the bar at the back of the restaurant, where cash tills and a telephone was also located.

Isis raised her eyebrows. 'It can't be for me. No one even knows I'm here.'

'He definitely asked for you,' the waiter nodded earnestly, 'I can bring the phone over here, or would you like to come . . . ?'

Isis glanced over at Frank before shrugging. 'Just take a message.'

'Right.'

Mark was glancing about the restaurant. 'Could be some-one here on a cellphone.'

'Yeah, but why?' Isis looked suddenly worried.

The two bodyguards were glancing about them. 'Kind of strange,' was all Frank would say.

Then the waiter was returning. 'I asked to take a message but he cut off.'

Isis looked up. 'Did he say anything at all?'

The waiter pulled a face. 'He said, "This is for Isis and Jordan Hampshire", but then he just hung up.'

At that moment the whole restaurant exploded in a crash of glass. Both of the large front windows shattered, with jagged shards of glass flying far back into the restaurant and flames leaping from table to table. Suddenly everyone was screaming. For a moment, Mark was too bewildered to move. It was as though some invisible, destructive tidal wave had burst through the window at the front of the restaurant, throwing whole tables of people on to the floor, leaving them lacerated, bloodied, crying out in shock. Further back, diners were scrambling from their tables in panic, looking about, wild-eyed, confused about what was happening and where to flee.

The two bodyguards instantly sprang into action. Frank picked up Holly, Denzil had his arms round Isis and Mark. They were running towards the rest rooms. Others in the restaurant were starting to move quickly too, as fire spread rapidly. The low canopy of fishermen's nets was ablaze, smoky flames leaping up to the ceiling, setting off the shrill clang-ing of a fire alarm. Hustled through the restaurant, Mark noticed a smashed wine bottle on the floor in a fast-growing puddle of paraffin fire.

They were soon in the corridor leading to the rest rooms, then out through a fire escape door through which several of the waitering staff had already fled. Outside, in the blazing sunshine, the bodyguards kept on running.

'Gotta get out of here!' Frank shouted over his shoulder, keeping Holly's face pressed firmly into his neck.

Mark looked about at the bloodied faces and hysterical screaming people as bedazed diners scrambled outside. It seemed wrong to be running away from all of this, doing nothing to help. But the bodyguards were heading directly back to Isis's Range Rover in which they'd all come.

Sensing his hesitation, Denzil kept tugging him by the arm. 'They might be waiting out here to pick you off.' Denzil couldn't get the door opened fast enough, thrusting the two of them inside.

'Mommy!' cried out Holly, scrambling from the front into the back seat, between Isis and Mark. Isis clasped her tight, as Frank quickly checked under the car, and its bonnet. Then he was back inside, engine started and pulling away at high speed. Isis closed her eyes, her face drawn and pale. Mark looked back at all the people they were leaving behind, standing in groups of pain and shock. Holly started to cry. While Frank concentrated on getting away as fast as possible, Denzil was keeping up 360-degree scans. There was a strange silence in the car, with the three of them huddled together like survivors from a shipwreck, while the two bodyguards constantly searched about them on high alert. Then as they got back to Isis's house and the gates began to open, she looked up at Mark, eyes filled with fear.

'Better call Hilton.'

He nodded.

'Tell him they're in LA.'

Hilton was round at Isis's within an hour. He'd been working at his Pacific Palisades home and when Mark called he'd got into his car and come over straight away. En route, he'd put in a call to the Los Angeles Police Department, telling them what had happened.

He arrived to find Isis hugging Holly on the sitting room sofa, Mark pacing up and down, and bodyguards stationed both out at the front and at the back. Wordlessly Hilton walked over to Isis and Holly, giving them both a hug, before turning to Mark and squeezing his arm. Even in casual attire he was immaculately groomed, sporting a linen jacket, deep blue shirt and beige Daks flannels.

'What about the special agent,' Mark was wry, 'who was going to tell us everything before it happened?'

'I know,' he acknowledged Mark's disappointment, perching on the arm of a sofa opposite.

'So much,' added Isis, 'for One Commando only operating in Britain.'

There was a tense pause which seemed to go on for ever. Mark flashed a glance, first at Isis, then Hilton, then back to Isis again.

'What?' demanded Isis.

'You didn't tell her, did you?' Mark blazed at the other. 'You gave me your word – that's what you said! And you didn't tell her!'

'Tell me what?' Isis's voice rose as she clutched Holly to her.

Hilton had fixed Mark with an impenetrable stare.

'Last Friday, before I went to London, I found out that Larson operates an international network. I told him.' He nodded towards Hilton. 'He promised me he'd talk to you about it. Said it was better coming from him.'

'I had every—' began Hilton, only to be cut short by Isis, face flushed and eyes blazing.

'You kept that information—'

'I had every—' repeated Hilton, voice raised.

'You bastard! You knew damned well I would have dropped Berkeley Square.' Isis was anger incarnate. 'Instead you put Holly's life and my life at risk for some photo-opportunity—'

'It's not like that!' Hilton managed.

'Oh yes, it is like that!' At her side, Holly began to sob.

'I had every intention of telling you.' Hilton got up from the sofa arm and began pacing the room.

'When?' demanded Isis. 'When we were both lying on a mortuary slab?'

'Today's incident was very unfortunate.'

Eyes ablaze, Isis was shaking her head vigorously.

Mark's voice, furious but controlled, cut in beneath both of theirs. 'It was also completely avoidable.' He regarded Hilton bitterly. 'You lied to me. You told me not to speak to Isis. You said you'd do that yourself. I trusted you and you let all three of us down.' He glanced at Holly and Isis. 'It makes me wonder what other lies you've been peddling—'

'Now let's get real—'

'Like your story about the Biographical Notes. All an innocent misunderstanding, you said.'

'As it was!' Hilton regarded him with piqued indignation.

'Which just happened to generate acres of press coverage. Is there nothing you won't stoop to for media space?'

'You're way out of line!' Hilton's voice was raised so high he was almost shouting. 'Something difficult has happened and now you're fantasising about other stuff that just isn't there.'

'If there's no "other stuff" why won't you tell me about Isis?'

Hilton and Isis exchanged furious expressions before Hilton replied, 'That's an entirely separate issue.'

'I don't think it's separate. It's all part of you and your information control. And I'm sick of it! You feed me a line here and a line there to shut me up. You treat me like some goddam puppet that'll dress and sing and shave its head and do any damned thing you choose.'

Hilton's expression was withering. 'I did warn you about image management.'

'Managing my image is one thing. But I won't be patronised!'

'And you're being paid rather a lot of money.'

'Yeah,' snorted Mark, 'danger money. But as far as I'm concerned, you can shove it! This endorsement isn't worth all the money in the world.'

'That goes for me too,' chimed Isis.

Across the room, Hilton struggled to regain his customary poise. 'I hope you've both thought very hard about what this means—'

'I've been thinking about nothing else,' Mark nodded towards Isis, 'her neither.'

'Don't forget the police are working on this.'

'Exactly,' turning for the door, Mark nodded towards Denzil, 'and look how bloody hopeless they've been.' At the door he looked back, fixing Hilton with a challenging stare. 'Seems to me if there are any answers to be found out, I'm going to have to keep looking for them myself!'

16

Los Angeles
Wednesday, 29 September

Hilton Gallo had put phone calls in to Blake Horowitz, Ross
McCormack and Leo Lebowitz and of course Elizabeth before
he'd even got on to the Pacific Highway into town. They
must drop whatever plans they had for the evening, he told
them. They had a huge amount to do in a very short space
of time; tonight was going to be a late one.

'You've all heard the news.' He glanced round the sombre
assembly in his office an hour later.

'Last straw?' asked Ross McCormack in a tone of resig-
nation.

'She wants out and there's nothing I can do to stop her.
I've played my hand. Overplayed it.' Hilton shrugged, in an
uncharacteristic gesture of helplessness, remembering Mark's
furious expression as he'd stormed out of Isis's house a short
while earlier. He could hardly believe that his masterpiece
– this spectacular deal – was crumbling before his eyes. Then
nodding towards the plastic file on McCormack's lap, 'Where
are we on timing?'

'We've already missed the deadline on some of the
editions in South East Asia and two mainstream European

titles. We could pull out of the rest first thing tomorrow, but it'll be a bloodbath.'

Hilton was glancing up at the clocks ranged about his office wall. 'It already is tomorrow in Europe. You'll get on the case when they start getting in to work?'

Nodding wearily, McCormack wondered what kind of career he'd have left in a few hours' time.

Catching his eye, Hilton responded, 'At least what happened this afternoon satisfies the requirement Blake noted last time.'

'Evidence of intimidation?' Blake looked grim. 'I'd say so.'

'You're putting out the withdrawal announcement immediately?' asked McCormack.

Hilton shook his head. 'I have a better idea.' Then observing the surprised expressions of his colleagues, 'I've spent months putting together this deal. I don't want GCM to be the agency that pulled out of the world's biggest endorsement – firebomb or not.'

They had all fixed him with expressions of intense concentration.

'The solution I have in mind,' he continued, 'is to turn the tables. Get Berkeley Square to release them from the deal—'

'Why would they do that?' McCormack's very blond eyebrows were raised.

Lebowitz had already seen where Hilton was heading. 'Public opinion?' he queried.

Hilton nodded. 'We'll pile on the pain in the next twenty-four hours. Bring overwhelming pressure to bear on the Berkeley Square Board so it becomes . . . an easier decision for them to withdraw the contract than to continue it.'

'Going to take some doing,' McCormack couldn't help observing.

'Of course. But the best result under the circumstances, no?'

They worked frenetically for the next five hours, fuelled only by hastily eaten Thai take-outs and strong black coffee couriered in by security. In his office, Blake Horowitz burned the midnight oil drafting new documents that would replace Isis and Jordan's current endorsement agreement and that would be legally binding in both USA and UK jurisdictions. The new documents provided for all options from the best-case scenario – Berkeley Square releases the two clients from all obligations, no strings attached – through to postponing the arrangement contingent on the arrest of the One Commando hierarchy.

Ross McCormack meanwhile was reviewing agreements with each of the twenty-five magazine titles yet to go to print with Nile advertisements. Having scrutinised the details of terms and conditions relating to postponement and withdrawal penalties, he was drafting alternative faxes and e-mails to each title, one of which was to be sent to each in twenty-four hours' time. Hilton's get-out was, he had to admit, an inspired piece of opportunism. If it came off, and Berkeley Square could be persuaded to withdraw, he'd be the happiest man in Hollywood – spared to fight another day. But could Hilton do it?

Up on the sixth floor, he and Leo Lebowitz were pulling out all stops to ensure that it did. The psychology was simple: to create such a powerful tide of opinion against what had happened, that by the time it came for Hilton to speak to Jacques Lefevre, Berkeley Square would get a huge benefit in PR terms from making the grand gesture. Carving up GCM's client list between them, Hilton and Lebowitz placed calls to all the biggest names in Hollywood, asking if they'd be prepared to give a reaction to the media about what had happened to Isis that day. Even though it was late on Wednesday night, most of their clients felt an undisguised, vicarious horror about what had happened to Isis and Jordan, and they were only too happy to oblige.

Within an hour, Lebowitz was contacting all the major media networks, offering quotations, down-the-line interviews and TV appearances for a gathering line-up of A-league movie stars, music performers, TV show celebrities and other showbiz luminaries. Provided with a ready-to-run celebrity story on a plate, the media were soon swinging into action.

Shortly after ten p.m., the focus of Hilton's attention switched to GCM London. Rousing a sleepy Stan Shepherd from his bed, just after six on Thursday morning UK time, he quickly updated him on developments and asked him to prepare a hit-list of GCM clients in the UK and Europe. It was too late to get into the Thursday morning papers, of course, but TV and radio were a different prospect altogether. While taking on for himself the unhappy task of having to wake up most of his biggest British clients from their slumbers, Hilton had Shepherd begin contacting major UK radio and TV stations, offering big names from Hollywood for live interviews.

It didn't take long for the momentum to develop. The limitless appetite of the media for any kind of celebrity news was always a certainty. When half a dozen or more major celebrities were prepared to be interviewed – doing their own careers no harm in the process – the result was guaranteed. Shepherd's track record of relentless networking also paid off. Speaking to a contact in one of the television news rooms, he discovered that the Home Secretary, the person with ultimate responsibility for law and order in Britain, was being interviewed on *Breakfast News*, Britain's most watched early morning news programme. Calls to the Minister's private secretary, and the hasty drafting of an appropriate soundbite, ensured that the Home Secretary himself weighed in against 'the utterly vile and reprehensible terror campaign of One Commando'.

In recent weeks, Shepherd had also been making friends with the PROs of mainstream animal rights lobbies, most of whom were desperate to distance themselves from the terrible damage One Commando was inflicting on the public image of their cause; Presidents and spokespeople from as diverse a range as Animals First, the RSPCA and even the Animal Liberation Army were coming forward to protest against One Commando's activities. Soon after ten-thirty, Hilton looked at his watch. Things were progressing well, but he could see he was still going to be tied up for several hours, drumming up support in Europe.

He called in Elizabeth.

'I need you to liaise with the police here to find out what in God's name they're doing. The Sheriff in charge is George Varley. Check with Mark to see if he's been in touch with them.'

'Shall I try Bennett in London as well, for an update?'

'Don't even bother,' he was dismissive, 'but keep Hanniford in the loop.'

Elizabeth tried Varley's phone several times, finding it engaged, before dialling London. Hanniford was unperturbed to be called so early in the morning. Before Elizabeth had even spoken, he was commiserating with her on the latest news which he'd heard on Radio 4 earlier that morning.

'So you've heard,' she was brief. 'I just wanted to keep you updated – and find out if you had any more news.'

'Not at this end. What are the police saying in LA?'

'We're still waiting for them.'

'They'll be liaising with Scotland Yard—'

'Who'll be liaising with MI5.' Elizabeth let out a sigh of frustration. 'Surely someone must know what's going on?'

She meant it as a rhetorical question. But Hanniford replied with assurance, 'Oh, someone knows very well.'

'Home Secretary?' she ventured.

'Close,' replied the other. 'He doesn't have time to keep up with the progress of every single case, but his spin-doctor is sure to know about prickly media issues. Try Peter Campbell. He's the only one with the whole picture.'

Elizabeth registered the name. She was sure she'd heard Hilton mention Campbell in the past. 'Can't you ask him?'

'Only about Lefevre.' Hanniford anticipated her request. 'It would be wrong of him to disclose anything beyond that and I wouldn't want to ask it of him.' There followed a considered pause. 'But I suppose I could give you his direct line. Hilton Gallo could call him directly. I shouldn't really be doing this, but in the circumstances . . .'

After taking down the spin-doctor's telephone number and finishing her call to Hanniford, Elizabeth tried Varley again. This time, his phone rang.

'I've just been on the line to Isis,' said Varley after she'd announced herself. 'I was about to call Mr Gallo. We've got them.'

'You've got the bombers?' Elizabeth raised her voice for Hilton's benefit, before switching her phone on to loud-speaker. Hilton made his way swiftly into her office.

'Booked them just over forty-five minutes ago in Culver City.'

'Was one of them Bengt Larson?'

'No. Why should that be?'

'He's the guy that attacked me.' Hilton spoke now.

'These punks aren't One Commando.' Varley was dismissive. 'Never been to London. Don't even have passports.'

Elizabeth and Hilton exchanged looks of disbelief.

'I've just come out from interviewing them. Fall into what I call the "social misfit" category. Spoiled kids who've had it too easy and wanted to do something to get themselves noticed.'

'Are you saying,' Hilton spoke carefully, 'these people have no connection at all with One Commando?'

'That's exactly what I'm saying. It's a copycat.'

'You're sure,' asked Elizabeth, 'they're not just covering for him?'

'Believe me, they're not covering for anyone. I've put the frighteners on them and they're not holding back. Their parents made sure of that.'

'Parents?' asked Hilton. 'How old are they?'

'Didn't I mention? They're both seventeen.'

Hilton exchanged a look of bewilderment with Elizabeth before asking, 'But – why Isis and Jordan?'

Varley let out a grunt of contempt. 'They've seen all the One Commando stuff on TV. Decided they wanted to get into the headlines themselves.'

'And how did they know they'd gone to Panama Jacks?' asked Elizabeth.

'Followed her from home. They've been staking out her house for the past two days.'

London
Thursday, 30 September

Jasper Jones's footsteps were brisk as he walked back to his flat from the Angel Underground station. Having spent the day in Paris on business, he'd returned to Heathrow on an early evening flight. It had been after changing at Paddington from the Heathrow Express to the Circle Line that he'd unfolded his copy of the *Evening Standard* to discover, right in the middle of the front page, the Jacques Lefevre announcement. The headline had electrified him. We've *done* it! had been his initial, triumphant reaction, as he'd glanced round at his fellow passengers, many of whom were reading the same article with inscrutable expressions. We've just forced Berkeley Square to walk away from the biggest endorsement deal in the history of the beauty industry. What a coup! What a triumph! He'd had to suppress the sudden rush of adrenaline as he'd stared at the ghoulish photograph of Jacques Lefevre in his black suit and black sunglasses, the white of the bandages showing down the sides of his face. It was the kind of image picture editors from every national newspaper would be sure to plaster all over tomorrow morning's editions. An image which would be seared into the public consciousness.

Once he started reading the article, however, Jones's initial excitement quickly changed. It wasn't Isis and Jordan Hampshire who'd abandoned the endorsement, he realised; Berkeley Square had ended it themselves. Far from suffering the humiliation of a major celebrity walk-out, Berkeley Square were being portrayed as the good guys, releasing stars from their contracts to spare them 'future intimidation'.

One Commando had yet again been outmanoeuvred in the media by Berkeley Square. While a litany of 'One Commando violence' was repeated, there was no detail about the systematic abuse and torture of animals by Berkeley Square as evidenced in all the AFL material distributed to the media. The only reference to that was a sentence to the

effect that 'alleged evidence of animal rights abuse was generally accepted as faked'.

Jones wondered how Larson would react to this latest turn
of events. The two would have to speak soon. Since yesterday morning, Jones had given considerable thought to that
biggest and most unexpected twist of all – Larson's revelations about Isis. In a journey through an Aladdin's cave of
surprises, that had been the most staggering surprise of them
all. How best to use the new information was something
Jones had thought about without coming to any certain
conclusion – but the Lefevre announcement put a very different perspective on things; now he had no doubt at all about
what needed to be done. If *Rolling Stone* magazine's 'Pop
Queen of the Year' thought she didn't need to bother about
One Commando again, she was very much mistaken.

Making his way swiftly home, eager to get in touch with
Larson, it was only when he had the front door key in the
lock that he remembered. Christ, yes! Gail would be upstairs,
waiting for him. Yesterday afternoon as they lay together in
a state of post-coital bliss, she'd suggested they spend the next
evening together. If he lent her a spare key, just this once,
she'd come round in the early evening and prepare something for supper – she'd give him a nice surprise, she'd
suggested meaningfully. He'd been in no mood to refuse.
Gazing across the satin sheets at her delicious nakedness,
Jones had been thinking that she was the woman of his dreams
– or almost. His only regret was her deficiency in the intellectual firepower department. She had no interest in current
affairs and didn't appear to read anything more demanding
than *Hello!* magazine – her casual acceptance of the status
quo really couldn't be more different from his own focused
intensity.

He made his way upstairs, and before he'd even got to

the first floor he could smell the results of her labours in the kitchen – a delicious aroma of garlic and coriander wafted through the house.

'Hello, darling!' he called out, not wanting to startle her. He needn't have bothered. In the kitchen she was oblivious to his arrival, all other noises drowned out by the hissing of the frying pan and the music blaring from his Sony portable which she'd retuned from Radio 4 to Melody FM.

Opening the kitchen door, he looked across to where she was standing at the bench dressed in his red silk bathrobe – and under it, a set of lacy black underwear designed with only one purpose in mind. Despite the urgency of his wish to speak to Larson, he couldn't help grinning.

'Hello, darling!' he repeated from the kitchen door.

She turned with a smile. 'My poor baby!' She pulled the pan off the stove and hurried over to him. 'So late! I was getting worried about you.'

They kissed hungrily, Gail pressing her body against his and running her fingers through his hair. When they pulled apart, she asked him, 'I hope Paris put you in a romantic mood?'

'I'll be feeling more ... romantic after a drink and a shower,' he replied.

She beamed at him. 'I'm sure that can be arranged,' she murmured, walking over to the cupboard where he kept his Laphroaig. Taking out the bottle she splashed a generous measure into one of his crystal tumblers.

As she did, he glanced round the kitchen. 'You've found everything?'

She nodded. 'Brought some stuff over myself.'

Then, as he looked back at her, 'Don't worry, I'm not about to move in. Spare key's back in your study.'

He shrugged. 'I'm not complaining.'

As she handed him his drink, he regarded her appreciatively – his red gown wrapped about her perfect figure; the tantalising glimpse of cleavage clad in black lace; her flawless features, made up to perfection, and the mane of tousled blonde hair. All this, and she wanted to cook for him too.

'While you're busy here, I'll just . . .' He gestured upstairs.

'Fine.'

'I've got to make a couple of calls as well.'

'Just don't be too long.'

Then as he was leaving the room, 'Oh. I brought the mail up from downstairs when I got in.' She motioned towards a pile of envelopes. Glancing over it, Jones's attention was immediately attracted by a large padded envelope which had evidently been personally delivered. His name was printed on it in Larson's distinctive hand. Collecting the envelope, he continued on his way upstairs to his study where he closed the door, put the glass of whisky down on his desk, and turned to the video player in the corner. It must be the Alan Brent video. Larson's interrogation of the secret service spy. Fumbling with excitement, Jones ripped open the stapled envelope and seized the video inside. He was in so much of a hurry to watch it, he didn't notice that the envelope had been opened and re-stapled. The holes of the new staples matched, but not exactly, those of the originals.

He was soon watching the tape, which was indeed the interview of Alan Brent. He marvelled at the quality of the recording. Larson had done an extremely good job of it – the light and camera angle could hardly have been improved on. As Larson had already told him, Brent had been sweating like a pig while Larson strode about him, clad in black. His answers to Larson's questions were weak, evasive – and Larson had shown no mercy. Why had he tipped off the police about the Gallo operation? How long had he been an informant? Was he an undercover agent for the police or a secret service? Jones watched, utterly engrossed as Brent squirmed under pressure, rivulets of perspiration pouring down the sides of his face and neck, heavy spectacles repeatedly slipping down his nose.

Now Larson was beating Brent around the head. Brent's glasses had slipped off again, one time too many for Larson, who angrily flung them to the floor, stamping on them with the heel of his boot. Brent cried out in protest, only to be struck heavily across the face. His terror was visible after that. His already pallid features had gone white as a sheet and his lips were quivering with fear. Taking a sip of his single malt, Jones watched intently as Larson told Brent he'd been found guilty and was to be executed.

Jones had thought Larson would have switched off the video camera at that point. The agreed purpose of the taping had, after all, been to give Jones a chance to see how Brent reacted to questioning, to provide a second opinion on whether or not he posed a security threat. But events had got ahead of themselves. Now the video showed one of Larson's sidekicks armed with handcuffs and a sturdy rope. There was a final desperate struggle as Brent tried to flee – not that he had a hope in hell. Then he was being trussed up like an animal about to be put on the spit.

'Be grateful we're not cutting your tongue out first,' Larson said, quite audibly.

There was a chilling theatre to the hanging. Brent pleading, crying out for help, which earned him another crack across the face and a heavy knee to the stomach. Then they had taped his mouth up. He was forced to climb up on the execution chair, where the knot of the rope was carefully adjusted about his neck. When the chair was kicked out from under him, he fell with an unceremonious crack, and dangled, limp, from the end of the rope.

It was one of the most intensely engaging pieces of action he'd ever seen, thought Jones, taking another long gulp of Scotch, and switching the video player off, before collecting up his study phone and dialling the latest contact number Larson had given him.

In Helsinki, where he'd spent the evening pumping iron at the local gymnasium, Larson had just returned to his safe house, a small flat in a high-rise apartment block, when his phone rang. He checked the display for the number of the incoming call, before answering.

'You've seen the news?' asked Jones.

'We wanted Isis to end it,' the other replied, 'not Lefevre.'

'Exactly.' Larson's frustration with Berkeley Square was self-evident. Even so, Jones thought he should be explicit. 'There's still been no acknowledgement of animal testing, let alone a promise to change things. It's the most ruthless cover-up I've ever seen.'

'So what do we do now?' Larson asked, voice flat. 'Tell the AFL we have failed as badly as they did?'

Jones searched his pocket before pulling out his cigarettes. 'Oh, I don't think we have to do that just yet. There's also the Isis information.'

'What use is it to us now? She's no longer involved.'

'Then we'll just have to re-involve her.'

'You mean—'

'Quite simple, the way I see it.' Jones extracted a cigarette. 'She tells the truth about Berkeley Square, or we tell the truth about her.'

Larson thought about this for a moment. 'Sounds very simple,' he responded, eventually.

'The best ideas always are.' Jones lit up.

Larson realised Isis would be desperate to keep secret the dramatic revelations about her private life which Brent had discovered and he had subsequently confirmed. And with no further obligations to Berkeley Square, why shouldn't she come out and tell the world what was going on?

'Just imagine the headlines,' Jones prompted him. '"Isis condemns animal torture in Spain. Berkeley Square forced to close Madrid operations." *Then* we'll see the tables turned. All of a sudden Berkeley Square will be in the corner and then you'll see the media turn.'

'But what about our agreement?' Larson asked. 'Only to go for targets who are ultimately accountable?'

Jones had wondered if Larson would go there. It was a subject to which he'd already given serious thought.

'You're right to ask,' he said now. 'The way I see it, Isis and Jordan Hampshire might not be directly responsible for torture. But they are for joining the conspiracy to hide the truth about it. In my book, that amounts to the same thing.'

So absorbed was he in his conversation with Larson, Jones hadn't heard the creak on the landing as Gail made her way, barefoot, upstairs. He had no idea she'd been hovering outside his door, listening intently to his conversation. Though the moment he'd put the phone down, having discussed plans with Larson in detail, she'd returned downstairs, waiting for the sound of his study door to open before calling out, 'Would you like another drink, Jas?' She appeared at the bottom of the stairs, the bottle of Laphroaig in her hand.

Jones paused, glancing into his empty tumbler. 'That would be good.' He decided he did have something to celebrate – not that he was about to tell Gail. Far from being floored by Berkeley Square's tactical advantage, he'd persuaded Larson that while Lefevre had won a battle, he had yet to win the war.

'Actually,' he reached out for Gail's shoulders before she'd reached the top of the stairs, admiring all six feet of her pure, blonde perfection, 'there's something I'd like even more than another drink.' As he leaned to kiss her, she responded, trailing one hand down his front to his crotch.

'You've finished for this evening, then?' she whispered, putting down the bottle of whisky.

'Not quite.' Pulling the cord around her waist to unfasten the knot, he'd soon brushed the bathrobe off her shoulders so that it fell in a wreath of crimson about her bare feet. She stepped up beside him, a voracious expression on her face. Taking his glass and putting it on the carpet, she stood before him in her designer underwear and began unbuckling his belt. His breathing quickened as he looked down at where she was bending in front of him, the outlines of her beige nipples showing through the intricate pattern of black silk. Undoing the buttons of his trousers and tugging them down his legs, as she slipped under his final layer and took him in her hand, she met his eyes with a look of unabashed lust.

17

Los Angeles
Friday, 1 October

The fax came through on Isis's private fax line sometime between two and three in the morning. The fax machine was in the mixing room of her studio, downstairs and through two closed doors from her bedroom. A light sleeper, Isis was aware of the sound of paper feeding through the machine. But she didn't fully awaken. Having registered what the noise was, she simply went back to sleep. It wasn't unusual for her to get faxes overnight; GCM offices in London and Europe frequently sent over stuff. When she woke up the following morning, she didn't even remember that she'd heard it.

After too many nights of troubled sleep, the last two had been blissful; eight hours right through, with no tossing and turning waiting for sleep to come, no wakening in the middle of the night, unable to banish her fears till dawn. Jacques Lefevre had banished them for her. She would never forget his appearance on TV: there'd been an audible gasp of shock from the media corps, accompanied by a flurry of flash cameras as he'd appeared through the door of the Berkeley

Square boardroom. It was his first public appearance since the attack and he was dressed in a dark suit and wearing large black glasses, the bandages covering his eyes clearly visible beneath. Led to a microphone by his secretary, his steps had been slow and tentative. Once he'd been introduced, there was nothing faltering in his voice, however. In the briefest announcement, he outlined the One Commando threat against Isis and Jordan Hampshire, and explained that he had concluded that nothing could justify allowing a continued risk to their well-being.

All the world's media knew it was an admission of defeat. But Lefevre's tone had been one of defiance. He had implored police forces to use every means at their disposal to arrest One Commando. Never, he declared, had corporate Britain been so held to ransom by a small group of militant extremists. This was about more than simply the protection of a handful of individuals, or even one company. One only needed to visit Russia and other Eastern European states to see what happened when terrorism and blackmail were allowed into the economy; the preservation of the free market system was at stake.

It wouldn't have mattered what Lefevre said; his sheer presence, standing there in his black glasses and white bandages, was enough to evoke powerful feelings of sympathy and outrage. But his speech was stirring and impressive, spoken to a media corps which had been unnaturally silent, hanging on his every word.

And his words had a specially profound meaning for Isis. She watched, heart in her mouth, taking it all in with complete absorption. When the news item had finished, she'd raised her hands to her eyes, silent tears of relief and exhaustion trickling between her fingers. Her oppressive burden lifted, for the first time since signing the endorsement deal she'd felt free. Her own long, dark night, she thought, was over.

Since that release yesterday, she'd felt very different. She'd had her first 'normal' day in weeks. It had been like having her life back again.

She'd gone into Unum for a hastily arranged final recording session. Then on impulse, she'd booked a hair appointment and had Frank drive her to her favourite beauty salon for the full treatment; facial, manicure and massage. She'd just lost one and a half million dollars and she was going to have to be extremely persuasive next time she met the bank manager. But she also felt invigorated, renewed.

She'd set up a series of business meetings for today, Friday. She planned to spend time with her accountant, her lawyer, her financial adviser. But as it turned out, she never got to see them. Having dressed and put on her make up, she'd gone through to her office to get together the papers she needed for her meetings, when she noticed the fax on the machine. She picked it up. Although it took her only a few seconds to read, she stared at it as though in disbelief for a full half minute. Then she walked over to the telephone, picked it up and began dialling.

The worst had happened. The discovery she'd feared for her entire professional career had finally been made. And yet a curious calm had come over her – almost as though she was watching all this happen to somebody else.

Hilton had been finishing off a breakfast meeting at the Mondrian when her call came through. Hastily excusing himself, he stepped out of the room. Isis told him about the overnight fax, before reading it out: '"Tell the truth about Berkeley Square's animal testing,"' she read out, '"or we will tell the truth about you. You have forty-eight hours."'

But it was the two words at the top of the page which

carried the impact. Two words pointing to the secret she'd successfully kept hidden from view for the past eighteen years. One Commando had found it out and now there seemed no escaping from it.

At the other end of the phone Hilton paused, deep in thought, considering the situation before Isis murmured, 'Just when I thought it had gone away. But it's never really gone away, has it? Not from the day I started out.'

'You're right,' he answered, realising that denial would serve no purpose, 'it has always been a possibility.'

In her sitting room she turned to face the sea. 'After all that's happened these past few weeks, I just wish I could lose myself. I don't feel I can cope with this any more—'

'You've done exactly the right thing calling me,' he said. Having reached a decision, his voice was now charged with resolve. 'And this is something we're going to handle together.'

She was still in a state of shock, he realised. Probably still anaesthetised to the full force of the news. That would hit her later. In the meantime, it seemed to him they now had only one remaining option, one last resort; he had to make sure she didn't do anything to blow it.

'There's just no end to it!' she was saying. 'Every time we close a door, they find another way in. And now the genie's out of the bottle.'

'It isn't yet,' he was firm.

'You think I should make a statement about Berkeley Square?'

'Even if they did test on animals, which they don't, you can't give in to blackmailers. They'd only come back for you.'

'Then what . . . what am I to do?'

'Last time I was in London,' Hilton's tone was serious,

'when they had me all bound up and lying on the bed, I thought – this is it. End of the line. There's no way I'm going to get out of this. But,' he paused, significantly, 'I *did* escape. I got out unhurt. The secret service agent in One Commando tipped off the police. I was only moments away from serious injury or death. But it wasn't allowed to happen.'

'The point being?'

'The point being that with an MI5 guy active in One Commando it's way too soon to give up. He saved me from . . . a fate worse than death. We can count on him to make sure this information about you stays under wraps.'

'We can?' She was distracted.

'Yes. I'm calling the British Home Office right away.'

Within moments of Hilton getting back to his office, Elizabeth had placed the call on his behalf. She'd been right in thinking her boss knew Peter Campbell. The two had attended an image management conference in Berne several years earlier, and had kept in occasional contact ever since. Not that she expected Campbell to do Hilton any favours; his reputation as an information control freak preceded him.

'Peter Campbell's on his way to a cocktail function at Downing Street,' she told him before putting through the call. 'I managed to track down his car phone number with Hanniford's help.'

'Thanks,' Hilton's face was sharply etched with worry, 'put him through.'

'Peter, its Hilton Gallo from GCM, Los Angeles. Francis Hanniford suggested we call you.'

'Ah, the Berkeley Square issue.' Fresh from a party to celebrate four years in power, and seated in the back of the Home Secretary's chauffeured Daimler, his spin-doctor, resplendent in an evening suit and sipping a glass of hot water with a twist of lemon, was his customary acerbic self.

'We need to know what progress is being made on One Commando,' continued Hilton. 'Scotland Yard are telling us nothing.'

'Procedural guidelines,' responded the other.

'And in the meantime, my client, Isis, is under threat.'

'But I was given to believe,' Campbell was puzzled, 'that the endorsement matter was settled?'

'Berkeley Square walked away from it – only because One Commando are still at large.' Hilton was firm. 'Now they're trying to blackmail Isis into supporting their ridiculous claims about animal testing. They have uncovered personal infor-mation about her which they're threatening to release. They must be stopped.'

Campbell blew on his glass of hot water thoughtfully, before replying, 'Regrettably, Hilton, neither the Met nor Interpol have reported any great progress. Larson and his cohorts are highly mobile and extremely difficult to detect given their constant changes of disguise and identity.'

'But what about Intelligence?' At the other end, Hilton found his frustration hard to conceal.

'Rear-view mirror stuff. Very little that's predictive.'

'Surely your agent can give you a steer?'

'Agent?' queried the other.

'Your undercover agent!' Hilton was exasperated. 'The MI5 guy.'

'I'm not sure I understand.'

'Francis Hanniford has already told us,' Hilton's tone was weary, 'there's no need to keep up this charade.'

'What charade?'

'I personally was attacked by these thugs—' his voice rose in anger, 'now my client is directly at risk—'

'Look, Hilton,' Campbell audibly pulled rank, 'I can assure

you there is no obfuscation going on from my side. Let me be quite categorical about this. There is no intelligence agent working inside One Commando.'

Hilton was shaking his head. 'But Francis Hanniford told us—'

'If dear old Francis has chosen to believe that, it's very much his affair. He's never brought the subject up with me or I would have put him straight.'

Hilton's unusual display of anger turned into an even more extraordinary desperation. 'But there's *got* to be an agent,' he insisted, 'who else tipped off the police when they tried to attack me?'

'That's something being investigated. It certainly wasn't Intelligence.'

'Are you saying,' he was finding all this too incredible to believe, 'there has never been an agent?'

'That's exactly what I'm saying.'

'And you're no closer now to apprehending One Commando than you were after the Lefevre attack?'

'Regrettably, no.'

'So what in God's name are we supposed to be doing?'

'That's really not for me to advise.' In the back of the Daimler, Campbell took another sip of his lemon water. 'All I would say is that we are dealing here with extremely dangerous criminals.'

When Hilton ended, he sank his head into his hands. Across the desk from him, having listened to every word of his conversation, Elizabeth felt, by turns, guilt and a rising nausea. It was she who'd originally been misled by Hanniford into believing in the existence of a secret service operation. Hanniford had seemed so certain, so confident. Now she realised how much of GCM's strategy had been founded on a fundamental error.

'No agent?' Her voice was barely a whisper.

Hilton shook his head without looking up.

'When Isis finds out—'

'She can't,' Hilton looked up, directly into her eyes. She didn't know if it was undisguised anger or ferocious determination in that gaze – but she knew he must not be crossed.

'If we tell her, we take away her hope.' His eyes bored into hers. 'And that's all she has left.'

Mark emerged from the swimming pool of his Beverly Hills home, seizing a beach towel from a nearby chair and drying himself briskly, before squeezing the water from his hair. He'd never thought of himself as a keep-fit fanatic. But this morning as soon as he woke up he knew he needed to do something, anything, to burn off the nervous energy he felt building up inside him.

Ever since his row with Hilton he'd been edgy and uptight. In spite of Lefevre's announcing that the Berkeley Square deal was off he'd felt in his gut that he hadn't heard the last of One Commando. There was just too much going on. For one thing, what was this 'background' of Isis's and why wouldn't they tell him? What would Vinnie do with the rug pulled out from under him by Lefevre? And the biggest puzzler of all: why was One Commando so convinced that Berkeley Square tested on animals, when the rest of the world accepted they didn't?

Lloyd had paid an unsolicited call on AFL offices posing as a potential recruit, and picked up anything and everything they'd ever published on Berkeley Square. He'd given the handful of fliers to Mark when he'd dropped him off at Heathrow on Monday night.

'Take a look at these,' he'd suggested, 'interesting reading.'

The photos were disturbing all right. Close-ups of rabbits, scarcely recognisable with their shaven fur, inflamed eyes and bodies punctured with tubes and needles. The pictures of chimpanzees were even worse – Mark found himself averting his gaze from the scenes of grotesque cruelty. Around these images, the accusations were equally sensational; all these photographs had been taken inside the laboratories of Berkeley Square's Research and Development unit, located in an industrial suburb of Madrid. An unnamed AFL activist gave a full, first-person account of his visit to the facility, including how he'd circumvented lax security measures, getting close enough to shoot dozens of photographs.

A different leaflet comprised first-hand interviews with former workers from the plant. Photographed in silhouette to protect their anonymity, in every case they had left the laboratory as soon as they had been transferred to the animal testing unit, nauseated by the systematic mass suffering inflicted on animals.

Taken as a whole, the evidence seemed compelling. Photographs, interviews – plus there was a video, Mark knew. Could it really all be just a hoax, he wondered? If so, what sick kind of individual would spend hours faking photographs of animal torture, and making up horror stories? And why pick on Berkeley Square? None of it made any sense.

Lloyd had also picked up stuff from Berkeley Square, like glossy brochures devoted to Berkeley Square R & D. Flicking it open, he encountered the genial face of Dr Andrew Craig, Head of Research and Development, described as an eminent bio-pharmacist, who'd formerly held senior positions in several major pharmaceutical companies as well as serving on British Government advisory committees. His introduction to the brochure was upbeat without being self-important, describing methodologies used by Berkeley

Square as 'leading edge' and emphasising the principled nature of the company's policies on genetic modification and other contentious issues. 'It is a source of personal pride', he noted, 'that Berkeley Square's laboratories in Madrid are not only at the very forefront of technological development, but that the Company's endeavours are informed by an enlightened philosophy of corporate responsibility and ethical leadership.'

Looking from the AFL leaflets to the Berkeley Square stuff and back again, for a long while Mark wondered what to make of it. Either Berkeley Square had succeeded in putting up an elaborate smokescreen, he decided eventually, or One Commando were motivated by reasons which just seemed inexplicable.

Now as he headed back up to the house, he found Mrs Martinez in the kitchen preparing a late breakfast. A full English fry-up would be ready in half an hour, she told him. In the meantime, he decided to check out his internet access to the OmniCell computer on which all Vinnie's telephone conversations were being recorded. Wouldn't do any harm keeping tabs.

In the study he logged on, quickly finding his way to the address Lloyd had given him, and entering the security passwords they'd agreed. A file log opened up showing that since the chip had been installed, Vinnie had made no fewer than forty-seven calls! Taking a swig of his beer, Mark wondered wearily if it was even worth trawling through them. Clicking open the first one, he was surprised, however, by the quality of the recording. All of a sudden his study was filled with a call Vinnie had evidently made from his car, after leaving the Lamb two nights ago, warning the manager of some club he could be slightly late – he'd been with an important client. Yeah, yeah, thought Mark, pull the other one. He didn't recognise the manager's voice, but the music in the background was Metallica and the recording was so clear he could even hear Vinnie shifting gear. He read the time label – 8.28 p.m., Monday, 27 September.

Mark found to his relief that by simply moving the cursor down the page, he could click open the next message without having to listen to all of the first. And it didn't take long to assess if a call was going to be of any interest. He wasn't surprised to confirm that most of Vinnie's conversations were purely social, with a few business calls thrown in. But the fourteenth call was very different. It was an incoming call. And as soon as he heard the accent he knew it could only be one person. The conversation, at nine-thirty a.m. this morning, London time, was brief:

Larson: I am putting you on standby.

Vinnie: (*Bitterly*) Oh, yeah? Like there's still something happening.

Larson: Why shouldn't there be?

Vinnie: Berkeley Square have pulled out! It's all over the papers!

Larson: They can't walk away from it as easy as that. There's still no admission of guilt.

Vinnie: You're the only one who seems to think they're guilty.

Larson: (*Growing heated*) How can I deny what I've seen with my own eyes?

Vinnie: They've cancelled the endorsement so I don't see what you've got on them now.

Larson: Let's just say I have some very powerful material on one of our targets. Information that's been kept hidden for many years and would be highly damaging if it came to light . . . (*Dryly*) . . . as

damaging as if the truth is told about Berkeley
Square.

Vinnie: You must be talking about Isis. But it's not her
that interests me, mate. It's that fuckhead, 'Jordan
Hampshire'.

Larson: (*After a long pause*) Believe me, if there's no Isis,
there'll be no 'Jordan Hampshire'. And there'll
be no Isis after this.

Minutes later Mark was sitting in the back of the Lincoln.
He ordered Denzil to get out to Malibu immediately. He
didn't care what he did. How many speeding tickets he
picked up. Just get the hell out there as soon as he could.
Unlike the last piece of information he'd got on One
Commando, this time he wasn't trusting it to Hilton. There
weren't going to be any delayed reactions or PR spin. This
time he'd make sure Isis got it straight. The recorded conversation with Larson was all he needed to know that Isis and
he were caught up in something that went way beyond an
endorsement. As much as he was attracted to her, he wasn't
going to let her take him for a fool. There was another whole
dimension to this, something that Isis and Hilton were
concealing. But the time for game-playing was over. He
needed to know, right now, just what the hell was going on.

Isis was alone in her sitting room when he arrived, and
she'd looked up in surprise when Juanita showed him into
the room.

'One Commando have got something on you and they're
threatening to use it,' he told Isis urgently, the moment they
were left alone.

'Hilton spoke to you?' she queried.

Mark stopped in his tracks. 'No. I found out myself. Less
than an hour ago.'

Isis turned away. She was more traumatised by the fax earlier that day than by anything that had happened during her entire singing career, and the timing of Mark's visit couldn't have been worse.

'It happened this morning,' she told him.

'What happened?'

'The blackmail,' her voice was taut. 'It's not good enough that we're no longer endorsing Berkeley Square products. Now they want us to tell the world that Berkeley Square tortures animals. If we don't, they're threatening to release information.'

So events had already overtaken them, thought Mark. All the more reason he should know the whole truth.

'What information, exactly?' He stepped closer towards where she was sitting.

She averted her eyes. 'Personal stuff. Stuff about me.'

'You mean, the stuff you and Hilton don't want me to know about?'

When she didn't answer he continued, 'It's not just about you. It's about me, too.'

She flashed an irritated glance. 'What *are* you talking about?'

'About our CD, Isis. And about my career.' He met her eyes and held them as he tried to reason. 'I've moved countries for it. I quit my job for it. I've put everything into it and now it's being threatened. I think I have the right to know—'

'The right?' she demanded, rising from the sofa. 'Don't lecture me about rights. Nothing, and I mean *nothing* gives you the *right* to meddle in my private life!'

'I'm not talking about *meddling*!' The sudden heat of her anger made him resentful. 'I just want to *know*—'

'And I'm telling you you can't know!' she told him. 'My private life remains private!'

Their eyes locked in blazing exchange before he lashed out. 'Just as bad as Hilton, aren't you?' he was furious. 'Keeping me in the dark—'

'That's not true!'

'"Managing information",' he taunted.

His criticism stung – because she knew it to be true. But what choice did she have? She couldn't tell him now, in a moment of crisis. If she told him, she'd spend the rest of her life wondering if he could keep the secret.

'I've done a lot for Hilton and you. Changed my name. My appearance. I've played along with the sham romance. I didn't want any of that. And you're quite happy to take, take, take—'

'I don't have to listen to any more of this!' Isis marched past him towards the door.

'Spent your whole career running away from the truth, have you?'

'You know what the problem with you is?' At the door she wheeled round with an accusatory gesture. 'You're out of your depth. Out of your league. You're like a small boy in short pants with no idea what you're into.'

'Oh yeah?' Mark shouted after her receding figure, 'And what about you, Isis? Tagging me along and dumping me when it suits you! All your fans might think you're something special, but I know different – I know better! When it comes down to it, you're nothing but the bitch from hell!'

18

Moments later, Mark heard the door to her bedroom wing slam shut. Standing alone in the lounge, after she'd stormed out, he trembled with rage. How dare she treat him like this? After the lengths he'd gone to – for both their sakes – trying to get a fix on One Commando. And this was his reward!

The very last thing he'd have expected was a reaction like this. And the news that One Commando had already issued a blackmail fax had taken him completely by surprise. What did it all mean? If One Commando was intent on blackmail, why had Larson put Vinnie on standby? And surely the secret service agent inside One Commando must know what this information was? Most of all, Mark just wanted to know what they had on Isis that was supposed to be so threatening.

He paced up and down the sitting room for some time, thoughts in turmoil, trying to make sense of the senseless. Gradually he began to calm down. 'My private life remains private,' he mused. She was terrified about whatever it was coming to light. The fax from One Commando must have come as a huge shock. Even though he felt completely justified in wanting to know what was going on, he began to wonder if he should have handled things differently. Maybe he could have been more sympathetic? Perhaps he needed to make more of an effort to understand what was going on in her head?

Hoping to make amends, Mark set off along the passage in the direction of the bedrooms. He'd never been down this end of the house before and didn't really know what was there, except bedrooms and a staircase leading down to Isis's basement studio. Reaching the bedroom wing door, he knocked loudly, but receiving no response, opened it and continued. On the right side of the corridor, a series of windows gave panoramic views of the ocean, while rooms led off to the left – a couple that seemed to be guest rooms, then Holly's, then a master suite he took to be Isis's. Yet again receiving no reply to his knocking, he put his head round the open door of the bedroom and found it empty.

Continuing further down the corridor he came to a small sitting room – evidently her personal retreat. In contrast to the opulence of her main sitting room, this place was decorated with rustic simplicity – deep red walls, kilim-style rugs and rattan furniture including a large cushioned armchair drawn over to a balcony overlooking the sea. There was still no sign of Isis. Glancing about the room, Mark took in the carelessly scattered cushions, the basket of seashells, the pine shelves cluttered with silver-framed photographs, mostly of Holly. There was a row of books too, including the Betty Bailey biography of Isis, together with a selection of music and showbiz titles and some fiction. A large, wide tome with 'ISIS' running in glitzy capitals down the side stuck out from the others; curious, he pulled it out, discovering it was a photo album of her *Aphrodisia* world tour, specially presented to her by GCM.

He was about to slip it back on to the shelf, when he noticed behind the first row was a second line of books. He could see a few of the titles: *Child Abuse in America: Fact v. Fiction*; *A Sob in the Dark: Coping with Physical and Emotional Abuse*; *Why Hurt People Hurt People*. Instead of putting back the Isis book, he leaned over and lifted out *Journey out of Darkness – A Manual for Self-Realisation*. The book fell open on its title page, on which he found a dedication written, in an elegant hand, at the front: 'For Isis – Never forget: As you think, so you become. With sincere good wishes, Dr Robert Weiner, Salmacis Hospital.'

Staring down at the book, Mark flicked through its pages. It felt wrong to be nosing around in this way but neither Hilton nor Isis would tell him anything. Perhaps this book was the key. The hidden books all pointed to the same subject, and as he glanced at the chapter headings of *Journey out of Darkness* he wondered if he'd discovered something of significance. Then something slipped out from between the pages of the book and fell to the floor. He leaned down to collect a single-page letter. It was written on fine bond paper, yellowed and brittle with age, and signed 'Mom'. As he picked it up a few phrases caught his eye: *I know I have failed you . . . tried to keep your father from you . . . recover from surgery.*

'What the hell d'you think you're doing in here!'

Mark jumped back guiltily and looked up to find Isis striding down the passage towards him.

'I came looking for you.' It sounded unconvincing as he said it. 'I thought we should—'

Isis was already upon him, grabbing the book and letter from his hands and pointing to the door. 'Get out!' she demanded, mighty with rage.

'Isis! We're both in this together!'

'Just get out of my house!' She pointed to the door. 'And don't you ever, *ever* let me find you in here again!'

London
Friday, 1 October

DCs Brewer and White had received a reply from Records, and soon discovered more about the restraint order, now eight years old, against Alan George Brent. According to the terms of the court order, Brent was forbidden from going within one hundred yards of any Berkeley Square building, director, or senior executive. The homes of a number of executives were also included in the ban.

The moment DC White saw Berkeley Square on the printout, he hurried through to report to DS Morris who, in turn, contacted DI Bennett. Bennett instructed Morris to check Brent's home, while he pursued other lines of enquiry. As soon as he hung up from speaking to Morris, Bennett picked up the phone to Berkeley Square's Human Resources Director, Francis Hanniford.

'Mr Hanniford, it's DI Bennett, Scotland Yard,' he announced himself. 'During the course of our enquiries, we have come across someone who we have reason to believe may be involved in One Commando activities against your company. Does the name Alan Brent mean anything to you?'

At the other end of the line, Hanniford groaned.

Brent's house had only one bell. There was no response when the policemen rang, not from Brent's place nor from either of the neighbours. They decided to break in through the bay window at the front. It was standard, covert police procedure; easy to get into, and no trouble to repair. Using the roll of thick, sticky paper and the collapsible steel baton they'd brought specially for the purpose, they soon rolled over the glass, and smashed round the edges of the window before removing the paper and hauling themselves through the now-open frame.

They found themselves in a large front room which, in most homes in the area, would have been used as either a lounge or a large bedroom. This one though was piled from floor to ceiling with brown cardboard boxes. They were neatly arranged with code numbers written in thick black pen on the outside of each box, as well as a month and a year. Some of the dates went back over ten years, noticed DC Brewer. Squeezing through the narrow space between rows of boxes, the policemen made their way into the main corridor leading through the flat, opening the door into another room which proved to be similarly stacked with boxes. DC White led the way through to a kitchen and bath-room – even these rooms had been turned into warehous-ing. Raising his eyebrows he murmured, 'Expensive storage facility. Rents for two-bedroom flats in this area are anything from two hundred a week up.'

DC Brewer was already unfolding the flaps of a cardboard box on the floor beside him. When he'd got it open, he let out a low whistle. DC White soon made his way over. Inside there appeared to be a pile of publications, the top one a pornographic magazine – X-Cess – its cover a lurid portrait of two women dressed in black latex, squatting above a man who was manacled and spreadeagled in what looked like a sado-masochist torture chamber. Lifting up the magazine, Brewer found more editions of X-Cess – in fact, the box was packed full of them. The two detectives quickly carried out random checks of other cardboard boxes in the room, and in other rooms of the downstairs flat. It soon became apparent that all of them contained hard-core pornography, magazines and videos going back more than a decade.

Climbing upstairs to the upper flat, past shelves stacked with yet more cardboard boxes, they called out several times before forcing their way through the locked door. Making their way inside, it was only to encounter yet more rooms of brown cardboard boxes, stacked from floor to ceiling.

In silence, the two detectives surveyed the kitchen, a squalid mess of fast-food cartons and condiments, before ascending the final flight of stairs to the attic room. There they discovered a double bed shoved into one corner, a creased, grey duvet flung to one side to reveal stained yellow sheets. On one side of the bed was a digital alarm clock with a red button that flashed every second. DC White wrinkled his nose as he glanced from the bed to the clothes strewn across the floor, a few stashed in a black bin liner which evidently served as a washing bag. Other clothes and belongings had been discarded carelessly on a threadbare carpet. A torn leather sofa and lava lamp gave the place the feel of a student dive that had been caught in a time-warp. Several empty bottles of vodka and cans of Sprite lined up beside the sofa confirmed the impression.

But the other end of the room was a different matter entirely. The whole facing wall was a mass of electronic equipment, the purpose of which was suggested by the tangle of wires leading from them to a row of five telephone sockets in the wall. A black, imitation-ash desk sagged under the weight of further equipment – scanners, a printer, fax machines and modems, all co-ordinated through a state-of-the-art keyboard and monitor.

DC White turned to his colleague. 'Quite a set-up he had here,' he mused.

'We'll have to dust the place for prints.' Brewer was more

cautious about confirming this as the home address of the murder victim they'd found in Olympia.

The other shrugged, 'Yeah, yeah. Classic underground porn operation. I've seen this kind of thing before, down the East End.' He gave Brewer the benefit of his extra years of experience. 'They assemble more electronic equipment than you can shake a stick at, then steal mountains of videos and photos from other internet operators and load it on to their own sites.'

Brewer glanced about him in surprise. 'You mean one bloke can run the whole thing out of his bedroom.'

'Technically speaking,' the other nodded, 'but you'll probably find he was just an agent for a larger underground set-up.'

Glancing at a pile of 'First Fist' videos, DC Brewer thought aloud, 'Wonder if there's any kiddy stuff in here.'

'Doubt it.' White was opening a desk drawer, rummaging through the contents. 'Mainstream operators don't tend to get mixed up with paedophile rings. Don't need to. Can cash up big time without going so high-risk.'

'So why d'you think he was strung up?'

'That, old son, is one of life's great mysteries.' Then, enigmatically, 'My guess is that it had nothing to do with his . . . money-making activities.' He glanced about with a caustic expression.

White had opened a desk drawer and was flicking through some of Alan Brent's papers, while Brewer looked about the room more closely. Behind a ceiling-high wall of boxes, Brewer found a filing cabinet and quickly had it open. The Berkeley Square files were meticulously ordered at the back of the second drawer. They included a company organisational chart, showing its different divisions, with photographs of the executives in charge. Several of these had been

circled in red, including Jacques Lefevre's. Calling out to
White, Brewer looked through the other files. Brent had an
'assassination list' of half a dozen Berkeley Square executives. Further information on each target included all contact
details including home addresses. The two policemen
exchanged a wordless glance before collecting up all the files
from the cabinet, bagging them carefully, and heading back
for the police station. There, they reported to DS Morris.

'Looks like our Alan Brent ran an underground porn operation on the Net,' White told his boss when the three of
them were in his office, behind closed doors. 'Unbelievable
operation. Three floors of hard porn.'

'What about Berkeley Square?' Morris was impatient.

'Found an assassination list.' Brewer gestured to the bulge
of files. 'Berkeley Square corporate structure. The lot. No
doubt he wanted to persuade his lords and masters to settle
a few old scores.'

Morris raised his eyebrows. 'Now we've got Bennett and
the whole of Scotland Yard breathing down our necks.'

'So what's the story with Brent and Berkeley Square?'
asked White.

'Former employee. Seems he was recruited by the
company to develop an IT idea he dreamed up at university
– some sort of allergy diagnoses using a computer. After a
few years, when the program was about to be marketed, he
and Berkeley Square had a falling out over who owned it.
He said the idea was his, but Berkeley Square held the patent
and collected all the cash.'

'Did he take it to court?'

'Tried to. His lawyers told him to settle out of court – he
didn't have a case. Berkeley Square paid out a hundred grand
in goodwill.'

Brewer's eyebrows twitched.

'Brent wanted more. He started threatening directors. Phoning them at home in the middle of the night – that sort of thing. Which is when they slapped the restraining order on him.'

'And he signed up with One Commando?'

'Seems so.' He paused before continuing, 'Bennett's convinced One Commando hanged him.'

'Motive?' asked Brewer.

'Round his neck,' shrugged Morris. '"Spy". They may have thought he tipped off Scotland Yard about Gallo. Maybe they were worried that his day job would compromise their activities.'

'Doubtful.' White was shaking his head. 'He still wanted to get One Commando to go for his own targets in Berkeley Square.'

While DC White exchanged a thoughtful expression with his boss, it was young Brewer who scratched his head. 'But, sir, if Alan Brent didn't tip off Scotland Yard,' he asked, 'then who did?'

Helsinki
Friday, 1 October

'What if they don't say anything?' demanded Larson. It was coming up for twenty-four hours since he'd faxed the demand note to Los Angeles and there had still been no response. Not so much as a word from either Isis or Jordan Hampshire on the subject of animal rights abuse by Berkeley Square.

'That's something we need to take very seriously,' replied Jones, who'd taken care to close his study door when Larson came through on the mobile. Gail was along the corridor in the bathroom, getting ready for a dinner party to which they'd both been invited.

Larson digested Jones's observation in silence. Persuasive though he believed his demand idea had been, ever since he'd sent the fax to Isis from a cellular telephone, he'd found himself wondering – what if they refused to play ball? What if they said nothing at all? Now he told Jones, 'I want to make a plan of action if we don't hear from them by the end of the deadline.'

'Sensible,' nodded Jones, slipping a hand in the pocket of his red dressing-gown as he paced the semi-darkness of his study.

'I can drop an envelope off to the local Reuters office. In an hour the whole world will know the truth about Isis.'

'An interesting thought.' Jones paused, meeting his own eyes, reflected in a gilt-framed mirror, with a hard stare. 'But what would that do for the cause?'

At the other end, Larson hadn't anticipated this reaction. 'I thought the whole point of the information was—'

'To trade a truth for a truth,' interjected Jones. 'But if, like Monsieur Lefevre, they find themselves incapable of telling the truth, then I would suggest we are left with only one alternative.'

As Larson absorbed this he added, 'If I can make a suggestion, Bengt, it is that we consider playing from our strengths. We've tried reason. We've done our utmost to persuade them. Maybe it's time, again, to do what we do best.'

Larson stared out of the window of the high-rise apartment, to where the sun was still high on the horizon even though it was eight in the evening. It was a long while before he spoke, but when he eventually did, it was in that tone of sardonic certainty that had drawn Jones to him at the very beginning.

'Yes,' mused Larson, 'I would enjoy a bit of foreign travel.'

Los Angeles
Friday, 1 October

Staff at GCM had never seen Hilton Gallo so agitated. Their CEO's legendary serenity had turned out not to be disaster-proof after all – but no one knew the reason for his current disquiet. Elizabeth Reynolds knew the discovery that there wasn't an MI5 agent working inside One Commando after all had a lot to do with it. And she felt a heavy burden of responsibility for having passed on Francis Hanniford's assumption that there was an agent as a statement of fact. But she knew that there was something else troubling Hilton; something had happened out at Malibu he wasn't telling her about.

Instead, he'd summoned Leo Lebowitz to his office. As Lebowitz made his way through Elizabeth's office, he'd raised his eyebrows. She shook her head. 'I'm out of the loop on this one,' she admitted, as he knocked on Hilton's door and walked in.

Inside, Hilton was pacing up and down by the windows.

'You guys have worked out some options?' he demanded, the moment Lebowitz appeared.

The other nodded. 'Dusted down the crisis strategy we worked out years ago for just this kind of eventuality. We're pretty much boxed into reactive mode.'

'Reactive? Shouldn't we be out there doing something?'

Lebowitz regarded his boss's agitation with concern. He'd never seen Hilton so perturbed.

'Very simply, we have two options in dealing with the media,' he began to explain, deliberately calm. 'The first is to hunker down in reactive mode – which isn't to say we do nothing, but we keep all the action under the surface. We prepare for a revelation of the full facts and have all our ammunition prepared and targeted in case we need it. The

second option is to go proactive. Get the news out ourselves
on the basis that we *theoretically* have more spin control.'
He held Hilton's gaze steadily. 'Now, we can go that route,
sure, but I would very, very strongly advise against it. Too
high risk,' he said, shrugging. 'What if it turns out One
Commando don't have the full story?'

'They've got enough,' countered Hilton, 'they could work
out the rest.'

'Maybe. Maybe not. I know it's tenuous, but what if they
don't know the significance of the discovery themselves?'

'Leo, please. Remember who we're dealing with.'

'Or what if', Lebowitz persisted, 'Interpol close down One
Commando before they've had a chance to get the story
out.'

Again, Hilton was shaking his head. 'Cloud cuckoo land.'

'The point being that once we've gone out with the story,
we can't reel it back in.' He paused, looking over to where
Hilton was staring out of the window, 'There's a terrible
finality to it. We can't unsay what's been said. Ever. And
the benefit of getting this particular story out ourselves is
marginal to say the least. The basic facts are sensational
enough before journalists even get—'

'Do we have to put out . . . the whole story?'

Lebowitz was shaking his head. 'It's the whole story or it's
nothing. We can't go out with a fudge. That would be court-
ing disaster.'

'Surely there must be a sympathy card?'

'Believe me, Hilton, if the need arises we've got the full
sympathy *pack* to play, but the only way it'll work is if the
other side put out the story first.'

'The other side.' Hilton was shaking his head. 'If . . .' then
shrugging, 'when One Commando put the story out, just
how bad d'you think the damage will be?'

Lebowitz nodded. 'I've put just that question into research this morning. The panel results so far aren't looking good. In fact, they're terrible. We're getting a strong sense of disappointment about the lack of trust . . .'

Hilton was following him intensely, Lebowitz's words seeming to affect him viscerally.

'What that research doesn't take into account—' he started.

'I know,' Lebowitz nodded, 'it's different when it's for real. But even allowing for all that,' he sighed heavily, 'it's the very worst piece of news that could come out prior to a record launch. There wouldn't be anything of a record launch left.'

Lebowitz's words were heavy with significance; it was as though with every word he spoke, Hilton was diminished. Folding his arms against the back of a sofa, Hilton leaned down to rest his head against it.

'Can't you give me anything, Leo?'

Lebowitz knew he must not allow Hilton any illusions.

'All the feedback I'm getting is that if the full story comes to light,' he hesitated only slightly, 'it's curtains for Isis, and for Jordan Hampshire,' he exhaled heavily, 'over before it began.'

19

—

London
Friday, 1 October

Vinnie wasn't sure this was the right bloke, to begin with. They'd agreed to meet outside the open-air theatre in Regent's Park at one-fifteen p.m. Hurrying along a path, he spotted the figure sitting on the bench, reading that day's copy of the *Financial Times*, as he'd said he would be. Right place, right time, thought Vinnie, but something about the man he was due to meet struck him as odd. Wearing chichi sunglasses and a designer suit under an elegant Burberry, he wasn't anything like Alexander Heindl. Vinnie had been imagining someone a lot bigger and tougher and more military in appearance. This guy looked like a yuppie.

As he approached him, his footsteps were less certain. The other man looked up.

'Vinnie Dobson?'

'That's right.' Vinnie paused, hesitant.

Then the other man was getting up from the park bench. 'Let's take a walk. Hedges have ears.'

He was only half-joking, thought Vinnie, glancing at the thick bushes behind him. There was something very earnest about this guy. Intense.

'I've heard a lot about you,' Jasper Jones said now as they made their way among the lunch-time strollers in Regent's Park.

'From Alexander Heindl?'

Jones paused a moment before replying, 'Yes. From Alexander. He tells me you've been very helpful.'

Vinnie had no idea where this was leading. He didn't know why this bloke wanted to meet him and was irked at being ordered across town on some mystery mission. No sooner had Heindl told him about this guy, than the man had phoned himself to set up the meeting.

'So you're about to go to America?'

'So Alexander keeps saying.'

His irritation didn't escape Jones. They walked on a few more yards before he asked, 'Looking forward to it?'

Vinnie thought about Mark making all that money – a multi-millionaire overnight. Plus he was screwing Isis into the bargain. The prick thought he'd got away with it. Like he could just turn his back, cut Vinnie out of the deal and everything would be hunky dory.

'Oh, yeah,' Vinnie turned to Jones, 'very much.'

The other smiled. 'Good,' he murmured. 'Good.' Then, pausing, he turned to face Vinnie. 'Tell me, what are you looking forward to most of all?'

Vinnie shook his head. 'Getting that prick Watson.'

'That's Jordan Hampshire's real name is it?'

'Yeah.'

'And you used to be his manager?'

'Damned right I was.'

'What have you got against him?'

'Did the dirty on me, didn't he? I was his manager for years, right? Worked hard to get him known on the local circuit. Then along comes GCM and their recording deal with Isis and that's it. Kaput.'

'But you can't blame him for accepting a deal like that.'

'I can blame him for cutting me out of it.'

'You mean, you didn't get—'

'Not a bloody thing,' Vinnie snorted. 'They cut me out completely.'

'How much do you think you should have been paid?'

'Three hundred and fifty grand, maybe more.'

Jones raised his eyebrows. 'That's a lot of money.'

'You're not joking, mate.'

'Surely,' he regarded Vinnie intently, 'you should be taking legal action.'

'Get real!' snorted Vinnie. 'What chance do I have against GCM?'

'There's legal aid available.'

Vinnie was shaking his head vigorously. Whose side was this bloke on anyway? 'Too complicated for that.'

'But surely a contract is a contract. If Jordan Hampshire broke the terms—'

'That's the whole point. We didn't have a contract, did we?' whined Vinnie. It was the first time he'd admitted it to anybody, but it didn't matter so much telling this bloke who he'd never even met before.

'You managed his business affairs, but you didn't have a contract?' the other was incredulous.

'Not written down or anything. What we had was a gentleman's agreement. An understanding.'

'Has he offered to pay you—'

'Nothing.'

'No form of . . . compensation?'

'Nothing!' Vinnie repeated, louder. He could feel the

anger building up in him. The violent, all-consuming hatred which came to him every time he thought about Mark Watson. And something in this bloke's manner gave him the feeling that the other wanted to know just how mad he was right now with his famous former client.

Jones regarded Dobson's visibly rising anger with satisfaction. His face was colouring and fury coming into his eyes. All he needed was a gentle push.

'Tell me,' he asked Dobson in a sympathetic tone, 'how do you feel about Jordan Hampshire right now?'

'How am I supposed to feel?' Vinnie exploded. 'After all he's done to me I hate the prick! He's stabbed me in the back. Stolen my money. He's turned my life into a fucking nightmare!'

Jones nodded encouragingly. 'And seeing that he hasn't paid you money you feel is rightfully yours . . . ?'

'He's going to pay for it all right,' Vinnie menaced. 'I'm going over to LA and One Commando will be right behind me. They'll get that son of a bitch and by the time they're finished with him and Isis they'll both wish they'd never even heard of GCM!'

'What are you planning to do to them?'

'You'll have to ask Alexander Heindl that, but you know what happened to that French bloke?' He smirked. 'That was just the warm-up.'

Less than fifteen minutes later, Jones left Regent's Park alone, heading in the direction of Marylebone Road, while Vinnie Dobson made towards Baker Street. Slipping his hand in the pocket of his Burberry, Jones felt the video recorder stashed in his pocket and turned it off, before removing the cord that led from the back of his overcoat to the camera concealed behind his glasses. A most productive session, he thought, strolling the short distance to the main road, and waiting for a cab heading east. Dobson had been an easy turn. Larson had primed him well for the meeting and he hadn't held back. It was all there: the motivation, the planning, but most of all the emotion, turbulent, vindictive, in your face – and nothing whatever to do with the cause of animal liberation.

Beverly Hills

Mark spent most of the car trip back to Beverly Hills in silence. Eyes closed and expression weary, he reflected that his visit to Malibu had been a complete disaster. He felt bad, very bad, about how Isis had caught him in her private sitting room, going through her personal library. But he felt completely justified in trying to seek her out. And just as he owed her an apology for intruding into her privacy, she still owed him an explanation about exactly what One Commando had on her. But after what had just happened, he reckoned his chances of getting it weren't too good.

The moment he'd got in the car, he'd written down the name of that doctor so he wouldn't forget it: Dr Robert Weiner, Salmacis Hospital. He'd also noted the names of some of the book titles while he still remembered them. And the phrases from her mother's letter: *I know I have failed you . . . tried to keep your father from you . . . recover from surgery.*

It all seemed to point in only one direction: Isis had been abused as a child. The man who, more than any other, was responsible for her protection, had instead betrayed both instinct and his daughter's trust, his treatment of her so savage that she'd required hospitalisation. Hardly surprising, Mark supposed, that Isis was so much on edge, her emotions running so close to the surface. It was hard even to imagine her feelings.

The more he thought about it, the more his discovery seemed to explain things. Like the moments of closeness they'd shared, first at the restaurant, then later at Unum studios, moments when he'd felt the overwhelming, intuitive force of mutual attraction – only to be rebuffed with a casualness that denied the slightest hint of involvement. Isis had conveniently hidden behind the on-camera, off-camera explanation. But it seemed to Mark that the real reason was far more complex and had to do with Isis's feelings about intimacy, which took her far back into her past.

What he couldn't understand, right now, was her paranoid fear of having her past revealed. Of course it would be traumatic to have the whole world find out about the part of her life that made her most vulnerable. But it wasn't as though she was the perpetrator of some terrible crime. She was the victim, for God's sake! Wouldn't the public response be a wave of sympathy and support. Surely it wouldn't mean the end of her career!

Mark just couldn't work it out. Try as he might, he could think of no explanation for her desperate desire for concealment. Unless, of course, she was trying to protect her father. But who was her father, and what kind of power did he have that both Isis and GCM were so determined that the truth should never come to light?

Deep in thought, Mark paid no attention to their progress from Malibu back home. Though in the front, Denzil was clearly in a conversational mood. Oblivious of Mark's discovery earlier in the day, not to mention events at Isis's home, he was irrepressibly upbeat.

'So, you must be feeling safer now with the endorsement

deal behind you?' he asked, the moment Mark opened his eyes and glanced out of the window.

'I guess.'

'Those punks, they have to be pretty damned crazy, unhinged, to do what they did to that French guy!'

Mark nodded. He wasn't exactly in any mood to be reminded of One Commando's exploits.

'What I don't get,' Denzil chattered on, oblivious to his expression, 'is why those guys think Berkeley Square do things to animals. No one else does, do they?'

'No,' agreed Mark, 'they don't.'

'The whole world's gone looking at this factory down in Spain, and they ain't found nothing.'

Mark thought about the AFL fliers he'd had scattered across the coffee table earlier in the day. The gruesome photographs of the rabbits and the chimpanzees. The photo of the laboratory gate with the Berkeley Square sign outside it – the laboratory that Berkeley Square denied had anything to do with them.

Turning into his street, the Lincoln cruised up the winding tarmac towards the top of the hill. As they neared the top, Mark couldn't help noticing that, during the course of just a few hours, the neighbouring property across the road had changed yet again. Gone was the mediaeval castle look, and instead it had been transformed to a Southern horse stud. White palisades were driven into the ground, giving an impression of ageless permanence, and over the recently erected traditional pole gates hung the authentic-looking estate sign 'Bluegrass Creek'. Viewed in isolation, it looked exactly as though it had been transported here directly from Kentucky.

'Changed again,' Mark nodded across the road.

'Amazing what a piece of fence and a sign can do,' agreed
Denzil. 'Creates this whole idea . . .'

He carried on chattily as he brought the car to a pause,
waiting for the electric gates to open. But Mark wasn't listening. Instead he paused, transfixed by what Denzil had just
said: *Amazing what a piece of fence and a sign can do.*

Suddenly it struck him: what if there *was* a lab near
Madrid, testing on animals? And what if someone had put
up the Berkeley Square sign outside? Maybe One Commando
had set the whole thing up to *look* like a Berkeley Square
facility. Maybe the sign shot they'd used on their video wasn't
anywhere near Madrid. But then Bengt Larson and his
cohorts were smart operators. Surely they would have realised
they'd never convince anyone? And why continue to go for
Berkeley Square, when they'd failed to convince anyone
about their torture claims?

As soon as he was back in the house he hurried to the
study where he switched on the computer. The moment
Eudora Light was open, he was tapping out an urgent letter
to Dr Andrew Craig, whose e-mail address he'd found in
one of the Berkeley Square brochures. Explaining who he
was, Mark hurriedly related the new idea he'd just had,
before scanning in the photo of the 'Berkeley Square laboratory' from one of the AFL leaflets he'd brought back with
him from London. Was there anything that identified the
building in the photo as a place near Berkeley Square's real
Madrid laboratories, he wanted to know? Were there any
distinguishing features suggesting where this plant, if it
existed, really was to be found?

Checking to make sure the e-mail went through, Mark
stared at the screen as he worked through the implications.
It seemed a long shot, but what, he began to wonder, if One
Commando were themselves the victims of deception?

Las Vegas
Sunday, 3 October

The gym of the Golden Millennium Hotel was large, anonymous and well-equipped. Bengt Larson had been on the treadmill for the last twenty minutes, the speed gear shifted to maximum. When he ran he tried to clear his mind of everything but running. Focus, he always ordered himself, whenever he found his mind caught up in thoughts. Keep your focus!

Since last Tuesday it had been harder than usual to retain a steel mental discipline. He'd been living for an item on TV or radio news. A piece in the papers perhaps. But the forty-eight-hour deadline he'd given Isis had come and gone – and still no statement on Berkeley Square. Despite all the evidence, the leaflets and the video, a copy of which had been sent direct to GCM. Despite the photos which demonstrated, beyond any shadow of doubt, the systematic abuses of Berkeley Square. In the end he'd had no choice. He'd had to come to America, to play out the final act.

If his detailed planning had been meticulous before, this time round it was even more rigorous – it had to be. His carefully chosen team of just three others were not only One Commando veterans who could be trusted and who were in peak physical condition. Each of them also had a specialist expertise. De Clerque from Amsterdam was the explosives guru. Guittard from Marseilles knew everything there was to know about security systems. And Harris, in Washington State, was highly trained in martial arts and had the kind of underground network in the US required for procurement. Not to forget their special guest.

As always, Larson had assembled as much detail about the operation as possible, though several important factors were still unknowns. This operation, he'd never been in any doubt, would be the most challenging since One Commando had begun. It was the most high risk, and the potential for things to go wrong was greater than on any mission he'd organised in his life. But unlike any other operation before, the potential impact of this one was huge. So huge, in fact, it went way beyond his imagination.

20

Who was Isis's father? Why was she trying to protect him? Mark had been working on the questions since late last week. And he reckoned he knew a way to get them answered. Back home in London on the OmniCell helpdesk, he'd had a lot to do with the debt collection department. Businessmen and private individuals who ratcheted up huge loan accounts or overdrafts which they couldn't repay, were sometimes tempted to 'disappear', change their names, leave the country, go underground. It was the debt collection department's job to track them down. Speaking to the blokes in the department, Mark had got to know the ways they traced people, using paper trails, computer systems, old-fashioned sleuth work on the telephone. The more difficult jobs, he knew, the company had subcontracted to tracing agencies. Those agencies were international. They were able to track down debtors who lived in the most remote corners of the world, sometimes years after they'd left Britain. If he could get a tracing agency on to the job of tracking down Isis's father, he reckoned he'd soon find out why his daughter and GCM were so desperate to protect him. He speculated a bit himself. What if her father turned out to be a politician, or some big business tycoon? Then he thought of the Italian name; it would be scarier, much scarier, he supposed, if he turned out to be some figure from the Mafia underworld.

He'd had to wait out the weekend before getting hold of his mate in OmniCell's debt collecting department. To his intense frustration, it was still more time before he had the name and telephone number of the tracing agency OmniCell used in Florida.

In the meantime, he'd had two e-mails from Dr Andrew Craig at Berkeley Square's facility in Madrid. In the first one, Craig had thanked him for his 'interesting idea', saying he'd circulated to all staff the photo from the AFL leaflet which One Commando claimed was Berkeley Square's. Should anyone be able to identify the building, he assured Mark, he'd let him know. Craig's second e-mail, sent on Monday morning, consisted of just two lines; a secretary in R & D thought she knew the building; it was opposite where her husband worked. Craig had sent her out with a digital camera.

Then there were the recordings of Vinnie's endless telephone calls. Painstakingly sifting through them all each morning, Mark had come across only one that alerted his suspicions. An incoming call from someone who didn't give his name, but only said that Alexander Heindl had said they should meet. They'd made an arrangement to get together in Regent's Park. Mark had never heard Vinnie mention this Heindl bloke before and it all seemed very mysterious. But maybe it was just Vinnie wheeler-dealering. Maybe it had nothing to do with Isis and him.

Mulling over his different lines of enquiry, Mark also kept wondering about Dr Weiner of the Salmacis Hospital. Might he be worth putting in a call to, he mused, if only to confirm his area of medical expertise? Mark supposed he'd find Salmacis somewhere in Miami, where Isis had grown up, and he wasn't wrong. Operator enquiries had soon given him the number of the hospital.

'Does Dr Weiner work there?' he asked, sitting behind the desk of his study. It must be many years, he realised, since the doctor had treated Isis.

'Dr Weiner sometimes consults at this hospital, but he has his own practice,' the receptionist told him.

'Do you have the telephone number there?'

'Please hold, sir.'

A short while later he was dialling a different number. As it rang, he glanced at his watch. He didn't know exactly how many hours Miami was ahead of LA, but it was now nearly three, so he guessed it must be early evening over there. He doubted very much if he'd catch Dr Weiner in. He'd probably have to call back or leave a message.

'Weiner,' replied a brisk voice at the other end, almost immediately.

'Oh,' Mark was taken aback, 'hello . . . Dr Weiner.'

'Yes?'

He hadn't expected to be speaking to him, not directly or so soon. Now that he was, he realised he hadn't worked out what to say to him. 'Actually, I'm phoning about a friend.'

'Ah.' Robert Weiner's tone changed in an instant into counselling mode. 'Does this . . . friend want to see me professionally?'

'You see, I need to find out what you do first, I mean, your area—'

'I know what you mean,' the other responded smoothly, well used to dealing with nervous patients. In a few jargon-free sentences, he explained before asking, 'Now, was it something along those lines?'

At the other end, Mark sat for a few moments, shocked to the core. He'd had his suspicions, from the titles of the books in Isis's private library. But hearing Dr Weiner tell him out loud, listening to him use those words with the fluent ease of practice made him realise just how very little he really understood.

Putting down the receiver Mark took a great sob of air before burying his face in his hands. It was a long time before he emerged from the study.

Las Vegas

Vinnie fiddled with the worry beads in the pocket of his leather jacket as he strode through the lobby of the Lucky Nugget Hotel. It was filled with fruit-machines. Glancing about at the tacky surroundings, he viewed with disdain all the fat Americans perched on stools, feeding quarters into the machines. Bunch of dumb fucks, he thought. Didn't they know you could never win against a one-armed bandit? He, meantime, had seen what he was looking for. Flashing red and gold signs had arrows pointing in the direction of the gaming salon – a vast, dimly lit expanse of tables, where people were playing roulette and poker and blackjack. The cool, air-conditioned interior was heavy with cigar smoke interlaced with ribbons of perfume. Cocktail glasses clinked from the nearby bar. There was money here – the place was filthy with it. And by the time he'd finished, a whole wedge of it was going to end up in his back pocket, of that he was certain. He knew a system. One of the regulars down at the Lamb had shown it to him. Apparently, the bloke who'd invented it had bust so many casinos, he was banned from all the main gambling houses in Monte Carlo. Plus there was the fact that Vinnie was feeling lucky. Very lucky. The kind of feeling that made him believe that things had finally started turning his way.

Heindl had called him about the trip late the week before.

'We need you to fly out in twenty-four hours. Do the recce,' he'd said.

At the other end of the phone, Vinnie had decided to try out the plan he'd been working on.

'Twenty-four hours.' His tone was sharp. 'You gotta be joking, mate.'

Heindl had assured him this was no joke. And he was on standby.

'But I can't just ... take off at such short notice,' he'd blustered.

'Why not?' Heindl had asked.

'Something's come up – a deal. I need to be here. If I don't I could lose big money.'

At the other end Larson's expression hardened. So that was the game. He should have guessed.

'Like how much?' he asked Vinnie.

'Five grand.'

'That is a lot of money.'

'Exactly my point.' Vinnie admired his own negotiating position.

Then Heindl was saying calmly, 'I'll have five thousand pounds in cash for you when you check in at Heathrow airport tomorrow night.'

Hanging up, Vinnie had punched a fist into the air with a yell of triumph. Yes! Five big grand in less than five minutes. Plus the satisfaction of knowing Mark Watson was about to see his ass – bigtime. He was back on a roll!

True to his word, Heindl had left five grand in an envelope together with his ticket, which he collected from an American Airlines desk at Heathrow. Vinnie had been surprised to find he wasn't flying direct to Los Angeles. His ticket took him to New York instead, where he'd been instructed to take a cab into the city, then a train to Boston, before catching another flight west.

When he'd finally arrived in Las Vegas, it had been nothing like he'd imagined. As he'd been driven into town from the airport, the taxi driver had taken him past all the famous hotels and gambling palaces, all emblazoned with flashing signs and spectacular special effects, from erupting volcanoes to cascading waterfalls. This place was dedicated solely to twenty-four-hour entertainment, mostly of the gaming variety – Vinnie reckoned he could get used to it. He was blown over by his hotel room – massive, deep-pile carpet and with two king-size beds all to himself. Heindl had left him a note. He was to keep a low profile until he appeared down in the lobby next morning at nine sharp.

Now as he swaggered across the casino, he headed for the money exchange to cash in some of his freshly minted cash for a pile of roulette chips. 'Make it a thousand dollars,' he bragged to the dark-suited woman behind the desk, who shoved a pile of counters in his direction. Then he was glancing round for a table to play at, before checking out one with a few spaces free. Double or quit, that was the game he'd learned. Keep it simple and get out when you're ahead.

He'd no sooner sat down than one of the cocktail waitresses in a black, crotch-length skirt and leather tassel top was offering him a glass of champagne. He hadn't realised it was free. Ooh, Mama, he could get used to this, he reckoned, taking a slug. After he'd made his pile, he might cruise the bar. Everyone knew American women just loved an English accent. The croupier, an ageing Oriental with a gold tooth and glittering rhinestone waistcoat, was spinning the wheel.

'Place bets!' he ordered in a shrill voice Vinnie didn't

much like the sound of. Well, fuck him, thought Vinnie, fuck them all. He shunted fifty bucks on to red. Start as you mean to continue, that was his line, he reckoned, downing another mouthful of champagne. He was in with the big time boys now, and nothing could stop him. Vinnie Dobson was invincible.

Pacific Palisades

Hilton Gallo was sitting at his bedroom escritoire, putting the finishing touches to a GCM Tokyo takeover proposal, when the telephone rang. Varley announced himself.

'There's been a development you should know about.'

'What's that?'

'In the past twenty-four hours, three forged EU passports have been used at different entry points into the US. The French think all three documents were commissioned by Larson.'

'How come?'

'For the past three months they've been monitoring the activities of Barend Rousseau, master forger in Paris. Specialises in providing fake ID. Last week he prepared forged EU passports for three men. The gendarmerie believe they were collected by Larson.'

'When you say "believe"?'

'They have CCTV bugs in Rousseau's offices. Picture quality isn't great, but the image of last week's visitor is an eighty per cent match to Larson.'

Hilton considered this for a moment before asking, 'If the passports were fake, why weren't the terrorists arrested?'

'The fake passport numbers were only loaded on to the computer *after* the men were inside the country.' Varley was clearly embarrassed. 'But by then . . .'

'D'you know where they're heading?' he could hardly bear to hear the answer.

'Got a trace on one of them. He had a connecting flight to Denver almost immediately.'

'Denver?'

'Unlikely that was his final destination.'

'He's heading west,' observed Hilton, 'which means the other two are headed this way too.'

Varley didn't argue.

'You have some way of tracking them?'

'No, sir. I think it's safe to assume they will all have booked onward flights in different names. The only reason we got the one in DC was because we caught him on airport cameras. He was late for his onward flight and was in such a hurry it made him easy to follow.'

'Well, what if—?'

'Viewing tapes from Denver?' Varley pre-empted his next question. 'That would be an overwhelming task.'

There was a long pause before Hilton said, 'So all we know is that the three of them, who *might* be members of One Commando, *might* be heading to Denver?'

'I know it's tentative, but in the circumstances . . .'

Hilton walked across the white carpet of his bedroom to where his window looked out into the darkness of the ocean. Only a few distant lights signalled the presence of ships in the night. Hilton thought quickly.

'Have you spoken to Isis?' he asked Varley.

'Not yet.'

'I don't think you should. It would be better coming from me.'

The police officer was hesitant.

'Her psychological state right now is very fragile,' continued Hilton. 'My concern is that if this news isn't pitched a particular way, it could push her over the edge.'

'Right.' Varley had read all the newspaper stories about Isis, the same as everybody else. He knew she lived in Lalaland, and like other big-name stars was to be treated with extreme caution. The last thing in the world he needed was to wake up to the headlines that she'd been admitted to some clinic with a nervous breakdown because he'd passed on the latest inconclusive Interpol report.

'In that case, I'll leave it to you.'

'Good,' nodded Hilton, 'and you'll let me know as soon as you have more news?'

'You can be sure of it.'

Hilton replaced the telephone receiver, but didn't go back to his writing desk, pausing instead, deep in thought. In the game of information management, timing was everything – and right now he didn't have time on his side. It would be another twelve hours before Unum Records gave *Nile* the final sign-off, and although all the noises coming out of Sam Bach's office were positive, the show wasn't over until Ariel Alhadeff had given the record the official thumbs up. He couldn't risk Isis high-tailing it out of town – if she did, and was unable to fulfil any final changes Unum demanded, then everything they'd both worked to achieve in the past six months would be put at risk.

He hadn't told her about the non-existence of the MI5 agent because he hadn't wanted to take away her hope. Now the ethics of disclosure loomed in his mind yet again. He'd always regarded himself as a straight-shooter. In a town in which every truth was relative, he'd made every effort to be punctilious in his client relations. But he pondered on Varley's latest news; Isis was anxious enough already, he reflected, without getting more alarming calls with information she couldn't do anything about. How was she supposed to react? Leave Los Angeles every time people with fake passports came into the country? And even if she did take off to some high-security bolthole, how much safer would she really be anywhere else, compared to her Malibu fortress?

All the same, he couldn't pretend the information didn't add yet a further disturbing dimension to the blackmail crisis – one he didn't much care to think about. If he could just get over tomorrow's Unum meeting, he decided, then he'd pay her a personal visit and get everything out in the open.

It was only a few hours away, after all.

Beverly Hills

Mark sat in the upstairs bar of his Beverly Hills mansion. Perched on one of the leather-padded bar stools, he flicked restlessly through the fifty-eight channels of his TV set while sipping on a vodka. After his short exchange with Dr Weiner, he didn't know what to think. As soon as he'd recovered from the initial shock of confirmation, he'd picked up the phone again and had started to dial Isis's number before reconsidering the whole idea. He wasn't ready yet, he decided. What exactly was he going to say to her? He needed to get his head round things first. He needed a drink.

That had been a couple of hours earlier and he'd been unable to focus on anything since. The more he thought about it, the stranger it seemed, but time and time again his thoughts kept coming back to the same point: why? He found it impossible to make sense of. His own family background and experiences were so far removed he just couldn't under-stand it. And he reckoned there was no way he was ever going to unless she explained it to him – and in her current frame of mind he couldn't see her doing that.

He wondered how he'd be next time they met. Tomorrow morning they had the meeting down at Unum to listen to the final mix of *Nile*. He'd been told it was an important meeting. Leo Lebowitz had phoned to advise him that the top Unum brass would be there and recommended he go 'in character', wearing some of the garments already picked out for the Jordan Hampshire wardrobe. He wondered how he'd react when he saw Isis. He played through their last scene in his mind. He'd have to carry on as though nothing had happened, at least while all the others were about. But would there be time alone with her afterwards? And what should he say? He wanted it out in the open between the two of them. But getting to that point was just too difficult and right now the very thought of it overwhelmed him. Pouring himself another drink, he walked over to one of the armchairs and dropped into it. *Seinfeld* was on TV and waves of studio laughter only confirmed his exhaustion.

When the telephone rang it took him a while to get to it. The secretary of Dr Andrew Craig was putting her boss through.

'I thought you'd be interested to know,' the brisk brogue of Craig's voice also conveyed excitement, 'the secretary I referred to in my e-mail visited the facility. And I've just been there myself – less than ten minutes away. It *is* the same place as in the AFL flier.'

Mark raised a hand to his forehead. 'And the animal testing?' he asked wearily.

'Nothing to identify the site from outside,' reported Craig, 'but the owner of the plant next door says it belongs to Voisier Laboratories.' His tone was acerbic.

'You know Voisier?'

'Oh, aye,' confirmed Craig. 'Monsieur Voisier is well known in the industry for his . . . methods. Notorious, one might say.'

Tuesday, 5 October

Isis could tell something was different from the moment she saw him. And it wasn't just the Jordan Hampshire clothes which he'd doubtless been ordered to wear by GCM. The difference had more to do with the way he was hardly meeting her eyes. Was it guilt, she wondered – or resentment? Since she'd ordered him out of her house last Wednesday, her own feelings had been running high. More than anything though she'd felt anxiety knotting her stomach as she worried about what he might have seen.

She'd been walking down the corridor as he'd been about to return the Isis photo album to the shelf and caught sight of the second, concealed row of books. As though viewing it all in slow motion she had seen him reach behind for the book that Robert had given her, flick it open, and then her mother's letter had fallen to the floor.

It had all happened in a few instants. Not enough time for Mark to have read any of the text. But had he realised the significance of the second row of books? Had it got him wondering? The possibility of it was added to her already deep concerns about blackmail and the more she thought about it, the more agitated she became. It seemed to her that she was finally about to lose control of her secret. After years of keeping the lid on, of relentless and rigorous management by GCM, she now had the deep-down sense that everything in her past was about to burst into view.

With Holly back from a visit to her father's though, there had been no question of Isis revealing any of her true feelings – she didn't have the luxury of being able to fall apart. Instead she'd just had to pretend, as she was pretending now in this roomful of suits. All the Unum big guns were here from Ariel Alhadeff downwards, not to mention the GCM team – Hilton, Leo, Andy Murdoch and even Blake Horowitz which was unusual for a final-mix session. They'd all had copies of the final-mix since the weekend, so the purpose of today's meeting was as much to finalise launch plans as to showcase the music.

As Sam Bach skipped selectively through the tracks, highlighting different aspects of the CD and emphasising its inbuilt market appeal, there were appreciative nods from around the table towards where she was sitting with Mark at one end. The two of them had, of course, heard this stuff so many, many times over the past few weeks that they were way past the point of being objective. The initial excitement they'd felt about the music itself had long since been replaced by concerns about phrasing, acquainted as they were with every nuance of melody, every syllable of the lyrics. All the same, seeing the effect the music had on the gathered suits from Unum and GCM was encouraging. Isis thought back to her first pre-release meeting just before the album *Isis* had come out and remembered how, after weeks of intensive work, it had felt, finally, that everything was coming together.

Glancing briefly at where Mark was concentrating on some remark by Ariel Alhadeff, she felt a pang of remorse. If it hadn't been for the dark cloud hanging over them right now, she thought, Mark would be feeling that same excitement. If it wasn't for all the trauma that arose from her past he would also have been feeling the same sense of achievement, anticipation, even mild euphoria that she'd felt when she'd first sat in on a meeting like this. It was impossible to guess what he really was thinking at this moment. He had deliberately withdrawn into his own world. If only they could return to the carefree intimacy they'd shared at the recording studio.

When the meeting ended, all the Unum suits dispersed in a rapid flurry of handshakes and congratulations. Walking down the corridor to the secure parking facility behind the Unum building, Isis asked Hilton if there'd been any news from the police. He glanced down at the floor, shaking his head. Nothing substantive, he told her, but, delivering a meaningful gaze, said he'd be in touch with her later in the day.

During this time Mark was walking behind them, appearing to be absorbed in the cover of the *Nile* CD. Outside in the parking lot they donned sunglasses, Hilton and Lebowitz making their way towards a stretch limousine, Isis heading across towards where Frank was standing beside the open door of her Range Rover. Mark's limo was parked near hers, Denzil behind the wheel. But they were still some distance away when he said, 'We need to talk.'

She glanced over at him. His voice was tight, almost choked. It was hard to tell what emotions were going on behind those dark lenses. Her footsteps slowed. 'You hardly said anything back there. What's the matter?'

'It's, uh, it's . . . important.' How was he to put this? Ever since he'd stirred from his armchair, early this morning, he'd been wondering what words to use. He still hadn't come up with any ideas by the time he had to leave for the meeting. Maybe there was no nice way of saying what he so desperately needed to say. As the two of them crossed the tarmac, the sun blazing down on them, he battled for expression, before finally blurting out, 'I know what they've found out about you. Your . . . past, I mean.'

Isis halted. Her instant reaction was one of disbelief. How could he know? Turning to him, she found herself replying, 'That's impossible!' She was shaking her head determinedly.

'No, it's not.'

'You *can't* know. Hilton and Lebowitz wouldn't tell anyone
– not in a thousand years.'

'It wasn't Hilton or Lebowitz who told me.'

'Then who did?'

Denial was one thing he hadn't expected. He realised
warily he was going to have to get into the detail he'd most
hoped to avoid.

'Well . . . no one exactly. I kind of worked it out for
myself.'

'Oh, yeah,' she allowed herself a grim smile, 'and what
conclusion did you come up with?'

'I spoke to Dr Weiner.'

Isis's expression suddenly froze. As she fixed on Mark from
behind her sunglasses, her face rapidly darkened.

'You got his name from the book?' Her anger was quickly
building. This was even worse than she'd feared.

Mark stepped back. 'You weren't going to tell me, were
you?' he tried, defensively.

'So you snooped?'

'You didn't give me much choice—'

'You snooped!'

'I didn't want to, but—'

'Do you realise you've just put my entire professional
career on the line?' In fury, Isis was vehement. Terrifying.
'Your spying could destroy everything I've worked for my
entire life. And blow away your chance of a career with it!'

'But I haven't spoken to anyone!' he protested.

'So it was all telepathy?'

'Not even Weiner knows I found out about you.'

'You're talking in riddles, Mark.' She stepped closer, prod-
ding him in the chest with her index finger. Although she'd
lowered her voice he was in no doubt about the ferocity of
her anger. 'You'd better tell me how you *did* find out.'

'Okay,' he held his hands up, 'I did get his name from the book. I saw the other books you had there. I put two and two together. I phoned to ask him about what sort of work he does—'

'I trusted you,' Isis managed between clenched teeth, 'and this is how you reward my trust.'

'That's why we need to talk!' He was desperate.

'There's nothing left to talk about.'

'But there's so much other stuff—'

'Why don't you keep on snooping then? See what else you dredge up!' She about-turned and stormed away from him.

Mark hurried after her. 'Isis, please!' he was begging her, 'be reasonable!'

Shaking her head, sunglasses flashing in the midday sun, it was impossible to get through to her. He'd expected her to get upset – but he'd hoped for a very different outcome. He'd wanted them to talk about it, for Isis to realise there was no point in blocking him out any longer. Most of all, he'd wanted her to tell him why. Why had she done it? What had been such an irresistible compulsion eighteen years before? He wanted to understand this woman who so intrigued him. But she was already stepping into the back seat of her Range Rover, with Frank slamming the door behind her. She wasn't looking at him as the car pulled away with a screech.

21

In the Range Rover, Isis fought to keep back the tears until they'd left the Unum lot. The desperate fury of her reaction to Mark concealed an even greater turmoil of anguish beneath. Already pushed to the brink by One Commando and their blackmail demand, now came the confirmation that Mark knew her secret too!

When she'd arrived in Los Angeles fourteen years ago, she'd had only one simple wish; to put the past behind her. But it seemed to her now that everything she'd done since getting here had been building to this moment. It was as though some perverse power beyond had conspired to return her to that time in her life she most wanted to forget, forcing her to confront what she so desperately wished to leave behind.

She had stashed Gabby's magazine article in her locker. During breaks in class and after school she would return to the locker again and again to read the article, especially all the stuff about the other girls who'd been through the same ordeal as she had. Every time she read it, she felt the same heady mixture of emotions: surging, liberating relief at the discovery that she wasn't the only one in the world suffering this torment; deep fascination at the description of how doctors and psychologists had helped others like her to recover. But there was a terrible fear, too; she knew that once she'd decided to do something about it, there could be no turning back. And at the age of fifteen, despite all the suffering, it was hard, very hard, to turn your back on everything you knew.

What really prompted her to make the call was Gabby's funeral. Five days after the accident it was held at St Columbus's and everyone was there from school, from church, from the Italian community. Because she and Gabby had been such good friends, the Carboni family sat near the front. Isis could see Gabby's sisters and parents and grandparents sobbing during the Mass, which set her off too. She stood there, throughout the service, tears streaming down her cheeks, and there was nothing she could do to stop it. The worst was when the headmaster stood at the front of the church and spoke about how everyone felt about Gabby at school. He told the mourners that Gabby had been more than simply a conscientious student and athlete; what had made her exceptional was that she'd gone out of her way to help others. He talked about some of the things Gabby had done, things that Isis and most of the other kids had no idea about. In those few short minutes during the funeral the whole congregation came to realise just how special Gabby had been. And after the headmaster had finished speaking, Isis made a promise to herself; she was going to make the telephone call to the people mentioned in the article. She was going to do it, not just for her own sake, but because she felt she owed it to Gabby as well. Gabby had pointed her in that direction, and the fact that she'd died so soon afterwards seemed, to Isis, like a kind of omen. A sign that she should do something.

The following day at lunch-time, instead of sitting under the trees in the courtyard waiting for the two o'clock bell to summon her back to class, she finished her sandwich, went to her locker, wrote down the telephone number in Biro on the back of her hand, took a few coins and slipped out of the school gates. There was a telephone box a few hundred yards down the road and it was working – she knew, because she'd tested it on the way into school this morning. Fortunately it was empty when she arrived. Heart pounding in her chest, she felt shaky as she picked up the receiver and began dialling. This was the most daring, the scariest thing she'd ever done in her life. And how was she going to explain herself? She could hardly find the words.

She was a little breathless when a woman answered the helpline. And relieved to be asked only where she was calling from. This was a national helpline, explained the woman, and she put Isis's call through to someone in her local area. There was a bit of a wait as she was transferred, then another ringing tone. A male voice came on the line. Isis would have preferred to speak to a woman. In fact she was thinking of hanging up and phoning back some other time. But the man sounded very gentle. And he didn't ask her any questions except whether she could arrange to come into an information centre in downtown Miami. He didn't even start to talk about her problem. He told Isis when advisers would be at the centre and said he hoped they'd see her there. And that was it. No pressure. No need for her life story. Just the offer of help. Walking back to the school gates, Isis had felt suddenly lighter, as though a heavy burden she hadn't even been aware she was carrying had been lifted from her shoulders.

'Thank you, Gabby!' she whispered, looking up at the sky. 'Thank you, thank you, thank you!'

Her first chance to go to the centre came the following Tuesday afternoon. Her mother had taken a part-time job at the local delicatessen, and her father never got home from work before six. School ended early, so she'd be able to make it into town and back home before either of her parents returned. She thought carefully about what clothes she should wear, before opting for her best jeans and a sweatshirt. The man on the phone had told her where the centre was – she could picture it exactly in her mind – so she hadn't needed to write it down. She simply caught a bus that took her straight there.

The centre itself was up two flights of steps on the first floor above a hairdressing salon. The reception room had a warm, cushioned feel about it with pastel-coloured walls and soft, comfortable furniture. As she walked across to the receptionist, she noticed posters on the walls to do with drug problems and unwanted pregnancies – and realised this centre wasn't only for people with problems like hers.

The woman at Reception looked up with a friendly smile. 'Is this your first visit?' she asked.

Isis nodded.

'You'll need to fill in one of these. It's completely confidential,' she assured Isis, handing over a form on a clipboard. On the form was a list of subjects on which you could receive counselling. Isis ticked the appropriate one for her, filling in her age and a few other details before handing the form back to the receptionist with a blush. Even though she hadn't actually spoken, it was the first time she'd admitted her problem to anyone apart from Gabby.

The woman glanced briefly at the form. 'If you sit down, someone will see you soon,' she said.

About twenty minutes later she met Robert Weiner for the first time. Although she had no idea what to expect, when the woman at Reception showed her along a corridor and told her to take the first door on the right, what she found wasn't like anything she had imagined. It was a large room that seemed like every teenager's fantasy. There were no chairs or desks – it was all beanbags and deep-pile rugs, posters on the walls of the big names in pop, an impressive-looking stereo system covered in flashing lights, and even a billiard table at the other end of the room. Standing in the middle, dressed casually in jeans and a checked shirt, was a man who introduced himself as Robert Weiner. He had a friendly look about him and a sensitive face. It was only much later that she discovered he was one of the leading experts in his field. It was just as well she didn't know it this first time, because she was intimidated enough by just being here. Though Robert immediately began to put her at ease, offering her a cool drink and then, as he went to get it, suggesting she pick out a record from the collection by the stereo. She browsed through the records in the rack before pulling out one by Abba which had long been her favourite LP.

When Robert returned to the room they both sat on bean-bags facing each other. They chatted a bit about music, what she liked and what she didn't. She was amazed he seemed so up to date with all the groups and the records that were doing well in the charts – he seemed genuinely interested in it all. But she also knew that, sooner or later, they'd have to get on to the reason she was visiting. Studying Robert's features carefully, she decided he was all right. Even though she was still embarrassed to be here, she reckoned she could trust him – he made her feel safe.

'You're probably feeling a bit nervous,' he said finally, glancing down the form which the woman from Reception must have given him. Then, meeting her anxious expression with an encouraging smile, 'Well, congratulations! Just coming here takes a lot of courage. There are plenty of people out there who would like to come, maybe even know they should come, but they put it off because it's such a difficult thing to do.'

She looked down at her hands. She was glad he realised that. It *was* difficult – not so much getting away from school and her parents, but having to speak to an expert, someone she'd never met before, about the most intimate part of her, the dark horror that had dominated every day of her existence for more years than she cared to remember. As though reflecting her own thoughts, he continued, 'For most people I see, this isn't a subject they can talk to anyone else about.'

Isis nodded vigorously. 'I had a friend, and she knew, and we used to do a lot of stuff together. But she died in a car accident ten days ago.'

'I'm very sorry,' Robert spoke softly.

'She was the only one.' Isis bowed her head. 'She was the one who showed me the article.'

There was a pause before Robert said, 'And you don't want her to die in vain, right?'

Looking up, she met his eyes. She hadn't put her feelings into those words, but what he said was exactly how it was.

'Right now you're probably feeling all alone with this,' he continued, holding her gaze, 'but it's important you realise that there are plenty of people who have exactly the same issues to deal with that you do.'

She looked at him in disbelief.

'You haven't ever talked to anyone about this except your friend, right?' he confirmed. 'So how do you know there aren't lots of other girls out there, maybe even girls you know, who are also not talking about it? Keeping it to themselves?'

He had a point – in theory. But thinking about all the kids she knew at school . . .

'Every day I see at least five different people who feel just like you do. Multiply that by twenty days a month and twelve months a year, that's twelve hundred women every year. And I'm only one practitioner – there are at least half a dozen like me in Florida alone.' He gave her a few moments to let the information sink in. That was a lot of people, thought Isis, and she never would have guessed. She was sure he wasn't lying to her – why would he? – but it just went against everything she'd ever thought about herself. Until Gabby had shown her that article she'd imagined she was the only one in the whole world with this problem. She'd always thought of the situation at home as being one that was hers alone.

'When did it first start—?'

'It's always been like this.'

Robert hadn't even needed to finish the question. He was making a note, nodding. 'With most people there's a turning point.'

Isis immediately thought back to the day when her father and Mr Bazzani had arrived back home unexpectedly.

'When I was twelve,' she said.

'Do you want to tell me about it?'

Isis had never told anyone the full story, not even Gabby. She'd only told her a part because she'd been so ashamed. Now, just thinking about it, the colour rushed to her cheeks.

'You can take all the time you need,' Robert told her.

It *did* take her a while to get started. To explain about Gabby's locker and how she'd seen the brassière – but had always intended to give it back. Once she started, though, the words came out in a torrent as she relived the scene in her mind, experiencing again the emotions she'd felt all those years ago: the erotic self-indulgence as she'd savoured the forbidden pleasures of Gabby's black lace bra and her mother's crimson lipstick – like living in a dream as she'd sat in front of her mother's dressing mirror. Then the visceral shock as she'd looked up to discover her father and Mr Bazzani standing at the door. Time standing still as their eyes met in the mirror, hers shamefully self-conscious and fearful, her father's blazing with a powerful mix of devastating fury and unbridled reproach. Then he'd swooped down upon her, ripping the brassière from her body and using it roughly to wipe the make-up off her face. Next, he'd flung her on the bed, face down. Mr Bazzani had pinned her by the shoulders as her father wrenched her pants down her legs. Not a sound had been uttered until that moment. Not a word exchanged, or necessary, as she'd struggled hopelessly to escape from their clutches. Then the screaming had begun.

Tears rose to her eyes as she recalled what had happened. Robert gently reached over to take her hand. The simple act of remembering had unleashed all her pent-up emotions. Every detail of that primal horror flooded back through her in cruel, vivid detail as she relived the terrible experience of that afternoon – and all the experiences that had followed. Tears rolled silently down her cheeks, before Robert handed her a box of tissues.

'Don't hold back,' he advised her in that serene, authoritative voice to which she was to become so accustomed in future months. 'Let all the hurt come out.'

It was the first time she'd ever been told by an adult it was okay to cry. In her family weeping, except in grief, was regarded as a sign of pathetic weakness. Her father was forever castigating her for her sensitivity, her inability to conceal the fragility of her emotions. But different rules applied with Robert, she was beginning to learn. Robert not only understood her vulnerabilities, he wanted to see them; it was the first time she'd felt fully accepted for who she was.

It was the first time, too, she began to see her family with a detachment of which she'd been incapable until then. Robert asked her a lot of questions about her parents, and in so doing made her realise that their idea of the world wasn't the only way it could be seen.

'The clients I see who have it hardest usually come from families who are very conservative, or where there is a deeply engrained ethnic culture, or whose education is lower than the national average. When these factors combine, in cases such as yours, it makes the issue extremely difficult to deal with.'

Isis nodded. She was still feeling shaky after the catharsis of reliving her ordeal, still getting used to the novel idea that instead of being all alone and taking the blame for her situation on herself, she was part of a much larger group of people going through the same private agonies.

'What about your mother?' Robert asked.

Isis shook her head. 'I think . . . she wants to change things. She tried to pretend it wasn't happening at first. She doesn't understand.'

'Of course. And there are divided loyalties. No matter how much she might want to help you, she probably feels that taking sides against your father won't help matters.'

Isis looked at Robert hopelessly. 'So what must I do?'

Robert reached over to give her shoulder a reassuring squeeze. 'Coming to see me is the best possible thing you could have done. You see, my job is to provide my clients with choices. And you do have choices. You can either carry on as you are—'

Isis was shaking her head defiantly.

'Or we can help you change things. But I must warn you, when I talk about change, I mean complete change. A change in almost every single aspect of your life, not just things at home.' His gravity was inescapable as his eyes held her gaze. 'You need to be completely sure that's something you can cope with.'

'Mind if we swing past Varley's office for an update?' Hilton looked across the expansive back seat of the GCM stretch limo.

'Sure,' nodded Lebowitz, already dialling the office to find out what news had broken during his two-hour absence. 'Good meeting,' he gestured in the direction of Unum Music as he raised the cellphone to his ear.

'Very good.' Hilton looked out of the tinted glass window before adding in an ironic tone, 'Leaves us free to play cat and mouse with One Commando.'

Lebowitz was soon talking to one of his colleagues, while Hilton checked his pager for messages. Traffic was light and it wasn't long before they were heading down Santa Monica Boulevard in the direction of the LAPD building. Though before they got there, Lebowitz had come off the line and looked up at Hilton sharply.

'Seems like there's been a breakthrough at the Berkeley Square end. The lab where they're supposed to be testing on animals? Belongs to a private company called Voisier Laboratories. Not ten minutes from Berkeley's own facility in Madrid.'

'One Commando set it up to look like Berkeley Square?' asked Hilton.

'Seems so.'

'But why would they want to do that? Why not just go after Voisier?'

'Who's ever heard of Voisier?' Lebowitz shrugged.

'I guess.' Hilton remembered Bengt Larson's face pressed

closely into his at his Green's suite. For all Larson's highly drilled efficiency, there had been a fanatical desperation in his expression, a genuine anger. It hadn't seemed like an act on his part; somehow the notion that Larson was pursuing Berkeley Square in full knowledge of the company's innocence didn't ring true.

'So what's being done?' he asked after a pause.

'They're setting up a press conference in Madrid tomorrow – Lefevre and Lord Bullerton double act. It'll be held at the Berkeley Square facility and the media will no doubt make a stampede for Voisier immediately afterwards.' He pulled a droll expression. 'Wouldn't like to be their PR man.' Then as Hilton absorbed this, 'Oh, and you'll never guess where the supersleuth work came from.'

'Not Bennett?'

Lebowitz shook his head. 'No. Our Mr Watson.'

'You're saying—'

'Shrewd cookie. Worked out that maybe there was something going on, but it was being dressed up to be misleading.'

'Nice of him to tell us.'

'Went direct to Andrew Craig.' Lebowitz shook his head, his tone sardonic. 'We pay him all that money and still he doesn't love us.'

'I think he stopped loving us when we put him into play.'

'Always the way.' Lebowitz shrugged, matter-of-factly. 'They never understand the price of fame.'

Sheriff Varley had little new to report when they stepped into his office. The fake passport holders hadn't been tracked beyond Denver. In Britain the police were still far from making any arrests. And latest Interpol computer reports had generated little of real value.

Lebowitz quickly updated him on the latest discovery about Voisier. 'After tomorrow,' he declared, 'the whole world will know One Commando's game.'

'Not that that will stop them,' added Hilton. 'They still have the information on Isis which they could release at any time unless', he fixed Varley with a purposeful stare, 'you do something.'

Varley sighed heavily. 'Mr Gallo, you know that blackmail is an issue we take very seriously. But my main concern right now is the safety of your clients.'

'Precisely,' returned Hilton. 'And even though you have a group of dangerous, armed terrorists headed directly towards them, you appear incapable of action.' This conversation, Hilton couldn't help thinking, was becoming strongly reminiscent of his fruitless discussions with DI Bennett at Scotland Yard.

'That's just not true,' Varley looked him in the eye, 'all squad cars in the vicinity of Malibu and Beverly Hills have been put on special alert. They're watching your client's home—'

'I was thinking in terms of arrests.' Hilton's gaze was hard.

'How can we arrest them when we don't even know for sure they're in the country?'

At that moment Hilton's phone rang. Extracting it from his jacket pocket, he recognised the number of GCM's guest house on the display.

'Mark Watson,' he murmured, before answering.

After Unum, Mark had returned home where he checked the OmniCell computer for an update of Vinnie's latest calls. That was when he'd heard the one from Larson saying he was to be sent on a recce to Los Angeles. Vinnie had got five grand out of the deal – that would have pleased him no end, thought

Mark grimly – but there were no other details about when he was flying out, or what this 'recce' was to involve.

And there had been one other thing. 'Alex', Mark noted, was what Vinnie had called Bengt Larson. Could this be the 'Alexander Heindl' alluded to in a previous conversation – the one setting up that mysterious meeting in Regent's Park?

One thing he was sure of was that he must tell the police. He needed protection. And he wanted to know how to handle Vinnie's arrival. This was the first definite evidence that One Commando were on their way to LA – but exactly why, he couldn't work out; they had tried to blackmail Isis and had failed. So why didn't they tell the world about her dark secret? What was stopping them shooting down her career overnight? Unless, of course, it had all been a bluff.

Hilton Gallo was his first stop, to get the details of his LAPD contact. As it turned out, Hilton was meeting Sheriff Varley when he called. After swiftly explaining the situation, Mark heard Hilton relay his discovery to Varley.

'Where is your client at this moment?' Varley reacted instantly.

'Beverly Hills. GCM guest house,' responded Hilton.

'We've got to get him out of there. Put him somewhere secure.'

'Like where?' asked Hilton.

'A safe house.'

'Can't get safer than Isis's,' proposed Lebowitz.

'What kind of security does she have out there?' Varley demanded.

'High-level electronic security systems. Armed-response crews within five minutes. She's had every security firm in town go over the place,' Hilton told him.

'She wouldn't want me under her roof,' Mark said down the phone.

'Oh, I think we could persuade her.'

'Damned right,' nodded Lebowitz, 'it'll play well in the media: "Jordan and Isis are *à deux*".'

'Just great!' Mark's tone was bitter. 'My life's under threat and, still, the only thing he's worried about is what the papers say.'

'I don't think that's strictly true.'

'Ask Varley what I'm supposed to do when I get the inevitable call from Vinnie Dobson?'

A few minutes later, Mark slammed down the phone, heading upstairs to his bedroom to pack a suitcase. He'd agreed to go over to Isis's until Varley and his men had made alternative arrangements – probably a safe house out of town.

They'd discussed, in detail, what they'd do if Vinnie called. They'd gone over the conversation between Vinnie and Larson, detailing what had been said. If Vinnie was being sent on a 'recce' they didn't want to alert his suspicions, said Varley. Mark should invite him round. Fix a time – and tell the police immediately. They would then set up an operation and have people in place so that once they knew where Vinnie was, they'd close in on him.

By the time One Commando arrived in town, Varley told Mark confidently, they'd find themselves with an LAPD welcoming committee.

The two-car convoy sped down the Interstate 15 from Las Vegas to Los Angeles. Chevrolet Luminas from the same car-hire firm, they were unremarkable and attracted no attention during the six-hour trip through the desert, then through the Los Angeles sprawl; Arcadia, Pasadena, Riverside, en route to the apartment in Santa Monica. In the first car, Harris and de Clerque sat in silence almost the entire duration of the trip, Harris driving while de Clerque sat up front with him. Behind them on the back seat, two small suitcases contained nothing more suspicious than clothing and toiletry bags.

As the only US-based member of the team, Harris had been in charge of procurement for the whole operation and everything they needed had already been installed in the safe apartment. A former Marine who'd been dismissed from the armed forces after being court-marshalled for 'imposing undue discipline' during a mission in Somalia – he'd shot dead five tribespeople who'd refused to play ball – Harris was now a furniture salesman in Seattle. The job was the perfect cover; people came in to see him, and he went out for frequent 'measurings' without arousing the slightest suspicion. Often to be found at the back of the showroom behind the closed glass door of his office, on the phone or sending and receiving faxes, Harris had never moved many sofas.

De Clerque's requirements had been the most challenging. He'd sent through specifications for Pentolite detonators, Cordex, P4 plastic explosives and a timing device. Harris's long-established underground network had come up with nearly everything on the list, but certain items of South African manufacture had been more difficult. In the end, de Clerque had been forced to source the devices in Holland, disassemble them and courier them over to Harris, for reassembly and testing.

As for Guittard, most of his list of electronic equipment had been readily available. Harris hadn't had any difficulty with the shopping list, picking up a lot of it over the counter from Radio Shack. The telephone interceptor had been more difficult, but available from a counter-surveillance operator in Boston. Also in the Santa Monica apartment was the small but carefully selected arsenal of weapons ordered by

Larson: four Glock 17 automatic pistols and two MP5s; six-inch-blade hunting knives in leather sheaths; two-wave radio sets; dark-coloured trousers, shirts and jerseys bought from Sears; ski masks and combat boots.

Preparations had been made far beyond the apartment. Harris had made arrangements to scramble getaway vehicles with a single telephone call, ensuring a range of several routes was available at any one time. Like every other One Commando operation, Larson had emphasised, this one was to be surgical. They were to penetrate all defences to the target, do the business, and get out again before anyone knew what was happening. The Lefevre mission was a textbook example. Gallo's would have been too, had it not been for a spy in their midst. But this time, Larson told Harris coldly, there was no Alan Brent.

Harris had also carried out the reconnaissance. Ever since Isis and Jordan Hampshire had become targets, he'd been keeping their two residences under close surveillance. All their movements were monitored, particularly security arrangements, the drill followed by security personnel, the location of CCTV cameras, and everything else there was to know about how the two stars were protected. Jordan Hampshire's Beverly Hills home was, Harris had soon discovered, an open book. The rudimentary alarm system could be disabled simply by cutting off the electricity mains. The security guard's quarters were easily isolated. There were no bars or security glass in any of the windows.

By contrast, Isis's home had the reputation for being a fortress of security arrangements – a reputation well-deserved from what he'd been able to detect through the Szirowski Optic binoculars from out to sea. Apart from employing an on-site guard whose living quarters were inside the house, she was also linked to an armed-response service, which guaranteed a fully mobilised cadre of crack security personnel within twelve minutes of her pressing any one of a number of panic buttons located throughout the house, or of key entry points being breached. The link to the service was by radio, not landline; deactivating the system would require elaborate planning. Then there were the on-site challenges. Two alarm systems in different parts of the house. The double-gate entry intended to isolate all visitors between outer and inner grilles before they gained access to the house. Steel security screens controlling access to various corridors. Plus Isis had once told an interviewer she was well armed – if that was true, the locations of her weapons were unknown.

Harris's big surveillance breakthrough had come ten days earlier as he was pacing about the furniture showroom. Playing on one of the televisions was one of the endless documentaries on celebrity – this one about the homes of the rich and famous. Harris had looked up when there had been a mention of Isis's house and how she'd transformed it from a modest beachfront cottage into a sprawling mansion split over several different levels, and including her own studio. There'd followed interviews with the architect and some camp interior designer who'd discussed the creative dimensions of the job amid much limp-wristed arm waving. The thought had suddenly hit him: Isis would have required planning permission from the City Hall Planning Department to carry out all this work. Surely they would have required full details of the project, including floor plans? A telephone call to the Planning Department quickly confirmed this. When he was told records of previous planning applications were confidential, he wasn't concerned. He simply had several of the clerks in the planning department tailed for a few days, before choosing the one whose lifestyle aspirations appeared most out of proportion to his modest salary. An offer was made

and a deal done: it wasn't long before he had in his possession a detailed floor layout of Isis's house, which he e-mailed
Larson. From there, the plans had gone to de Clerque and
Guittard. By now, all four of them were intimately acquainted
with her house.

During their time in Las Vegas, Larson had gone through
his usual rigorous pre-op training, focusing on the main challenge of this operation – Isis's security systems. They faced
the most complex logistical problems ever and, equipped
with floor plans, photographs and videos of relevant interview clips, in Larson's suite at the Lucky Nugget they'd
mapped out as many different scenarios as they could fore-
see, working out their *modus operandi*, roles for each of them
that were flexible enough to be adapted to whatever circumstances they faced.

As usual, Larson's outward demeanour had been one of
implacable calm. But beneath the impenetrable expression
he harboured a concern that had never troubled him on
previous operations. This was One Commando's biggest and
most daring mission to date, with its highest-profile targets
ever. It would have a much, much greater impact than the
attack on an anonymous businessman in central London.
When the bodies of Isis and Jordan Hampshire were found
in her Malibu home, a global tidal wave of hysteria would
follow. The story would dominate the world's media. There
would be condemnations and condolences, weeping fans
depositing a mountain of bouquets at her gates; endless trib-
utes would be played on radio and TV stations. It would
become one of those pivotal events, like the assassination
of John F. Kennedy or the death of Princess Diana – people
would always remember where they were when they heard
about the double murder of pop's greatest sex icon and her
lover. And he, Bengt Larson, their executioner, would inherit

their fame. One Commando's notoriety would become as powerful as their celebrity had been, making him the most feared guerrilla leader in the world – a man of whom even his father would be in awe.

It was ironic, he thought as he sat hidden behind his reflective Ray-Bans in the back seat of the second car, that the key to his ambitions and this whole raid came in the form of the undisciplined, self-opinionated loser sitting in the passenger seat of his car.

Vinnie Dobson had been in a state of sullen bitterness since being escorted from the roulette table the night before. His instinctive reaction had been outrage: he could do what he liked, he complained loudly to the man he knew as Alexander Heindl, his voice raised. This was a free country. The croupier was staring across at him and others round the table were looking up, bemused. Then Larson had seized him by one arm and Harris by the other, and he remembered being told how plain-clothed security men patrolled casinos all the time, and how he couldn't afford to attract their attention because he was staying at the hotel under a false name and using a false passport.

He'd allowed himself to be escorted back through the lobby and up in a crowded lift till they came to Larson's floor, where they were the only ones to step out.

'That's a thousand bucks you made me leave behind!' He turned to Larson in undisguised fury as he was led down the corridor.

Larson ignored him.

'What the fuck d'you think you're playing at?'

Harris's American voice was cool and cautioning. 'Mind what you say.'

'*You* mind what *you* say!' snapped Vinnie as Larson pulled out his card key and opened the door of his suite.

Once inside, there was no holding Vinnie back. 'I'm doing you fuckwits one hell of a favour coming here. If I back out of this, you're stuffed. Completely stuffed.' He glowered first at Larson, then Harris, both of whom watched him without expression. 'You both know that,' he interpreted their silence as deference. 'You need me a whole lot more than I need you.'

'Is that so?' Larson came towards him, stopping less than a foot away so that his tall, muscled body towered over Vinnie's. 'I think you've completely misjudged the situation,' he said in that strangely contorted accent of his.

Vinnie was forced to raise his head so that he could meet Larson's eyes.

'You did us no favour coming here. We paid you five thousand pounds to release you from non-existent contracts.'

'What d'you mean, non-existent—!'

'We looked into your activities in London.' There was contempt in his voice. 'There was no big deal in the wings. Since Swerve you haven't cut anything except a sympathy contract from GCM.'

'That's not true!' Vinnie's voice quavered between anger and fear.

'Don't tell me what's true and what's not true. Your demand for money from us was extortion.'

'Get out of my face.' Vinnie tried brazening it out, reaching out to Larson with his arm. But Larson wouldn't budge.

'Just because I'm here doesn't mean you own me.' He tried pushing Larson away with both arms now.

'It means you'll do exactly as we say.' Larson's voice was toneless. 'And I don't tolerate indiscipline. Harris?'

In a single motion Harris, who had acquired a black belt in judo after three years' intensive study in Japan, had seized Vinnie by the arm, brought it up behind his back and forced him to the ground where he yelped in agony.

'Stop it!' he cried. 'You're going to bust my arm!'

'So what if we do?' asked Larson.

Vinnie hadn't stepped out of line since. He'd sat in one room of Larson's suite while the others planned the operation in the other, occasionally having him order in something from room service for them. Larson had given him a book to study, *Close that Tele-sale*; he expected Dobson to have thoroughly familiarised himself with the techniques it covered by the time they left Las Vegas, he said. Vinnie had protested, saying he didn't know anything about tele-sales and didn't need to. To which Larson had replied that he was about to close the sale of his life: when he phoned Mark Watson, wanting to visit him in Isis's home, the answer must be 'yes'.

Larson had been staring out of the car window at the barren landscape for most of the trip. Up front, in the passenger seat, Dobson continued to flick through the tele-sales book, distracted. He'd been left in no doubt how important it was that Mark should agree to meet him. Everything else depended on it – all One Commando's elaborate preparations would be as nothing if he didn't play his part. But that wasn't something directly within his control. Although he'd left Mark on cordial terms outside the Lamb in London, he couldn't guarantee how he'd behave in LA. For once, Vinnie felt his bluster desert him.

Finally, unable to take the silence any longer, he turned round to face Larson, his voice rising in desperation. 'What if, I mean, what if he doesn't say yes?'

It was a while before Larson responded. 'He must,' he said in a level voice. 'If he doesn't, you won't be going home. You won't be going . . . anywhere.'

*   *   *

Mark had only just stepped into the hallway of Isis's home when his mobile phone went off.

'Mark, me old son,' came the voice from the other end.

'Vinnie!' He didn't have to feign surprise. While he and Varley had discussed what he'd do when this call came through, he hadn't been expecting it nearly so soon.

'Didn't really think I'd call, did you?'

'Well, I—'

'Only joking!' Vinnie acted out his usual life-and-soul persona. 'So guess what? I've just made my first transatlantic crossing. First of many.'

'You're in America?'

'Even better. I'm in LA!'

'Really?' Mark was aghast as he looked through the open front door to where Denzil was parking the Lincoln, oblivious to his conversation.

'Too right,' Vinnie was saying. 'And I'd like to see you.'

'Sure!' Mark tried to project enthusiasm. 'Would be good.'

'So what are you up to?'

'Well, we've just had the album signed off,' began Mark, 'we'll soon be in rehearsals for the tour—'

'No. Now, I mean.'

'Right now?' This was happening too fast! He wasn't ready for this and, more to the point, were the police? They hadn't been expecting the call for a day or two, maybe more. Deep down, he supposed, he'd hoped that if he and Isis disappeared from view for a while the One Commando problem would go away; how could their cause be sustainable once the Voisier scam was publicly revealed?

But there was no escaping the voice at the other end of the phone.

'Right now,' he said cautiously, 'I'm in Malibu.'

'You're at Isis's then?'

'Yeah, why?'

'You know how much I'd love to meet her.'

'I don't know if that's such a good idea.' Mark made a play for time. 'She's not feeling too good at the moment. In fact she's in bed.'

'Sick, huh?'

Mark paused before saying, 'That time of the month.'

'But *we* could still meet,' persisted Vinnie.

'I'd like that, Vin. But I've got to be at a function in town at six. By the time I get home, I'll have to head right out again.'

'Oh,' Vinnie digested this in silence before saying, 'the thing is, I'm only here for a couple of hours.'

'How do you mean?'

'Heading to Las Vegas.'

'You flew all the way here just to play blackjack?'

'I've got some business to attend to as well.'

That'd be right, thought Mark. Maybe Vinnie had been sent on his recce so they could all hole up somewhere and work out their operation. Maybe that was the plan.

As though confirming his suspicions, Vinnie continued, 'We can meet up properly, in a few days when I get back. I was just hoping to see you quickly. Couldn't I drop in to see you, just for ten minutes?'

Mark thought of his conversation with Varley. Surely it wasn't beyond the capabilities of the LAPD to get some plain-clothes cops out to Malibu in half an hour? Someone who could trail Vinnie back to wherever his new-found friends were hiding?

For a moment as he paused, mind racing, he thought that the timing of Vinnie's call couldn't have been worse. He hadn't seen Isis since earlier in the day at Unum – Christ knew what kind of reception he was going to get.

And he could just imagine what her reaction would be when he told her he'd invited a known One Commando spy for afternoon tea. But right now, it seemed the best thing to do. Hadn't Varley himself told him that when Vinnie asked to meet him, he should say yes?

Eventually he said, 'Well, I guess if this is the only chance we have . . . Do you know Isis's address?'

22

When Isis emerged from the bedroom wing to find that Mark had arrived, and that a One Commando agent was on his way to her home, her already dark mood grew rapidly worse.

'Why the hell—?'

'Just following orders,' he said with a bleak grimace. He didn't much care that he was on her home ground. Vinnie's imminent arrival and the accompanying police operation were far too important to get hung up with her mood swings. Besides, after her temper tantrum outside Unum Music, he reckoned he didn't owe her any favours.

'I've got to tell Varley what's happening.' He picked up her hallway phone, extracted the policeman's number from his wallet and commenced dialling.

'Is that Sheriff Varley's office?' Mark didn't recognise the voice at the other end.

'No, Simmo, a colleague,' replied the other. 'Varley's stepped away from his desk for five minutes.'

Mark exhaled heavily. 'It's Mark Watson. Do you know about One Commando?'

'Fully briefed.'

'I'm at Isis's and have just had the call from Dobson,' he said quickly. 'He's coming here in thirty minutes.'

'You're both in the house?' confirmed the other.

'All three of us – there's also Holly, Isis's daughter.'

'Stay where you are.' His voice was imperative.

'You'll be able to send in—?'

'Of course. Just stay where you are,' the other repeated. 'We have the situation under control.'

Mark hung up, looking over at Isis's expression – a mix of anger and apprehension.

In the back of the specially equipped courier van heading out towards Malibu, Harris switched the microphone off his headset, before leaning forward to where Larson was sitting in the driver's compartment.

'I've just intercepted a call. They're on to Dobson.'

Larson flashed a look of urgent enquiry.

'It's okay, it's okay.' Harris nodded. 'I told them to stay put.'

When the buzzer of the gate intercom sounded, Mark looked into the monitor by the front door. Vinnie was standing alone – he must have come out by taxi, thought Mark, picking up the intercom before letting him through both sets of gates. Then he opened the front door and stood waiting for him to appear, unlocking the steel grille behind the door with the key kept next to the gate monitor.

'Jordan Hampshire!' Vinnie greeted him in a facetious tone as he approached the front door. 'So here we are, both of us in Lalaland together.' He extended his hand as he stepped towards Mark.

Mark played along with the put-on joviality as best he could.

Then Vinnie was exclaiming, 'This place is like Fort Knox!'

'Yeah, well, has to be.'

'Electronic controls for everything, right?'

'Something like that.' Mark waved in the direction of the gate intercom as he led him through the hallway into Isis's sitting room. 'You're in luck. Isis got up a short while ago.'

'Oh, great!' responded Vinnie, though Mark didn't miss the twitchiness about him, the distracted expression on his face as he glanced about a hallway crammed to the rafters with security equipment. He could look all he liked, thought Mark, it wasn't going to help. Even if he'd cased out every device in the house, in just a few minutes Varley and his men were going to arrive – the beginning of the end for One Commando.

In the meantime, they were to play along with the pretence of normality.

'Come through to meet her.'

'Yeah.' Vinnie followed him, scanning round the room.

Leading him out on to the balcony, Mark watched Vinnie carefully as he reacted to the presence of Isis, whose expression was hidden behind large Versace sunglasses. Standing a short distance away, Frank was watching Holly who had gone down to the beach immediately below.

'Isis, this is Vinnie Dobson from London,' said Mark.

Vinnie extended his arm and was shaking her hand more vigorously than was polite. 'I'm your number one fan,' he said.

How many times had she heard that, Mark couldn't help wondering. Aloud he said, 'Vinnie's only here for a short while, then he goes to Las Vegas.' He turned to Vinnie.

'That's right,' Vinnie was nodding, 'I've got to be out of here soon. But I couldn't pass through LA without looking up me old mate. I was the one who discovered him, you know?' he couldn't resist.

'Really?' Isis's eyebrows darted above her sunglasses briefly. 'Oh, yes. Knew he was going to turn into a star!'

There was an awkward pause while Isis regarded her unwelcome guest coolly through her sunglasses. Then Vinnie was saying, 'You know, right now,' he was apologetic, 'I need a loo.'

For just a moment, Mark and Isis exchanged a look of mutual bemusement before Mark was saying, 'Sure.'

Turning Vinnie away he led him back through the sitting room into the hallway.

'It's called the bathroom over here,' he said, pointing him in the direction of the visitors' bathroom. 'Second on the right.'

Hilton Gallo was in the Columbia boardroom pitching a major new motion picture development to the assembled suits when, back at GCM, the phone call came through from Varley. With neither Hilton nor Elizabeth in the office, it was his secretary, Melissa Schwartz, who picked up the call. Was his message urgent, she asked Varley, having explained that Hilton was out of the office. There was no mistaking the seriousness of Varley's tone when he replied. This was extremely urgent and of critical importance too.

Moments later Melissa was typing a message to appear on the pager Elizabeth carried with her at all times. Only in the most extraordinary of circumstances would she consider interrupting a meeting as important to the agency as this one. But these were extraordinary circumstances.

Elizabeth felt the pager vibrating in the pocket of the handbag pressed against her leg under the boardroom table.

While one of the Columbia execs was engaged in a spirited defence of the studio's latest budget-busting space movie, she leaned down, slipped the pager from her handbag and read the message, before scribbling it on a piece of paper which she slipped to Hilton, sitting beside her.

Hilton quickly excused himself from the meeting, to the evident astonishment of both the Columbia and GCM teams.

'Life or death issue,' he explained, heading for the door.

Outside, he commandeered the nearest phone and quickly dialled Varley.

'What is it?' he demanded.

'We got a fix on one of the group – the guy who changed at Denver? He terminated in Las Vegas. From that we back-checked and picked up another guy, also in Vegas.'

'So they're all there.'

'That's our assumption,' Varley spoke quickly. 'There's something else you should know. We've run ID on both men. De Clerque's wanted by Russian police, he's heavily involved with a St Petersburg Mafia group. He had explosives train-ing from a former KGB sabotage team, and has blown his way into three banks in the last eight months. The other guy, Guittard, is a digital security wonk. Ex-Marconi and a technology runner between the IRA and Tripoli. Someone wealthy must be bankrolling these guys.'

Hilton listened to Varley with a hard-eyed intensity. 'What's being done?'

'We're searching for them, of course. But trying to find four men in Las Vegas . . .' Then, after a pause, 'We need to get this information to—'

'Of course,' Hilton replied swiftly. 'And protection?'

'I've fixed a safe house for both your clients. Santa Ynez. It's being prepared to take them tonight.'

'In the meantime—?'

'Our squad cars are patrolling Broadbeach—'

'We're way past that stage.'

'Only a few hours ago you assured me she had the highest level security of any home in California?'

'We can't just leave them like sitting ducks!'

'Get your clients to pack their bags,' Varley didn't disguise his impatience, 'and we'll be round to collect them.'

Vinnie Dobson had a good look at the gate entry and intercom console as he walked through the hall to the bathroom. As soon as he heard Mark out on the balcony talking to Isis, he about-turned and went back to it, quickly scanning the CCTV image, the intercom receiver, the array of buttons and lights on the panel.

Walking in here had been dead easy! Straight through the open gates and in through the front door. After all the contingency planning bullshit One Commando had gone on about, he'd expected masked gunmen and razor-wire at every turn. Instead, it had been like stepping into the home of any other multi-millionaire. He'd quickly noticed where the two bodyguards were standing – he'd been warned to expect them and told that under no circumstances was he to attempt a gate opening if either of them was around. But one was out on the balcony right now, and the other floating about like a spare part in the sitting room. 'If you can't perform the gate opening from inside, cut your visit to less than ten minutes then leave,' the man he now knew as Larson had ordered him. 'We'll get in when they open up to let you out.'

No need for that, thought Vinnie, trying to decide which button to push. As soon as the gates had opened, he knew, they would cut off all the electricity and phone lines so that none of the security systems would function. It wouldn't take them long to get up the driveway and into the house. They had the whole thing drilled down to split-second timing.

Suddenly the phone was ringing and he felt under pressure. He couldn't hang around here – he could hear footsteps heading in his direction. Taking a chance he pushed both green buttons on the entry console before stepping away. Mark was in the sitting room picking up the phone.

'Mark. I need Isis.' Hilton's voice was imperative.

'Hold on a second.' Mark was about to put the receiver down when he heard a click on the line. The unmistakable sound of another receiver being lifted. But how could that be? Denzil and Isis were on the balcony. Frank was downstairs. The other two lines went into the hall and Isis's bedroom. His bemusement turned to outrage, however, as Vinnie appeared in the doorway holding the cordless receiver from the hall.

There was a smirk on Vinnie's face as he came towards him – a sly, challenging expression. About to shout at him to put the phone down, Mark heard the telephone line click dead – and instants later was aware of movement out of the corner of his eye. Glancing out of the window, he saw to his horror the gates opening and four men in dark clothing pounding up the driveway.

Vinnie pounced, knocking the receiver to the floor and shoving Mark against a bookcase. Hearing a noise from inside, Denzil was already storming in from the balcony, seizing Vinnie by the shoulders and throwing him off Mark, on to the floor.

'They're coming through the gates!' gasped Mark.

Denzil looked up to see figures nearing the house.

'Frank!' he screamed as he ran to the balcony door, 'bring her up!'

Mark was scrambling over to Isis who'd jumped up from where she'd been sitting, her face frozen with terror. Frank rushed up the steps from the beach carrying Holly, and shoved the child into Mark's arms.

'Behind the security barrier!' Frank ordered, hurrying to join Denzil.

Mark led Isis into the house, carrying Holly and shielding her eyes. To get behind the security barrier, which could be lowered to isolate the bedroom wing, they had to go through the hallway – immediately outside which their body-guards were now in hand-to-hand combat with two dark-clad intruders. For a moment in the sitting room, Mark paused in indecision. Then he decided they should get through while they still had access. He and Isis had hardly started their dash through the hall when they both found themselves twisted back and falling to the floor. As they fell, they caught sight of a tall man with short-cropped blond hair and cool blue eyes. He must have come in from the balcony. Holly had fallen on top of Mark and rolled on to the carpet.

'Run to your secret place!' screamed Isis.

Above them, Larson barely glanced as she sprinted out of the room.

'We get her later,' he told Isis, expressionless, poking her in the chest with his boot, pointing his automatic pistol from her face to Mark's and back again.

Outside the front door, Denzil had defied Harris's judo training with several well-placed blows to the head – but Harris now had him on the floor where the two were locked in struggle. Meanwhile Frank's brawn had been too much for Guittard whom he'd sent reeling down the steps. Then, catching sight of where Larson had Isis and Mark pinned down, he moved stealthily through the hallway and up behind Larson, delivering a powerful blow to the small of his back, sending him buckling across the sitting room. Isis sprang up immediately, running through the hallway and down the corridor to the bedroom wing. Scrambling to his feet, Mark found his escape blocked by Larson who'd seized him by the ankle. Frank began hammering Larson's outstretched arms. Seeing that Mark was about to escape, Vinnie, who'd watched Larson's capture of Isis and Mark from the corner with a smug satisfaction, grabbed the nearest weapon he could find – an oak fruit bowl – and ran over, intending to bring it down heavily on Frank. Frank ducked out of the way, so that the full force of Vinnie's blow struck Larson on the shoulder. Larson yelped with pain in the same instant that Mark broke free, following Isis into the bedroom wing. Immediately he was in the corridor, he pressed the button operating the steel security grille which began to slide down from the ceiling. Then he ran to find Isis.

Isis had rushed to Holly's bedroom. They had regular security drills, once every two or three months. They'd pretend the house was under attack and they'd follow the directions of the security firm that had installed their systems. Behind the steel security grille, the bedroom wing was safe, with windows providing an escape route out. As a last resort, they could bunker downstairs in the studio, access to which was protected by additional security measures. Now Isis sought Holly in her special hiding place – a cupboard in her bedroom which had a false bottom. But she wasn't there! Nor was she in any of her other cupboards or under the bed. Hurrying to her own room, Isis had called out for her daughter, searching in every place she could think, before trying the guest bedrooms.

By the time Mark appeared, Isis was desperate.

'I can't find her anywhere! She's not here!' She glanced about, wild-eyed. 'Unless—' She looked behind where the steel grille was descending, to the guest bathroom. As a game, Holly sometimes hid in the washing basket, pretending to have gone missing. Following Isis's gaze, Mark ducked beneath where the steel security screen was already more than halfway to the floor. As he hurried across the hall he could hear the sounds of combat from the sitting room. In the guest bathroom, Mark called out for Holly, opening several cupboards, before finding her huddled up and trembling with fear, in the washing basket. Seizing her, he carried her outside. The grille was getting closer and closer to the floor. He wouldn't have time to clamber under it with Holly in his arms. Instead he put her down on the floor, held her by the wrists and swung her in an arc that sent her flying across the polished wooden floor under the gate to where Isis was waiting, just moments before the grille lurched to a halt inches above the floor – and lights went out throughout the house. Sweeping Holly up in her arms, Isis looked through the steel bars at Mark with a mixture of profound gratitude and anguish, just as Larson stormed through from the sitting room.

'Like a rat caught outside its cage.' He seized Mark by the back of his shirt, flinging him heavily on to the floor.

For a moment, Mark lay paralysed on his stomach, all the air forced out of his body. As he lay there, gasping and unable to breathe, he looked out towards the front door, where Larson's three dark-clad accomplices had overwhelmed Denzil and Frank, and were dragging their two unconscious forms into the house.

Larson had Mark's hands behind his back and was taping up his wrists while shouting out something to one of the others about the inside security barrier. De Clerque quickly moved over to the grille and was packing plastic explosives on to the four steel bars from which it was suspended. Dragging Mark away from the area, Larson tugged him along the hallway and into the kitchen, where he began taping up his ankles.

'You're wasting your time,' Mark gasped. 'Whatever you do, the whole world will know the truth tomorrow.'

'You speak nonsense.'

'Berkeley Square are holding a press conference. Madrid. Tomorrow.'

Larson flipped him over so that his back arched painfully over his bound hands.

'That's good.' He'd seized Mark's ankles and was wrapping them tight with tape.

'How can it be good? They'll know you framed Berkeley Square! They'll know the testing went on at Voisier.'

'What is this Voisier?' Task completed, Larson shoved Mark's feet away in contempt, flashing an angry glance at him. 'The video was of Berkeley Square!'

As Larson stalked out of the room Mark stared after him. Was it all a bluff? he wondered. But why would he bother? Larson's anger seemed like a flash of fervent outrage. It wasn't put on.

He could hear them in the hallway fixing explosives in place. With the two bodyguards inside and the front door closed, there'd be no sign from the outside of the house that anything was amiss. Despite the hitches, the operation was running with clean, surgical efficiency. With both electricity and phone lines cut, there was no way he or Isis could contact people outside – even if they could get to a phone or panic button. But surely Hilton would have raised the alarm after his abruptly curtailed phone call?

Raising his head as far as he was able, and taking short,

panting breaths, he glanced about the kitchen searching for something, anything, with which to free himself. Drawing up on to his knees, he found that he could shuffle backwards very slowly. Behind him, next to the space under the kitchen sink, was a unit of drawers. He didn't know what was in them, but it was worth a try.

From outside came the sound of a muffled crack, followed by a great reverberating clanging which shook the whole house, as the steel grille fell from its supports on to the floor.

'Bring them here!' Larson ordered, before darting back to the kitchen to check up on Mark.

The cacophony of the steel gate crashing had made Mark lose his balance and tumble once again on his face. When Larson looked into the kitchen he was lying, prostrate and gasping.

Within seconds of the grille coming down, there was an ominous hissing. Two of Larson's men quickly returned, clutching their faces.

'Tear gas!' screamed Harris, hurrying out of the corridor into the hall. He and Guittard who had run in first and had taken lungfuls of it, were doubled up in agony, faces in their hands. Glancing about him, Larson tried to keep his rapidly rising anger in check. If he'd known she'd had gas installed, it would have been very, very easy to have brought masks. One gap in intelligence and now he had two men incapacitated and a no-go zone created, while his target was free to escape from the other end of the house.

Seizing dishtowels from the kitchen, he handed one to de Clerque.

'You and I go in and get them,' he ordered.

Then, glancing into the sitting room, where Vinnie was sitting sullenly in one corner, 'You look after your friend.'

Mark was back on his knees as soon as they'd left, and

inching back towards the drawers. He didn't know how long he would have before Vinnie appeared. Only moments. But he had to get there – it was his only chance.

He could feel one of the drawer handles against his knuckles. He managed to pull it towards him without falling forward, and search inside with his fingertips. There were linen napkins and napkin rings, other smooth round objects he couldn't identify. Then the handle of a knife. Seizing it hurriedly, he fell on his side, sliding his legs from under him so that he was sitting with his back to the drawers and legs out in front of him, the knife clasped in his hands behind him.

Running his fingertips up the blade, however, he soon discovered that what he'd retrieved was a cheese knife. Its only sharpness was at the twin tips of the blade. Nonetheless he began jabbing through the tape that wrapped his wrists together, piercing and tearing and working frantically at the bindings, until Vinnie appeared in the doorway.

Vinnie had a bruise all the way across his left cheek from where Larson had thrown him against a table. It had come up in a dark, crimson weal and had started to bleed though he affected not to notice.

'So, Jordan Hampshire,' he leaned against the kitchen door-frame, 'bet you don't feel such a big-shot now, do you?'

Behind his back, Mark kept working on the tape. But he had to keep his movements carefully controlled.

'You just don't get it,' he shook his head.

'Oh, I get it all right,' sneered Vinnie, 'thought you were so clever using me to get what you wanted. Big money. Big house. The Queen of Pop. But I'm the one who put you there.' He pointed to himself. He was on a roll now – which was just what Mark needed. He was ranting on about how much he'd done for Mark, how he'd put him on the map.

All the while he was talking, Mark kept up the piercing and tearing. Piercing and tearing. He was making progress, he could feel it. The bindings were getting looser.

As Vinnie vented his spleen, Mark hastily glanced around him. It was one thing getting his hands free, but with his feet still bound, how was he going to get past Vinnie? He needed to work things out – to use his brains. He knew that with the tear gas canisters off, Isis and Holly could be in only one place. She had explained to him how they'd only ever use the gas as a last resort, before bunkering in the downstairs studio, which was not only soundproof, but airtight too. But how to reach the two of them? And how to get them all out of here?

After a while he interrupted Vinnie's monologue, 'It's not all how it seems, you know.'

'Oh, yeah?'

'The clothes I wear. The haircut. None of that's my stuff. They make me do that for the media.'

'Oh, sure, like you've got no control.'

'Too right!'

'You're the big star but you've got no say.'

'Not a lot of say.'

'Why do I find that so hard to believe?'

'D'you think I'd go and stick a fucking stud in my tongue, then?'

'That'd be right,' said Vinnie.

'It's the truth.'

'Get out of it!'

'Well, what d'you think this is, then?' He opened his mouth.

Shaking his head, Vinnie walked over towards where he was sitting, 'Where is it, then?' he demanded, leaning down to look in Mark's mouth.

In that same instant, Mark reached over, his hands now free, to a spray can of industrial bleach that Juanita kept under the kitchen sink. He squirted the contents in Vinnie's eyes. Staggering back, Vinnie howled in pain as Mark quickly pulled himself to his feet, seized a carving knife from the top drawer, and slashed through the tape around his ankles. With Vinnie doubled up in the corner, Mark thought quickly. Isis and Holly would have locked themselves into the downstairs studio. Larson and the other man searching for them in the bedroom wing would quickly realise they'd gone down there. Secure as the studio was, it couldn't withstand plastic explosives. If they tried to escape by car, that would only prompt Larson and the other one to wait outside and attack the moment they emerged from the garage. Suddenly he had an idea.

Five minutes later, the garage door started to judder open. Larson and Guittard scrambled outside to halt a getaway. Inside, they could hear the Range Rover kicking into life. Meanwhile Harris and de Clerque, recovered from the tear gas, had seized Holly and, despite her futile efforts to break free, emerged from the house and were running up the driveway with her struggling form. Or so it appeared. Larson didn't notice the two dark-clad figures immediately, focused as he was on the opening garage door. But once alerted, he shouted for them to stop. This wasn't part of their plan! The three targets were to be isolated *inside* the house. Something was going wrong!

But his two comrades continued to the top of the driveway. The first one disappeared from view and the second, carrying Holly, was about to turn the corner out of view, when he suddenly collapsed to the ground. The bullet had been a clean shot, directly through his left shoulder. As he fell, he released his grip of Holly, who scrambled away from him, rushing towards the first dark-clad figure. Ripping off the ski mask and black hood, Isis faced the rapidly approaching line of police officers.

'Don't!' she cried out, grabbing Holly to her. 'It's us!'

As Mark lay on the ground, bullet wound bleeding, he looked back at where the remote-operated garage door had opened sufficiently to allow room to climb under it. Guittard was already scrambling inside. Urging him on, Larson glanced up the driveway when he suddenly saw Mark's prostrate body – and realised he'd been duped.

Abruptly, he turned from the garage, setting off swiftly down the beach towards the neighbouring property. It was only moments before the line of police reached the top of the driveway. A volley of fire pursued Larson as he dodged and weaved between Isis's house and her neighbours. Then, struck by a bullet, he was thrown off his feet and collapsed in a heap on the sand. Watching all this from where he lay on the ground, Mark felt his face wet with blood, and a strange, pounding sensation in his shoulder. Moments later, he blacked out.

By the time Hilton and Lebowitz arrived on the scene, a dozen squad cars with flashing lights already blocked the entrance to the street, a hundred yards up from Isis's house. Two ambulances were at the gates and a fire engine down the driveway. Rapid-response media vehicles jammed the street and two TV helicopters were circling overhead – police had already cordoned off the property to a fast-gathering crowd of reporters, neighbours and prying passers-by. Explaining who he was, Hilton demanded to be taken to his clients.

He'd been suspicious the moment Mark answered the phone. Something in the other man's voice hadn't sounded right. Then he'd been disconnected and the moment he called back he got an extended ringing tone. Realising the phone line had been cut, he immediately dialled up Varley, telling him what had happened. Varley promised to take immediate action.

Hilton had taken the lift downstairs, ordering Elizabeth to get Lebowitz to join him. The two of them had headed out frantically through the traffic, Hilton phoning Isis's place continually, but to no avail.

As he and Lebowitz appeared, escorted by a reluctant police officer, Varley came out towards them.

'Are they okay?' Hilton's face registered an uncharacteristic tumult of emotion.

'Thank God, yes,' nodded Varley. 'Mark Watson's taken a hit in the shoulder – on his way to hospital, but nothing serious. Isis and Holly, they're being treated for shock.' He gestured towards the house.

'What the hell happened?' demanded Lebowitz as they strode towards it.

'One Commando took out the bodyguards and disabled the security systems.' He glanced behind him. 'Survival in those circumstances,' he was shaking his head, 'quite frankly, it's a miracle—'

'So how—?'

'Two of them were badly teargassed. Crawling on the floor apparently, when Mark Watson knocked them out and grabbed their uniforms.'

'When did your boys get here?' asked Hilton.

'As soon as you phoned I got on to control,' said Varley, 'but they already had six squad cars on the way. You should have told me you'd already—'

Hilton was shaking his head vigorously. 'You were the first person I called.'

The two men halted abruptly, exchanging a long, hard stare that seemed to last an eternity. Before, finally, Varley whispered the question that had stopped them both:

'Then who tipped them off?'

23

Elizabeth Reynolds was at his bedside when Mark came round from the general anaesthetic. He'd been rushed to Emergency where surgeons had operated immediately on his shoulder. He'd suffered only minor damage; the bullet had passed under his skin and through his biceps before exiting, only just missing his humerus bone and brachial artery. It would be several months before the muscles knitted back together and he'd have to wear a sling for the first few days as a precaution. But no lasting damage had been done.

As he blinked open his eyes and focused on Elizabeth's face, she reached out and squeezed his hand.

'Take it easy,' she murmured.

He felt his eyelids close heavily.

'They cleaned you all up and stitched you back together. You're going to be fine.'

He smiled, exhaling slowly before asking, 'How's . . . Isis and . . . ?'

'They're both okay. Shaken. But okay. It's all over now.'

She took his hand again. 'Larson's dead. The others are in jail.'

He opened his eyes to look up at her flawless features and the blonde hair that framed her face. He was still floating from the anaesthetic and Elizabeth appeared dreamily angelic amid the white walls and white sheets of the hospital room. Taking in what she'd just told him, he recalled the events of the afternoon like a sequence out of a movie. The arrival of One Commando through the gates. The desperate struggle in the house. How he had realised the only possible escape route was through diversion and disguise.

'It's all . . . surreal,' he managed, after a while.

'Don't think about it – you don't have to. Just relax.'

But closing his eyes again Mark found that he *wanted* to think about it. He didn't want to 'just relax'. Even if Larson had been killed and the rest of One Commando were out of action, there was still too much that was unexplained. Even in his drowsy, drugged-up state, he recalled Larson's anger when he'd told him, while struggling on Isis's kitchen floor, about Voisier Laboratories. It hadn't been the anger of being caught out or proven wrong, Mark had thought even at the time – but the anger of being contradicted. Larson passionately believed he *had* videotaped Berkeley Square's labs in Madrid. It wasn't just a cynical set-up; it was the real thing. And no doubt that was how he justified the attack on Lefevre – and the horrors he'd planned to inflict on Isis and himself.

Which was another thing Mark didn't get: One Commando had the inside story on Isis and had threatened to use it. So why hadn't they gone ahead and carried out the threat? Why hadn't they told the world about her private past and left it to the media to tear her apart. Flying out to LA on a military adventure was a risk he just couldn't understand them taking.

The key to all his questions, Mark thought in his anaesthetic haze, was bound up in the biggest mystery of all: who had tipped off the Los Angeles police? While being loaded into the ambulance, he'd been told of the eleventh-hour alert – exactly the same as the British police had received just before Hilton Gallo was attacked in Green's. Someone outside One Commando knew what was going on. And for reasons Mark couldn't fathom, he'd decided to tell the police – not far enough in advance to prevent the attack from happening, but with enough time to ensure they were quickly on the scene.

Thoughts giddy and disordered, Mark moved restlessly on the hospital bed before he looked up directly at the ceiling. There *was* another person outside of One Commando! There had been the conversation when that guy with the made-up-sounding name had set up the meeting with Vinnie in Regent's Park. If the call could be traced . . .

'I need to get to a phone.' He felt down his body with his right hand, and found he was wearing some kind of gown, as he looked over at Elizabeth again.

'We've spoken to your mother,' she reassured him. 'She knows you're going to be fine—'

'No it's – it's something else. I must get hold of Lloyd, my brother.'

Elizabeth was glancing at her watch. 'But it'll be the middle of the night—'

'Doesn't matter.' He was already struggling to get up. 'This is important.'

'All right, wait.' She sensed his determination. 'I'll call a nurse and see if we can put some pillows behind your back. You can use my cellphone.'

*   *   *

London
Thursday, 7 October

It was after midnight when the sleek convertible pulled up in the quiet Islington street and from out of the driver's door stepped the dark-suited figure of Jasper Jones. Since Malibu he'd been working even more intensely than ever. He hadn't had much sleep and the long hours and frenetic pace had put dark bags under his eyes. But the lack of sleep hadn't bothered him. Almost every waking moment for the past two days had been spent focused on One Commando and the Isis secret. Adrenaline charging through his system, he'd seldom felt so driven, so close to his goal.

He let himself into his house and made his way up the stairs, stepped into the sitting room and threw his jacket over the back of the sofa before switching on the TV news channel through force of habit. The drama at Isis's house had been all over the media, of course, the final end-game like something out of a mega-budget Hollywood blockbuster. With Jordan Hampshire lying wounded in a hospital bed and a One Commando trial inevitable, the whole saga was set to run and run.

In the meantime, Isis's secret, undoubtedly the most explosive confidence to which he'd ever gained access, had yet to be revealed; he was the only one now who knew it. Because the only other person with any idea about his real involvement in One Commando was now lying in a mortuary in California. All in all, thought Jones, he couldn't have scripted the whole thing better himself.

In fact his only cause of regret was the end of his budding romance with Gail. Last night he'd been at home, fixated on CNN, when the doorbell had rung and in came Gail, with two bags from Marks & Spencer replete with food.

'Surprise visit!' she announced cheerily. 'I thought I'd cook us both supper.'

He'd barely been able to suppress his irritation – or keep his eyes off the TV screen.

'Don't look so ecstatic.' There'd been an ironic note in her voice he'd never heard before.

'Sorry.' He turned back to her. 'It's just that I have a lot of work to do tonight.'

'Oh, work, schmurk. Can't you give it a break for once?'

Jones had felt the heat rising to his face. 'Don't presume to tell me how I should spend my time!' he snapped.

She stood, staring at him open-mouthed, bags of groceries dangling from both hands, before about-turning and walking back to the front door.

'Look, I'm sorry,' he went after her, 'that came out—'

'It's all right, Jas, perfectly all right,' she glanced over her shoulder with a toxic smile, 'I'd rather find out sooner than later.'

'Find out what?' Alarm was added to his mixed emotions.

'Don't play the innocent.' At the front door she swivelled round and pointed a long, exquisitely manicured finger in his face. 'You're seeing someone else, aren't you?'

He reacted to the accusation with amusement and relief. 'Seeing someone else?' he repeated, incredulous. 'I don't have time to see you, so when the hell am I supposed to be seeing someone else?'

'If you weren't such a two-timing bastard you would have time to see me!' she argued, tears in her eyes.

For a moment he looked her up and down, taking her all in. She was perfect, he thought yet again. Just the look he went for, and tailor-made for the passenger seat of his Saab. Pity he had to let her go, but if she wanted to believe in her outlandish fantasies, then good luck to her. He didn't have the time or the inclination to whisk her upstairs and molly-coddle her and tell her that everything was going to be fine.

'Look, Gail,' he began, 'I'm not seeing anyone else. I've no *desire* to see anyone else. I think you're a great girl and that we've got a wonderful thing going between us. You just have to understand that sometimes I have to work incredibly long hours.'

'I thought you were an agency director?' She was suspicious.

'I *am* a director.'

'So, you must have a choice?'

He shrugged. 'You'd think I would but—'

'And you choose to put your work above me?'

'It's not like that!'

'Then how is it?'

'It's—' he stood before her, spluttering, trying desperately to think of something to say.

'You know,' she'd opened the front door, composure having returned, 'I think I'd prefer it if you *were* seeing somebody else. At least I'd have the satisfaction of knowing I'd dated a man with balls!'

She turned, slamming the door behind her, and stalked down the pavement at high speed. He hadn't made any effort to go after her. What was the point? Within moments he was back in front of the TV, completely absorbed in a live report from LA.

Tonight he hadn't long been home when the phone rang. Even for Jasper Jones, calls at half past midnight were outside the ordinary. It crossed his mind that this might be Gail. But from the other end came the panic-stricken tones of Lindy Laburne, Animal Liberation Front's key spokesperson.

'I've been trying you all night,' her words came out in a

torrent, 'something terrible's happening and I just don't know what to do.'

'Why don't you tell me?' he asked, his tone cool and condescending.

'I've heard on the grapevine that Berkeley Square have set up a media conference in Madrid tomorrow. The lab we've been campaigning about – turns out it belongs to Voisier.'

'How unfortunate.'

'We've staked everything on this,' her voice rose, agitated. 'I just don't understand how it happened.' She ranted on for quite some time before demanding, her voice near the point of hysteria, 'So what do we do?'

'Nothing we *can* do,' Jones told her, crisply. 'We can't stop Berkeley Square holding a media conference.'

'But I mean, surely . . . how could we have got it so wrong? You went there yourself!'

'I did indeed.'

'So did Alexander when he took the video.'

'Exactly.' Then, after a pause, 'I don't understand it at all.'

Laburne let off steam for a few more minutes before realising that any further discussion was futile. Putting down the receiver at the other end, Jones shook his head. Silly bitch! The only surprise, so far as he was concerned, was how long it had taken them to work it out.

The decision to pick Berkeley Square had been quite fortuitous. In his early days in the animal rights movement he'd invested considerable time checking out animal testing allegations, and one of his searches had taken him to Madrid. Rumours had been circulating of a laboratory carrying out the most evil excesses, and with the help of local sympathisers, and relentless questioning, he'd eventually tracked it down in a sprawling industrial zone. Far behind an outer security fence, the building was heavily fortified and regularly patrolled by a private security firm. He'd gained access posing as an out-of-hours delivery operator for long enough to fire off half a dozen surreptitious photographs. While there he had also caught sight of a package addressed to Voisier Laboratories.

It hadn't surprised him. Jean Voisier had already been run out of his native Belgium by anti-vivisection campaigners. Having had to close down in Bruges, it looked as if he'd simply decamped to Spain where he'd continued his lucrative and barbarous testing. Returning for a few external shots the next day, Jones had been on the way back to his hotel when he'd got hopelessly lost in the unfamiliar, anonymous maze of factories and chimneys and security fences. He'd paused to consult a map, and when he'd looked up he'd found himself directly outside a Berkeley Square plant.

That had got him thinking. A campaign against Voisier Laboratories back home in London wouldn't be exactly headline-stopping. No one outside the animal rights movement had ever heard of Voisier, a tiny sub-contractor in the vast machine of the cosmetics industry. Plus there was the fact that Voisier was in Madrid, not Manchester. And what were the rights-sensitive chattering classes of Britain supposed to do, apart from write stern letters to their MEPs? They couldn't boycott Voisier products. They couldn't protest outside Voisier offices – there weren't any. All in all, his photos would provoke nothing more than a storm in a teacup.

Berkeley Square, on the other hand, offered limitless possibilities. It was synonymous with middle England – the Nightingale product range had been much loved by generations of ladies of a certain age. The company's glossy advertising promoted all the values – sensuality, gentility, refinement

– that his photographs most sensationally contested. The idea that all those many litres of eau de toilette and parfum had their genesis in this cruel, clinical hell on earth was an outrage.

So the decision had been easy. He'd photographed Berkeley Square's own sign and, on his return to Britain, he'd commissioned a duplicate to be made. Then, hours before Larson's subsequent video break-in, he'd personally attached it to the anonymous external fence of the Voisier plant, before removing it afterwards.

He hadn't, of course, been at all surprised by the media's reluctance to accept AFL allegations. His main challenge, as he'd always known, had been to keep Bengt Larson determined, motivated, and in the game. But it had been easier than he'd feared; in the face of universal condemnation, Larson had continued to believe his own eyes. No one's fool, he had *seen* the sign. He *knew* the plant was Berkeley Square's. Outright denials by Lefevre and Bullerton only inflamed his passions all the more.

Right from the very start, Jones had expected revelations about Voisier's Madrid facility to bring an abrupt halt to the One Commando campaign. But until that happened, he'd been only too happy to run with the show as far as it went – which, as things turned out, had been beyond his most wildly optimistic expectations. Tomorrow's Berkeley Square media conference was, he considered now, the icing on the cake. Making his way across to the drinks cabinet, he selected a twenty-five-year-old bottle of port, before pouring out a glass for himself. Time for a celebratory nightcap, he decided. Berkeley Square would be setting the scene for him, with One Commando revealed in the very worst and most duplicitous light. It was all just perfect for his purposes.

Lloyd got into work early, and spent the morning going through Vinnie's telephone conversations. Mark had told him about the call setting up a meeting in Regent's Park, but hadn't been able to give him a date; Lloyd was having to screen through every single call on the computer.

As he got into the routine of listening to the first few seconds of each, he thought about how Vinnie himself was now sitting five thousand miles away in a police cell. He'd read the details of his part of the attack in the paper on the way into work. Taking part in an armed break-in with the intention of committing grievous bodily harm carried penalties of several years in jail which, the paper's legal experts were saying, would almost certainly be spent in America.

Mark, meanwhile, was being lauded as the hero of the day, whose quick thinking had saved not only himself, but Isis and Holly from an unimaginable fate. An enterprising paparazzi photographer had, with the aid of his telephoto lens, snapped a photograph of Mark, arm in a sling, while in hospital – a photo which had been plastered all over today's tabloids.

Head bent as he listened to each sound-bite, clicking the cursor forward, Lloyd worked with unusual intensity and speed. On the phone, Mark had gone to great lengths to stress the urgency. Although the media seemed to believe the show was over for One Commando, according to Mark there was something much bigger than the future of One Commando at stake. There was someone, right here in London he believed, who had a particular knowledge he could use to achieve everything that One Commando had failed to achieve – and without any of the risk. He could knock Isis off her pedestal and destroy her career by making known a particular piece of information. Just who this bloke was, and what motivated him, wasn't something Lloyd had discussed on the phone, but he thought about it a lot as he went through all the recordings. If there wasn't any risk involved to this man, why had One Commando launched their high-risk strike in Malibu? Just how closely was this guy working with One Commando? And had he been known to everyone in the group, or just the now-dead Larson?

He found the recording eventually. The conversation itself was of less interest than the telephone number of the incoming caller, also digitally recorded. Having copied the call on to a floppy disk, and written down the incoming telephone number, Lloyd quickly typed a code on the keyboard – and watched the entire directory being deleted. In less than a minute, he'd wiped out all trace of his illicit operation.

The Regent's Park caller didn't use an OmniCell number – that would have been just too easy, reflected Lloyd. Not that he was especially perturbed. Many of the industry's 'propeller heads' like himself knew each other. They met at exhibitions and conferences. They moved from one company to another. They traded information. With the caller signed up to a rival network, Lloyd realised it was time to call in a few favours.

It was halfway through the afternoon before his call into SatLink was returned. His SatLink mate, a former OmniCell colleague who'd moved companies, had been tied up in meetings. Lloyd had to do a lot of grovelling; confidentiality of customer records was the Holy Grail of the industry and never to be passed off lightly. Assuring his contact that his interests were entirely non-commercial, Lloyd had had to pull out all stops to persuade him. But the information did come through shortly before five; the user name was one

Jasper Jones. The phone was registered for personal use, with a billing address in Islington. The moment he had the information, Lloyd logged out of his computer and headed for the door.

Los Angeles
Wednesday, 6 October

Isis emerged from the bathroom of the lavish Peninsula Hotel suite, glancing across to where Holly was kneeling at the coffee table in the sitting room, with a colouring-in book. Hair still wrapped in a towel, and wearing a hotel dressing-gown, she made her way over to her daughter.

'Darling!' She sat on a sofa behind her. Turning, Holly climbed up and nuzzled into her lap.

'Did you sleep okay?'

'Snug as a bug in a rug,' replied Holly.

'Good.' She hugged her tight.

They had the whole floor to themselves, no one knew they were here, and there were police guarding the lift doors to make sure it stayed that way. After the attack, emergency medics from the ambulance had treated Holly and her for shock, then they'd gone back inside the house, but only for long enough to pack a few bags; they needed to get out of there. Hilton had made arrangements with the Peninsula, and the police had blocked off the media convoy. Arriving at the hotel they'd made their way, under protection, directly to the lifts and come straight up. Her doctor had arrived within half an hour and prescribed her some pills they might both need to get to sleep, as well as mild tranquillisers. But neither of them had taken any medication – they hadn't needed to.

Traumatic though the events of the previous day had

been, they had also been powerfully cathartic. For the first time Isis felt free of a direct threat to her life. The prospect of physical horror which had been with her ever since she'd heard of the Lefevre attack, was now gone. Although there was no escaping the intuitive sensation that things weren't completely over. That foreboding which she'd sensed ever since signing the Berkeley Square endorsement was still present in her consciousness, leaving her with the strange sensation of a life 'on hold'. She no longer felt directly threatened – but nor did she feel completely free. She had no desire to return home, but she wasn't sure whether she wanted to take off on holiday either – something that Hilton kept suggesting. As for Holly, it was hard to tell. She seemed to have taken it all in her stride – she'd even made a joke about it, as though the One Commando attack had had all the reality of a computer game. But what was really going on beneath that irrepressible exterior might not reveal itself, Isis knew, for some time.

Isis had also kept wondering about Mark. She'd tried calling him in hospital – only to find that he'd discharged himself. His cellphone had been switched off and it was only when she finally got hold of Mrs Martinez that she was told he was on his way back to England to see his family. She badly wanted to speak to him. Her feelings for him had gone through a profound change with the attack – she knew she owed him both Holly's life and her own. She recalled vividly every detail of what had happened – the risk he'd put himself under to rescue Holly from her hiding place; the way his escape plan had been the means of their release from siege.

She recalled too, with remorse, her own fury when he'd told her, outside Unum Music, how he'd discovered her secret. She'd been guilty, she realised now, of extreme self-ishness. Even before the attack he'd deserved some kind of explanation; after the way he'd acted during it, she really felt the need to explain herself.

When the telephone rang, it was answered for her by their hotel butler.

'Message from Mr Lebowitz,' he said, coming through a short while later. 'He says you should watch CBS.'

The Berkeley Square item had already begun on the news by the time she'd switched on the television. In the foyer of Berkeley Square's much-publicised Madrid facility, the media corps was evidently larger than had been expected, judging by the crush; Lord Bullerton, Jacques Lefevre, and Andrew Craig were pressed against a white wall, while television lights blazed and flash cameras caught their every gesture. The purpose of today's session, Bullerton told the tightly packed assembly, was to clarify recent allegations made against the company. What had been billed as an executive briefing, however, soon dissolved into a witch hunt; no sooner had Craig announced that the laboratory featured in AFL leaflets had recently been identified as one within a few minutes' drive of Berkeley Square than pandemonium ensued.

Clutching Holly to her lap, Isis and her daughter both watched as journalists bayed for the address of Voisier Laboratories – which Craig was only too happy to supply. Whereupon there was an instant exodus out of the door. The female CBS reporter announced that over twenty teams of reporters and TV crews had made their way in convoy to Voisier Laboratories. Reaching the inside security fence, their demands to speak to the owner resulted only in the rapid exit, a short while later, of a white Mercedes from the back of the factory. This had provoked the media corps even further; in less than a minute they'd forced open the gates and, ignoring the two dazed security guards, had made their way inside the factory.

'Some viewers,' the CBS lady said, 'will find the following scenes distressing, but they are by no means among the worst that we found.'

Isis turned Holly's face away from the TV as there followed the same vision of hell that Bengt Larson had videotaped – but which the British police had never allowed into public circulation. As cameras panned over the row upon row of tortured animals, the CBS reporter, barely able to maintain her composure, described how Voisier Laboratories had perpetuated this same horror once before in Belgium – before being forced to close down.

Mercifully, the next footage showed rescue teams, as well as volunteer vets and other animal welfare groups, removing the lab animals and driving them away to new and more hopeful futures. Some, explained an animal welfare worker, would have to be put down, their diseased eyes and infected wounds too ravaged to treat. But for the others, new homes would be found. One of the most heart-wrenching sights was a baby chimpanzee being reunited with the tortured mother from which she had been separated, apparently for weeks. The two of them, clutching desperately at each other, were said to be bound for a primate sanctuary in Zimbabwe.

'Will they be all right now, Mummy?' Holly wanted to know.

'Yes, my baby,' Isis cuddled her. 'For ever and ever.'

Now the CBS reporter was wrapping up with an interview with Andrew Craig. 'Tell me, Dr Craig, how did you find out that Voisier Laboratories were One Commando's real targets?'

'Jordan Hampshire worked it out,' Craig told the cameras in his bluff brogue. 'He wondered if animal testing was going on in a facility nearby. After that, it was easy.'

'You never knew before,' the CBS reporter asked in disbelief, 'that this was going on in a laboratory just a few kilometres from here?'

Craig delivered a stony-eyed glance. 'Do *you* know everything that goes on in your business district?'

'So,' she had to roll with the blow, 'One Commando attempted deliberately to mislead people?'

'Unless they were, themselves, misled.' Craig was dry.

The reporter looked astounded. 'You must admit, Dr Craig, that's a far-fetched proposition?'

'I must admit nothing of the kind. It is one possibility.'

'But who would want to mislead an animal rights group? And for what reason?'

Craig was looking into the distance contemplatively, before musing, 'For what reason, indeed?'

24

At the wheel of the hire car, Lloyd headed out in the direction of Ealing, Mark sitting beside him in the passenger seat. He'd arrived back in London the afternoon before and had gone straight to the family home in Lewisham. Their mother had been extremely anxious since the attack, and even though they'd spoken on the phone and he'd reassured her that he was all right, she couldn't wait to see him. She'd fussed and flapped about him, not letting him pick anything up and frequently asking him how he felt – 'It's just a damaged muscle, Mum,' he found himself telling her sharply after he'd been home a few hours.

But he knew he'd done the right thing coming back. Last night the three of them had sat down to his favourite childhood meal – grilled cutlets followed by strawberry cheesecake – and he'd produced a bottle of champagne he'd bought duty free. His Mum had toasted his health and success with *Nile* but, thought Mark, what they knew she was really toasting was the end of the One Commando threat.

Lloyd had taken today off work. Earlier this morning he'd

picked up the hire car – Mark had decided to treat himself to a BMW – before collecting his brother. Last night, as soon as their mother had gone to bed, Mark had looked at Lloyd and asked, 'Traced that number?'

Speaking quickly in a low voice, Lloyd had told him about his investigations. After getting hold of Jasper Jones's address, Lloyd had set out on a recce, directly from work. He hadn't really known, in his own mind, what he was expecting by staking out Jones's home. He supposed he hoped to catch sight of him. But by the time he got there, he wondered if he was too late. From what he could gather, walking past the street number, Jones occupied both floors of a terrace house; sitting on a concealed doorstep opposite and slightly down the street, Lloyd observed a light being switched on. Someone was at home, and unless Jones had a partner or housemate, that someone must be him.

It was cold and dark outside and, huddled up, pressing his knees to his chest, Lloyd had stared up at the house, and observed the occasional passer-by. He could never be a private eye, he'd reckoned, glancing frequently at his watch as the minutes ticked slowly past. After over an hour of this he wondered if he should just go home. It seemed pointless hanging round waiting for nothing to happen. Besides, Jones was probably settled in for the night and had no plans of going anywhere. He was about to get up when he heard the sharp click of stilettos on the pavement followed, a short while later, by the appearance of a tall, striking woman making her way purposefully along the opposite side of the street. She wasn't only highly attractive, as Lloyd observed when she walked under the streetlights, but even though she was carrying a couple of M&S grocery bags she conveyed an indefinable glamour, as though she was used to being watched. She had to be a model, he decided.

As her footsteps slowed, he was wondering casually which house she lived in, when she made her way directly towards Jones's front door. Halting, she pressed the buzzer; from across the street, Lloyd heard the sound of footsteps descending the stairs. Would he get a glimpse of Jones, he wondered? When the door swung open, would he stand in the entrance to greet her? But there were no hugs and kisses for public display. The woman was inside the moment the door had opened.

Outside, Lloyd had reflected that Jasper Jones was a lucky man. The woman had come armed with M&S bags and looked like she was set to cook supper – all very cosy. Was she a girlfriend? She didn't have keys to his house, so maybe things were still fairly new. Mulling over the possibilities, Lloyd heard raised voices only moments before Jones's door was opening again and out came the woman, still with the groceries, slamming the door behind her. The crashing of the door reverberated all the way up the quiet street as she stormed back in the direction from which she'd come only minutes earlier. Lloyd glanced between the girl and Jones's front door, expecting it to swing open at any instant, and for Jones to make an appearance. But there was no sign of him.

Lloyd thought quickly about what he should do: he could continue on here, staking out Jones's house. But if he did that, he'd lose the girl – and she could be useful. Besides, he decided, he could always come back tomorrow morning and catch Jones on his way to work.

Quickly getting up from where he'd been huddled in the shadows, he headed down the street in hot pursuit. She was easy to follow and completely oblivious to what was going on around her, absorbed no doubt in the row she'd just had with Jones. She caught the Underground at the Angel and he trailed her movements as she switched to the Piccadilly

Line, finding a seat and burying her head in a *Marie Claire* magazine for what was evidently to be a long trip. Sitting just two seats away from her, close up he appreciated her blonde good looks all the more – the high cheekbones, narrow chin, and radiant blueness of her eyes. He noted how she attracted a lot of attention in the train – she must be used to being stared at, he guessed, although she showed no sign of being aware of anyone else.

She got off at Ealing Common and, making her way down to the Broadway, turned left. Evening diners as well as visitors to the pub on the corner gave him cover as he tracked her into a residential street. Falling well back, he watched carefully as she extracted a bunch of keys from her handbag, making her way to the front door of a semi-detached house, and let herself in.

'I'm not sure if she's anyone useful . . .' Lloyd told Mark, after reporting this.

Mark met his eyes with a determined glance. 'You've done a great job!' he told him. 'And right now, we need all the leads we can get.'

Then, observing Lloyd's surprise, he got up from where he'd been sitting and paced the room, gesturing with his free hand while he spoke.

'The way I see it, what we've got right now is a real bugger's muddle. I'm having trouble trying to make sense of it all. Why did One Commando launch a high-risk operation in California, when they could have done far more commercial damage releasing the information they have about Isis?'

Lloyd followed his brother intently.

'How come Larson didn't know about the Voisier thing?'

'Are you sure he didn't?' Lloyd interjected.

'As sure as I can be,' he said. 'I was on the floor. He was

tying me up. I told him about Voisier. He just went mad—'

'Maybe—'

'Uh-uh,' Mark anticipated him. 'Not that kind of mad. More like he was angry I could even suggest it.' Mark paused, staring into the mid-distance before turning back to Lloyd.

'Then there's the biggest question of all.'

'Who tipped the police off?'

'Exactly.' Mark nodded soberly. 'Had to be an insider.'

Now, as they curved round the Chiswick roundabout, heading north towards Ealing, the two of them talked tactics. The way Mark saw it, they had only two options. They could follow up Lloyd's leads themselves. Or they could go to the police. Mark wasn't in any hurry to see all their own investigative work come to nothing – besides which, if they went to the police they'd have had to admit how Lloyd had broken the law bugging Vinnie's phone, which would get him into serious trouble at OmniCell. Going to see Jasper Jones's evening visitor seemed the best thing to do right now – though they both had their reservations; what if she slammed the door in their faces and refused to speak? Worse, what if she told Jones that they'd been round asking questions? All they could count on was the row Lloyd had witnessed two evenings before – and the impact of her opening the door to find Jordan Hampshire on her front step.

They parked the car a few metres from her home in the wide, tree-lined street. It was mid-afternoon and they knew that if 'the model', as Lloyd referred to her, had an office job, they'd have to hang around – and just hope she made her way straight home. But something about her made Lloyd think she wasn't a regular office worker – she'd just didn't seem the type.

They climbed out of the car into the chill afternoon. The sun was weak behind smudged banks of grey cloud, but at least it was dry. Making their way to the front door, Mark reached for the round, brass knocker and hammered three times. The two brothers exchanged a tense glance. Then there was a sound coming from inside, and a shadow appeared behind the frosted-glass panels of the door.

'Who is it?' came a woman's voice.

'Jordan Hampshire,' announced Mark.

'Yeah. That'd be right. And I'm Isis.' The voice was young and clear, and had the intonation of recently acquired refinement. As she moved closer, they saw blonde hair dappled through the frosted glass.

'Seriously! It's me.'

Evidently curious, and perhaps recognising his voice from TV, she carefully opened the door – on the chain – and peered out. Mark took a step back so she could see him, meeting the two wide blue eyes.

'Did the agency send you round?' she seemed not to believe what she was seeing.

He shook his head. 'Found my own way round. This is my brother, Lloyd,' he said, pointing. 'We need to ask you a couple of quick questions.'

She paused. 'What about?'

'A guy who lives in Islington. We only know him as Jasper Jones—'

'I've nothing to say about that tosser,' she snorted. 'I chucked him two nights ago.'

Relieved to hear this, Mark decided to risk it, 'The thing is, he may have been caught up in criminal activity—'

'Why don't you go to the police?' The eyes glanced from Mark to Lloyd.

He shook his head, 'I'm afraid it's not that simple.'

The door closed and they heard the chain being slipped back before she was opening the door. Mark had to agree with Lloyd – she *was* spectacular. About-turning, she took their entrance for granted and was leading the way through to the lounge. 'I can't believe it's you here,' she told Mark.

'It's me all right.'

'So what's she like?'

'Who?'

'Isis!' she replied, sitting on a black leather sofa and looking for all the world as if she'd just stepped out of a glossy magazine. 'Is she a moody cow like they make out?'

Mark remembered that, as far as 'the model' was concerned, Isis and he were an item. 'You know how it goes,' he and Lloyd sat down opposite, 'we have our moments.' He met her eyes. 'What couples don't?'

'That's not how it was with Jas,' she picked up on the cue.

'No?'

'I don't know what you want to know about him,' eyes narrowing she leaned forward in her seat, 'but I'll give it to you straight: he's a two-timing bastard.'

To their surprise, she didn't enquire further about criminal activity before launching into a tirade about Jasper Jones. How they'd met at Models Against Mink, and how he'd subsequently courted her. Clearly a girl that demanded drama, she told them of her suspicions right from the start. The furtive phone calls from behind closed doors. The unexplained absences.

'He might even be married for all I know!' Her mercurial gaze flicked from one to the other. She was enjoying the celebrity audience. 'I could tell you a few stories about men, believe me. A girl can't be too careful. She has to keep a close eye.'

Mark was nodding in agreement. As she'd been speaking

he'd already realised: at the very least, this girl was highly volatile, unhinged. He had a pretty good idea Lloyd was thinking the same thing too; this one was a 'rabbit-boiler'. Now he asked her, 'You kept . . . a close eye?'

'Have to, don't you? I listened to his phone calls—'

'How d'you do that?' Lloyd was surprised.

She shrugged. 'Changed the mode of his answerphone so it recorded incoming calls. There was nothing on the tapes – at least no female callers – but that doesn't mean a lot by itself, does it?'

'These tapes—?' Mark probed.

'I s'pose you'll be wanting them?' She tilted her head, coquettish.

'Well, it would be—'

'Only if you promise you'll give me your autograph.'

'That's not a problem.'

'And a photo!' She glanced over at Lloyd. 'Will you take a photo of the two of us. The girls will never believe this!'

She stepped across the lounge and was going through a cabinet drawer.

'Doesn't surprise me you think he's a crook,' she shuddered, collecting up a handful of micro-cassettes.

'No?'

'Always had his mind on something else. Always plotting and scheming. And people used to send in the most . . . kinky videos.'

Giving Mark the handful of micro-cassettes, she resumed her seat opposite.

'Sex videos?' asked Lloyd.

She screwed her face up, 'Just . . . kinky. S&M, I suppose. There was one I saw, and this bloke was being strung up by a rope by these thugs in black outfits and masks. Acted like he was being hanged. At least – I think it was acting.'

Mark gave Lloyd a sideways glance. 'But why, I mean, would people send that sort of thing to him?'

'It was his job, wasn't it? Videos.'

Mark shook his head, bemused. 'I've no idea what his job is.'

'Well, just shows you, doesn't it?' She rolled her eyes, leaning back in the sofa. 'He told me he was well known. Like, everyone in the industry was supposed to know his work.'

'So, what *does* he do?' Lloyd could barely contain himself.

'He makes documentaries. He calls himself,' she grimaced, 'the *master* of the exposé. He goes into things, undercover, and makes these fly-on-the-wall programmes . . .'

Opposite, Mark buried his face in his hands. It was a long, long time before he murmured, 'Of course!' His voice was husky. 'It had to be.'

Jasper Jones worked in the editing suite under the offices of Love Smith Ben David. It was late – after eleven, and he was pale and drawn as he sat going through video footage on several different monitors, an annotated script in front of him. Tonight, like the past few nights, would be a late one as he rushed the production through, but he wasn't worried by the lack of sleep – he was still living on adrenaline.

What had started as an idea for an engaging insider documentary had quickly developed way beyond that. The One Commando activity had burgeoned beyond his most fanciful dreams. Then, when he'd made the discovery about Isis's secret, that had been transformational. He'd no longer be hawking round a fly-on-the-wall series to the major TV channels. Christ, no! They'd be scrambling to buy not just the documentary, but the book rights too. This thing would be a multi-media extravaganza. Of course, there'd be rich pickings from the newspaper exclusive. He'd be able to expand his already sizeable investment portfolio. Yes, he'd be rolling in it. All the expense so far had definitely been worth it. And then there'd be TV awards, the talk-show circuit – overnight, he would become the most celebrated director and author in Britain.

He didn't look up immediately when he heard a noise at the door. Too absorbed in his work, it took him a moment to register that the last person had gone home an hour before. When he did look up, he half expected to find the night watchman, on one of his routine patrols. Instead, there was a young man in his mid-twenties in jeans and a jacket, standing eyeing him from the door.

'Mr Jones?'

'Who are you?' He was irritated by the distraction.

'The name doesn't matter,' the other stood, hands in his pockets, cocky. 'I'm with the AFL.'

'Who let you in?' Jones's annoyance grew. 'How did you get past security?'

The other pulled a droll expression. 'Your old boy wanted a smoke, didn't he? So he stepped outside for a while.' He shrugged. 'Open house.'

Jones's eyes flashed from the intruder back to the monitor. 'Well. Now's not a good time.'

'I bet it's not.' The other's tone was laced with sarcasm. Jerking his head towards the monitors he asked, 'Making your One Commando documentary, are you?'

Jones responded with a disdainful stare.

'No need to pretend with me, Mr Jones. You see, some of the others at AFL might be idiots, but I'm not.' He tapped his head. 'Worked it out, you see.'

'Did you really?'

'I reckon this Voisier thing didn't catch you by surprise at all. I reckon you knew about it all along—'

'Don't be so stupid!' snarled Jones. 'How on earth could I have known?'

'Maybe you put the Berkeley Square sign there yourself?'

Jones glared contemptuously across the room at the young intruder. He'd been prepared for all kinds of contingencies, but this had caught him unawares. Though he supposed he shouldn't be surprised by some kind of backlash from the AFL.

'Now look here,' his tone was imperious, 'you're welcome to your own opinions, but the fact of the matter is that I'm as shocked as you are by what has happened. This completely destroys everything we've been working so hard to achieve.'

'Not from where I'm sitting it doesn't.' The other took a step closer. 'The way I see it – it all makes for great TV. I mean, who's ever heard of Voisier? Who cares what they do to cute, fluffy animals? But Berkeley Square—'

'This isn't about TV!'

'Isn't it?'

'My involvement in the animal rights movement has nothing whatsoever to do with my professional career.'

The young man was shaking his head. 'Wish I could believe you, mate, but it doesn't add up, does it? I mean, take that Lefevre guy. He could have been knocked over the head, or shot or something and no one would have given a damn. But gouge his eyes out, well, that's a different kettle of fish, ain't it? That's prime-time TV. That was your idea, wasn't it?'

'I had no influence at all on what One Commando planned for Lefevre!' Jones blustered.

'Same with that attack in Malibu. It couldn't work, could it. It was never going to work—'

'Larson was the most capable commander I'd ever met. If anyone was going to do it—'

'Yeah, but not with the police coming after him,' suggested Lloyd.

'What on earth—'

'Both times,' he pointed at Jones. 'Hilton Gallo. And Malibu. Both times the police are tipped off just before the attack. Too much of a coincidence to my way of thinking.'

Jones felt his heart pound, his mouth go dry. This guy knew far more than he could have just picked up. He'd been working on it.

'Look, Mr Whatever-your-name-is,' he tried to brazen it out, 'this is all a wonderful conspiracy theory. Quite magnificent. The only problem with it is that it's complete rubbish.'

'I'll tell you why I know you're lying,' Lloyd continued calmly as he came towards him. 'What happened to the single most powerful weapon One Commando ever had? And don't pretend you don't know what I'm talking about.' He glanced at one of the monitors which had a frozen image of Isis in performance. 'Yes,' he nodded, 'her. What happened to *that* information?'

Jones sat back in his seat. It was impossible to assert himself as the other leaned over him.

'I'll tell you what happened,' continued Lloyd. 'Nothing. It was never used. You thought you'd keep it for yourself, didn't you? Make sure your production was the most sensational exposé ever seen?'

He stared down at Jones's face, only a few inches from his own.

'Got to hand it to you,' he smiled mirthlessly. 'You've had half the AFL dancing to your tune for the last twelve months. Larson's dead and his guys have been put away, and all this time you've been sitting here in your Director's chair choreographing the whole thing. They didn't know they were just actors. While they were all taking it for real, all you were interested in was a prime-time TV series!'

Sliding further down in his chair, Jones was becoming even more alarmed by the outpouring of discoveries. This intruder posed a serious threat to his plans. Arguing with him wasn't going to work. He had to be neutralised. Jones hadn't come all this way, paid out all that cash, for his plans to be ruined now. For a long while the two stared, unblinking, at each other as Jones tried to figure it out. Then he glanced away at an anglepoise lamp, before he asked in a businesslike tone: 'Why have you come here?'

Lloyd cocked his head. 'Why d'you think?'

'You're not like the others,' said Jones as though thinking aloud. 'I think you're here to cut a deal.'

Lloyd nodded. 'Keep talking.'

'You're looking for a pay-out.'

'Silence money, right?'

'Yes.'

'What kind of deal?'

'Fifty thousand pounds.'

'Puh-lease,' Lloyd was shaking his head. 'I'd get more than that from the papers. I want a cut.'

Jones looked alarmed. 'What kind of—'

'I'd say keeping all your secrets is quite a big job. I reckon it's worth about fifty per cent of takings.'

Jones looked up into Lloyd's face with an expression of undisguised loathing. As though he was going to hand over half his earnings to some self-styled sleuth from the AFL. Especially after he'd spent so much on this project already. Did this arrogant little upstart really think it came that easy? Eventually he said, 'Okay. Fifty per cent.'

'You can start by advancing me a payment right now.'

Jones held his gaze. 'It'd have to be a cheque. We don't keep—'

'A cheque's fine,' the other stepped back from him. 'I'm sure you wouldn't want it to bounce.'

'My office.' Jones gestured towards the door, rising from his chair.

Nodding, Lloyd made his way out of the editing suite. No sooner had he got to the door, however, than he felt a swingeing arc of pain in his shoulder and he was slumping down to the floor. Behind him, Jones had seized the anglepoise lamp. Using it as a club, he'd brought its heavy base crashing down on Lloyd with all his strength. Aiming for Lloyd's head, he'd missed and struck his shoulder instead. Now Lloyd was trying to scramble across the floor, away from him.

'You don't really think I'm going to hand over half my hard-earned cash to some jumped-up Sherlock Holmes do you?' he sneered at Lloyd who was jammed in a corner between the photocopier and a dustbin. 'Larson's been my lackey all this time – what makes you think I'm going to let a nobody like you—'

'It's too late!' cried Lloyd.

'Oh, I don't think so.' Jones pressed down his foot on Lloyd's chest.

He already had a plan. There was a service elevator just outside. Once he'd knocked this one out cold, he could get him down to basement parking and into the boot of his car with no one around to notice a thing. He'd make sure the offices were left neat and tidy before heading for the municipal dump. Larson had once given him a lecture about body disposal. There was a Glock pistol concealed beneath the driver's seat of his Saab. In less than an hour, this whole unpleasant incident would be over.

Now as he raised the anglepoise again, Lloyd screamed out, 'I'm wired!'

'Nice try, sunshine.'

Jones was bringing the lamp smashing down towards where Lloyd was trapped, when he suddenly buckled, the anglepoise smashing through the glass panel of the open photocopier as he stumbled forward.

'He's right.' Jones heard a familiar voice behind him.

Lurching round he found himself face to face with Mark Watson.

'Yeah, it's me.' Mark noted Jones's aghast expression with grim satisfaction. Then gesturing towards Lloyd, 'Quite an actor, isn't he, my kid brother?'

Jones glared from Mark to Lloyd and back again. 'What's this?' He was bewildered.

'You should know.' Mark regarded him coolly. 'It's what you do best, Mr Jones. It's a sting.'

Jones stepped forward, seizing Mark by his shirt. Using his good arm, Mark pushed him back. 'I wouldn't do anything more if I were you.' He met his eyes with a grim smile. 'The boys in blue are already on their way up.'

When the lift door opened downstairs ten minutes later, the night watchman didn't immediately grasp what had happened. All he knew was that the police had arrived half an hour earlier with a warrant for access to several floors of the building. Nothing like this had ever happened on his shift before.

Of course, he knew who Jasper Jones was; many nights Jones had been the last one out of the building. 'All locked up, sir?' he'd ask if Jones left by the front door. Jones would generally grunt some form of acknowledgement.

Tonight, when Jones stepped out of the lift, the watchman

didn't notice that he was attached to a policeman by a pair of cuffs.

'All locked up, sir?' he called out as usual.

But tonight, Jones didn't reply. Quick as a flash, the policeman answered on his behalf. 'He will be, for about fifteen years.'

Maldives
Monday, 11 October

On the verandah of the beachside bungalow, Isis reached out her hand to where Mark was sitting opposite. They had just finished a delicious dinner, and as they sat relaxing in the sultry night, the only light came from a bowl of floating candles on the table – and the turquoise glow of phosphorescence from the coral reef offshore. Palm fronds rustled gently along the beachfront and from the darkness of the vegetation all about them came the ethereal cadences of crickets.

'Four days.' Isis's eyes glinted in the darkness. 'Feels more like four weeks. It's like LA was a different era.'

Mark leaned back in his cane chair. 'I s'pose in some ways it was. It'll be a very different LA we return to, thank God.'

Soon after the Jones arrest, Hilton Gallo had dispatched them both for a week's rest and recuperation. A hurried consultation with GCM's travel agency had produced this private chalet in the Maldives, where they were guaranteed seclusion. There was no radio or television to intrude into their thoughts. And only with some reluctance had Isis agreed to leave the telephone connected. For one whole week, it was just the three of them.

They had spent the first three days on the beach, soaking up the sunshine, unwinding from all the tension and drama of the past weeks. Mark and Isis had helped Holly build extravagant sandcastles and, as the days wore on, the three of them had become closer and closer. Holly would march into Mark's bedroom in the morning and drag him blinking into the sunshine to play games on the sand. Isis would look on in amusement from the verandah, glad that her daughter seemed to be emotionally unscathed by the traumatic events at their home, and impressed at Mark's easy way with her child. They had taken a boat trip out to look at the corals and exotic fish. There had been something magical about swimming among beautiful, vividly coloured creatures with Holly and this man who had saved their lives.

She wished that she hadn't put up so many barriers when she and Mark had first met – it was because she had felt attracted to him and feared the consequences. When they had been recording *Nile* the sexual tension between them had been electric, but she had felt powerless to act on it. Threatened by it even. For those two days in the studio they had enjoyed a fleeting intimacy but then the whole nightmare with the AFL had taken off, and their uneasy alliance had been tested to breaking point. She had treated him badly, she knew, and as she got to know him better now, she realised how lucky she was that he hadn't just turned his back on her. It was a sign of their feelings for each other that they had managed to come through it all together. And under the blue skies of this tropical paradise, they were gradually rediscovering their earlier closeness – a friendship that was daily growing into something deeper.

Last night, their third night together, after Holly had gone to bed, Isis finally found the strength to tell Mark what she knew he'd been so desperate to hear. She had already made her mind up, of course; a sense of obligation. Besides, he already knew her secret; what he deserved to understand was *why*.

It hadn't been easy going back into it, revisiting the trauma she'd spent her whole adult life trying to put behind her. But for Mark, hearing Isis's side of the story had been revelatory. His gaze had been unfaltering as she'd related the most extraordinary experience of anyone he'd ever been close to – made all the more extraordinary by the spectacular heights of achievement she'd subsequently reached. The private agonies she'd suffered gave him a new understanding. And as he knew more, as she'd told him of her most intimate fears of the past, her father's brutality and her mother's silent acquiescence, he'd been ashamed of his own initial reaction to the discovery. Instead of aversion, he'd felt a welling up of admiration at her courage.

'There's something I don't understand,' he'd said, earlier in the evening. 'Holly.'

'John and I adopted her.'

'So that whole thing about phoning John when you were in labour—'

Isis smiled, shrugging. 'Leo Lebowitz. Who else?'

They had spoken for hours and from the heart. Now that there were no barriers from Isis's side, their conversation flowed with an easy effortlessness – there suddenly seemed so much to talk about. After they'd finished, in the early hours of the morning, and Isis had fallen asleep, exhausted, on the chalet sofa, Mark had picked her up in his arms, and taken her through to her bedroom. Putting her to bed and drawing the covers over her, he'd looked down at where she slept with an overwhelming tenderness.

Tonight, he felt a return of that same tenderness as he held her eyes across the table. And not only tenderness. Lifting Isis's hand to his lips, he kissed it.

'You're so beautiful, Isis,' he told her. 'You've always done it for me.'

She looked over at him questioningly. 'Even now?'

'Even now.'

Getting up from the table, he came round beside her and she rose to her feet. They kissed, with searching, passionate kisses, his hands descending her back as he held her to him.

'So,' he broke apart after a moment, 'I'm not just some small boy in short pants any more, caught up in something out of his league?'

She met his grin with a chuckle. 'Yeah? And what happened to the bitch from hell?'

They both laughed before he kissed her again, then reminded her, 'There are no cameras here.'

'This isn't for the cameras,' she replied, her hands roving down his body. Then, eyes meeting his, 'And it never was . . . only for the cameras.'

'Now there's an admission!'

There could be no mistaking his arousal – or hers – as they clung together in their awakening desire. Wordlessly, he put his hand round her waist, and led her across the verandah, to her bedroom.

Los Angeles

'One never likes owning up to a mistake, but I have to eat my words, Leo,' Hilton faced Lebowitz, who was sitting opposite him on one of his cream sofas.

Lebowitz returned a quizzical expression.

'There was a time back there, just ten days ago, when I was convinced we'd be unable to contain the Isis story. Remember you said we shouldn't be pre-emptive because you never knew what was round the corner. Well, you were right and I was wrong.'

Lebowitz shrugged with a wry smile as Hilton put aside

the report he'd been sent by Scotland Yard, detailing Jasper Jones's arrest.

Hilton was shaking his head. 'Who would have thought the enemy was a documentary maker?' Then, after a reflective pause, 'D'you reckon he can do us any harm from behind bars?'

Lebowitz shook his head. 'Zero credibility,' he replied. 'No one will believe a word he says now.'

'Meantime he's just delivered us more pre-launch publicity than we could have dreamed of,' beamed Hilton.

The arrest of Jones had given the One Commando story yet another unexpected twist to which the media, on both sides of the Atlantic, hadn't failed to respond. With the launch of Isis and Jordan's album less than ten days away, public obsession with the couple had never been greater.

'I've stood the crisis team down,' Lebowitz told him, 'and the Isis files are back in secure holding.'

Hilton met his eyes. 'No need for damage limitation after all.'

'None,' agreed Lebowitz, 'her secret is still safe. You know, after this, I can't help thinking it always will be.'

EPILOGUE

Father Marvin Robieri was proud of what had been achieved at St Columbus's. During the past decade the Italian community, to which the church belonged, had prospered. And St Columbus had prospered with it. The church roof appeal had been the start of the transformation, though the urgently needed replacement of the dilapidated roof had soon been followed by other construction work, which Father Marvin had, for a very long time, been offering up for Divine Blessing.

It was living proof of prayer in action, Father Marvin would frequently remind his congregation. First there had been the new St Columbus Hall, where youth group meetings, community events and other informal gatherings were held, giving the church an even more active part in the life of the community. Then there was the Outreach centre in town, where trained counsellors were on duty, twenty-four hours a day, to help those whose lives were being torn apart by drugs, alcohol and domestic violence. Most recently, a suite of offices had been added behind the Hall, to accommodate the growing number of pastoral and administrative staff required by the burgeoning activities run by St Columbus.

The development of the St Columbus website had been one of Father Marvin's more rewarding projects. Always technologically minded, he had been inspired by a visit to St Columbus's by a group of pupils from Milan to create a forum within which his local congregation could stay in touch with friends and family in the old country. He'd been amazed by the number of visitors to the site from all over the world, starting on the very day of its inception. The two terminals he had installed at the back of St Columbus Hall for e-mail purposes had proved so popular that he'd swiftly ordered another three, and a Communications Room had been created. Adding to the website in every way he knew how, Father Marvin had come to regard it not merely as a tool for communication, but also as a repository for everything that was important to the life of the Church. All its activities and history were now instantly accessible to anyone, wherever in the world they might be; it was a way of putting his own community on the virtual map.

It had been a long and onerous task, going through records since the Church had begun, collecting information and either keying it or scanning it into his computer. But there would be people, out there, who would find his work of value, he had no doubt. And if, through his labours, he drew just one single person into the fold, all his efforts, he would remind himself, would have been worthwhile.

Having inputted all the community records – baptisms, marriages and funerals – since St Columbus had begun, he found himself beginning to wonder if there was any further need to keep the many boxes of ageing files and papers which were now easily accessible by computer. What was the point? While he was required by law to keep certain records, most of the material cluttering up the new admin offices fell way outside that category.

In the end he decided to make his own rule; any records that were over ten years old which he wasn't required to keep, he would discard. It was an important task and one that required discretion – which was why he'd taken it upon himself to go through every single one of the ageing records.

The job had already taken several months, and he was less than halfway through. It was something he fitted in between all his other more urgent activities, and he'd usually find himself in the admin offices late in the evening, after a function in the Hall, spending an hour or two clearing out more boxes. He would go through every page of each file. Not a single document was to be consigned to the black bin-liner at his feet until he had looked at it to make sure it shouldn't be kept. And whenever he doubted the relevance of a piece of information, he kept it.

While Father Marvin was sometimes to be heard describing his task of clearing out the archives in wearied tones, it was one that wasn't entirely a burden. Much of the work was routine, but there were plenty of memories and nostalgic reflections too as he sifted through the paperwork: a baptismal notice which conjured up the image of anxious parents sitting outside the vestry; names which recalled faces of those in the community with whom he'd had dealings in the long-distant past, forgotten till now.

This particular night he came upon a set of programmes for a carol concert held at the church twenty years before. There must have been thirty of them wrapped around with an elastic band. Extracting one, he opened it up and glanced through it. He supposed he must have had a hand in producing it, though he couldn't really remember. Below the list of carols were printed the names of all those who had appeared, including the organist who'd been at the church for thirty years – now, sadly, passed away, several members of the congregation – had they really all been together for that long? And of course the children. They were mostly just a blur of names – even for Father Marvin who was well known for his excellent memory. One or two names did stand out. Those kids who'd gone on to achieve great things with their lives. And those whom he remembered for less gratifying reasons – problems with the law, parents, authority of all kinds.

Now as he scanned down the list he paused at a name which instantly brought an altogether different memory; he could remember watching the poor kid walking past St Columbus's on the way home from school, day after day. Always alone. It had been there from the start to those sensitive enough to notice it, but as the child reached puberty, the differentness was inescapable. Father Marvin had felt his heart go out, his compassion aroused – though he had a policy of never directly intervening in the lives of his congregation unless asked. Instead, he'd suggested the idea of the carol concert to the mother, Rosa Carboni, who'd duly sent her child to take part in the choir. Father Marvin had looked for opportunities to nurture the poor kid, whom, he remembered now, had possessed a remarkably good singing voice. He'd hoped, perhaps to open a door, to create a point of contact. But after the carol concert, the child hadn't returned to choir.

Now that he thought about it, Father Marvin realised he had no idea what had happened after that Christmas. The father, a tyrannical brute by all accounts, had died some years ago. The mother suffered from Alzheimer's and he'd visited her in hospital several times though she hadn't remembered him. But what had become of the child? Father

Marvin searched his memory; no, he couldn't remember anything, though he could recall the blank faces of friends of the family whom he'd once asked. It was, he reflected, just one of life's many mysteries which he'd continue to live with – what had happened to little Marco Corrado Carboni?